YAGRUMA NIGHTS

Rodolfo Labourdette

TRANSPERSONAL PRESS

Yagruma Nights

A Transpersonal Press Book
Published by arrangement with the author

Printed in the United States of America

First Transpersonal Press edition published in 1996

Cover design: R. Fernández-Trujillo

Book design: Debra Doyle

Library of Congress Catalog Card Number: 96-060475

ACKNOWLEDGMENT

This novel's original manuscript was written in Spanish, my mother tongue. I am deeply indebted to my good friends John Epperson and Ed Widener for their most valuable help and assistance in the English translation of this work.

R. Labourdette
May 1, 1996

This book is a work of fiction inspired by the author's own experience and historical events. The characters featured in this book are purely fictional.

The Author

CHAPTER I
THE PADRE TEMPTED

When I was a youngster, my maternal grandmother had the habit of taking me with her into the parlor of the house each evening after dinner, to sit down with me by the open window and enjoy the coolness of the night. I listened with pleasure to the family stories she used to tell me, especially those about my French grandparents, whom I never knew.

Etienne Barreau, my grandfather, had been an associated priest in the parish of Urrugne, a small town in the old French Béarn. My grandfather adored women and, according to the town's gossips, had put the horns on quite a few of his parishioners.

His good luck, and the cassock, had gotten father Barreau out of many of problems that his lust had caused him. But, like the Spanish proverb says, "The pitcher keeps going to the fountain until it gets broken." In one of his trips throughout the region, in the small town of Soublette, Etienne Barreau met Jeannette-Marie Ribeaux, a stunningly beautiful young woman whose father happened to be the town's mayor.

The clergyman fell for her immediately, and since he was a good-looking sort of fellow and had a way with words, Jeannette-Marie and the priest soon became lovers. Unfortunately, and in spite of all the precautions that the couple took, a few months after the romance started the belly of Jeannette-Marie began to swell. Her father, upon realizing that the young lady "had someone growing inside her", used his influence with the bishop of the diocese who, fearful of a scandal, and through intimidation and threats, forced my grandfather to hang up his vestments and marry Jeannette-Marie.

On the day of the wedding, as soon as the ceremony was finished, Jeannette-Marie's parents told their daughter never again to set foot in their house which she had dishonored, and Monsieur Ribeaux warned his brand new son-in-law not to expect any kind of help from him. "Not one franc! Not a penny!", he shouted.

Lady Luck had abandoned my grandfather. It was true that, a few months before, upon the death of his mother, he had inherited some money, but as time passed, the francs were disappearing without him being able to find any kind of work to support himself and his wife.

The offense that he had committed against the Ribeaux, one of the oldest and most respected families in the region, had closed all the doors that he came upon in search of work. My grandfather, as we say in Yagruma, was left out in the street, without resources, naked in the open air.

Desperate, unable to count on the support of his father in law, who hated him, watching his meager resources dwindle away and rejected by his former parishioners, the ex-priest made the decision to write to his uncle, Agustín Barreau, who had emigrated to America many years before. Uncle Agustín lived in Helena, a city in the Republic of Yagruma, an island nation in the Caribbean, south of the Florida peninsula.

In his letter, my grandfather told his uncle about the situation he was in and implored his help. Weeks later the answer arrived, in which uncle Agustín expressed his regrets about the misfortunes that his nephew was suffering. In his letter he stated that, in spite of what people said, he and his wife were not rich. All they had, he assured Etienne, was a modest income that permitted them to live decently.

Of course, added uncle Agustín, Etienne was not only his nephew, but also the only relative that he had left, and he felt obligated to help him in any way that he could. If Etienne wanted to come to Yagruma to start a new life, he had business contacts in Helena that could probably offer him work. He ended the letter saying that Etienne and his wife could live with them until they were able to support themselves.

As for my grandfather, it wasn't very difficult for him to come to a decision. He arranged an interview with his wife's father, and after begging and humbling himself before him, he secured a loan from the old man for the cost of the fare for himself and Jeannette-Marie. A month later, the ex-priest and his wife embarked on a steamship that touched at the port of Helena.

Agustín Barreau had made a fortune in Helena, as a loan shark. The old whiner, always afraid of thieves and kidnappers, used to swear to everybody that he was far from being wealthy; and so that people would believe him, he and his wife lived modestly, without luxuries, while the mountain of money that they had in the bank kept growing and growing.

With the help of his uncle, Etienne found a job with "Helena Victuals, Inc.", a commercial enterprise of very solid reputation, where Agustín had money invested.

Since their arrival in Helena, my grandparents had been living with uncle Agustín and Saturnina, his wife, but as soon as my grandfather began collecting his salary from Helena Victuals, Agustín put the pressure on his nephew and forced Etienne to move, pretending that he was doing him a favor.

"Married couples need their own place to live", he told Etienne, "Besides, you have to get used to the idea that your playboy days are over".

Two months later, Jeannette-Marie gave birth to a son, my future father, who was baptized with the name of Cesáreo. Uncle Agustín and Saturnina agreed to be the godparents. By then, Etienne had rented a modest dwelling on the left bank of the San Juan River.

Agustín Barreau and his wife had never had any children, and Saturnina, bit by bit, began to fall in love with the toddler.

Shortly after the infant was weaned, she asked my grandmother to bring him to her house everyday. She made Jeannette-Marie leave Cesáreo at the Barreau's for many hours. Finally, the child was spending most of his time in the house of his godparents, who took care of everything that little Cesáreo needed.

Although Etienne and his wife worried that they might be losing their son's affection, they did not confront Agustín and Saturnina, because, with the small salary that my grandfather earned at Helena Victuals, their taking care of the needs of the child was to them, a real life saver.

My grandfather often complained about stomach pains that he thought were caused by intestinal gas. One morning he had a pain so strong that he fell to the floor, almost fainting. His appendix had ruptured, and he died of peritonitis the following day in Helena's civil hospital.

Those who saw Jeannette-Marie commented that, though shedding tears and dressed in mourning, she did not appear to be devastated by the loss of her husband.

Several days before Etienne's death, for the first time since she left France, Jeannette Marie had received a letter from her mother that made her remember fondly, the comfortable old mansion in her native country, where she had been so happy. Memories of the good old times came back to her mind. The summers in St. Jean-de-Luz, the seasons in Biarritz, the trips to Paris...and here she was now, leading a meager existence in this wretched village!

That philandering priest had really made a mess of her life!

The truth was that Jeannette-Marie, for some time now, had made the decision to leave Helena for good and try to get back to France. If her parents didn't want to help her, so much the worse! She would get the money out of Benigno Merino, her husband's former boss, who already had his eye on the widow of his deceased employee, or, if she had to, from uncle Agustín, who had made a pass at her on one occasion.

Benigno Merino, who was excessively timid when it came to women, hesitated to approach my grandmother directly. But, one day he showed up at her house, bringing with him an envelope containing two hundred pesos which he begged her to accept "in the name of the firm". It was, as he put it, a little assistance that he had been able to obtain for her.

Upon leaving, the Spaniard, nervous and in a cold sweat, told my grandmother that he would be back soon "to visit and to see how things were going".

The situation with uncle Agustín began one afternoon when my grandmother stopped by to see Saturnina and found that "auntie" had gone shopping. But Agustín, who was home alone, greeted Jeannette-Marie with a lusty embrace, much bolder than those that he dared to give her when his wife was present.

"Saturnina won't be gone very long", he said, "Wait for her till she comes back". And seeing that Jeanette Marie had taken off her shawl, he added, "Why don't you make us a cup of coffee while you are waiting?"

Jeannette-Marie, who was accustomed to making the coffee when visiting in Agustín's house, went into the kitchen and put the water on to boil.

Then, while she was searching the shelf for the strainer and the coffee, he came up to her from behind and, while groping her buttocks, kissed her on the neck, with kisses so furious they felt like bites.

The young widow whirled around to face him, blind with rage, swearing that she would tell Saturnina. But, quickly remembering her fate, she concluded that it would be wise to keep uncle Barreau as an alternate in case Merino failed her.

However, even if she couldn't get money from either of these men, Jeannette-Marie had firmly decided to leave Helena for Sabana, the capital city, where she would do anything to survive.

"It doesn't make any difference to me", she said to Consuelo Morgado, her only friend and confidante, "I would rather be a whore and eat steak in Sabana than be honest and eat sweet potatoes in Helena".

Jeanette Marie had not touched the two hundred pesos that Merino had given her. She put it away for "essentials" when she got to Sabana, just in case that she couldn't squeeze any more money from Merino or Agustín

After very careful consideration, Jeannette-Marie wrote her father a letter in which she acknowledged her past mistakes, stating her repentance and saying how sorry she was for the errors she had committed, for which she was paying so dearly. In the end, she begged her parents to forgive her and let her return to Soublette, to her ancestral home.

She waited, anxious and fearful, for several weeks that seemed an eternity to her, until the answer finally arrived. Her parents had agreed to forgive her and gave her -and only her- permission to return to the family mansion. They would be sending their daughter a money order for the passage back to France and for traveling expenses.

Their reply filled her with happiness, eliminating her fears and anguish. At last she no longer had to even consider going to bed with Merino, or selling her body to the highest bidder.

She didn't even wait for the money to arrive from France, the two hundred pesos from Merino were enough to get process started. Jeannette-Marie hired old man Estornino, one of the few lawyers in town that was capable of keeping a secret, to apply for, and obtain, her passport at the French consulate in Sabana.

Her son didn't figure at all into her plans. In Jeannette-Marie, the maternal instinct was completely missing. If at any time she came to reproach herself for her self-centeredness, she justified everything with the excuse that her child did not love her, but instead Agustín and Saturnina, who had raised him.

"What the hell, the damn kid wouldn't be lacking anything!" she rationalized. They surely would designate him as their heir! Leaving her son with them, she was doing him a favor. When Cesáreo grew up and understood things, he would realize that his mother, if she abandoned him, did it for his own good. He would thank her for it!

The money from France arrived a week later, and a few days after that, Jeanette-Marie had her passport all in order. My grandmother, then, spoke to Carmenate, the coachman, and instructed him to come and pick her up at day break, promising him a five peso tip if he would keep his mouth shut, which he promised to do, and did, because at that time five pesos could buy a lot of things.

Nobody, not even her only friend, imagined what she was planning to do. The evening before her departure, Jeannette-Marie went, as was her custom, to the Barreau house to see her son, to dine with them and chat with Saturnina. Shortly after dinner she left, with the pretext that she had a headache.

Very early the following morning at the train station, she took the Sabana express, and a few days later the steamer that would take her back to France left the port of Sabana.

Jeannette-Marie Ribeaux never returned to Helena, nor did she ever want to know anything further about her son. Saturnina, after writing her several letters that were never answered, became convinced that my grandmother, upon leaving, had shaken the dust of Helena from her shoes.

Months later, aunt Saturnina was worried sick about the damage that might be inflicted on little Cesáreo if the child was told the truth. But, upon realizing that he hadn't even seemed to notice that Jeannette-Marie was no longer visiting them, Saturnina called him to her room and let him know, as tactfully as she could, the story of his mother desertion.

The boy, however, showed neither pain nor surprise, not even curiosity as to why his mother had left him. His full attention was centered on a toy he had been longing for, which had just been delivered to the house. It was a big papier-mâché horse, a present from Saturnina to lessen the impact of the sad news upon the child.

Saturnina had not yet realized the kind of person that Cesáreo really was, and she wouldn't listen to anyone that tried to open her eyes about him.

Present in that child were almost all the detrimental qualities that can be found in a human being. Not only was he a hypocrite and a liar, ill-disposed and fiercely egoistic, he also had an early inclination to grab what was not his.

One day, when he was in the third grade, they called Agustín from the school, because Cesáreo had been accused of stealing the lunch money from one of his classmates, whose mother was raising hell, threatening to go to the police so they would "put the thief in the reformatory".

On another occasion, Cesáreo was found in his uncle's bedroom, where Agustín caught him in the act of stealing change from his pocket book.

Cesáreo's sexual precociousness was also outstanding. He was barely eleven years old when he was found masturbating while spying on Apolonia, the maid, through a hole that he had drilled in the door of the servant's bathroom.

Agustín got out his belt to give him a thrashing, but Saturnina thrust herself between them, shielding Cesáreo from his uncle's wrath.

"Can't you see he is only a child?", she yelled at her husband, "He doesn't know what he's doing! You have to talk to him about the facts of life!"

Finally, Cesáreo Barreau, chosen by fate to be my father, was legally adopted by Agustín and Saturnina, thanks to the efforts of the latter, who pushed, coaxed and threatened her husband until he consented to the adoption.

My father-to-be finished primary school with very good grades. He went to the "Colegio Edgardo Medeles Vito", the most expensive private school in Helena. Everybody got good grades, provided, of course, that the students' tuition was paid punctually.

At the "Colegio Edgardo Medeles Vito" they gave my father more outstanding grades than there are pork sausages in a ten foot long string. But, in spite of that, when Cesáreo took the high school entrance examination, he flunked the test.

Saturnina puffed up with anger at the injustice that had been perpetrated against her son, and ordered Mr. Barreau to go to Helena High School immediately and see to it that those "wise parrots", as she called the teachers, would be able to clearly understand that the son of Saturnina Díaz de Barreau, simply, was not to be failed.

Helena High's teachers were, for the most part, a wretched crowd that got paid at the end of the month only to see themselves penniless a few days later. Then they would go to the loan sharks, to whom they were indebted for life.

And many of these teachers were indebted to Mr. Barreau. This made it easy for him to convince the members of the examination tribunal to give "corrected" grades to Cesáreo. Now my future father had great grades to go with his great expectations.

Thanks to the increases in the price of sugar during World War I, the fortune of Agustín Barreau and his wife had multiplied. Following the advice of his friend Benigno Merino, Barreau quit the usury business and invested all his money in sugar, farm and commercial financing, and the importation of European goods. Now he was a respectable business man, and streams and rivers of money continued to flow.

Cesáreo, the adopted son of the new millionaires, had no problem in graduating from Helena High School. Certainly, those niggardly and starving teachers were not going to stand in front of Agustín and Saturnina to tell them that their son had to study in order to graduate, something that Cesáreo had never done, nor would ever consider doing.

As time passed, Cesáreo's hypocrisy and malice intensified, and became more refined. In Helena High, because he was the son of Agustín Barreau, his teachers always gave him the highest grades, and since they were all a bunch of sycophants, they praised him to high heaven every time they met his adoptive parents on the street.

The day Cesáreo graduated from high school, he reminded Saturnina of her promise to send him to college in the United States. She managed to gain admittance for Cesáreo to attend the Golden Mine College of Commerce in Pennsylvania. This was to be a two year program especially created for the sons and daughters of wealthy Spanish-Americans.

Cesáreo never finished his studies at Golden Mine. In Yagruma, with the free fall of the price of sugar and the subsequent failure of the banks, the so-called "golden days" passed into history, and those who in a couple of years had become millionaires, passed, as in a nightmare, from opulence to poverty.

Greed had blinded Agustín Barreau. When the price of sugar began to fall, he could have sold all his stocks and made a decent profit. But he didn't, with the illusion that the market was going to recover and that he, then, would have an even bigger windfall. But the price kept falling precipitously, and the old whiner saw his fortune disappear virtually overnight.

Aging Barreau, defeated and tired, didn't have the strength to confront the catastrophe. He realized that he could no longer find the energy to fight the battle of life. The idea of being an old man leading a deprived life terrorized him and he began obsessing about it. He saw himself begging in the streets of Helena, ridiculed and insulted by those who, until recently, had adulated and flattered him servilely.

One afternoon, after telling Saturnina that he was going to spend a couple of hours going over some accounts, he went to his office and locked the door from the inside. After leaving two letters on his desk, he took out his revolver.

Putting the barrel in his mouth, he could taste the bitter gun metal. As his trembling lips held tightly to the cold steel, he slowly depressed the trigger. Barreau's life and brains splattered throughout the room.

In one of the letters, addressed to the police, Barreau explained the reasons for his suicide. The other was for María "La Chumba", a woman who, for more than forty years, had been his mistress. In neither of the letters did he mention his wife or his adopted son.

Neither Barreau's suicide, nor the loss of the fortune that he had accumulated, were enough to even subdue Saturnina, who had a temper of steel.

While the economic bonanza lasted, she had, without Barreau's knowledge, been putting aside in a hiding place, all the money that she was able to get out of her husband, so as to have a reserve, in case some day it was needed. When that day arrived, Saturnina had ten thousand pesos in her nest egg, a fortune for those times!

One of the first things she did was to call Cesáreo, telling him about Agustin's death. She also informed him that they were penniless, and that she didn't have the means to continue paying the Golden Mine College of Commerce. After all, with what was left to her, she told him, they barely had enough to put food on the table.

She added that she was sending him the money for the return fare to Yagruma and advised him that, as soon as he returned, he would have to look for a job, since all she could offer him was room and board.

She didn't tell Cesáreo anything about the money she had hidden away. Perhaps, with the years, she had begun to know this adopted son after all.

Yagrumans who had no political, military or family connections, found it impossible to obtain decent employment. My father came to this conclusion after spending several months running around Helena and the countryside looking for a job, with no success.

He even went so far as to change his family name from Barreau, which in French is pronounced "Barró", to Baró, which is conformable to the Spanish language. He got it into his head that with a Spanish surname it would be easier for him to find work in Yagruma. But he was wrong.

Cesáreo had worn out several pairs of shoes, and was getting down to the last one he had. Trotting around the streets of Helena, he would visit the local politicians as well as many of the associates of the late Agustín. Then, one afternoon, while walking through the city park, he came across Dr. Onofre Riverón, alias "Bemba'e Toro", his old friend and classmate at Edgardo Medeles Vito.

"Bemba'e Toro" had become a doctor of education. Since he was the son of a local politician who controlled tons of votes in the south of the province, he had been named, first professor, and then, director of Helena's Normal School for Teachers.

After an enthusiastic embrace, and the customary exclamations, the two old friends, who hadn't seen each other for many years, sat down on one of the benches in the park. They relived old memories and told each other what had been happening in their lives. My father also talked about the crisis that he was going through in looking for a job.

When Cesáreo mentioned that he had been studying in the United States, Dr. Riverón showed real interest.

"Do you speak English, Cesarito?", he asked.

"Well, I am no Shakespeare", answered my father, "But I can get by".

"What do you know! It looks like I may be able to solve your problem!", exclaimed "Bemba'e Toro", "The English teacher that we have in the Normal School is an old guy who has a foot in the grave. Yesterday they took him to the hospital, and the doctors are giving him no more than a couple of weeks. Are you interested?"

"Is the Pope a Roman Catholic?", retorted Cesáreo. "But, wait a minute, my friend! I didn't graduate from college. Don't you have to have a diploma to teach at the Normal School?"

"To teach French, English, and that kind of things, no!", replied the other, "You know enough English to get by, don't you?"

"Well, yes", admitted my father, cautiously, "Enough to get by..."

"OK, then, it is a deal!", concluded "Bemba'e Toro", "Tomorrow, you report to the Normal School, so you can start subbing, and that way you can make a little money. I'll take care of the paperwork. Father is going to Sabana in a couple of days, to see Senator Caballería, and I am going to talk to him so you'll have a little pull. The old man always remembers you; he really liked you!"

And so that's the way it turned out. The father of Dr. Riverón, at his son's insistence, used his influence with the senator, and within a few days after the death of the old teacher, Cesáreo Baró was appointed professor of English at Helena Normal School.

For Cesáreo, who was a born actor, it wasn't very hard to convince his students and his fellow teachers that his command of the English language was better than Rudyard Kipling's. As the old saying goes, "in the land of the blind, the one-eyed man is king".

Although my father liked women more than he liked French Vanilla ice-cream, he was very careful not to get involved with any of his students, aware that a scandal could cost him his job.

But, when my future mother made her appearance in the English class, his good judgment vanished and he fell for his new student the moment he laid eyes on her. Dominga Oropesa, at fourteen years of age, had the body of a voluptuous woman of twenty, that would have provoked excitability in a castrated Trappist monk.

Dominga's jet black hair cascaded past her shoulders and its bluish reflections sensually framed an angelical face that would have bewitched King Tut's mummy. The attraction was mutual, my grandmother told me years later. Dominga confessed to her that, as soon as she laid eyes on the teacher, she had fallen for him like a ton of bricks.

The romance didn't take long to develop. In the beginning, the two met after school, in one of the classrooms, under the pretext that Dominga needed tutoring. And as they became more involved, things turned into a Greco-Roman wrestling match.

Unfortunately, these trysts were becoming endangered. Titina Polanco, a friend of my mother's that was also a student of professor Baró, perhaps jealous that he hadn't noticed her, went to "Bemba'e Toro" with the gossip.

The director, then, called my father to his office and told him that the affair had to end, or, he would have no other choice but to fire him, in spite of their friendship.

Cesáreo was a man that made quick decisions without taking into account anything other than the urgency of the situation. Dominga had gotten into his blood, and if the only way to have her was to marry her, then so be it!

A few days later, Cesáreo went to the house of the widow Oropesa to ask for the hand of Dominga. It surprised him to find that the old lady didn't put up any resistance. She only expressed some reservations at the difference in ages, because papá was fifteen years older than my mother.

Unfortunately, to afford a wife and a home one needs money, and my father was always flat broke. Concerning credit, he was in debt up to his eyeballs, and a major portion of his paycheck went to pay interests to the loan sharks that were constantly after him.

The man had a talent for persuasion. He also had a serious, grave face that fooled the most clever ones. It wasn't very hard for him to deceive my grandmother, and get the poor old lady to permit the newlyweds to come and live with her for a while.

He invented a tall tale that he was waiting for the sale of a piece of Barreau's real estate which was left to Saturnina. As soon as the litigation came to an end, he assured his mother-in-law, he would be paid a considerable amount. At that time, he would use the money to move into his own home.

My grandmother swallowed the story and consented to the pair staying with her until the land was sold.

CHAPTER II
PLEASURE REIGNS

I was born on the twenty first of November, the Day of the Presentation of the Blessed Virgin and also the date on which the Catholic Church celebrates the Patronage of Our Lady. My mother, who was a Roman Catholic in her own way, as she used to put it, wanted me to be baptized with the name of Patrocinio. But my grandmother insisted that they give me the name of Miguel, in memory of her deceased husband. My father reluctantly agreed.

The same day that I came into this world there was a monumental scandal in Helena; something that, with the passing of time, became a local legend. That was the day that that Pocholo gave birth.

"Pocholo" was the by-name given to Manolo del Jardín, the only social columnist in Helena whose reviews were published in a newspaper of national circulation. And Pocholo was always ranked among the important people of the city, along with the mayor, the chief of the military district and the president of the court of appeals. Pocholo's chronicles, under the title of "Waves of Helena", appeared daily in "The Marine Herald", a newspaper published in Sabana that was to be found all over Yagruma.

For Helena's petit-bourgeoisie, becoming part of the local high-life was an official seal of distinction, a most longed-for accomplishment. And in order to enter such an exclusive circle they needed Pocholo, because, according to an unwritten but rigorously observed rule, only those whose names appeared regularly in the "Waves of Helena" could be considered members of my hometown's high society.

Pocholo, who was in his early forties at that time, was gay, and very flamboyant in his homosexuality. He owned a beautiful villa, called "Villa Coral", on the outskirts of Helena, and he lived there with his companion, Serafín Cordeiro, better known as "Springfield". Cordeiro, formerly a military man, had been charged with sodomy and kicked out of the army several years before.

In addition to the parties that he gave to celebrate his saint's day and his birthday, Pocholo, romantic soul that he was, celebrated the anniversary of what he called "their union". On these occasions, his neighbors witnessed a long line of boot lickers, flatterers and brown-nosers, each loaded with presents, parade in front of Villa Coral.

Those who wanted to earn the good will of Pocholo had to spend real money, because, as he himself said to his friends, whoever showed up with cheap gifts, would suffer his everlasting disdain.

They say that "Springfield" complained about Pocholo's not being able to bear him a child, so the latter, to please his companion, began to pretend that he was pregnant. He went around the house dressed as a pregnant woman, complete with a false stomach made from a pair of pillows. To make his performance even more realistic, he rejected "Springfield" when he made advances.

"No, Serafín, no!", he yelled, so that the neighbors would hear him, "-I can't do it, in the state I'm in! Serafín, leave me alone..!!"

Pocholo wanted to give birth on the twenty first of November, the date that the pair had first met. That first meeting took place at an afternoon tea given for her friends by Blanca Lisa Perdices de González Tavernier, one of Helena's most distinguished social leaders.

For the day of the birth, Pocholo and "Springfield" organized a fiesta to which they invited the most select and flowery of Helena's society. Among those was doctor Antonio Montt, the fashionable gynecologist, who was to assist Pocholo in the terrible moment of childbirth.

When the day of the farce arrived, at nightfall, the automobiles full of guests began streaming into Villa Coral, and soon after, spurred by lust, and under the influence of alcohol and occasional "touches" of cocaine, the whole crowd began to lose its composure. The first brawl took place when Doctor Omar Arcilla, judge of the district court of South Helena, discovered his wife, Josefina and Perfecto Lima, the manager of the American Bank, devouring each other behind the living room curtains.

As night arrived, the debauchery had reached its climax. The guests were vomiting in the bathrooms, in the corners of the living room, and even in the flower pots. Many were giving themselves up to the love exchanges that were the salt and life of the parties in old Helena.

All of a sudden, "Springfield" came running out of the room where Pocholo was lying. His hair was all messed up, his eyes were unfocused, and terror was written all over his face. They say the man played his part very well.

"Doctor, it's time!", he screamed, "The contractions aren't stopping! Oh, Holy Mother!"

The women began shrieking as though it were really happening. Doctor Montt, who was quite drunk, got up with some difficulty from the sofa where he and Pura Miranda had been fondling and caressing each other, and headed toward the room where the "birth" was to take place. The rest of the group, who didn't want to miss the spectacle, followed him, but the doctor, who was in a bad humor, turned them back, yelling like an animal.

"Get the hell out of here!", he roared, "Wait outside! I'll tell you when you can come in!"

From inside the room came the screeches of Pocholo, who, playing his part, screamed like the devil, acting out the trauma of childbirth. Doctor Montt went in, closing the door behind him.

The screeches continued for some minutes. All at once, all sound ceased, leaving the guests in unnatural anticipation. Doctor Montt burst through the door dressed in a white surgeon's gown stained with red to proudly announce the miracle of birth.

"Pocholo has had a baby", he proclaimed very seriously, "The child and the mother are fine. You can go in and see them now".

The guests rushed into the room, where in a large double bed, they found a swooning Pocholo, barely covered by a rose colored negligée, cradling in his hairy arms a beautiful baby doll. Ceferino Pratts, the agent in Helena of "El Hechizo", the famous Sabana department store, donated it for the grand performance.

Unfortunately, not many of the guests had the opportunity to congratulate the proud couple, because, at that very moment, a squad of police, with the "Black María" and everything, made its appearance at Villa Coral. In the blink of an eye, the villa was surrounded and some of the guests, who tried to escape by jumping over the patio wall, were nabbed by the police.

Captain Jerónimo Folgueiras, followed by sergeant Abundio Jaramillo and a group of policemen, entered the living room and announced to everyone that they were all under arrest for public scandal, disturbing the peace, sexual promiscuity, sodomy, drunkenness and "anything that the courts deemed pertinent". The captain had a weakness for the legal jargon.

Pocholo's neighbors had called the police, complaining about the orgy taking place in Villa Coral, and captain Folgueiras, a real tough peasant who didn't believe in high society, scooped up the whole crowd. As sergeant Jaramillo said, "even the cat wound up in the can".

Well then, in Yagruma, as is true all over, justice is for the underdogs, and there were none of those among the guests of Pocholo. Every one of them "knew somebody". Pocholo, of course, had his society column, and that made him unassailable. Phone calls were made to the mayor, the district colonel, the president of the court of appeals, and to senator Nivaldo Caballería, whose niece, Daniela Guerra, had been removed from Pocholo's bathtub, where they found her, naked, with two men, also nude, who were lathering her from head to toe.

As usual, he who has a godfather gets baptized, and he who doesn't remains a heathen. Pocholo and his guests all had "godfathers", and since no serious crime had been committed ("just some high-class buggers and queers having a little fun", as colonel Pérez said), the authorities decided to ignore the whole incident. The colonel called the chief of police, the president of the court of appeals put a lid on the unfortunate affair, and the bishop of the diocese warned all the priests in Helena that those who dared to even mention the name of Pocholo during mass would be sent to new parishes in the swamp.

All the necessary arrangements were made: the records of arrests were annulled, the legal proceedings that had been started were dropped and all those imprisoned were set free.

Everything was kept quiet. Senator Nivaldo Caballería sent his private secretary, Julito "Iron-eater", to clamp down on the local reporters, making sure that the Villa Coral scandal didn't come out in the newspapers. But the leaders of Helena knew very well that, no matter how hard they tried to cover up the scuttlebutt, they couldn't avoid word getting out, and that people would be talking about it all over town.

Even forty years later, the stories of Pocholo's pregnancy and childbirth still circulate around in Helena.

Meanwhile, my mother went into labor at eight o'clock in the morning, but it wasn't until fourteen hours later that I had the misfortune to appear in this miserable world. As was customary, my father had sent for an old midwife who was very well known in the city. In addition to childbirth, she did abortions and restored virginities, services that were in great demand in Helena. Albertina, as the old midwife was called, did everything she could to get me out of Dominga's belly, but seeing that the situation was getting complicated and more that she could handle, she told my father that he had better get a doctor.

"The child is coming out backwards", explained Albertina, "and is becoming entangled in the umbilical cord. There is nothing else I can do".

After thirteen hours of labor, with my mother moaning in the dark room, my grandmother on the verge of a heart attack and aunt Lidia fainting away, my father had no choice but to get moving. He called a taxi and went looking for doctor Montt, his old friend and companion of parties and whoring. When he got to the doctor's house, the physician had just arrived. It had been a short time since his release from the precinct where he spent a good part of the evening.

Doctor Montt was exhausted, ashamed of himself and still under the effects of the drunken party. But in view of my father's predicament, he took his bag and together they went to the house where I was fighting not to be born.

I had the dubious honor to come into this world the same day as Pocholo's pantomime, and because of that questionable distinction I paid dearly.

My grandmother told me that doctor Montt was unable to use his right arm for several days, because of the pain and inflammation caused by the hours he spent pulling on the forceps until he finally, freed me from Dominga's uterus. The doctor couldn't, or didn't know how to use the forceps as well as he should have. During one of the attempts that he made, my skull was crushed.

If I hadn't been brought to this world the same day as Pocholo's pantomime, my destiny would have certainly been different. The doctor wouldn't have been half-drunk, worn out and aggravated by all that had happened to him, I would have escaped injury, and my childhood would have been entirely transformed.

I was three months old when a famous surgeon, in Sabana, patched up my head, saving my life. This doctor warned my parents to be careful that I didn't receive any bumps in the back of my head. Thanks to that I spent my childhood enclosed in the household where I was born, looking out of the window at how the other children did everything that had been denied to me.

My grandmother, who had been a teacher when she was young, taught me to read and write when I was only four years old. Then I discovered the world of books. In the living room of the old house was an extensive and select library that had belonged to Florencio Marcial, a Sabana journalist, who was a close friend of my great-uncle Sóstenes.

Concerning Marcial, he got into big trouble when he tried to blackmail a powerful politician. The journalist left for Mexico, where he went into hiding, because the politician's goons were after him to tear his head off. Marcial, who had the moral fiber of a condom, was, nevertheless, a cultured man, and not wishing to lose his books, before leaving for Mexico he sent them to Sóstenes for safekeeping until he could return to Yagruma.

Marcial never came back, because they killed him in Mexico. Now his books were gathering dust in our living room, as no one ever opened them. Finally my grandmother gave me her permission to begin looking through the books, warning me to be careful not to damage them.

From that day forward, I spent all my time in the living room, reading. When a visitor arrived, I would take my book and go into any empty room where I could be alone and read in peace. The other kids could have their bicycles, their roller skates and their games. I had my books.

The house of my maternal grandmother, where I was born, was a decaying Spanish colonial structure at the back of which flowed the smelly, greenish waters of the San Juan River. The current carried with it the outflow of thousands of toilets and the wastes of the local slaughter house.

With the passing of the years, the humidity had softened the plaster on the walls. There were big patches of something like a viscous drool. The dirty and damp facade showed the deterioration caused by the passage of time and lack of maintenance. Sometimes even today, I think I can smell that particularly repugnant odor that one could not ignore upon entering the house. My mother called it "the smell of an open sore".

I remember that the parlor was separated from the other rooms by beautiful double doors of stained glass that depicted scenes of the Crucifixion. Some of the panes had been broken and were now held together with adhesive tape. It had a very large keyhole, and through it I spied on my aunt Lidia and her fiancé, Chuchú, the army corporal.

Chuchú and aunt Lidia sat in some old wicker rocking chairs grouped in one of the corners and there, thinking that nobody could see them, they hugged and kissed, and fondled each other.

The whole house reeked of poverty, melancholia, and despair. The cracked cement patio was separated from the neighbor's house by a dark gray wall, eight feet high. There, in a large, weed-infested tract, a couple of crotons, a dwarfed pine tree and a guacamaya shrub fought for survival. These plants never completely died, because when they began to dry up, my grandmother would sprinkle a little water on them to prolong their agony.

My grandmother, my mother and aunt Lidia did the cooking, and scrubbed, washed, ironed and cleaned house. Sóstenes, who always had plenty of money, paid most of the household expenses.

His wife, Goya, spent the whole day with her ass stuck in a chair, reading magazines or listening to radio programs.

In order to prevent flooding of the patio during Helena's torrential rains, they kept the sewer drain uncovered. This allowed hordes of cockroaches to roam freely all over the house, whether it was night or day!

From the pipes that drained down to the river came packs of rats that entered the house through the basement windows. Ever since my uncle Barbarito committed suicide by taking permanganate, my grandmother was horrified by anything that was poison. So that not even against the rats would she think of using it.

The old lady had some big rat traps, a sort of cage of heavy wire, in which she put as bait some pieces of rancid cheese. When a rat was captured, my grandmother took the cage out into the patio and left it there, under the scorching sun, where they would suffer a slow death. When ever possible, I gave a helping hand to my grandmother in this battle. I sharpened an old knife, and attached it on to the end of a stick with some tape. Becoming an expert with this homemade spear, I killed so many rats with it, that they started calling me "Jack the Ripper".

As far as the old house is concerned, apart from the books and the rat hunting I have very few pleasant memories. I remember, though, that at the end of the day I liked to wait, leaning on the window sill, for the sunset to tint with scarlet and copper the quiet neighborhood. At dusk, I enjoyed watching the bats when they came out, shrieking and flying about the patio until they vanished, like ghosts, into the night.

Sóstenes, my great-uncle, acted as head of household and was the only one that seemed to have any amount of money. Sóstenes took care of the major part of the expenses to the delight of my parents. Goya, his third legal wife, a snub-nosed woman with no neck, flaunted her enormous and gelatinous breasts, even though a large black, ugly wart was visible between them.

Before marrying Goya, Sóstenes was a two-time widower. Engracia, his first wife, had committed suicide, and Dolores died of cancer. As for Dolores, Sóstenes, who at that time had become involved in naturopathy, had wanted to cure her by having her eat only raw vegetables, and taking her to a witch doctor in a nearby village. Finally, my grandmother, seeing that the poor woman was getting worse by the day, convinced Sóstenes, by begging and pleading with him, to put Dolores in the hands of the doctors. But by then it was too late, and Sóstenes was left a widower for the second time.

Shortly after the death of his second wife, Sóstenes became involved with a mulata, for whom he rented a room in a tenement house that was close to where we lived. Pastora, Sóstenes' sweetheart, was a close friend of Juana "Palangana", a young woman who lived in the same tenement house. Juana earned her beans by "cleaning the saber" of José, the owner of the neighborhood "bodega".

Sóstenes and José were buddies, and often went out carousing together. Everybody in our house criticized this, especially my father, who was the moralizer in our family group.

When several days had gone by without Sóstenes visiting Pastora, she stood on the doorway of the bodega, which was very close to my grandmother's house, and screamed at the top of her lungs, so that of course everybody could hear:

"Sóstenes, what's the matter? Have you run out of steam?"

And if José or Juana told her to shut up so as not to make trouble for the old man, she screamed her answer:

"I want to be cruel! I want to be bad and cruel!!"

And, lowering her voice, she said: "That Sóstenes is a bastard!"

When Sóstenes got married to Goya, he brought her to live with us, and his visits to Pastora became difficult because Goya was very jealous. She didn't miss a footstep of the old man, so that, in order to solve the problem, Sóstenes took Pastora out of the tenement on Santa Erenia and rented a room for her on Moratín Street, far away from us. The truth is that the old man spent a lot of money. As a youngster, I was left with my mouth open upon seeing how Sóstenes put his hand in his pocket and pulled out rolls of bills that would choke a horse.

Sóstenes was an inspector with the Bureau of Tobacco and Alcohol, an agency of the Treasury Department. My great-uncle had been instated in his job by a resolution of the Supreme Court, which meant that he was permanently connected to the gravy train.

Everybody knew that the Treasury agents were the bureaucratic elite of Yagruma. Those from other Departments could be bribed with small amounts. But with the Treasury the situation was different. For the Treasury could create great "difficulties" for the industrialists, as well as the merchants.

Arturo Menéndez and I were school chums. Arturo, with whom I got along very well, was a distant relative of mine. His father and my mother were second cousins. Arturo and I studied together almost every day at his house.

Higinio, Arturo's father, was a bleary-eyed man, with a purplish nose. From his pock-marked face sprouted a black mustache that, like his nose, was always dirty. The government of president Arau Santín had rewarded Higinio's revolutionary merits, giving him a Treasury inspector's job. Higinio and Sóstenes worked together for almost two years, until Sóstenes was finally transferred to another zone.

Higinio liked to bend his elbow. On one occasion that I went to study with Arturo, I found his father in the living room, sitting on a rocking chair. A bottle of rum "Totí" and a glass were on a little table beside him.

"Arturo has gone off on an errand, but he'll be right back", he informed me, "He said to wait for him".

I sat down in another rocking chair in front of him. Although he wasn't drunk, he had to have put away several shots, because he was running off at the mouth more than ever. He began to try to get me into a conversation with him, talking about Sóstenes.

"Everybody wants to work with Sóstenes", he assured me, "That old guy knows a lot! I had months that I made more than a thousand pesos when I worked with him!"

I played dumb, putting on a blank face. "A thousand pesos! Nobody earns that much except congressmen!"

He looked at me as if thinking: "What an idiot!"

"I'm talking about making money, son!", he exclaimed, "Real money! One looks for a pigeon every day, in this business!"

He sprawled out in the rocking chair, took a big gulp of rum and lit a cigarette of the kind that in Yagruma we called "chest-breakers" and also "supersticks".

"Let me tell you how Sóstenes and I used to operate", he said, "Suppose we had orders to conduct an audit on a distiller. So we arrive and begin the inspection. Sóstenes, who has fabricated a reputation of being tough and incorruptible, lets me do the talking and gets down to work, without saying a word. He wouldn't crack a smile even if they tickled him".

He put the glass to his lips again. He still had it in his hand and was ready to put down another shot.

"That Sóstenes, he is smarter than the lizards!", he went on, "He always finds out how the water gets in the coconut!"

"And, how did that alliance of yours work?", I wanted to know.

"You'll see", he replied. "You don't have the least idea of the fierce face that Sóstenes could put on! While he was doing his thing with the account books and papers, I was getting together with the storekeeper, or the president of the company, or whoever, until I gained his confidence and he lowered his guard"

"Then Sóstenes would come up", he continued, "And show the guy all the discrepancies that he had found, and he would tell them that that was illegal. To put the fear of God into him, he began talking about the penalties, the severity of the judges, the possibility of a jail sentence...all that shit!"

"Finally he would say that there wasn't any other way out but that he had to "write it up", and with that he would turn around and start filling out forms".

"And that's where you came in, right?" I asked.

"Of course!", he replied, "Now the guy is hanging on the ropes, and then I say to him that everything in this life has its remedy. Then he, tells me that he is going to make us a gift of two hundred pesos if we can fix the problem".

"And then I tell him: "Look, as far as I am concerned, that's fine. I'm not a hog! Today for me, tomorrow for you!"

"But when the guy is believing all this and thinks he is going to get it all cleaned up for a lousy two hundred bucks, I let loose the line: `Well, now, the problem isn't with me, it's my partner. That old guy has a tough skin! He doesn't even trust his own mother!"

I was enjoying the story, above all remembering that Sóstenes, at home, when we were seated at the table, used to tell us about the many occasions where he had been offered bribes that his moral principles kept him from taking.

I spoke again to Arturo's father, who was now sort of glassy-eyed and lighting another "superstick".

"Well, and then what?', I asked, "The guy raised the offer?"

"He went up a little ways", answered Higinio, "First he gave a big sigh, and then swore that if he had screwed things up a little, it was because the business wasn't going too well at the time. That sales had dropped, that his partner had turned out to be a womanizer, that if this, or that if that, and finished by going up to three hundred bucks".

"And you grabbed it right then, right?"

"None of that!", replied he, "This is the scene that was always played out. I pointed over to where Sóstenes was, and said: `Look, my partner, the old guy, is no slouch. Look at him: English muslin, American shoes, gold watch! What else! I wouldn't confront him with this problem for anything less that five hundred pesos'!"

So that explained to me how Sóstenes always went around with the big roll in his pocket." And so how did it all end up?", I asked, just to say something, but already guessing the answer.

"How was it going to end up?", he replied drunkenly, "For that guy it was better business to pay up and let us have it! It was cheaper for him! Besides, we arranged everything for him. We sold him peace of mind!".

"How did you divide up the money? Fifty-fifty?"

"Well, not exactly", answered Higinio, "Sóstenes put aside one hundred pesos that went to the big boss, in Sabana. At least, that's what he told me! The rest of it, yes, we went half and half".

I would have liked to continue pumping Higinio to learn more about the activities of Sóstenes, but the alcohol had begun to have its effect on him, and the distinguished public servant, leaning back in his rocking chair, closed his eyes and passed out. He wasn't pleasant to look at, because his nose had begun to drip again, and the discharge ran down onto his mustache, where it was forming a crust.

CHAPTER III
A BIG ROLL OF THE DICE

Once my newlywed father had installed himself in my grandmother's house, Cesáreo never again spoke of moving. Whenever my grandmother wanted to know how long this situation was going to last, he came up with a different story. He would say he had had to bring new charges against some of the defendants in the case, or that he and Saturnina had been forced to go on appeal before the higher court, or that they had to levy judgment against a third party, etc., etc.. In short: lies upon lies. He invariable ended by assuring his mother-in-law that it wouldn't be much longer until he, along with Dominga and their son, would be leaving.

My grandmother also had to push my father to come up with his share of the household expenses. That was like a battle between a lion and a tied-up lamb, because papá mastered the difficult art of living on the cuff.

When several weeks had passed without Cesáreo dropping his guard, my grandmother took him aside, very discreetly, and all blushing, in a low voice, she faced him with the problem.

He then got himself lost in web of explanations and excuses and ended up finally giving her only a fraction of what he owed, promising to pay her the rest as soon as his next paycheck came.

Those promises were never kept, and the scene would repeat itself the following month, and the next, and the next...After some time, my grandmother stopped asking him anymore about the litigation involving the Barreau property, convinced, that it was another story invented by my father.

Years later, friends of papá told me that Cesáreo was quite a Don Juan. According to them, he would make passes at anything in skirts. Like the gypsy in the song, father believed that even the ugliest woman has something nice to offer, and though short and paunchy, he was convinced that he was a ladies' man.

Besides being a womanizer, papa carried in his veins the gambling vice. What he liked most of all was poker, but he would not turn down baccarat, black jack, or three-card monte. When there wasn't anything doing in his usual haunts, father went to Bachicha, an ill-reputed section of Helena. There, in the back room of Pantaleón's "bodega", he dove into dominoes, craps, and even the old shell game. He even bet on the license plates of the cars that went by.

Papá, who during the first few months of his marriage only had eyes for my mother, soon returned to his Don Juan activities.

Sóstenes, Aunt Lidia and my grandmother's friends had frequently seen him standing on street corners or hidden in the doorways of the stores, talking with Cuca Moreno, a swinging spinster who lived around the corner from us, and also with María Liras Forza, a middle-aged divorcee, also known in Helena's social circles as "The Nymph".

Whenever anyone came to my mother with gossip that they had seen papá on the street with another woman, she would know how put on an indifferent face and assured everyone that she wasn't afraid that her man was running around.

“What's your problem, sister?”, she would reply, "He and I, we each have our day. I send him off to those whores, but I have the best part first".

My father, on the other hand, was more jealous than Othello. When relatives from the countryside came to visit, especially my mother's cousins, who were tall, real good-looking guys, Cesáreo ordered his wife to shut herself up in the bedroom and not leave until the visitors left.

"They don't come here with good intentions!", he would say, "They are coming here to see if the women are going around hot to trot!"

During the years that he was a professor at the Normal School, papá began to enjoy the fact that his students, as was the necessary usage in those days, had to address him as "doctor".

Almost every evening we went to Saturnina's house, and on the way we had to pass by on the sidewalk in front of the Casino Español, at whose doorway was always "Burro Triste", the doorman.

"Burro Triste" had a daughter who was a student of papá's.

When my father passed by, the man would respectfully greet him with a "Good evening, doctor!"

As for me, I have to confess, it made me very proud to hear that papá was called "doctor". It was something that made me feel important.

The city of Helena was known as "The Parnassus of Yagruma", for having been the cradle of a series of literary celebrities, especially poets.

In Helena, a group called "The Literary Circle" got together every week. It was comprised, for the most part, of starving lawyers, dirt-poor school teachers and local journalists.

According to its members, the purpose of the "Circle" was to keep alive Helena's glorious literary tradition. "Pocholo", occasionally, reviewed the meetings in his column, which was, probably, the main reason why the poor bastards kept holding them.

Actually, the "Circle" was nothing but a mutual admiration society in which the "learned" members spoke, read their works and discussed their intellectual reveries, among mutual eulogies and congratulations. Then, on the way back to their homes, they tore the hide off each other.

My father went once in a while to those "intellectual feasts", as "Pocholo" called them, because he was convinced that it gave him stature.

Papá believed that the Jews and the blacks were the natural allies of communism. And he was convinced that President Mechado was the only leader capable of holding back the red wave on the Island.

These ideas he expanded upon in his classes, at home and in the casino, earned him the dubious fame of being a "mechadista", and cost him his teaching job when the Mechado regime fell.

His teaching position was given to an old drunk who had the revolutionary merit of being the father of the mistress of some army corporal, promoted to lieutenant colonel in the wake of general Bautista's rise to power.

Cesáreo took things philosophically, always insisting that it was his civic attitude that caused him to lose his job. Meanwhile, although he didn't have two nickels to rub together, he didn't despair.

I had to go to Saturnina's every day, to pick up the bag of coffee and the two packs of cigarettes that she provided for him. Cesáreo was a chain smoker and also a coffee-addict who used up a pound of coffee daily. Without the stuff, the man would be climbing the walls, and Saturnina, after all, still cared for her adopted son.

Papá stayed in bed until noon, smoking, drinking coffee and reading "The Marine Herald". At which time he would get up, have his lunch and, if he could swindle a couple of pesos from Sóstenes or Saturnina, he would go down to the Casino to play a game of dominos. He didn't return to the house until dinner time, when papá assured us that he had been diligently searching for work.

A year later Saturnina died, leaving in her will a few thousands pesos to Cesáreo Baró, her adopted son and only heir. My father, as long as the money from the inheritance lasted, continued to live without lifting a finger, until the day he realized that he had spent almost all of the money that Saturnina had left him.

The situation that faced us in the house got worse by the day. Months went by that he didn't give my grandmother any money for household expenses. Finally a letter came from my school, telling my parents not to send me there anymore unless the back payments were made.

Besides that, Sóstenes and my grandmother made it very clear that they were fed up with taking care of him, and that he either found some work, even if it was a job in a pool hall, or they would kick him out of the house.

"My daughter and my grandson are my own blood", said my grandmother, "Food and a roof over their heads they will have here as long as I live. But as for you, we won't stand for any more of your trickery, so, you better watch what you are doing!".

As if that were not enough, Sóstenes made father's life miserable with the cutting remarks and insults that he threw at him when we were sitting at the table at dinner time.

I remember that once, while we were sitting at the table, eating, I gave my mother a sharp answer. Sóstenes looked at me with a fierce face.

"You will respect your mother!", he bellowed, "Look how you have raised this kid! Even I respect your mother!"

And looking out of the corner of his eye at my father, he added: "And in this house, for better or for worse, I am the one who puts food on the table".

At other times, Sóstenes would talk about the qualities that should be present in anyone who considered himself a man.

"A man that can't support his home isn't a man!", he declared.

If my grandmother, trying to calm things down, tried to justify anyone found in such circumstances, Sóstenes would reply:

"Those are not men! Those are just `things' with pants!"

My father sat there with his eyes fixed on his plate and kept on eating as though he had heard nothing, an attitude that irritated me, because I would have liked to see him get up and smack that old bastard across the face. Later, I understood that, in his situation, my father had no choice but to bear his humiliation. That was the price he had to pay for the plate of food that was placed in front of him.

His only release, in situations like this, was to shut himself up in the room with my mother, to vilify Sóstenes and my grandmother and swear that as soon as he got a job he would leave the house forever.

My father finally did get a job, thanks to his old friend, Dr. Montt. The good doctor was the director of the Medical Association of Helena, Inc., which owned the "Workers' Medical Center" and the "Polyclinic of the Proletariat", two clinics that specialized in the treatment of workmen's injuries.

"El Trapiche" and "La Cigarrera" were two of the most important insurance companies in Yagruma. Their general agent in the province of Helena was Don Cleto Echegarrúa, an old cheat who did business with the Medical Association of Helena, to whose clinics he sent all the injured workers covered by policies with the companies that he represented.

Don Cleto had not been feeling well lately. At first he didn't think it was anything important, but when he began to have nausea, and pain in his bowels, he decided to see his personal physician, Dr. Bonifacio Areces, who diagnosed his problem as cancer of the pancreas. A terminal case, because it had progressed so far.

Echegarrúa, who had a tremendous fear of death, refused to accept the diagnosis and left for the United States, where he checked into a world famous hospital that specialized in the treatment of cancer.

In my hometown, nothing could be kept a secret, and the case of Don Cleto Echegarrúa was no exception. Everybody knew that he was at the point of death, and there were many already trying to get his position that would open as soon as the old guy kicked the bucket.

The word was out that the two insurance companies were looking for someone to replace their ailing agent. But Dr. Montt got ahead of all of them.

Montt had a sister who was married to Cardenio Porrúa, executive vice-president of "El Trapiche", and an important stockholder in "La Cigarrera". The doctor talked to his brother-in-law about my father, portraying him as the man they needed, and recommending him as a person in which the insurance companies could place all their confidence.

Dr. Montt arranged an interview for my father with Don Cardenio and several executives from the two companies. Cesáreo impressed them with his verbosity, his impeccable attire and the fact that he had lived in the United States. His reputation as an anti-Communist, that the doctor had taken upon himself to recount, was an added virtue in the eyes of those businessmen.

Papá, with the last pesos of his inheritance from Saturnina, put on the clincher, inviting them all to have lunch with him at "La Aragonesa", one of the most famous and expensive restaurants in Sabana.

When Don Cleto finally died, my father was already installed into his office, on Independence Street.

It seemed as though his new activities had brought about a change in Cesáreo. Now he was a different man. He got up at seven o'clock in the morning, arrived to his office at eight, took care of all the urgent business, and was involved with his agents until noon, when he went to lunch. About one thirty or two he was back in the office, where he spent the rest of the afternoon receiving clients. He also had conferences with the directors of the clinics, doctors, lawyers, and others whose lives revolved around the insurance business.

Sometimes he took a rented car and went to the countryside to talk to local agents about cases of special interest to his companies. At least, that's what he told my mother whenever she raised a big fuss any time that he appeared back at the house after two or three days of absence on what my father said were business trips.

My mother complained about being entombed in this big old house, like a cloistered nun, and she swore that she would go crazy if it lasted much longer.

But Cesáreo was always able to calm her down, assuring her that they would soon be leaving Helena, because his bosses were so happy with the fantastic job he was doing that they were going to promote him, transferring him to Sabana.

And when this happened, he promised that he would be taking her to the United States, where they were planning to send him to take a special course in insurance at a university. My mother swallowed everything that Cesáreo told her.

Things went along that way for almost two years. Papá complained that his workload was increasing by the day. His excursions to the countryside became more frequent, so he hired a secretary who would take care of the paper work and office routine while he was away.

One morning, my father left his room carrying a couple of suitcases. The night before, he had announced to Dominga that he was leaving Helena the next morning, on a business trip.

Papá told her that he would be gone for more than a week, because he had to see several important customers, widely scattered over the province.

He was having a last cup of coffee that mother had made for him, when the taxi that he always used on these occasions arrived. Fat Florentino, the chauffeur, put the suitcases in the trunk. Then, papá kissed my mother, promising that he would phone her. And as the car went around the corner, my father turned around and waved good-bye to us.

Two days after father had left, his secretary, sounding very upset, called Dominga to tell her that the police had been in the office, looking for Cesáreo, and that they were heading for our house.

A short time later two officers arrived and searched the house from top to bottom, to the delight of Sóstenes, who said that he had always had the premonition that my father would end in jail. My grandmother and aunt Lidia, nevertheless, watched this spectacle trembling and crying, consoling Dominga and me.

My mother assured the officer in charge that papá had left Helena on a business trip, which the policemen found to be very funny, because they broke up laughing at hearing that.

To my mother's questions they answered that a warrant had been issued for the arrest of my father, and that, if she wanted to know more, she would have to go to the courthouse and talk to the clerk.

Needless to say, when my mother heard this, she had an emotional breakdown. She screamed so loud that she could be heard all over the block, and the fainting spells came and went, in spite of the attention that my grandmother and aunt Lidia gave her.

She went to the courthouse that same morning, where the clerk explained to her what had happened. There had been charges of fraud and mishandling of funds made against papá by many of his clients and also by the insurance companies that he represented.

Among the many duties that my father had as general agent for "El Trapiche" and "La Cigarrera", were the collection of insurance premiums and the payment of claims to the workers. Papá had absolute control of the bank accounts that "El Trapiche" and "La Cigarrera" had open to their general agent at the Helena branch of the Yagruma National Bank. Through his hands passed a huge flow of money. Cesáreo decided that if he took a little bit from here and a little bit from there, and plugged up the holes with another little bits from there and here, nobody would ever notice.

The man, who was handling a pile of money, let gambling and womanizing drag him down. These were the two vices that dominated him and took him from one crazy thing to another. On those "business trips", he mixed business with the pleasures of whoring, gambling, and spending lots of money that didn't belong to him.

Over a period of close to a year he had been maneuvering the money that came in, taking some today to cover that which he had mishandled yesterday, and so on and so forth. But, as usually happens with those games, the moment finally came when there wasn't any more money.

So, fatally, the moment came in which he found himself short five thousand or more pesos that he needed to cover a "hole" which he had to take care of the following week.

In such a short time there was no way for him to dream up a solution to the problem; the idea of going to jail and having to try to protect his ass at the prison's showers terrorized him. He still had a couple thousand pesos left, so he decided that the best thing that he could do would be to leave the country before the time bomb exploded.

And that's what he did, leaving my mother and me high and dry with no resources in that rat-infested house.

Months later, Dominga received a letter from Sao Paolo, Brazil. It was signed by my father, and in it he begged us to forgive him and asked Dominga to do everything possible to send him some money, because he was going through hell. He ended the letter promising that when everything cleared up he would return to Yagruma, because, according to him, mother and I were his whole life. "See if you can send me at least three hundred dollars", he added as a postscript.

But my mother, who was enjoying her delightful, recently recovered freedom and had found someone who would provide what she most needed, tore up the letter into little pieces and threw it into the waste basket.

"What a son-of-a-bitch!", was her only comment.

After that letter we knew nothing further about my father. I don't know if he returned to Yagruma or if he stayed in Brazil. We never heard anything more of him, nor did we try to find out what had finally become of Cesáreo.

Sóstenes, Goya and aunt Lidia, who hated papá, couldn't hide their satisfaction to see that "the parasite", as they called him, had disappeared from the family scene.

As for my mother, not much time went by before we began to see her each afternoon leaning on her elbows at the window, with her makeup and lipstick on and her hair all done up, clad in a very tight dress that accentuated all her curves.

There she stayed, smiling and casting feverish looks at all the passers-by of the male sex that interested her, until my grandmother called her to dinner. Later, after dark, she went with her friend Charo Pita, or with aunt Lidia, to the city park, to look for the man that she knew sooner or later would bite the hook.

It seems that mamá didn't like to sleep alone, after having enjoyed, for twelve years, the pleasures that papá had given her.

Finally, another man appeared in her life. He didn't belong to Helena's middle class, nor was he a member of my hometown's "intellectual" community, but he knew how to satisfy my mother's needs, which was all that she was looking for.

Mother's new boy friend was Máximo Abelló, a man of peasant origin that owned two of the buses that traveled the route Sabana to Helena to Matadero

Beach. According to grandmother and Aunt Lidia, Dominga began flirting with Máximo the same night that she met him at a carnival that the parish held for the benefit of our senior citizens, and she even let him take her home.

Several days later they met again while they were strolling in the park, and it was there that the romance definitely solidified.

They never spoke of marriage because Máximo, who was already married and had children, was not prepared to face up to the consequences of a divorce. Besides, my mother was not interested in getting married all over again.

The only thing she looked for was a serious man who could satisfy her, with discretion, in what she called "a woman's needs". And Máximo, ever since the first night that she went to bed with him, surpassed her wildest dreams. So, Dominga decided to stay with this lustful boor who knew so well how to fulfill her erotic fantasies.

In order to avoid gossip and people talking, they avoided seeing each other in Helena. They met in Sabana, where inns and motels were everywhere.

The affair, nevertheless, only lasted a few months. One night, when mamá was coming back to Helena after having spent the day in the capital with her lover, the bus in which she was traveling collided on the highway with a big truck overloaded with cattle, turned over and burned.

The bus was one of those buses made in Yagruma, consisting of a truck chassis on which was built a body of planks and sheets of tin.

Many of the passengers were trapped in their seats or between the twisted iron of the bus and died a charred death. Among those was Dominga. Her body, totally burned, could only be identified by her dental records.

I remember the day that they buried what was left of her. One of Sóstenes' buddies, a local poetaster, gave the eulogy, and while I was listening to them send my mother off to heaven, I realized that the only thing that I felt was an intense desire to go back to the house and shut myself up in the living room with my books.

Back in the house, aunt Lidia hugged me and kissed me, which was a very rare thing for her to do.

"Poor little fellow!", my grandmother said, "He's been left all alone."

I was twelve years old when my mother died, and was ready to take the high school entrance examinations. But Sóstenes, as he never tired of repeating, was the boss of the house, and tried to convince my grandmother and Aunt Lidia, who had taken charge of me, that there wasn't a single reason why I should attend Helena High School.

"Why should he waste his time?", he said to them, "He won't be able to go to the university, which is the only thing a high school diploma is good for. Who's going to pay the college expenses?"

"When he graduates from high school, he will be able to study for some career on his own", ventured my grandmother.

"And starve to death! Right?", cried Sóstenes, "Lawyers are a dime a dozen, and I know clerks, and even some laborers, that hold doctoral degrees! What he should do is go to work and make a man of himself!"

"And is he the only one to end up stupid?", put in Lidia, "All of his friends will be attending high school!"

"His friends have their parents to worry about them!", replied Sóstenes, bothered by the unexpected resistance on the part of the two women, "But this kid isn't my son! I am giving him room and board because, after all, he is a relative. But that's as far as I'm going! He isn't going to stay here as a freeloader!"

"Miguelito is still a child", countered my grandmother, "Besides, what kind of work would he do?"

"Jorge is looking for a boy to clean up the store and run errands", answered Sóstenes, "I can talk to him so he'll take Miguel".

Manuel Jorge, another of Sóstenes' friends, was an old, pint-sized man who had a drugstore on Cabildo Street.

"Is that the future that you want for your grand-nephew?", exclaimed Lidia "You are going to put him to sweeping floors! I can't believe it!"

"Today he'll sweep and clean up", responded Sóstenes, "Tomorrow he will learn, with Jorge, how to make pills and fill prescriptions...and in a few years he'll be a pharmacist's assistant!"

"Great!", answered my grandmother, "In other words, when he turns forty he can look forward to earning sixty pesos per month!"

"Well then, what the hell do you ladies want?", yelled Sóstenes, really getting mad, "Why dump all this on me? For God's sake! Stop giving me shit!"

After a moment of silence, seeing that the two women were looking at him hatefully, Sóstenes sweetened his tone a little.

"And why doesn't he go to the Normal School, and become a school teacher?", he suggested, "That's only four years!"

"Oh, is that right?", replied aunt Lidia, "And what is he going to do with a teacher's certificate? Spend twenty years sucking up to some politician, making points to see if some day they give him a classroom? And for what? So that some day they send him to Remanganaguas so he can earn eighty pesos per month that won't even keep food on the table!"

"OK, how about business school?", proposed Sóstenes, "Or isn't that good enough for the son of the Marquis of Baró, either!"

"That's enough of that!", exclaimed my grandmother, "Miguelito isn't like his father! Besides, to keep books for those bastard "gallegos" for the shit they pay, you don't have to sweat out four years in the business school!"

All of this discussion took place in the living room, and I, who had enclosed my self in what used to be my parents' room, to read in peace, didn't miss one word of what they spoke. One of my favorite fantasies had always been to murder Sóstenes by putting ground glass in his coffee. In that moment I swore that if the old man got his way, the following day he would have his intestines perforated.

But as luck would have it, grandmother and aunt Lidia convinced Sóstenes to accept a deal that they proposed: I would attend high school, and when I got my diploma I would go to work. The university, of course, was a crazy dream that I would have to agree to forget. If when I finished my studies in the high school I wished to continue living with them, then I would have to contribute to the household expenses.

Sóstenes, for his part, promised to give me food and a place to live during the five years that my studies were to last, but no money for clothes or for books. If my grandmother or aunt Lidia could, or would want to, that was their affair.

Sóstenes called me the following day and informed me of what they had decided to do for me. He made it clear that he was giving me one chance, that's all, to take the high school entrance examination. If I passed, then the agreement was in effect; if not, I would be sent to work at Manuel Jorge's drug store.

I agreed to whatever he said. What else could I do?! But something inside me made me feel sure that, by one means or another, I would know how to arrange things so that I would be able to study at the University after I got my high school diploma. Come hell or high water I would become a professional!

CHAPTER IV
IN HIGH SCHOOL

There were High School entrance examinations twice a year, in June and September. The death of my mother, which happened about the end of May, plus the period of uncertainty that followed while my relatives decided what to do with me, kept me from taking the June examination.

So I spent the whole summer reviewing for the test, which I finally took, and passed, in September. A couple of weeks later, the new school year opening took place.

The students at Helena High School could choose between attending classes in the morning, from seven until noon, or going to the afternoon session, which went from one to six. Since I knew that neither my grandmother nor Aunt Lidia would have the money to buy my text books and schools supplies, I went to see Jorge, the druggist, who hired me, part-time, to sweep the floors, wash flasks and bottles and run errands, for fifteen pesos per month. The work was from two to six, so I had to attend classes during the morning session.

My clothes, then, were Sóstenes' old clothes which, though fixed up for me by my grandmother, never fit me very well. My shoes were too old and full of holes, but with three dollars that Jorge advanced me I could buy a pair of rubber sneakers.

The first day of school, Adrianito Gómez Mazas, the Mayor's nephew, who was in our class, looked at me askance and laughed, whispering something to a very pretty and tastefully dressed girl who was sitting beside him. I later learned that that beauty was Mary Macías del Sol, the daughter of a local dandy.

As if complying with an unwritten rule, the students that composed our class divided up, from the beginning, in two groups: one, small, formed by sons and daughters of well-to-do families; the other, quite large, made up of kids from the lower classes.

There was no communication between these two groups. They pretended to ignore each other, although, when their members converged in the hallways of the High School, one could see, in the looks that they exchanged, how much they hated and despised each other.

The small group, the "good kids", sat at the front of the class, right up against the professor's desk, to impress on him the elegance of their clothes and their impeccable conduct.

The rest of the class left a couple of empty rows between them and those of the "high society". Behind this space, which was like a no-man's land, were the "rabble" and the "trash", as we were called behind our backs by the little aristocrats. One had to have balls to survive in this section, because among the people in this group, although brothers in poverty and despair and united in their hatred of those up ahead, existed, nevertheless, divisions and rivalries which often exploded in open confrontation, in the classroom as well as outside of it.

The trouble-makers arrived to the classroom well supplied with pieces of chalk, paper clips, spit balls, and other projectiles of that sort, to throw at the "mamma boys" when the professor had his back turned. Some of the underdogs would tie a well sharpened pencil onto their shoe strings and, sitting behind the other students, stuck it in the rear end of whoever was sitting in front of them.

In Yagruma, getting a teaching job was possible only for those who had good "connections" or money enough to buy the appointing. Those without "pull" never got the job, even if they happened to be smarter than Albert Einstein.

With a few honorable exceptions, the teachers that we had earned neither the respect nor the affection of the "rabble" and the "trash". We knew that Helena High School educators cared only about their paychecks.

The professors kept an attitude of total indifference toward the underdogs, and one of complete servility toward the children of the bourgeoisie.

It was not that they openly looked down upon the "rabble": they simply ignored us. For our teachers, it was as if we did not exist. On the other hand, they went out of their way to take care of and to placate the elite, the relatives of politicians, military officers and the well-to-do, of which there were quite a few in our class.

All of this, combined with the mediocrity of most of the teachers and the ineptitude of some others, made the classes horribly boring.

After attending the few classes that we liked, we used to leave the High School in small groups and go to Helena's central park. There we sat on wooden benches, under the elms, to smoke and tell dirty jokes. Once in a while, before heading back to school, we would stop at a store and have a glass of beer, or a shot of firewater with sugar and lemon.

The only good memories that I have of my times as a student in Helena High School are of moments like those.

CHAPTER V
WHORES AND MEMORIES

Some of the students took pornographic novels to the classrooms with them, which they passed around to their classmates, who read them while the class was in session.

I'll never forget the day that Sócrates Govín, a mulatto that was seated beside me, started to read, in a History class, one of those novels, whose title was "Madame Madness' Boudoir". When reaching one specially intense passage, Govín, who had gotten excited with the reading, could not contain himself and released a

"Holy shit..!!"

that was heard in every corner of the classroom. It provoked a flood of laughs and whistles in our group, and even some of the "grandees" in the front rows were giggling. But one of them, a little Lord Fauntleroy named Jaimito Alba, turned around toward us and, with a straight face and a serious tone of voice, protested.

"We can't pay any attention with all this noise", he said. Govín stared at him for a few seconds.

"You tell me that outside", he answered.

The teacher, who didn't want any problems in his class, especially if a member of Helena's aristocracy was involved, intervened.

"OK, that's enough now!", he yelled, "Govín, what's the matter with you?! What is it that you want? You want to be suspended?!"

"No, sir, excuse me", answered Govín, appeasingly, "It got away from me, sir. There won't be any more!"

The professor breathed a sigh of relief, thinking that the storm had passed, and turned back to the blackboard. But Govín arranged to pass to Jaimito a note that read: "I'll be waiting for you out in the street, you fairy!"

The news spread, and that day all of us were waiting for Jaimito Alba to come out, and see Govín smack him in the face.

But Jaimito went to the main office and called home for help. So, when we got out, the Alba family's Packard was already there, parked in front of the building.

Standing next to the car was "Canturo", the chauffeur, a black man over six feet tall who had earned a reputation as an amateur boxer. Seeing "Canturo", Govín lost his desire to fight, and we left, disappointed, because we would have given anything to see that little aristocrat leave the high school with a broken nose.

Of all the girls in the class, Mary Macías del Sol was the one I liked the best. I fell for her, although everybody told me that the possibility of Mary taking any notice of me was as preposterous as Rita Hayworth falling in love with Sócrates Govín.

Mary was the daughter of Doña Corina del Sol, Helena's richest heiress, and her husband, Antonio Macías, a handsome, brainless, and ignorant parasite whom Pocholo del Jardín, in his society column, used to call "Helena's best-dressed man". Gossip had it that Antonio earned his keep by "servicing" not only his wife, but also his widowed, millionaire mother-in-law, Doña Pilla Pérez del Sol.

Among my classmates at the High School, only the sexually active guys were considered "real men". But, in those times, in cities like Helena, those who wanted to play the game had no choice but to go to the brothels.

To be a "macho", one had to become a whorehouse rat. Otherwise, they would call him "señorito", "little virgin", "mariconcito", or even worse names.

I decided that frequenting the whorehouses and joining the "macho" crowd might be a way for me to gain some stature in Mary's eyes, so I decided to go and get my feet wet.

Arturo, with whom I talked about my plans, wanted to go along, and I agreed, because I did not like the idea of walking through the red light district all by myself. We remembered the stories that we had been told about the dangers lying in wait for those high school students that dared venture alone in the area.

Helena's red light district was down by the docks, in a section known as "La Marina". It occupied eight blocks of run-down old houses and miserable shacks with small gratings about the size of a person's head set into the doors at eye level, behind which stood the prostitutes to call out to any man that passed by.

The day before the big adventure we went for a walk through the area, to familiarize ourselves with the streets and to lose our fear of the place. We got to La Marina about one o'clock in the afternoon, a time at which, according to Sócrates Govín, the ladies of the evening were taking their siesta, so as to be in good shape by nightfall, when their work began.

While walking by Manzanares street we happened to see one of them, a short, rather plump woman who, to escape the suffocating heat of her shack, had taken a stool outside.

There she sat, by the door, fanning herself with a piece of cardboard, when Arturo, to show his machismo, decided to insult her, and on passing by, he shouted:

"I smell a whore around here!"

But the woman didn't pay the least bit of attention to him. She didn't even look at us. Sitting on her stool she just kept on fanning herself, impassively, with her eyes fixed on the dark gray clouds that were slowly invading the incandescent sky.

The following day, at seven o'clock in the evening, Arturo and I met in front of City Hall, as we had agreed, and headed for La Marina.

Helena lay wrapped in a soft violet light. A warm breeze, bland and gentle like a caress, came from the sea and made me shiver, I didn't know why. Upon entering Manzanares street, and seeing again the rows of filthy shacks and run-down houses, I began to think that I would feel a lot better if, instead of this place, I had gone to the breakwater, to watch the setting sun paint purple and gold the quiet waters of Helena bay.

Now the neighborhood had begun to take on some life, and one could hear the cries of the prostitutes calling to the men from behind the gratings.

Arturo and I walked through the sad alleyways, surrounded by the shadows that the few street lights couldn't disperse. We were full of apprehension, hearing the women that whistled at us from behind their doors, trying to allure us with promises of indescribable pleasures.

But we couldn't make up our minds. The simple fact was that we were afraid. We were afraid of syphilis, of gonorrhea, of the bad things that all "grown-ups" had warned us would happen to boys that went to bordellos.

Time was running out on us. The clock at San Carlos Cathedral had struck eight o'clock. It had been now almost a whole hour that we had been wearing out shoe leather going up the street-down the street, and we could not keep on like that.

What the hell, you had to be a man! At that moment we heard the voice of a whore calling us.

"Psstt! Psstt! Blondy! Come on in, blondy, you are going to get tired!"

Since my hair was light brown, and Arturo's was black, it appeared that she was calling me. I liked that, I must confess, and I stopped in front of the door, looking directly at the grill and holding back on Arturo, who wanted to keep on walking. Again the voice came to us.

"Come on, blondy, come on! You are gonna like what I've got here for you!"

"What do you think?", I asked my companion in adventure, who was silent, shuffling his feet in the dirt.

"Go into that pigsty?", exclaimed Arturo, "Not for me, brother! That's a hotbed of infection!!"

"Chico, we've got to make up our minds", I answered, "We came here to do a little sinning, right? Well, let's get it over with!"

At that moment I saw, out of the corner of my eye, that the prostitute's door had opened to let in a customer, who responded to the woman's cries. If we kept on standing there, like idiots, there would soon be a line of guys waiting in the hovel, increasing our chances to leave there with a disease, and so I told Arturo.

"Well, how about it?", I pressed him, "Are we going or not?"

He certainly was in a demurring mood. "Suppose we get crab lice!", he answered.

"What about it?", I cried, "That's nothing! With mercury, you can get rid of that in three days! Well, what do you say? Are you going with me, or are you going to stay here?"

All of a sudden, Arturo exploded. "What did we have to get into this for?", he whined.

I could see that his was a lost cause. "You are not up to this", I said, "Why don't you go home?"

With that, he had the excuse that he needed to be the offended one. "Well, I'm going then, brother!", he cried, "And I feel OK about it, yes sir! I'm better off at home, with my dog, than wrapped up with one of those whores!!"

So, he turned his back to me, and with quick steps disappeared down Manzanares in the direction of the park. As for myself, the truth is that I felt like going with him, but the memory of Mary, and the hope I had that she would pay attention to me after hearing that now I was one of the "machos" of the class kept me there. I didn't fool around any more: I went up to the shack and knocked on the door.

"Who's there?", responded a hoarse voice, coming from behind the window.

"I would like to talk to the girl", I replied, following the instructions that Govín had given us.

"She is busy right now", was the answer, "But come in, son, she'll be finished in a few minutes".

The door opened, and the owner of the hoarse voice signaled for me to come in. It was an old woman of about sixty years, with a wrinkled face, dressed in a transparent gown that revealed her flattened breasts and the shadow of her pubis.

I stood still in front of the open door, without the courage to enter; a nauseous odor, like that of boiling innards, came from the inside of the hovel.

"Come on in!", said the madam, "Don't be afraid, we don't eat people here!"

There was no time to change my mind now. I took a step backward, cast a last look at the stars shining above in the tropical night and, taking a deep breath of the jasmine-perfumed air, went into that den of inequity. The woman shut the door after me.

"Now, my little man", the old whore said then, "You take a seat and relax. Rosa will be ready for you in a few minutes".

I sat down on one of the two decrepit rockers available in the small and grimy living room. Ten or fifteen minutes later the curtains from the back of the shack opened slowly and a man came out. Without a word, the madam opened the door of the miserable dwelling and let the customer out.

Then, from behind the curtains, came a nude, pleasantly plump young woman with the thickest black triangle under her belly button. She smiled as she held out her hand to lead me into her den.

"Come with me, honey", she whispered into my ear, "You will remember me, always!"

Indeed I will always remember the Rosa from that dank and dirty shanty shack. In those few moments of youthful passion, she taught me many things. Sometimes, even today, when the trade winds blow in from the sea, I can smell and feel Rosa in the tropical breeze.

The following day, after telling Govín and the other "machos" of the class the story of my "debut', I officially became a member of that select group, and their girlfriends took charge of spreading the news to the other girls. But as for Mary, I couldn't get a single glance. One day, entering the classroom, I saw her standing by the door, and I searched for her eyes with mine. Then I knew how the invisible man must have felt. She looked at me without seeing me, as though there was nobody in front of her.

Turning half around, I left the classroom and the school, heading for the park. I sat down on a bench there, under the elms, with a small bottle of cheap rum that I had bought on the way.

I didn't go to any classes that day. The following day I saw her entering the classroom, escorted by Adrianito Gómez Mazas, and I didn't feel my heart racing within my breast, as it had before. Mary had disappeared from my dreams, for good.

CHAPTER VI
OPPORTUNITY CALLS

In Yagruma, during my time, one had to study for five years to get the high school diploma. There were four years of secondary basics, plus a fifth year of pre-university specialization in letters or science, depending on the career that one had decided to follow.

I did the fifth year in letters, and Arturo, who wanted to study medicine, opted to specialize in sciences.

One Good Friday my grandmother sent me to the grocery store to buy some cod fish. When I got there I saw, in addition to Juana "Palangana", two stevedores from one of the crews that loaded the sugar barges at the warehouses on the river banks. They were having a few shots of rum and joking with "Snow White", a black errand-boy who, in one corner of the store, was beating a conga rhythm on the box he was using for a seat.

While I waited, leaning against the counter, a red Buick, long and shiny, stopped in front of the store, and a white-haired man with an aristocratic manner got out. He was wearing a suit that, even then, had to have cost him, at least, one hundred and fifty pesos.

"Oh, shit! Here he comes again!", murmured Juana "Palangana".

Doctor Manuel Galán was the president of the court of appeals of our province.

The judge entered the store. Seeing him, José, the grocer, came out of the back room and, throwing the piece of codfish that he had in his hand onto a sack of beans, jumped over the counter to greet the distinguished visitor.

"Good to see you, doctor! Welcome to my store!", he exclaimed, smiling servilely.

"What's up, big guy?", answered doctor Galán, trying to sound democratic.

"Twelve o'clock, guys!", squeaked Juana "Palangana".

"Snow White" jumped to his feet and rushed to a grimy radio set placed on one of the store's shelves. "It's time for Pancho Yarey!", he cried out.

"I'll fuck your mother today!!", was the rhymed retort from one of the stevedores.

Pancho Yarey was Yagruma's folk hero. A serial based on his life was being broadcast through the local radio station.

The storekeeper, infuriated, turned to face his customers.

"This gentleman is Helena's chief judge!!", he yelled, "Be careful with what you say!! Can't you show some respect?!"

José's words had a magic effect. The two stevedores hurriedly drank their last sips of rum and left without saying another word, while "Snow White" went into the back room, jabbering something that sounded like an excuse.

José turned back to talk to the judge. "Well, then, what can I do for you, doctor?", asked he, obsequiously.

"Have any good brandy in stock?"

"Of course we do, doctor! Carlos I! Best brandy from Spain!", responded José.

"Very good!", said the illustrious customer, "OK, then, send six bottles to my house. Oh, and six cases of German beer, too! Tell me, José, how are you fixed for Spanish sausage? I mean the real thing, you know!

"We have everything, we have everything!", answered the storekeeper.

Doctor Galán ordered Mallorca sausages, mountain cured ham, cheese, stuffed olives, anchovies and other delicacies.

"We are having a little party at home", he explained to José, "Can you send it all over this afternoon?"

"Of course, Your Honor! We'll send it over right now", was the answer.

"Great!", replied the judge, "Well, then, farewell! And thanks! Send me the bill, OK?"

"Vaya con Dios, vaya con Dios!", replied José.

Doctor Galán turned on his heels, left the store, entered his car and went off like a shot.

"Son of a bitch!", Juana "Palangana" shrieked, "On top of that, he has the balls to tell you to send him the bill! José, why do you wait on him? You know he is never going to pay that bill!"

"Because guys like those you can buy with a few bottles of brandy and a few pounds of sausage!", replied the storekeeper, "And you better keep them happy, for you never know when you are going to need them. At that price, justice is very cheap for me! Period!" He yelled, calling his delivery boy. "Manolo", he ordered, "Get the pickup ready. You have to take an order to judge Galán's house".

Yagruma's judiciary enjoyed special privileges. Their relatives and in-laws were always in the government's payroll, and no merchant would ever dream of sending them a bill for what they bought, on credit, in their stores.

Doctor Galán's visit to José was just an example of how grocers, shopkeepers and restaurateurs put up with the judges' plundering, in the hope to have the bench on their side, whenever necessary. Like José had said, the judges must be kept happy.

I began to feel, within my heart, a tremendous respect for those men of the robe, who lived such a sweet life in Yagruma, feared and brown-nosed by all. And one afternoon, washing flasks in Jorge's drugstore, I made the decision to become a lawyer, so that one day I could enter that sacred brotherhood and enjoy the "dolce vita" in our tropical paradise.

Finally, one day, about the middle of July, I went down the high school's stairway with the diploma in my hand and took a last look at the building. An indescribable happiness filled my heart. Never again would I have to set foot in those cursed rooms! Such was the hate that had accumulated in my soul against that place!

When I was back home with my diploma, my grandmother and aunt Lidia were bubbling over with happiness, and gave me a great hug. The poor old lady, behind Sóstenes' back, gave me five pesos so that I could go and "celebrate with my friends".

The ones that did not seem too impressed were Sóstenes and his wife. Goya did not take any notice of me, and Sóstenes only comment was:

"Well, it looks like we are getting to the point of this now!"

I knew that it would not be long before Sóstenes told me what plans he had for my future. That "now" meant that he did would not keep giving me free room and board.

As it turned out, one afternoon the following week, before I left for Jorge's pharmacy, Sóstenes, with a long face, called me into the dining room.

"We have to have a serious talk", he said, "Sit down".

So I did. Sóstenes sat at the other side of the table, facing me and, after clearing his throat, he began his sermon.

"I want to begin by saying", he stated, "That not only myself, but your grandmother and your aunt, are very happy to see that you have finished your studies".

At that point he hesitated, perhaps to give me a chance to express my gratitude for all the wonderful things that he had done for me. But, seeing that I did not open my mouth, he continued his discourse.

"For us", he went on, "You have been like a son, and that's the way we have always treated you. You can imagine how uncomfortable I feel, having to tell you what I am going to say. But we have to face up to the realities of life, no matter how unpleasant".

He made a pause, and taking a long cigar out of his coat pocket, proceeded to light it after biting off the end, all this with much pomposity and keeping his brow furrowed, as if the weight of what he had to tell me caused him real pain.

Knowing Sóstenes, I knew very well where he was going to end up with all these theatrics. "I can see what is coming, you mother-jumper!", I said to myself.

My great-uncle sucked on his cigar a couple of times, tried to frown even more, without quite making it, and continued with his harangue.

"You have never lacked for food", he said, "And you have always had a roof over your head. Do you know, Miguel, that right here, in Helena, there are many hungry orphans living in the streets?"

As far as I was concerned, the fucking orphans were not important to me. "Screw them!", I felt like answering, "Who told them to be born on this shitty island?" But, given my situation, I could not even think of having the pleasure of that response, so I assured Sóstenes that I was well aware of that tragedy, and that I felt very badly about it.

Sóstenes went on: "Do you realize how lucky you have been!? Can you understand what the love of your relatives has meant for you? During all these years you have had a family that has given you all your necessities!"

He was right, if by "necessities" he meant the cot that I slept on and shared with the cockroaches, and the diet of beans, rice and plantains.

What wouldn't I have given, just to tell the old fucker what I really thought of him, of the rat-hole we lived in and the freaking city in which I had had the misfortune to be born!

But reason prevailed. If I gave in to my impulses, it would probably end up by increasing the number of Helena's homeless, because Sóstenes would kick me out of the house.

Sóstenes' voice, now grave and solemn, resounded again in my ears.

"What do you say, Miguel?", he was asking, "Doesn't your heart tell you anything?"

I have inherited from my father the ability to cry without an onion.

"What can I say to you, uncle?", I answered with a faltering voice, letting a couple of tears the size of lima beans run down over my cheeks, "My family is all I have in this world! What would have happened to me if I hadn't had you? I could never repay you for all that you have done for me! May God reward you as you deserve".

I let two or three more tears fall down.

"Well, well, calm down!", said Sóstenes, patting me on the back of my hand, "Come on now, man, things aren't as bad as all that! Let's see, are you calmed down now?"

I nodded.

"Well", he proceeded, "It's about your situation in this house that I want to talk to you about. You remember the agreement that we made before you started going to high school?"

"Yes", I answered, "I remember it".

"Then, you will agree that you have to define your situation with us, isn't that so?", he asked. I nodded again.

"Then", he said, "Beginning today, according to our agreement, things have to change. Now you are not a child any more; you are a high school graduate and I think it is only fair that from today on you will be treated like a man. And men that are really men don't let others support them. Right?"

I had cried for nothing! Neither tears nor sighs had any effect on the old son-of-a-bitch!

"In other words", I replied, "Beginning today, if I want to keep on living here, I'll have to pay. How much?"

Instead of directly answering my question, he got lost in a round-about rambling.

"I talked to Jorge last week", he said, "He is very happy with you; he told me you are a good, responsible worker, and he wants you at the drug store, permanently, as his assistant. He is willing to pay you sixty pesos per month. You are going to be learning how to run things".

I didn't utter a word.

"Jorge is sure that you could get your license as a practical pharmacist in a couple of years", Sóstenes continued, "Then, you'll be able to earn more! Who knows? In about ten or fifteen years Jorge will be retiring, and if you have learned how to run things, and have saved some pesos, I'm sure he'll give you the chance to work out some arrangement with him so that you can end up with the drug store".

"Well, yes, Jorge has already talked to me about some of that", was my only comment. I would have gained nothing by telling him that, to me, the idea of spending the rest of my life in Helena, running the fucking pharmacy, was something totally abhorrent.

"But, tell me", I insisted, "How much will I have to pay to keep on living here?"

"Twenty pesos per month", he told me point blank, "Is that OK with you?"

The son-of-a-bitch was already planning to get out of me a third of the salary that I had not even begun earning yet.

"That's OK", I responded, while mentally sending him to hell.

Perhaps he had been thinking that I was going to ask him to lower the amount, judging from the contented look on his face when I accepted without protest. He got from his chair, smiling from ear to ear, came towards me and put his arm around my shoulders.

"I have always said", he exclaimed, "That we can be proud of you; now, with this, even more so!" And, then, in a jocular mood and probably thinking of the twenty pesos he was going to get out of me every month, he added:

"And you'll still have forty bucks left every month! You'll be able to save and also go dip your wick every once in a while! Did you hear that Nicolasa has a new pair of good looking gals that are really something?"

This was the first time that Sóstenes had ever said anything like that to me, but I was careful not to reciprocate.

"No!", I answered, briefly, "I haven't heard anything. So, uncle, if everything is arranged now, and there is nothing more we have to talk about, I am going over to the Menéndez house. Arturo is leaving for Sabana this afternoon".

"Sure, son, sure!", he responded affably, "Vaya con Dios!"

In my situation, there was nothing I could do, except bowing my head and take the full-time job at Jorge's drug store. I had no alternative. At least, the twenty pesos that I would give to Sóstenes every month assured me I would not be homeless.

It was painful to watch the few good friends that I had made during my five years in Helena High School go off to Sabana to study at the University. Above all, I knew that I would see less of Arturo, with whom I had always gotten along so well.

I envied him, really. Arturo's mother had a niece, Leticia, who lived in the capital. Leticia was the widow of doctor Serafín, a lawyer that, at the time of their marriage, was a member of the staff of the legal department of the Ministry of Commerce.

When president Arau Martín named a politician from my province as Minister of Commerce, doctor Serafín, who was able to get on the good side of his new boss, soon became, through sheer ass-licking, the minister's main toad-eater and right-hand man, a mixture of adviser, snitch, and procurer.

During his eighteen-month tenancy, Dr. Mazas, the new minister, who soon earned the nickname of "Black Market Czar", made himself a multimillionaire.

But Dr. Mazas was not held in contempt by the people of Yagruma, because it could be said of him what the Yagrumans used to say about one of their former and most popular presidents: "When the whale dives, people get splashed".

And the "Black Market Czar" also "splashed", generously, those who helped him to steal his millions. Among them, of course, was doctor Serafín, who purchased a sumptuous residence in an exclusive area, the most expensive Cadillac available in Sabana, and had accounts opened at "El Hechizo" and "Turn of the Century", the exclusive department stores.

Unfortunately, Serafín could not enjoy his riches for very long, because he had hardly tried out his air conditioned mansion when terminal cancer of the pancreas took him off to St. Peter's domains.

His widow did not want to remain alone in that splendid mansion. She sold it, and moved to a luxurious condominium. Leticia and Arturo's mother got along very well, so that when Leticia learned that her cousin had to move to Sabana to study medicine, she wrote to the Menéndez, offering the hospitality of her fabulous penthouse apartment to her cousin Arturo.

"Of course", she clarified in her letter, "You don't have to send me a penny. Thank God, poor Serafín left me very well provided for".

Leticia came to Helena frequently to visit her relatives, and I was introduced to her on one of these occasions. She was a beautiful brunette, still young, with a sculptural body, large brown eyes with an intense look and lips as red as crimson, always slightly open, exuding sensuality.

"It is going to be very difficult for Arturo to concentrate on his studies", I thought.

The day after I talked with Sóstenes, I accepted Manuel Jorge's job offer.

"Our Lady of the Miracles", one of the oldest pharmacies in Helena, had been established by Jorge's father in the year eighteen ninety-five. It was a huge, dark place, with an interior that reminded one of a cathedral.

In its enormous and tall wooden shelves were lined up rows of old-fashioned apothecary jars, relics of a bygone era, and artistic balloon flasks full of colored water.

The rear part of the pharmacy was what Jorge called "the laboratory". The living quarters of the druggist and his family were also located in this section.

Jorge, a parsimonious old bastard, never wanted to modernize the place. When he referred to the other pharmacies in Helena, for the most part modern, of contemporary style, he called them, derogatorily, the "fancy goods stores".

The pharmacist had been very successful with two medical formulas of his exclusive invention. One, which Jorge himself prepared in his "laboratory", contained calcium lactate, Phenobarbital, bismuth, magnesium and tincture of belladonna and was, according to its creator, the best there was to cure irritation of the large intestine.

The doctors prescribed it continually, because Jorge, at the end of the month, paid them a percentage on the total sales that each one had generated.

Jorge also made a pill that he sold under the brand name of "Vigoril". According to the ads that he put in the papers all over the island, those pills cured impotence, sexual apathy and something the druggist called "timidity".

The process of making "Vigoril" was very simple. Jorge bought bulls' testicles in the slaughter house and cooked them in a large oven in the pharmacy's yard. Then, with starch and other agglutinants, he prepared the dough from which the pills were made.

The druggist, in his ignorance, never stopped to think that the bulls' testicles, upon being cooked, lost all their hormonal qualities. Nevertheless, the pills sold like hot cakes, and all the newspapers in Yagruma published, in their advertising sections, the testimonials of those that gave their assurances that they were men again, and able to enjoy the good things of life, thanks to "Vigoril".

So I began to work as a permanent employee in the drug store. After a few days I was doing so well that it almost seemed as though I had never done anything else in my life, and Jorge told me that he was thinking of moving me up to get started making the famous "Vigoril".

But, as the old refrain goes, "Man proposes and God disposes". It seems as though God did not want me to spend eight or ten years cooking bulls' balls in "Our Lady of the Miracles".

One afternoon, Higinio, Arturo's father, showed up at the pharmacy. He greeted me with a wave, and went straight to Jorge, who was standing at the cash register counting the day's sales.

"That's how I like to see you, Don Manuel", he said, "With lots of cash in your hand!"

Jorge, hurriedly, put the money back in the register, "What a big fish we caught in the net!", he exclaimed, "Well, and to what do I owe this pleasure?"

"I would like to talk to Miguel", answered Higinio, "If you can loan him to me for ten minutes".

My boss turned to me. "Have you finished with that batch of "Vigoril?", he asked. And, when I said yes, he added, "OK, you may go with Mr. Menéndez".

"Let's go over to "El Paraíso", said Higinio, "We can talk over there". "El Paraíso" was a nearby cafe, gloomy and dirty. We sat down at a table, and Higinio ordered "café con leche", --steamed milk and espresso coffee, the Yagruman national drink-- and buttered toast for both of us.

My mother's cousin, as always, had a runny nose, and apparently did not have a handkerchief. He wiped his nose on the sleeve of his guayabera, and then went right to the heart of the matter.

"Look here, Miguel", he said, crushing out in the ash tray the stump of a big cigar that he had been smoking, "Wouldn't you like to go to Sabana to study, the same as Arturo and all the others?"

"Does the dead man want a mass?, I answered, "But, Higinio, you know very well what my situation is! You know Sóstenes!"

"Never mind that mother-fucker!", replied Higinio, "Listen, Miguel, I can get you the money so that you can go and study!"

For a few seconds I sat there, openmouthed. Recovering, I tried to say something, but he, with his hand, motioned for me to wait.

"I'm going to be honest with you", he said, "Arturo doesn't know anything about this. My wife and I want to help you, and not only because we are related. We are worried about Arturo. My son is a good boy, but he lacks determination, and he lets others lead him around. And, you understand, living with Leticia, I don't know how things are going to turn out for him!"

"But, Higinio, Arturo is not a child!", I replied, "What could ever happen to him?"

"What could happen to him!?", cried Higinio, "I wasn't born yesterday, Miguel! That woman has my son under her thumb!"

"So what?", said I, "What is the problem? That she and Arturo have a little fun together? Man, do you know what it is to have room and board and a good piece of ass in Sabana, all for free!? And with a sex machine like Leticia!!"

He was going to answer, but I stopped him with a gesture.

"Just think!", I added, "Let's assume that you are right about her. Arturo wouldn't have to go to a whorehouse to get laid, nor would you two have to worry about him getting syphilis or gonorrhea!"

I don't believe that what I had just said had much effect on him.

"I don't like what I have heard", he confided, "I have been told that only a few days after her husband died she was going out celebrating in the cabarets. And there is more! One of my friends told me that she's been "serviced" by some good-looking stud, the owner of "Cupid's Motel", the one near Pelayo's Pond".

"You have to realize", I replied, "That Leticia is a widow, free and rich, and she is offending no one. She can do whatever she wants with her body or her money. Besides, she doesn't have any children. Whom is she hurting? Nobody!"

Higinio wiped his nose and his mustache again, this time with the napkin, already soiled with café con leche.

"I don't know", he said, "I don't like the way that woman is leading her life. She's involved in that Sabana environment, with the big shots and the society people! And you know how it is there, with drugs, and orgies, and all that shit!!"

He stared at me. "My wife and I need your help", he said, "And, by helping us, you are going to help yourself, also!".

"Man, if I can, with great pleasure", I responded, without wanting to commit myself. "What am I going to get out of all this?", I wondered.

"I will arrange the means by which you can go to Sabana, to study", he replied, "If you promise to keep Arturo under observation, and report to me each month. And if you see something that you don't like, if you see that my son is going astray, you call me right away!"

I could not believe what I was hearing. "If you are that afraid", I suggested, "The best thing would be for Arturo to go to a boarding house. Make up a story for Leticia, tell Arturo that you want him closer to the University..! You surely can invent something!"

"If I did that", Higinio replied, "Arturo would give me the finger and keep living with her, no matter what I said. Believe me, Miguel, it is as if she had cast a spell on him. She has total control over Arturo".

"But you are into politics", I replied, "You are one of Chente's main men here, in Helena. You surely could make things tough for her, even use some muscle to convince Arturo to dump her...What the hell, Sabana is full of broads; Leticia is not the one and only hot fuck in the capital!"

Now, Higinio began to show his true colors.

"We have to be careful", he murmured, "I don't want to offend her. The last time she was here, Leticia told us that, since she didn't have any children, she was thinking of naming Arturo as her only heir. If we give offense to her, good bye inheritance!"

"The most likely thing", I said, "Is that you are seeing ghosts where there aren't any, and that Arturo, in that house, with that woman, will be happier, study more, and will be better off and more comfortable than if he were in one of those boarding houses for students they have in Sabana".

"And if it isn't like that?", asked Higinio, "And if I am right?"

"Man, that's what I'll be in Sabana for!", I replied, "If I see something that I don't like, I'll blow the whistle!"

"Then, are we in agreement?", he asked, extending his hand. I shook it firmly. "It's a deal!", I said.

"I knew you wouldn't fail me, Miguel!", he exclaimed. There was real relief in his voice. "And since I knew that, I have already spoken to Chente about your problem. Now, this is for sure: as soon as it is arranged, you'll have to leave for Sabana. It's been two weeks since Arturo left. Well, he hasn't dropped us a line. He has not phoned, either!

"And, why don't you phone him"?

"Because Leticia, invariably, is the one who answers", he said, "And she tells us that everything is going along beautifully and that Arturo is very happy. She always tells me that he isn't in the apartment. Liar! What's happened is that she has already started to cut his balls off!"

He stood there thinking for a moment, in silence.

"Come around to my house tomorrow night", he said to me, "About eight o'clock. If I am not there, wait for me!"

Higinio threw fifty cents down on the dirty marble of the table to pay the bill, got up and left the cafe.

Vicente Diago, alias "Chente", senator of the Republic and Helena's political boss, had just brought down old senator Caballería and managed to get elected in his place some moron whose claim to fame was having been one of Chente's most trusted bullies.

Diago had also managed to put in another of his "associates", Ciriaco Roque, as governor of the province, while two other "Diaguitos", as the cohorts of Chente were called, had been elected to the mayoralty of Helena and to the House of Representatives, respectively.

The election had been plagued by fraud and intimidation in the electoral colleges. By afternoon, Chente's partisans, full of rum and firewater, exploded out into the streets, punching anyone who had the audacity to protest that electoral farce.

Some malcontents and troublemakers had tried in the past to oppose Chente, who passed along the handling of these problems to his right-hand man, Adelardo Hernández, alias "El Cojito".

"El Cojito" specialized in firearms, and his favorite one was the Thompson submachine gun, .45 caliber, which he used to convince his boss' enemies that making trouble for Chente was not good for their health. The riddled bodies of three of them were found under the San Juan bridge, near the open market. Another body, also looking like a sieve, lay at the entrance of the nearby village of Santa Apolonia.

I left "El Paraíso" on the heels of Arturo's father. When I got back to "Our Lady of the Miracles" I found Jorge waiting for me. My prolonged absence had made him mad, and he gave me a hard time, calling me names. I listened calmly, while mentally telling him to go butt-fuck himself in the park.

He finally got tired of yelling at me, and went into the back room. Since it was now close to six o'clock, I cleaned up the utensils that I had been using, closed the drugstore and left without saying good-bye to my boss.

I could not sleep that night. The conversation that had taken place with Higinio was going around in my head.

I did not doubt that I could get, from Chente, the money that I would need to go and study in Sabana. Higinio was Chente's political delegate from the district of Peñas Blancas, where he controlled most of the voters.

He was one of those "sergeants" that politicians always tried to keep happy; Chente, surely, would not deny Higinio a special favor.

The following morning, when I arrived at "Our Lady of the Miracles", Jorge talked to me as though nothing at all had happened the day before. I spent the eight hours working mechanically, looking at the clock and counting, first the hours and then the minutes until six o'clock.

Finally the drugstore was closed, and I went home. Aunt Lidia and my grandmother noticed that something had happened, and they wanted to know what was going on. I told them that I had a headache, and went to the bathroom to do my daily wash-up.

After showering and dressing, I sat in the living room and tried to read a magazine until dinner time, but I couldn't stand it for more than a few minutes, because the house was closing in on me. I was desperate to know if Higinio had managed to get what he had promised me!

Unable to wait any longer, I went to the kitchen, where my grandmother was frying plantains, which Sóstenes really liked. She had to fry them every day, just for him, who devoured the plantains while the rest of us looked on with our mouths watering.

"I'm leaving, grandmother", I said, "I have to see a customer. Something about the drugstore! Don't save any dinner for me; I'll eat something at 'El Paraíso'".

The poor woman tried to convince me not to leave without eating. She wanted to give me a plate of rice and beans, but I did not want any. I gave her a kiss, instead, and left the house.

At eight o'clock sharp I was knocking on the door of the Menéndez house. Arturo's mother opened the door. She was a tall, thin woman, with horse teeth and thinning hair that did not quite cover a big cyst she had on her head.

"My husband hasn't arrived yet, Miguelito," she said, "He called a little while ago and said for you to wait for him, not to leave". For a few seconds she stood looking at me, as though she wanted to say something, and then appeared to change her mind.

"Come on in", she told me, "Sit down and wait for Higinio. He won't be long. How about some coffee?"

I was going to say no, for her not to bother, when at that moment we heard the outside door open and Higinio, with the pockets of his guayabera full of papers and the customary "superstick" between his lips, made his appearance.

"Well, how goes it?" was his greeting. He sat down in his usual chair, and turned to his wife

"Sweetheart", he said, "Why don't you make us a little coffee?"

"Right away, dear ", she answered, "But, first, tell me, did you get Miguel's problem solved?"

"When it comes to politics in the Peñas Blancas district, with whom do they have to deal?", responded her husband. "With Higinio Menéndez, right? Well, Chente knows that! He has to keep me happy!"

The woman looked at me, smiling, and left heading for the kitchen. Higinio could clearly see that I was about to explode with anticipation, but he still hesitated a few moments, because he was really enjoying my anxiety. Finally, out of one of his overstuffed pockets he produced an envelope and handed it to me.

"Read this", he said to me.

I opened it, with trembling hands. Inside the envelope was a written notification of the appointment of Miguel Baró Oropesa as clerk, fourth class, in the offices of the Ministry of Education, with an annual salary of one thousand three hundred and twenty pesos, "payable in twelve equal monthly installments".

By special administrative provision in the same notification, I was being transferred to Helena's Provincial Office of Public Works, as a typist in the office of the chief engineer.

In other words, Higinio had obtained for me a "pipeline", so I would be able to go and study in the capital.

I couldn't believe what I was reading. If what that paper said was true, I was going to get one hundred and ten pesos per month! I was afraid that it was a dream and someone would wake me up any minute!

Higinio's voice brought me back to reality.

"Well, your problem has been solved", he said, "Now, let's see, when can you leave?"

My head was spinning.

"I don't know", I answered, "I need a few days; I have to get my things in order, talk to Jorge, tell my family!"

Higinio was shaking his head while I talked.

"No, no, no!", he protested, "You and I have an agreement, and I have completed my part of it. Now it is your turn. You have to go right away, because I need you there".

"Well, OK, but I don't have any place to stay there", I said, "And even worse, I don't know my way around Sabana. Give me some time to find a boarding house!"

For an answer, Higinio took out a piece of paper from another pocket, scribbled a few lines and gave it to me.

"That's already taken care of!", he responded, "This is the boarding house that you want. It's only three blocks from the University. Go straight there and ask for Cachita Heredia; she is the owner. Tell her that you are my cousin, the one that I talked to her about".

"Higinio", I said, "The truth is that I don't know how to thank you! I'll never forget what you are doing for me!"

But something was still bothering me, and I decided to clear it up with my benefactor.

"Am I going to have to come to Helena every month to pick up my check? I asked.

"Don't worry about that", he answered me, "I'll take care of all those details. There will be a money order mailed to you at Cachita's house every month. Do you need something now in order to move?"

"No", I said, "I have some money saved up. Not much, but it will stretch for the first month".

"So, then what?", he asked, "When are you leaving?"

I thought it over. It was Wednesday evening, and I had to make Higinio happy. My hundred and ten bucks were in his hands.

"This Sunday", I answered.

Arturo's mother brought the coffee. I sipped mine slowly. "How sweet it is!", I thought.

CHAPTER VII
OFF TO EMERALD CITY

The following morning I got up earlier than usual. I wanted to talk to Sóstenes before the old man went out to begin his daily routine.

I found him in the dining room. He was sitting at the table, having breakfast, with his mouth full of bread and sausage and his mug of café con leche in front of him.

I didn't beat around the bush. I let the bomb fall without any preamble.

Of course, I didn't tell him about the nature of the agreement worked out between Higinio and me. I said only that Higinio had used his political contacts to solve my problem because, as a relative, he was feeling sorry for me. But I had the impression that the old buzzard did not quite buy that story.

To my surprise, he took it all very calmly. There were no insults, nor did he throw in my face "the rice and beans that he had been feeding me all those years!" He didn't utter a word, but kept on eating as though he had not heard me, finished his café con leche, swishing around in his mouth the last mouthful, which he swallowed, as usual, and finally got up, asking me:

"Well, when are you leaving?"

"Sunday", I answered, "Everything is arranged".

"Have you told Jorge yet?", he inquired.

"I am going to tell him later this morning", I replied.

"I imagine that neither your grandmother nor your aunt Lidia know anything about this", he said.

"No", I told him, "I'm waiting for them to come out of their rooms".

"That's good", he said, "Well, I have to go to work".

That was all we said to each other. He walked toward the patio, in the direction of the front door, but upon leaving the dining room he spoke to me once more.

"I hope you'll be happy", were his last words.

Apparently, my grandmother and aunt Lidia had gone back to bed after serving Sóstenes his breakfast, because it was close to eight thirty in the morning and they were still in their rooms. After a while, I thought that I should go to "Our Lady of the Miracles", to notify Jorge and collect the pay for the days that I had worked that month.

When I arrived at the drug store, I found my boss behind the counter, with a fearfully stern face. He didn't answer my "buenos días" and, when I started to speak, he cut me off:

"I knew all about it", he warned me, "Sóstenes came by here and told me".

"I am not planning to leave until Sunday", I said, "I can work today and tomorrow, while you try to find someone".

Jorge couldn't deny that he was a Spaniard's son. "I don't want you around here anymore!", he yelled, "I have given you an opportunity, I have opened up the future for you, and look how you repay me! No, thank you, we don't need any ingrates around here!!"

I wanted to explain the reasons I had to leave Helena, but the druggist was about to blow up.

"I don't need, nor want, your explanations!", he screamed,

"And if you haven't come here to buy something, do me the favor of leaving! I don't want you around here anymore!"

Jorge's stupidity filled me to overflowing. I was about ready to pick up one of the wooden chairs that was next to the door and throw it against the shelves, to shatter the beautiful apothecary jars that were the pride of their owner.

But I remembered that when Sunday arrived, I would be leaving Helena forever and I understood that violence would only create problems for me and delay my plans, so I contained myself.

"All right, then", I replied, "Pay me what you owe me for this month, and I'll leave!"

The man, without saying another word, went into the back room and came out a few minutes later with some bills and a piece of paper in his hand.

"I owe you for seven days", he said to me, trembling with rage, "That's fourteen pesos. But first sign this receipt!!"

So I did, and he gave me the money.

"OK", I said, extending my hand, "No hard feelings?"

Jorge acted as though he didn't see it.

"You'll have to excuse me", he answered, sharply, "I have things to do!" And turning his back to me he went into the back room again.

That was the last time I saw him. Years later, Jorge achieved the sad distinction of being among the first ones in Helena to face the firing squad in San Victorino castle, shortly after the rise to power of the tyrant Casto Cruz.

Back at the house, I found my grandmother in the patio, arranging her rat traps. I told her that we had to talk and that I would wait for her and aunt Lidia in the entry-room.

When they arrived, I let them know about the decision I had made, but this time it was not as easy as it had been with Sóstenes. Grandmother cried, but not aunt Lidia, who held back her tears, although I could see that her eyes were moist, as she dried them with a handkerchief.

"Oh, my son, and when are we going to see you again?", asked the old lady.

I told them that every two or three months I would be coming to Helena, to see them; I also promised that I would write to them frequently.

"It's for his own good, mama; it's for his own good", Lidia kept repeating to her mother, caressing her.

For the first time in my life I felt like crying, with a real flood of tears. After all, these two women were the only human beings that had given me a little love.

My aunt put her arm around me.

"Give me all the dirty clothes that you have", she said to me, "I'll have them ready for you this evening".

At noon I went to the bank and closed my savings account. During the time that I had been working for Jorge I managed to save sixty-three pesos that, with the fourteen that I had just received, would make seventy-seven. That would be enough to pay for the first month at the boarding house and other necessities until the money order from Higinio arrived.

Dinner that night was, as usual, poor and scarce, except for Sóstenes and Goya, who had their specialties: "palomilla" steak, ripe fried plantains, white rice, salad and dessert, while grandmother, Aunt Lidia and I had to settle for rice, red beans and sweet potatoes.

That was the last dinner I had in the house where I was born. Sóstenes didn't condescend to even look at me and Goya made several references to "those that bite the hand that feeds them", and also about the cats, "that don't look at whoever feeds them so they don't have to say thank you". Neither grandmother nor Aunt Lidia uttered one single word.

That night, when I retired to my room, I saw on my cot, carefully folded, the clothes that aunt Lidia has washed and ironed for me that afternoon, and I put them in a suitcase, together with my high school diploma. I had just finished getting my things ready when I heard a knock at the door. It was aunt Lidia.

"Your grandmother is not coming", she said, "Because she is too upset. But this is from both of us".

And she put some folded bills in one pocket of my shirt. I wanted to give them back to her, but she wouldn't let me.

"If you don't accept it, you are going to make us unhappy", she insisted, "And Chuchú, also. He contributed something, too".

Aunt Lidia leaned over and kissed me on the cheek. "God be with you, Miguel", she said, "Let us hear from you".

Again alone in my room, I counted the money that she had given me. It was twenty-seven pesos, in fives and ones. Now I had a total of a hundred and four pesos! I was rich! And, putting the small bundle of bills under my pillow so I could touch it with my hand once in a while, I undressed, lay down and tried in vain to get some sleep.

About five o'clock in the morning, tired of tossing around in bed, without having slept a wink all night, I got up, put on my clothes and, grabbing my two suitcases, left the house heading for the bus stop, in front of the city's central park.

The next bus to Sabana would be leaving at seven o'clock. I bought a one-way ticket and went to the cafeteria for breakfast.

My heart was beating so hard that it seemed like it was coming out of my mouth. Soon, the bus would be rolling down the road, through fields and places, toward the glittering capital.

The boarding house ruled over by Cachita Heredia was on San Gabriel Street, behind the University stadium.

At the end of the decade of the twenties, the house had been the residence of José Luis Ojeda, better known as "Cheo Majarete", who was a congressman and also a close friend of General Mechado, Yagruma's dictator at that time.

This mansion was among the countless ones ransacked by the mob that swept through the streets to sack, rob and kill the day the Mechado regime fell. "Cheo Majarete" was hiding up in the roof, but they found him and chopped his head off, right there.

How that white elephant of a house had come to be in Cachita's hands was something that nobody knew. The mansion hardly had the remains of its former splendor: the steps of the marble staircase were broken, the walls were dirty and greasy, with the plaster falling in pieces; the tile floors were scratched and, with the passage of the years, the frescoes on the ceilings and walls had faded.

When I arrived to the house, the front door was open. I got half way up the stairs, and saw that the screen door had been left ajar, so I did not have to ring the bell and wait for someone to come and open it for me.

The stairway led into an enormous living room, thinly furnished with an ancient sofa and three huge, moth-eaten old armchairs, with the seats worn out and grease stains on the arms and backs.

In one of the corners, a makeshift room had been improvised with plywood and two-by-fours, and to my right was a door that opened into a wide, long hallway, from which opened the doors of six rooms, three on each side.

At the end of the hallway I could see the dining room beside which, I imagined, would be the kitchen and the bathrooms.

On the other side of the living room, from an oversized covered balcony overlooking San Gabriel Street, someone spoke to me. It was a woman's voice, mellow and slow.

"What can I do for you, young man?"

"Señora Caridad Heredia?", I ventured.

"At your service", answered the voice, "Come in, come in!" Cachita was sitting on an old ottoman, in a corner protected from the sun by large green awnings, now faded. She was a big, fleshy woman, with folds on her neck, on her arms, and surely on her fat thighs, that I could visualize under the thin cloth of the robe that she had on, and that she used without any undergarments.

She stared at me for a few seconds, sizing me up.

"And, how can I help you?", she asked.

"I am Miguel Baró", I told her, "Higinio Menéndez's relative".

"Oh, yes, Higinio!", replied Cachita, "Yes, he called me the other day! I told him that we were all filled up here now, but since it was for him, I would open up a space for you, somehow!"

"I would appreciate it very much", I assured her.

"Don't thank me", she responded, "Thank Higinio! If I take you in, the truth is that I am doing it for him".

I would have liked to know the reason of Cachita's devotion for Higinio, but after thinking it over, I decided that it was none of my business.

"Well, thank you, anyway", I said, "And, so, tell me, what are the arrangements here?"

"The board is fifty pesos per month", Cachita informed me, "Paid in advance. That includes breakfast, lunch and dinner. The bed clothes are changed every two weeks".

"Be on time", she continued, "Anyone that comes late to the dining room, after I have cleared the table, doesn't get served. Another thing, visitors have to leave at eleven o'clock, and at twelve the gate is closed. Any questions?"

"If by any chance I had to return home after twelve o'clock, what would I have to do?", I wanted to know.

"Oh, if you are going to get in late, you have to talk to Bebo and make arrangements with him, to see if he'll open up for you", Cachita said. And, anticipating my question, she explained that Bebo was the house-boy, a young fellow who, according to her, though gay, was very serious and responsible.

"Well, now", I said, "If you will show me my room, I would like to get my things arranged". I took five ten-peso bills out of my wallet and handed them over to her.

Cachita lifted up from the ottoman her approximately two hundred fifty pounds of weight. "This way", she grumbled, "Your roommates have left for the morning, but they'll be back before lunch".

She assigned me to the second of the rooms on the left side of the hallway. The furniture consisted of four cots, an old wardrobe, three decrepit chairs, one of which had a broken leg, and a wooden rocking chair.

Between two of the cots was a sort of small table on which I saw, beside an alarm clock, a coffee pot, a small alcohol stove and the remains of a bar of guava paste. There were cigarette butts scattered all over the room, crushed cigar stumps in an ash tray and piles of books on the chairs and on the floor.

Evidently, the wardrobe was not big enough for all the clothes of the four occupants, because there were shirts, trousers and underwear hanging from nails and hooks on the walls of the room. A pair of shit stained briefs hung loosely from a nail over what was to be my bed.

"We have lunch at one", Cachita told me, as she was leaving, "Whoever is late, doesn't get anything". And she left, closing the door of the room behind her.

After I was left alone, I decided to hang up the little clothing that I had, but when I opened the wardrobe I saw that it was overflowing, and resolved to wait until my roommates arrived, so as to discuss the matter with them.

Underneath their cots I had seen suitcases and boxes where they could store some of their clothes and personal items.

Between the lack of sleep and the emotions of that morning, I felt I could not stay on my feet any longer. And since it was only eleven o'clock, I took off my shoes, threw into a corner the soiled underwear that was dangling over my bed, and lay down to rest.

I was wakened by the sound of a gong that seemed to come from the back of the house, and the noise made by people talking in loud voices, surely Cachita's guests going by in the hallway.

I got in my shoes quickly, went out into the hall and followed a group of students into the dining room, where there were two long tables made out of plywood sheets placed on top of saw horses. A huge refrigerator stood in one of the corners, and on a sideboard by the kitchen door I saw the gong whose sound had awakened me.

There were baskets of bread lined up on the tables, and three caldrons, one full of white rice, another of red beans and a third one whose contents I could not guess. Standing in front of the caldrons, ladle in hand, was a fat guy of about thirty, with yellow-dyed hair, lipstick on his lips, and a beauty mark painted on one cheek.

"Well, let's go, before it gets cold!", he cried in a high pitched voice, "Let's go, let's go, form a line!!"

The students, finally, got in line and began, plates in hand, to march past the caldrons, where the fat guy was serving. One of them, a pot-bellied young man with pop eyes, made a rebellious gesture when he saw what had been put on his plate.

"Put some more on there, asshole!", he cried, "That's not enough for me!"

The server threw the ladle in the bowl of beans and, spitting fire from his eyes, faced the student.

"You can put out that where the sun does not shine, you hear me!?", he spouted, "If you don't like it, leave it, you butter ball!"

"Don't be like that, Bebo!", cried someone from the back of the line, "Give Goyito a little more!"

"No, sir, I won't give him any more!", yelled Bebo "I've got my orders from Cachita to serve two full ladles to each guest! And even if that were not so, I want to teach this guy that, anyone that doesn't show me respect, is going to get a lot of grief!"

And, snatching out of Goyito's hand an extra piece of bread that the latter had just grabbed from one of the baskets, he said, "Let's go, get moving!"

Goyito stood looking at him for a few moments, clenching his teeth, as though he wanted to insult Bebo, but finally, thinking better of it, turned around and went with his plate to sit down at one of the tables, where he gulped down his meager lunch, swearing to himself. The other students had watched the whole scene, but with the exception of the one that had spoken before, nobody opened his mouth to defend Goyito.

Finally, my turn to be served arrived, and since I didn't know anybody in that place, I sat by myself, off to one side, and put away my scanty and uninviting lunch.

For a moment I thought of going out for a walk around the University, to familiarize myself with the area. But I still didn't feel comfortable there, so I decided instead to return to the peace and quiet of my room. Nevertheless, upon entering, I found Goyito there. He was sitting on one of the cots, eating crackers and guava paste.

"You are the new guy, huh?", he said.

"Yes, I am Miguel Baró".

He got up and we shook hands. "I am Gregorio Sánchez". And pointing with his finger to the package that he had on the bed, "Do you want some?", he asked.

He didn't have to twist my arm: I attacked the crackers and the guava paste.

"Things are tough in this place", I commented, "I, also, ended up hungry. But, how come nobody protests?"

"It's easy to see that you are new here!", replied Goyito, "When people complain, Cachita, calmly, tells them that, if they are not happy here, they can go someplace else, that it makes no difference to her".

"Well, then, why not go looking for a better place?"

"You've got a lot to learn", insisted Goyito, "You won't solve anything by going to another boarding house. Not at all. They are all the same as this one, if not worse. In Sabana, this is all you can get for fifty pesos a month".

"Have you looked around to see if you can find anything better?", I asked.

"Listen, pal", he responded, "I don't have to look. I know where we can find first-class boarding houses, with toilets that don't get stopped up, hot water at all hours and chicken every Sunday. But that, Miguel, will cost you, at least, seventy five pesos per month. Can you pay that? No? Neither can I! So then? We have to get screwed!"

The outlook, then, was not very encouraging for me. The idea that I would have to spend five years in Cachita's boarding house, or in some other one just like it, must have been reflected in my face, because Goyito tried to cheer me up.

"Don't let it bother you!", he advised me, "We don't have it too bad here, after all! On weekends we buy smoked herrings, sardines, some firewater...whatever, and we have our little parties. Besides, every once in a while we go to the whorehouses, to get laid, or to the "Hong Kong"...besides, like somebody said: `happiness is for those who can be contented with little'!"

Until just recently I had sheltered the hope that in Sabana, as a university student, my life would be a little better, but now, in the face of reality, that possibility was beginning to look like another vanishing dream. Frustration and despair lead me to confide my disillusion to my new friend.

"Don't let it get to you", commented Goyito, "Like I said, things could be worse. Your life is going to change here! This is Sabana, brother!"

Then he got up, grabbed a couple of books and left the room, saying that he had to go and study with a classmate who lived in one of the boarding houses on the block. Goyito was a second year medical student.

"He has problems of his own", I thought, seeing him leave, "Why should he worry about mine?".

I had brought with me some of my favorite books, and I spent the rest of the afternoon reading. Later on I went out to take a walk around the area, to acquaint my self with my new surroundings. When I thought that the following morning I would be at the University's administration building, filling out my enrollment papers, my hands got cold and my stomach cramped up.

When I got back to the boarding house, Bebo was already ringing the gong. The dinner was as nasty and disagreeable as the lunch we had at noon. It consisted of salty noodle soup, the eternal soupy white rice and some kind of low quality shredded meat. Upon finishing the miserable dinner, the guests went back to their rooms, to reinforce themselves with crackers and guava paste.

Back in ours, Goyito introduced me to my two other roommates. We began talking, in a short time the ice was broken, and finally we were exchanging ideas, opinions and information about the important topics in our lives.

Of my new friends, one was a country boy, tall and skinny, called Teodulfo Montes, who had come to Sabana to study to become a dentist. Teodulfo, who spent his time and his money drinking, whoring and playing pool, had not been able to get more than two or three passing grades during his first two years in dental school.

As one could expect, his father, upon learning what was happening, cut off his support and ordered him to return home immediately. But Teodulfo, after having had a taste of life in Sabana, wasn't about to return to his hometown, even if they put dynamite up his ass.

Teodulfo, who had been lucky enough to find a job in Sabana, kept on living at Cachita's, where he was the only one of the guests that had a key to the front door, and the only one who was not a student.

My other roommate, Ruperto Badías, was a third year law student. He was sitting on the rocking chair, over whose back he had a cane hanging.

He was the one who put a stop to the chatting.

"Gentlemen", he said, "The conversation is very pleasant, but it is midnight, already, and we have to get up early".

"Are we going to go to bed with an empty belly?", asked Goyito.

"All this guy thinks about is eating!", exclaimed Teodulfo, "Look at the belly on him! It looks like he is pregnant!"

"This is what's pregnant!", cried Goyito, grabbing his crotch with his hand.

"You can bend it over and shove it in your..!" Teodulfo could not finish, because Ruperto, cane in hand, stepped between them.

"OK, you guys!", he said, "Go ahead and scream and fool around and see if Cachita doesn't come! You know she has been climbing the walls, lately, ready to explode!"

It seemed that they respected Ruperto, because the others calmed down right away.

"We were just playing around", explained Goyito.

"Playing? Playing around you are telling me!?", exclaimed Ruperto, "Don't you think you are a little too old for that shit?"

He turned toward me. "If we don't give him something, he is going to spend the whole night screwing around and bothering us", he said, "Besides, we have to celebrate your arrival to this pigsty".

"What!?" Did you bring some brownies?", asked Goyito.

"Even better than that!", answered Ruperto, "I am to make you guys some café con leche!"

"I bought some crackers at Segundo's store", said Teodulfo.

From a cardboard box underneath his bed, Goyito took out some not very clean cups. Ruperto produced a can of evaporated milk and some ground coffee in a container, and soon after we were enjoying our modest repast.

Upon getting undressed to go to bed, I discovered that Ruperto was lacking his left leg, cut off almost up to the crotch. As naturally as if he were taking off a sock, he removed the artificial limb, that was attached to a belt with a kind of harness. Then he put it beside his bed and made a sign to Teodulfo to turn off the light.

Minutes later, all four of us were asleep.

The breakfast that Cachita gave to her guests was about the same as the rest of the food that she served there. With watered down milk, and coffee as clear as I have ever seen, the cook prepared a light-brown beverage which the students called "liquid filth". That, with the addition of a piece of bread with margarine, made our breakfast.

As soon as I had finished, I headed for the University, accompanied by Ruperto. We separated in front of the administration building, because I had to register as a new student, and he went on to his class. "We'll see each other back at Cachita's", he said as he left.

The first class I attended that day had, as a name, "General Theories on the Political Body". When I got to the classroom, the professor hadn't arrived yet, but the classroom was already full of students.

There were several empty rows of seats between the ones sitting in the first rows, close to the professor's desk, and those occupying the seats in the middle of the room towards the back. That made me remember the classrooms in Helena High School, divided by racial and socio-economic differences into two groups that deeply hated each other.

I couldn't help but notice the expensive clothes and the fine jewelry worn by the students of the first group. The girls, above all, were dressed as though they were attending a New Year's Eve reception at the presidential palace, rather than a class at the University.

Of course, I did not have to waste any time deciding where I was going to sit. I already knew where I belonged. I picked out a seat at the back, beside a big-nosed, skinny student who was dozing on his seat.

I began to examine the people in the room, especially the females. There were some very pretty ones. I was trying to figure out how to become friendly, when a beautiful young woman entered the classroom. She went straight to the front rows, but seeing that all the seats in that section were taken, opted for a seat a little father back, close to where I was sitting.

At that moment, voices were heard ordering the students to shut up, as the professor had just entered. Doctor Godín was a chubby little guy whose name appeared in the newspapers quite often. He frequently was a guest speaker in the main clubs and cultural societies of Sabana.

Doctor Godín did not bother taking the roll, nor did he excuse himself for his lack of punctuality, but immediately launched into his discourse, giving us an interminable tirade about the individual in society, the state, Rousseau, the social contract, and all kinds of related crap.

Shortly before the class ended, doctor Godín put aside his notes and began asking questions of the class. Finally, he gathered up his papers, which were spread all over the desk, grabbed his brief case and left like the devil was after him.

During the whole class, I could not keep my eyes off that girl that had sat near me. Now she stood up, smoothing out her skirt and picking up her handbag and books. Her eyes, between amber and green, were prominent in her tawny face, enhanced by wavy brown hair. Behind the tailor-made lace blouse, two full and high breasts jutted out. The skirt, which was not very long, showed perfectly formed legs attached to a voluptuous, upside down, heart shaped ass.

I kept looking at her until she left the classroom. Then, I realized that Big Nose was still there, but getting ready to leave.

I couldn't contain myself.

"Listen", I told him, "That girl that was sitting near us, in that seat...who is she?"

"She doesn't come to class very often", he answered, "I have heard she works for an American company. Like I said, we don't see her much around here".

"Do you know what her name is?", I asked.

"Perlita", he said, "Perlita Shell".

CHAPTER VIII
AGAIN, THERE IS NO FREE LUNCH

After a couple of weeks of attending classes I was really discouraged. I felt even more depressed now than in the days when I walked the streets of Helena, back from the slaughter house, pushing the cart where I carried the bloody masses of bulls' testicles with which Jorge prepared the "Vigoril".

One did not have to be too keen an observer to realize how things were in Sabana University Law School. The students of scanty means and obscure, unheralded ancestry, were like shadows in that place.

For the professors, these students did not seem to exist. The smiles, the deference, the praise and, of course, the outstanding grades and the academic awards, were for the descendants of the rich and the influential.

Ruperto, who had become a master of cynicism due to his years at the law school, found all this very natural.

"Only the stupid ones will not accept a reality that they cannot change", he told me once, "The `profs' are all practicing attorneys. Why do you think they are so nice to those assholes? Because they need the contacts, the relations, the influence, and the good will of mama, or papa, or uncle, who are VIPs and have pull. That's why they lick those bastards' asses!"

"For those old farts in the faculty", he went on, "Money is the only thing that matters in this life, and probably in the next. Do you know why, Miguel!? Because without money they can't live their sweet lives!! No Jaguars, no Mercedes, no club life, no mistresses, no trips to Europe!!!"

He stopped to light a cigarette. I was about to open my mouth to tell him what I thought of his reasoning, but the sound of the gong calling us to dinner put an end to the conversation.

Among the faculty members, the most hated one was, probably, Dr. Berardo Corcela, professor of Political Economy.

Corcela's examinations were always oral, and in order to pass them one had to memorize the class lectures to the letter. There were over a thousand pages of them, and if those being examined did not use exactly the same words and repeat them exactly as written, like parrots, they were failed.

Through the years, hundred of students had not been able to graduate, because of this professor.

The case of a student named Gabriel Fernández was famous, as he only needed to pass Political Economy to graduate. He took the exam twelve times, and twelve times Corcela failed him.

Finally, one day, stuffed full of benzedrine, with his eyes popping out of the sockets, his tongue hanging out, Gabriel, during his thirteenth exam was able to come up with exactly what Corcela wanted, and he left the classroom like a zombie, with the passing grade in his hand.

That night his friends, to celebrate the great accomplishment, gave Gabriel a celebration dinner at "The Three Belches", a restaurant that was very popular in the student community. At dessert time, the guest of honor, who was now completely drunk, assured the group that, as soon as he got back to his home town, he would talk to a santería priest that he knew and have him do a job on Dr. Corcela.

It was never known if Gabriel followed through with his threat, but that same year, during the September examinations, a student that Corcela had just failed waited for the terrible professor in the hallway, punched him in the face and threw him down the stairs.

The professor, after all, was a very lucky man. Instead of the fall killing him, as all of his students were hoping, he only suffered a broken leg.

Another screwball was Dr. Godín, a cultured man, but also a pedant.

In Yagruma, politics has always been the most important industry, and Dr. Godín, years before, had tried to involve himself in it, joining the enemies of president Mechado. But the man was cranky and ill-natured, and those defects have never been excused in Yagruma.

All that Godín could get out of the revolution was his professorship, plus an appointment as legal counsel in the Ministry of Public Works, where he only had to show up once a month, to collect his paycheck.

Dr. Godín did not have much luck in private practice, either. He had his law office in the old colonial section of Sabana, where he spent most of his afternoons playing dominoes with the building "super" and a couple of old guys that lived around the corner.

His laziness was proverbial. He missed classes frequently, and was late most of the times that he showed up. Often, he pretended to be annoyed with something that some student had said to him, using that as an excuse to put an end to the class. He would leave the room in a rush, spewing out threats and swearing, on his mother's grave, that he was going to get even with everybody at the exams.

Some veteran students maintained that Dr. Godín did not bother to grade the examinations. According to them, the professor put to one side the exams of the "privileged" students, who were assured beforehand of an outstanding grade, and stacked the rest on his desk.

He then took a fan, set it at full speed, and aimed it at the pile of exams, blowing them all over the room. Those that fell on this side of the fifth row of floor tiles got a D; those that landed between the fifth and seventh rows got a C; the ones between the eight and tenth were given a B and, finally, those who got as far as the door, which did not happen very often, achieved a grade of A.

Of course, the exams of the students that had been giving the professor a hard time received special attention.

I had to get in touch with Arturo so I could send the first report back to his father. I depended on Higinio: I had to keep him happy, so a couple of days after having settled into the boarding house, I called Leticia's house to talk to Arturo.

The woman who answered the phone told me that she was Eumelia, Leticia's maid. She informed me that "señor" Arturo had left for medical school and that "señora" Leticia was still in her room and had given orders not to be disturbed. I gave Eumelia the phone number of the boarding house, with a message for Arturo to call me as soon as possible.

He returned my call that night. We talked, and made an appointment to meet the following day, at ten o'clock in the morning, at the plaza in front of the Law School.

I got there about five minutes early, lit a cigarette and sat down on one of the benches, under the trees, to wait. But ten o'clock came, ten fifteen, finally ten thirty, and Arturo still had not arrived.

Tired of waiting, I got up and was about to cross the avenue to go back to school, when a red, fish-tailed Cadillac convertible of the latest model, with the top down and Arturo at the wheel, stopped by the curb.

"Let's go, Miguel, get in!", he cried.

"I can't!", I replied, "I don't have enough time. I have to be back in class in twenty minutes. Park it here and let's sit in the plaza!"

"The hell with your class!, answered Arturo, "Let's go, get in, I want to show you where I live! There we can talk all you want!"

"Can you bring me back?", I asked, "If I am not back at Cachita's at noon, I don't get any lunch!"

"Let's go, forget all that", he responded, "You can stay and have lunch with us. You know Leticia, don't you?"

"I met her once in Helena, at your parents' house".

"Great!", commented Arturo, "Well, get in!"

I had never been in a car like that one. Now, seated in the luxurious convertible, I could understand why someone, forced to chose between killing his own parents or giving up his "fish-tail", might pick the first option.

The car that Arturo was driving belonged, surely, to Leticia. His monthly allowance, though generous, would have never permitted him to afford such luxury.

My cousin was paying attention to his driving, keeping both hands on the wheel. Looking at him from the corner of my eye, I noticed an expensive gold watch on his left wrist. I could also see that the clothes he warc were more appropriate for a rich land owner than for a medical student.

It was clear that Arturo had fallen into the good graces of someone, and that someone had to be Leticia.

Leaving behind Sabana's nightmarish traffic, we came out on a broad, beautiful avenue along which stood sumptuous residences surrounded by fantastic gardens. Arturo, who had been silent for a while, opened up a little when we entered the avenue.

"I'm not asking you about my folks", he said, "Because it's been only two or three days since I have had news of them"

"From whom?", I asked, pretending interest.

"From Sócrates Govín. He was in Helena just a few days ago, and he ran across my old man at the bus stop".

"And how are your folks?", I inquired.

"Fine", answered Arturo, "You know my father. Always involved in politics, telling stories...same old bullshit!"

"Well, tell me about yourself", I asked, "How is it going with your medical studies? Are you still excited about it?"

He told me that he was, but it seemed to me that he answered in the same tone of voice as though he had said no.

After a while, leaving the avenue behind, we turned onto a street flanked by opulent mansions and apartment buildings. About a block ahead, Arturo entered into the basement garage of a luxurious apartment building, so splendid and showy that, in my opinion, it would have left the Taj-Mahal looking rather small.

He parked the convertible beside a real beauty, a silver gray Mercedes Benz. "Well, here we are!", he said, pointing with his finger at the Mercedes, "That's Leticia's car".

And, seeing that I didn't make any comment, he added, with a bit of vanity in his voice: "She bought it so she could let me have the convertible".

"Sure, and she bought both of them with the money her husband stole", I thought.

We went into the building and got into an elevator that took us to the penthouse. Arturo opened the door with his key, proof that he had the right kind of "connection" with his cousin, and we entered into a fabulous living room, furnished with elegance and good taste.

Leticia's housekeeper, who was in the living room polishing the furniture, stopped working for a moment to wish us "buenos días". She surprised me, because Eumelia did not look like most of the peasant girls that leave the farm for the city to work as housemaids.

She was a stunning female in her early thirties, with dark eyes and light brown, almost blond hair, in which a few strands of silver could already be seen. Her uniform, although loose-fitting, allowed one to discern a very well formed body and a pair of simply divine legs.

Our eyes locked, and something that I saw reflected in hers made my heart beat faster.

"Eumelia", ordered Arturo, without returning her greeting, "Tell 'señora' Leticia that my cousin Miguel is here".

The woman returned in a few moments. "The señora just went into her bath, sir", she informed Arturo, "She said she'll be with you in a little while".

He turned to me. "You are not in any hurry, right? We'll eat lunch a little later! We can have a high ball while we wait for her".

"Do you like scotch?", he asked, "If not, you tell me. We've got everything here". I would have preferred firewater with a little sugar, but I accepted the whiskey for fear of appearing like a country bumpkin.

"Eumelia!", he cried again, "Bring a bottle of Chivas Regal, glasses, and soda. Ah, and tell Epifanio to make a little extra effort today, because we have a guest for lunch".

"Epifanio is our gourmet cook", he explained. And seeing that I was still standing, he pointed to the sofa and ordered, "But, sit down, Miguel! Sit down and relax, man!"

I grimaced, and plopped my butt down on the edge of the sofa.

"Excuse me a moment", said Arturo. And he disappeared down one of the corridors that led off from the living room.

As I was left alone, I passed the time making a mental inventory of the porcelain vases, the original oil paintings and all the other wonderful things that were in that living room, trying to figure out how much money might have been spent on the stuff.

This important occupation was interrupted by the return of Eumelia, bringing the booze, the soda and the glasses on a large silver tray

"Your highball", señor", she said, presenting the tray.

"I am going to ask you a favor", I replied, "Leave off the señor! That's OK for Don Quixote".

"Oh, and how do you want me to address you?", she asked, smiling.

"Just call me Miguel".

"Listen to that", she exclaimed, laughing, "You know, you are the first Miguel I've met since I came to Sabana!"

Still, when addressing me, she used the formal Spanish appellation. "You don't have to use usted'", I replied, taking one of her hands in mine, "Address me by Tú!"

Slowly, but firmly, she withdrew her hand, and on her face I could see that she was afraid.

"No, no, don't!", she whispered, "If they catch me you like this, they'll kick me out!"

She was so pretty like that, pleading, with her beautiful eyes full of fear! Getting even closer to her, I put my arm around her waist and pulled her towards me. Eumelia pushed herself back, trembling, with her eyes wet.

"No, please...Miguel!", she implored, "They are going to fire me! I need this job! Please!"

Arturo's steps, returning from the living room, sounded on the marble floor. I separated myself from Eumelia, and went and sat down again on the sofa.

Arturo excused himself for his delay, and we drank and talked about the good old times when we were at Helena High until I began to notice that, with so much drinking on an empty stomach, I was half plastered.

"And the old bastard...!" I had begun to holler, referring to one of our old high school teachers, when Arturo made a sign for me to shut up. The queen of the palace had just made her entrance into the living room.

Arturo and I stood up. "You know Miguel, don't you?", he asked.

She hardly looked at me. "No, I don't think so", she responded icily.

Her depreciative attitude made my blood boil. "I had the pleasure of meeting you at the home of the Menéndez's, in Helena, last year", I said, "Don't you remember?"

"No, no, I don't remember", she answered, with a note of impatience in her voice. "Well, honey, whenever you are ready", she said to Arturo, who was fixing himself another highball.

It seems that when he saw Leticia's hostility towards me, Arturo decided to act up a little.

"What do you mean, when I am ready!?", he exclaimed, "But, Leticia, we are not going anywhere today!"

"Oh, boy, what a memory you have!", replied Leticia. She turned to me, with a smile as false as a three-dollar bill. "I don't know what I am going to do with him when he gets old!"

I couldn't imagine what kind of pretext that woman was going to come up with to get me out of her house, but now I was sure that I wouldn't be getting any lunch. Arturo had just whispered something to her that she did not like, because Leticia was screaming at him, mad as hell, without caring in the least that I was witnessing the show.

"All right!", she yelled, "I have given my word to Conchita and Polito that we were going to have lunch with them at the Casino, and play cards afterwards! And it is not in my best interests to offend them!"

"But, sugar", this loving expression escaped from Arturo, "I had invited Miguel to have lunch with us!"

"Well, that is too bad!", she exclaimed, "Why didn't you let me know in time? Look at the problem you have created!"

I felt wiped out, flattened by the shame of being the center of that boondoggle, and I could see that Eumelia, from the corner of the living room where she had withdrawn, looked sadly at me.

That son-of-a-bitch Arturo was standing beside the table with the drinks, and without saying a word, his eyes riveted on the floor, not daring to look at me. His attitude convinced me that he had changed, not only on the exterior, but also inside.

Leticia turned to face me.

"You...a...what's your name? Miguel? You understand the situation, Miguel? It really makes me feel bad, believe me, but we are going to have to postpone the invitation. Call us one of these days and we will be very pleased to have you here".

I could hardly speak, from the anger and shame that I felt.

"Control yourself", said the little voice inside me, "You have to keep Higinio's "pipeline" functioning".

Composing myself as much as I could, I answered that I understood everything, and that I was sorry to have caused the problem. "Well, then", I finished, "With your permission, I will go".

"Wait a minute, Miguel!", Arturo said, "Let me take you where you can catch the bus!".

I would have choked first! If I had been able to unleash my instincts, I would have killed both of them, and I would have cut off his balls and stuffed them in Leticia's mouth. But when I responded to Arturo, nobody would have known, from the tone of my voice, what I was thinking.

"No, you don't have to do that!", I said, "I remember where the bus stop is. It's only two or three blocks, and the walk will do me good!"

"But, listen, remember", he insisted, "You heard what Leticia said. You have to come and have dinner with us one of these days!"

"Sure!", I answered, "Don't worry, I'll call you. Well, see you soon!"

Two hours later I was back in Cachita's house. I had bought some bread at the corner store, and when I was back in my room I went straight to the drawer where I kept the guava paste. That was my lunch that unforgettable day.

CHAPTER IX
NINETEEN, AND ANXIOUS

I tossed around in bed all that night, without being able to sleep. It was not the snoring and farting of my roommates that caused the insomnia, but rather my recollections of Eumelia's big brown eyes, the curve of her firm, round buttocks, and the feel of her hands imprisoned in mine. Leticia's maid had gotten under my skin.

She had not been totally indifferent to my advances, judging by her reaction. So, the solution to my problem, which was to get Eumelia in bed with me, did not appear to be too difficult. But then, doubts and fears began to surge through me.

How would she react to the advances of an insignificant student? There were, surely, a string of guys after Eumelia, trying to make out with her, guys that could spend money on her. And even if she agreed to go out with me, where the hell would I take her? The little money that I had saved up would vanish away in one single night at the "Trópico Club".

"Cowardly dogs don't screw", I said to myself, "They won't get bitten, but they won't screw". The following morning I called Leticia's house. As I imagined, Eumelia answered the phone.

"Guess who is calling", I said.

She laughed. "I know who it is", she answered, "It's Miguel. Arturo is not here!"

"That's good. Listen to me", I replied, "This is going to be short. I don't want to cause you any problems".

"You can talk all you want to", she assured me, "I am all alone in the penthouse. The señora has left also".

"Eumelia", I said, "I don't have any excuse for my behavior with you yesterday. I am calling to ask you to forgive me!"

"There is nothing to forgive", she replied after a few seconds, "Nothing has happened between us".

"I have to see you", I said, "I have to talk to you. When can we see each other?"

"I think that would be a mistake", replied Eumelia, "Look, after you left yesterday, I was hoping that you would call me. I'll tell you the truth; I thought you were real nice. But after I cooled down and thought about it a little more, I decided that there could never be anything between us".

That woman's voice had an aphrodisiac effect on me. "I am lost, lost without you", I exclaimed, "Eumelia, I spent all last night thinking about you, wishing for you to be here, in bed with me!"

"Young man! You are going awfully fast!", she commented, in a joking tone of voice.

"Give me a chance, please!", I pleaded, "The only thing I ask is that you give me a chance to talk to you, so you will understand how I feel about you! Am I not worth a few minutes!? Do I interest you so little?"

She softened her voice a little when she answered me.

"It isn't' that, Miguel, it isn't that", she replied, "I really like you, but as much as you might want to deny it, you don't feel anything serious toward me. What you have is a big passion for me, and you want some place to put it. That's all there is to it!"

"A few moments ago you told me there could never be anything between us", I reminded her, "Do you want to tell me why?"

"How old are you, honey?", she asked.

"Nineteen", I replied, somewhat ashamed of my youth.

"I am thirty one", said Eumelia, "And I have a son who is sixteen. He is only three years younger than you! Besides, there have been some things in my life that I know you are not going to like. Think about this, Miguel. Even if you and I get involved now, all that passion that you are showing is not going to last very long. I titillate you, and you want me to rescue you. But there won't be any of that!"

My mouth and throat were dry, and I noticed that I was having difficulty talking. "Listen to me!", I interrupted, "You are mistaken, and I can prove it to you. But not on the telephone; I have to see you, because this kind of thing has to be dealt with face to face".

"I am really sorry", she responded, "But now you know how I feel".

I couldn't take her refusal. "Listen to me!", I cried.

"Think over very carefully all that I have said to you; if you change your mind, call me. I'll be right here, by the phone, waiting. If you haven't called in five minutes, good-bye then! I give you my word that I will not bother you anymore".

I hung up without giving her a chance to say anything. Five minutes passed by, and I got up preparing to leave, when the telephone rang. It was Eumelia.

"Four o' clock, this afternoon,", she said, "Is that OK?"

"Four o'clock is fine", I answered, "Where?"

"At my place would be best", she replied, "Write down the address".

What Eumelia called "an apartment complex" when referring to the place where she lived, consisted, really, of four rows of cheap apartments, built around a rectangular cement yard.

It was not quite four o'clock when I called at the door of number twelve.

"It's open", answered Eumelia's voice, "Come in!" So I entered the apartment, which was very small. It only had a bedroom and a minuscule living room, in addition to a very small bathroom and a tiny kitchen.

All the windows were sealed shut; an oscillating fan on top of a small table tried in vain to cool the place, which the sun, in that afternoon of tropical heat, had turned into an oven.

Eumelia got up from the sofa on which she had been sitting and came to meet me. She was beautiful in her black silk robe, adorned in a Chinese pattern of green and red.

I had not come here to waste time talking, and she, certainly, could not say much, because when she came up to me I took her in my arms, and passionately kissed and bit her eager lips. This time, Eumelia did not resist. She abandoned herself to my caresses and returned my kisses with hers.

I slowly removed her sash. The robe slipped gently to the floor and I began kissing her all over until she erupted into a sexual frenzy.

She pushed me over to the sofa; there, cupping her breasts in her hands, she offered them to me. They were so beautifully round and firm, with nipples like sweet rosebuds! I was ecstatic with anticipation.

"Bite me!", she pleaded, "Bite me hard! Until you see blood!"

Now, this was going to be a wild time. If I could just hold on and not bust my ass, this could be one hell of a ride.

Eumelia was, in my opinion, a case of sado-masochism. To get sexually excited, she had to be hit, kicked, defiled and insulted. When she reached her orgasm, she went crazy, screaming, vomiting obscenities and raking me with her nails and teeth.

We spent several months like this. I had to wait until she called me to tell me when we could see each other, and from those encounters I always left completely wiped out.

Arturo and I were having coffee one day, in the school cafeteria, when he told me that Eumelia had quit her job. According to him, she told Leticia that she had gone back to her husband, from whom she had been separated for a couple of years.

"The man was coming to get her the next day", Arturo informed me, "To take her back to his town".

"Is that right?", I said, casually, adding: "And where did they go?"

"I don't know", he answered, "She didn't tell us, and Leticia didn't ask, either".

That afternoon I went to the "apartment complex" and asked the "super" if Eumelia had left any message for me. The answer was negative.

"By any chance, do you have her new address?", I asked.

"No", he said, "All I know is that, a few days ago, an old guy showed up here in a pickup truck. She told me that the man was her husband. By noon, the two of them had loaded all her stuff into the pickup and took off without even saying good-bye".

I left the "complex" feeling a little sad. I knew I would never see Eumelia again. It would take some time to erase her completely from my mind.

Although I never went back to Leticia's house, I kept calling Arturo frequently to find out how things were going with him.

I also stopped by the medical school to see how he was doing in his studies and, in general, to get out of him as much information as I could about his life with Leticia. This was the material that I used to make up the reports that I mailed to Higinio.

Sometimes, for fear of losing my monthly income, I would put in some lies the size of a railroad boxcar.

CHAPTER X
STORIES: WOEFUL PASSION, POLICE GRAFT

I learned to ignore the strange and hostile character of the owner of the boarding house, who treated the students dryly and severely, as though she hated them.

When her guests complained that the food was bad and measly, that the toilets were stopped up and there was no hot water in the shower, she did not pay the least bit of attention. Any student that did not have his money ready at the end of the month she kicked out onto the street, and if the poor devil begged for a few days of grace, Cachita would give him this advice:

"Son, if you want charity, go to the shelter and see if the nuns will help you..!

Cachita was a widow. She had an unmarried daughter, about thirty years of age, called Rosalina, who was a school teacher.

Rosalina lived in the house with us. She was rather homely, cross-eyed, and had a face full of pimples, but that still didn't keep a medical student, named Filomeno, from taking her out and getting her pregnant.

According to Bebo, Cachita, upon learning what had happened to her daughter, got a revolver and went out looking for the seducer or, as she said, the "rapist", swearing that she was going to kill him if he did not marry Rosalina. But, as hard as she tried, she could not find him.

In the boarding house where Filomeno used to live, they told Cachita that the student, one morning, gathered up his things, paid his bills, called a taxi and disappeared with no explanation. He was never seen again at the University, nor in the area.

Cachita, who knew that Filomeno's family lived in Baracutey, a town in eastern Yagruma, found out their address and called them, threatening to take the "criminal" to court.

But Filomeno's father, who answered the phone, told her that he had sent his son to the United States, to study. He also warned Cachita that if she kept on bothering them, he, Don Marcos Balbón, would speak to his associate, Colonel Pérez de la Rosa, who happened to be Filomeno's godfather, and ask him to take charge of the matter.

That prompted Cachita to change her mind and forget Rosalina's defilement and her longing to get even with Filomeno. Because it was said of that Colonel that he killed people just to see the blood run.

Rosalina, who kept on living with her mother, gave birth to an incredibly ugly baby boy whom they named Remember. This name his mother really liked, because, according to her, it had "resonance".

But very soon the whole house was calling the child by the nickname that Cachita used when she was cradling him in her arms, singing him to sleep:

"Cucuíto", my pretty little boy, “Cucuíto", the joy of my heart,
"Cucuíto", sleep tight, my little one, "Cucuíto", my glory, my love!

And the poor child was stuck with this sobriquet for the rest of his life.

I got along well with my roommates. They arc part of the few pleasant memories I have of the years that I spent in Cachita's boarding house.

Teodulfo Montes, the former dental student, though a whore-monger and an elbow-bender, was a good friend to everybody, and splendid when he had a few pesos in his pocket.

Teodulfo worked in a store called "La Preferida", where he earned sixty five pesos per month, which was not enough to sustain the style of life he led in Sabana. Luckily for Teodulfo, his mother, behind her husband's back, sent him a money order every month.

One night that he had not gone out carousing, Teodulfo was telling us about his place of work, his fellow workers and his boss, the owner of "La Preferida". He was a Spaniard named Leopoldo Sousa, whom everyone called Polito.

"I've been working there for three years now", he complained, "And I've never had a raise! Busting my back for sixty five dollars a month! They can all go to hell!"

"Maybe the business isn't going too well", I ventured.

"That business!?, cried Teodulfo, "Rivers of money come in that store every day! Polito lives in a palace, in Almendrales Heights!!

"The thing is, brother, that you have been screwed!", observed Ruperto, "What you guys should do...!"

"One moment, one moment", interrupted Teodulfo, "Wait a minute, you don't know anything yet! The ones that are getting screwed are the Yagrumans! The fucking Spaniards take care of each other!"

According to Teodulfo, Polito Sousa favored two of his employees, Ignacio Carbonell and Antonio Fernández, just because they were Spaniards, the same as he was, while paying miserable wages to the rest, all native Yagrumans.

It was a established practice in that business, he told us, to advance money against their salaries to those employees that asked for it, money that was later deducted from their earnings on pay day.

Nevertheless, Ignacio and Antonio never had their advances deducted in full, and the balance that they owed went on accumulating each month. The "natives", however, did not enjoy this privilege.

Then, at the end of each year, Polito would tear up the receipts for the advances that the two Spaniards had not redeemed as yet, and forgave them the debt. As if that were not enough, Polito Sousa, last Christmas, had distributed bonuses among the employees, giving three hundred pesos to Ignacio and two hundred to Antonio, but only twenty pesos a piece to the Yagrumans.

It was close to midnight, and everyone in the room had had some of Ruperto's famed café con leche, when Teodulfo began to tell us the Polito Sousa story.

"When Polito arrived in Yagruma, from Spain", he began, "The hemp sandals on his feet and the beret on his head were his only capital. Soon after his arrival he began to work in "La Preferida", a pawn shop that belonged to a countryman of his, and after spending a quarter of a century behind the counter, he became a partner in the business".

"When the old pawnbroker died, with no wife nor heirs, the pawn shop passed into Polito's hands. He added to the business the purchase of old pianos that, after being repaired, reconditioned and tuned, Polito would sell for a price twenty times over what he had paid for them".

According to Teodulfo, Polito Sousa was now a millionaire. Ignacio, one of the store's veteran clerks told him the story of the sexual involvement of Don Leopoldo, as he had to be called these days, with Conchita Pérez, who, after marrying the pawnbroker, became Doña Concepción Pérez de Sousa.

"Polito still had the pawn shop", he continued, "When he met Conchita, who had just moved to the neighborhood, into a rooming house near Polito's".

"Conchita's husband, a mailman, could no longer work, because of two heart attacks that he had had, one right after the other. He spent his days in his room, on a big chair".

"Wasn't there anyone to help?", asked Goyito, "Friends, family, anyone?"

"The only relative that they had was a son, useless as hell. He couldn't even take a dog out to pee; a real jerk, lazier than an old fox!"

"Well, how did they manage to survive?", insisted Goyito,

Where did they get the money from? How did she connect with Polito?"

"Well, Conchita began taking laundry at home from her neighbors, but with what she made they barely had enough to eat. One day she did not get paid for some washing she had done, and she was counting on that money to buy food. Imagine!"

"And that was the day she met Polito!", ventured Ruperto.

"Exactly!", cried Teodulfo, "Brother, you got it! How did you know that!?"

"I've got second sight, brother!", answered the other, "Don't fool around with old Ruperto! Well, how about it? Are you going to finish the story or not?"

"I'm getting there! Conchita had a pair of earrings that she didn't want to get rid of. But since things were getting really grim, she grabbed them and went to Polito's pawn shop. Let me tell you that this happened more than fifteen years ago, and at that time Conchita was still a hell of a good looking woman".

"Well, go on! What happened?"

"Well, the old fucker, without Conchita even imagining it, had fallen for her like a ton of bricks, just by watching her pass by in front of the shop every day. He was a very timid man, and had never had the courage to make a pass at her. Man! When he saw that "she, in the flesh" had walked into his store, he began to shiver, and broke into a cold sweat".

"So, what happened? Did he take the earrings?"

"Not only did he not take them, but he reached inside his pocket, took out a roll of bills and gave Conchita fifty pesos to help her get by for a time, saying that he was at her service for "whatever she needed", because he was really sorry that someone like her would be in such a situation".

"And that's where things started heating up", commented Goyito.

"Just imagine! It didn't take long for Conchita to realize how the Spaniard felt about her, and she saw the skies open up! Right then she began telling him about the tragedy of her life, the drama that she was living, the hunger that they were suffering...!"

"Well, she really painted him a picture!", said Abilio Pardo.

Abilio was a policeman, assigned to the nearby station. He was also in the third year of law school, like Ruperto, of whom he was a friend. Abilio often came to Cachita's house to fool around and talk. He had just arrived, and was listening to the story that Teodulfo was telling.

"Well, then, how was it that they finally got involved with each other?", he asked.

"All I know is what Ignacio told me", answered Teodulfo, "He lives in the neighborhood, and is friendly with a few old hags and a couple of faggots that keep him well posted about what's going on around there".

"Polito", Teodulfo went on, "Was madly in love with Conchita. Well, the guy was a real goner! He was head over heels, but he wouldn't dare to make a pass at Conchita. What an idiot!"

"Now, every time that she needed money, Conchita took her earrings and went to the shop, to pawn them. Same thing as always: she left the store with money in her pocket and the earrings on her ears!"

"Then, what? How did they finally get it on? Did she arrange it?", asked Abilio Pardo.

"More or less! Conchita knew very well that Polito had fallen for her. It was a lot more that a simple infatuation: the man was completely crazy about her. Naturally, Conchita, who was no dummy, realized that Polito could be the solution to all her problems".

"And then, she let him have a little taste of that honey, eh?"

"Exactly! One afternoon she waited until six o'clock, which was the time that they closed the store. She knocked at the door and told Polito that she had to talk to him, but inside, because if any of the old ladies of the neighborhood passed by and saw them together, all kinds of rumor would get started, and she was a married woman".

"Trembling with emotion, he agreed, and they went into the back of the store, where he had his bed and a makeshift bathroom".

"How did she manage to get him over his shyness?", I asked.

"Look!", replied Teodulfo, "Conchita is a smooth operator! She is slicker than a snake! She began by telling Polito how grateful she was to him, and that, little by little, saving from what she earned washing clothes, she would be repaying him the money that he had given her".

"She would send it", added Conchita, "By her son, Bienvenido, because never again would she put her feet in "La Preferida".

"When Polito heard that, he broke out in a cold sweat, and his heart began hammering inside his chest. Still half-recovered from the shock, he asked Conchita what he had done to deserve such a cruel treatment, to which she answered that she couldn't understand how some men were so blind that they didn't notice the love they inspired".

"How couldn't you realize, just by looking at me, how I felt about you?", she complained. Bitterly adding that, since she was a married woman, her duty was to resist her impulses, and stay away from Polito.

"Because I'm afraid", she concluded, "That if I don't stop seeing you, I'll soon lose the control that, up to now, I have somehow managed to keep!"

"Saying this, Conchita pressed herself against him, rubbing her tits against his chest and caressing his cheeks".

"And from there to bed, right?", asked Goyito.

"Yes, sir! Screwing and Company, Incorporated! And when the money began to flow from Polito, Conchita kissed poverty good-bye!".

"But Polito ended up marrying her", exclaimed Abilio, "What about the sick husband?"

"God and Conchita took care of him!", explained Teodulfo, "God, because He sent her husband the heart problem, and Conchita, because she knew how to use it to get rid of the poor bastard".

"Let's see, let' see, how was that?", asked Ruperto.

"Like I told you, the guy had already had two heart attacks. He had one foot in the grave, and the doctor had told Conchita that stress and intense emotions would be fatal to him".

"Well, Conchita started wearing new dresses and shoes, and buying things for her son. She stopped taking in washing, she had money...Very often she wouldn't be back in the house until nine or ten in the evening, because she had been at the "La Preferida", with Polito".

"And the husband, who was not a complete fool, began to suspect something!", concluded Goyito.

"Naturally! But that's not all: Conchita arranged for a pair of old hags, friends of hers, who were the biggest gossips and troublemakers in the neighborhood, to visit the sick man and tell him what was going on between Polito and her".

"That night, Conchita arrived home later than usual, and the man, who had been waiting for her with a pent-up fury, grabbed her by the neck and threatened to kill her if what the old harpies had told him was true".

"Go on, man! What happened then?", insisted Abilio.

"Well, she gave him a big shove, and he fell to the floor. He lay there, choking, according to what Ignacio told us. Then, Conchita, very calmly, let him know that what he had heard was true, that, yes, she was the pawnbroker's lover"

“How did Ignacio know that?” asked Miguel.

“One of Ignacio's friends was outside, peering through the open window" he answered.

"The man", continued Teodulfo, "Who had managed to get up with great difficulty, began to run towards her, his fists clenched, but he could only cover a few steps: all of a sudden he pressed his hands against his chest and collapsed to the floor"

"He bought the farm, right?", someone asked.

"Not right then, no! The neighbors called a taxi, because Conchita hadn't moved a muscle, and they hauled him to the hospital, but when he got there he was already a dead duck!"

"Ready to push up daisies!", finished Abilio Pardo.

"To finish the story", continued Teodulfo, "A few weeks after the funeral, Conchita and Polito were married. Now, Conchita, who, although poor had always gone around with her nose in the air, didn't like being the wife of a pawnbroker".

"She made Polito change his business from money lending to the buying and selling of jewelry and fine furniture, and didn't give up until Polito bought the big mansion in Almendrales Heights, where they now live".

"Smart bitch, Conchita!", said Goyito.

"Oh, and that's not all!", added Teodulfo, "Now they are living the 'social life'. Just imagine: Polito is now vice-president of the Spanish Country Club of Sabana!"

"If a dog has money, call him 'Mr. Dog', right?", commented Abilio.

"How did Conchita's son take all this?", asked Ruperto.

"How was he going to take it?", answered Teodulfo, "The only thing that Polito couldn't buy him is brains; otherwise, everything: designer clothes, a sports car, money, trips to Spain...the asshole is in clover! And, listen to this: now, the son-of-a-bitch calls Polito 'Dad'!"

"My girl friend is a manicurist in ‘La Parisienne’", said Abilio, "And she sometimes does the nails for Conchita. She told me that the old girl has a ring with a diamond as big as a golf ball".

"Out of the worm's ass comes the silk", said Goyito, "Out of silk comes the woman's ass".

When Ruperto was a child, his parents often took him to visit his maternal grandparents, who lived in the countryside. One night, coming to a railroad crossing, the bus they were riding back home collided with a train.

There were many dead and injured among the passengers of the bus, but Ruperto's parents, miraculously, escaped with only minor cuts and abrasions.

Our friend, though, came out with his left leg smashed to a pulp, fractured in several places, and in such a condition that there was no option but to amputate it.

He, apparently, learned to accept the limp philosophically. We never heard him complain about his bad luck and never, in his behavior, did he show any bitterness about his destiny, that had treated him so cruelly.

Ruperto got around perfectly well, climbing up and down stairs with his artificial leg and his cane. He got on board those demonic Sabana buses, and jumped off them, with incredible ease.

He was planning to go back, after graduating, to his home town, where old lawyer Campos had announced that he would retire in a couple of years. One of Ruperto's uncles had promised our friend to lend him the money to buy Campos' law practice.

Ruperto and Teodulfo Montes liked whores and booze, and they often went out together. Ruperto, also, was one who enjoyed playing practical jokes on people. Teodulfo told us about the night when he and Ruperto, both drunk, went into a bordello in the Don Cristóbal section of Sabana.

Ruperto picked out the girl he liked, and went with her into one of the rooms. The woman disrobed in a matter of seconds and stood there, in the nude, but Ruperto, without taking his clothes off, asked her to turn off the light, because, as he said, he didn't like to display his private parts.

The prostitute was a real professional who had learned not to be surprised at anything, so she obeyed without objections, went to the bed and lay there while Ruperto, in the darkness of the room, took off his clothes and his artificial leg.

"Look what I have here for you!", he said.

And he placed the woman's hand on the stump that remained of his amputated leg. The whore, who wasn't overly intelligent, thought that she was touching a gigantic penis, and went into hysterics.

"You put that inside your mother, you son-of-a-bitch!!!", she screamed, "Bastard!! Mother fucker!!"

Ruperto, now afraid of having gone too far, turned on the light and tried to explain that it had all been a joke, but he only made the situation worse. The woman kept yelling at the top of her voice, spewing out insults and obscenities and calling for the pimp and the madam.

"Aurora!!", she hollered, "Jesús!! Look what this cock sucker has done to me! Jesús!!! Aurora!!!

According to our friends, it was very hard to calm down Jesús, who burst into the room, knife in hand, swearing that he was going to castrate Ruperto, to show him that "you don't fuck around with Jesús, in this whorehouse!".

Only after a lot of explaining, and giving them ten pesos as an "indemnity", were Ruperto and Teodulfo allowed to leave the brothel.

"Those shitheads took all the money we had!", said Ruperto. He turned to Teodulfo: "How about calling your mother and hitting her for twenty pesos? Otherwise, we'll have to jerk off until we get the allowance!"

Almost every evening, Ruperto, Goyito and I got together in our room, to talk. Abilio Pardo often joined these gatherings.

Abilio had been a cop for five years now. His ambition was to graduate as a lawyer, with which he would automatically have, according to police regulations, an immediate promotion to second lieutenant.

From him we learned about the graft in law enforcement, and some of the "goodies" that the agents of the law had available to them in the discharge of their duties.

"As a policeman", Abilio explained to us, "I can bet free, everyday, up to twenty five cents on numbers and charades, in every betting joint in my post".

"And how much is each bet?", I asked.

"You can win one peso and twenty-five cents for each nickel you bet".

"That's if one of the numbers you pick comes up", explained Ruperto.

"Well, of course", replied Abilio, "But since there are fifteen betting joints in my post, I always have a good chance to win. Every week I get, at least, three or four numbers".

"Do you have to divide it up?", Teodulfo asked.

"No!", replied Abilio. "That's for the cop on the beat! I don't have to share with anybody".

"And on top of that, you get your salary!", exclaimed Goyito, "You've got it made, brother!"

"In Yagruma, a police officer lives better than the average civilian", admitted Abilio, modestly, "I can't deny that".

"And how about the big fish?", I asked, "Don't tell me they don't have their `pipelines', too!"

"Of course they do! But the `heavyweights' deal directly with the big bosses, the ones that run the big operation. We are talking hundred of thousands of pesos each month, which they divide according to their rank, after a portion is set aside that goes to the president of the republic.

"For example, the chief of police gets more than the inspector general; the inspector general gets more than a district captain, and so on and so forth."

"What other graft you have got going?", asked Goyito.

"Well, you know", answered Abilio, "The grocers get hit once in a while: a few pounds of rice, some pounds of beans, a couple of gallons of olive oil, condensed milk...things like that! Coffee and cigarettes you get free, because nobody wants to charge you for them, so they can stand in good terms with you".

"Yeah, but you also hit the butcher!", observed Teodulfo.

"Well, yes, that's true!", said Abilio, "But that's an accepted practice!"

"And, how do you go about it?" I asked.

"Simple! I go into the butcher shop and, if there are customers, I greet the butcher, you know: `How are things going'?, `What's happening'?, `What's new, brother'? I ask him about his family...you know, that kind of shit! He, then, goes to the refrigerator, takes out a package that he already has prepared for me, gives it to me, and I leave!"

"And later, at the police station, you divide the meat according to rank, right?"

"No, none of that! That meat I keep; it's for the cop, for him to eat! No dividing!"

"And, what does the butcher put in the package?", I asked.

"Well, he always gives me a couple of beefsteaks".

"Filets?", joked Teodulfo.

"Shit! He tells me he is giving me the loin, but the truth is that he gives me round steak. To tell you the truth, I like the round steak, that's why I've never said anything to him".

"Do you get anything out of the whorehouses and the drug traffic?", Ruperto wanted to know.

"No! Hell, no! The bordellos and the drugs are controlled by the big fish. Not captains, not even majors. Colonels, generals and ministers, nobody else!"

Evidently, the caste system ruled in Yagruma, even in the National Police Force. The peasants, in this case, were the policemen on the beat, who got the bones while the aristocrats--the big brass--enjoyed the filet mignon.

CHAPTER XI
SINFUL NIGHTS IN THE CITY

Even though they called it "burlesque", the Hong Kong theater, located in Sabana's Chinese ghetto, was nothing more than a place where they presented pornographic comedies and showed "adult" movies.

Usually, when the spectacle was over, the horny bunch of students that frequented the place swarmed into the nearby whorehouses, to finish their wild night in real style.

I went to the Hong-Kong once, partly because of curiosity and partly to please Goyito and Ruperto, who insisted that I, as a university student, had the obligation to become acquainted with the place.

Admission to the Hong Kong cost one peso. There was nothing attractive or interesting about the theater, that reminded me of Helena's "Moderno" movie house, except that in the Hong Kong, behind the last row of seats, were a series of closed booths with venetian blinds through which one could see, without being seen, what was happening on the stage. My attention was attracted to a sign addressed to the public, written in large letters on the wall. The signs contained the following warning:

LAUGH, HAVE FUN, BUT BEHAVE PROPERLY IF YOU
DON'T WANT TO BE ARRESTED!

"Why do they have that there?", I asked Goyito, indicating the signs.

"It's nothing", he answered, "It's only because sometimes the guys get wild and they run up on the stage to grab the women".

On one of the passageways, a man with a cardboard box on his shoulder was selling pornographic books.

"Spicy novels!!", he cried, "Spicy novels!! `A Lustful Widow'!! Learn what happened to the sexy widow!!! Spiiiiiicy noooovels!!!"

The demand for the books was overwhelming.

I took a look around to see what kind of people were coming to this place. Besides the student crowd, there were vendors, porters and patrons from the nearby open market. I also noticed a few women who, according to Ruperto, had already made their arrangements with someone at the theater door.

The titles of the works that were presented at the Hong Kong were somewhat witty: "The Cave of the Owls", "The Little Red Light", "An ill-fated ass", "We lost our Pepita", "Frine's Fancies", "A Smart Nephew", and others of the same ilk.

The "comedy" they were showing that night, entitled "A Lucky Thief" was, simply, abominable. I couldn't understand, really, what it was about, because in addition to being devoid of the most elemental decency, it had no plot, no purpose or significance.

The main actress, a flabby forty years old, probably illiterate, judging by the way she assassinated the language, showed, as she undressed, a pair of sagging breasts and a fat flabby ass. Her leading man, some fifty years old, was plump and sweaty. The make-up on his face was excessive, and he wore a hair piece.

"He is a faggot", Goyito told me, when the thing made his appearance on the stage. The information, of course, was unnecessary, because just by looking at him one could tell the guy was a "pájaro".

The two "artists" became involved in a long and boring dialogue that was nothing but an endless exchange of obscenities and swearing, with the leading man trying to convince the heroine to take her clothes off, which she finally did.

When the woman was naked, the fat guy pushed her towards a nearby bed, without much resistance on her part, and there they set about simulating making love, with the usual panting and grunting, screams and indecencies.

It seemed as if the distinguished public was really enjoying itself, from the whistles, applause and shrieks that echoed throughout the theater. But when two popular comedians, Blackie Coco and Old Teruel, made their appearance on the scene, the house really came down.

The acting of these two was of the same caliber as the two already on the stage. After spewing out an assortment of obscenities when he saw what the pair on the bed were doing, Coco tried to climb onto Old Teruel, but Teruel put up a fierce resistance, using a vocabulary that would curl your hair. The public came apart applauding, bellowing, roaring.

The "comedy" was followed by a variety act which, had it not been for the sorrowful appearance of the performers, would have made me laugh. First on the scene was a tall, skinny woman with an enormous mouth, who delighted the audience with some stupid parody of a popular Mexican song.

At the end, a dozen burnt out, shabby looking women, dressed as cow girls, came on to the stage. They had toy guns on their belts.

These aging sylphs began dancing, wiggling their hips in time with the music that the Hong Kong's paltry combo was playing. When the dance was finished, they formed a line on the stage, in front of the audience, removed their clothes, and began to shoot their toy guns in the air.

"Well, you know what the Hong Kong is like now", Ruperto said to me, somewhat condescendingly, when we left the theater.

I didn't answer him, because as we passed by, my attention was attracted by the unusual presence of several masked men and women inside a booth with the venetian blinds open.

"What are those masked people doing?", I asked.

"Those are people who like to fool around, but don't want anyone to recognize them", explained Goyito.

"Why not?"

"Man!", he replied, "Because they are respectable people!"

The orgiastic night had its honorable ending on Gran Almirante Street, in a foul smelling bordello that was a regular stop of our friend Ruperto. I was lucky enough to get a cross-eyed country girl, with an enormous and hairy mole on her belly, and breath like an outhouse. She had also been blessed with a remarkably stupid face.

From her neck hung a chain with a saint's medal. Before she lay down with me, she swung the medal around to her back.

"Why do you do that?, I asked.

"So that the saint won't see the dirty work!", was her reply.

It was after two o'clock in the morning when we finally left the brothel. Ruperto had the idea for us to go and have a beer. Goyito, who was also a carouser, seconded the motion. I accepted, somewhat reluctantly, because all the experiences of that night had been anything but enjoyable to me.

We went to a tavern on the street corner and put away the first beer, and after that another, and another, and another, until we got loaded. Goyito got the urge to sing, and started bellowing:

"They say that I'm a drunkard,
That I'm going through this life
Like a lost soul..."

"Gentlemen!", exclaimed Ruperto, "We have to sober up! Let's go to the open market and get some fried rice!"

Goyito, who let Ruperto dominate him, thought this was a great idea, but I declined the invitation. To accept would have meant that we would get back to

Cachita's house at daybreak, drunk as the lord, because, knowing my friends, I was sure that the fried rice would be accompanied by another dozen beers.

Under different circumstances, perhaps, I would have gone with my friends. But it was now the early hours of Thursday, the day on which, the same as Fridays, I always went to class.

Those were the only days that Perlita Shell would possibly attend classes at the University, and for a filthy drunken spree I wasn't going to lose the opportunity of seeing her in the classroom, and enjoy gazing upon her.

My two companions became indignant when I told them that I was going back to the boarding house, to sleep. You can't reason with a drunk, and when I saw that they just kept on stammering and jabbering nonsense, I left the cafe and went to stand on the corner to wait for the bus.

After a short while I saw them leaving the joint, staggering and trying to harmonize on Yagruma's favorite drinking song :

"On the trunk of a tree, a young girl
carved her name, with sweet delight..."

An hour later I arrived at Cachita's house, convinced of two things. First, that the Hong Kong nights were not for me. And second, that I had no desire to be a bordello rat.

I finished the second year of law school with good grades, which was all that an obscure student like me could hope for at Sabana University Law School.

Although it had now been two years since I left Helena, I wasn't enthusiastic about visiting there during the summer vacation. I would have liked to see my grandmother, but I rebelled at the idea of having to live, even for a few days, under the same roof as Sóstenes and Goya.

I had decided to stay in Sabana when I received a letter from my grandmother that made me change my mind. In it, the poor woman complained that I had forgotten her, and also let me know that aunt Lidia and Chuchú were going to get married at the end of the month. She begged me to be at the wedding.

For some time my heart had been reproaching me about the abandonment of the only two human beings who had brought a little love into my life, and my grandmother's complaint sharpened that feeling.

The following morning I was on my way to Helena, asking myself how I was going to feel when I arrived back in my home town and was again in the house where I was born; or how it would be to go to the city park, as before, to sit on those grubby benches under the shade of the old poplars.

Walking once again the streets of Helena, I found that the town had changed. It looked more somber, more lacking in life than before. And when I arrived at the house of the rats, I had to make an effort to overcome the urge to turn around, run back to the bus stop and take the first bus to Sabana.

The house seemed smaller and dirtier than when I lived in it, with the front covered with green stains, caused by the moisture from the nearby river. The door of the house, peeling and full of spider webs, was open, showing the dreary entrance. Further in, I could see the gloomy patio and the skeletons of dead plants standing up in their ruined terra cotta pots.

My grandmother was in the kitchen, placing pieces of rancid cheese in the rat traps. The poor thing, after hugging me and kissing me, crying, put on a pot of water to make some coffee.

Aunt Lidia, she told me, was out shopping, looking for fabric for her wedding dress. Sóstenes and Goya had left for Aguilera, Goya's hometown, because the father of the old bitch had died, and they were going to the funeral.

While we were drinking our coffee, I told her about my life in Sabana during the past two years, about the University and my friends, and what I planned to do when I graduated. I could tell, as we were talking, that she wanted to tell me something, but hesitated to, although on a couple of occasions she was clearly on the point of letting it out.

"Grandmother", I promised, "I swear that I won't let so much time go by without seeing you again. Look, I'll be spending this Christmas here, with you!"

"Oh, son", she responded, "Things have changed! When Christmas comes I won't be in this house. I was going to tell you, in any case".

"What do you mean you won't be here!? Why not? What happened?"

She explained to me that Goya, who wasn't comfortable in Helena, had twisted Sóstenes' arm until he, finally, asked the Ministry for a transfer to Aguilera, which he had been granted because of his seniority. The Ministry had notified him that in less than a month the transfer order would reach him.

Meanwhile, Chuchú, who was stationed at Santa Apolonia, about thirty five kilometers from Helena, had been promoted to sergeant, and was being transferred to Los Remates, a town that was too far away for him to commute back and forth every day.

"And what about you?", I asked my grandmother, "What are you going to do? You can't stay in Helena, all by yourself!"

"If Sóstenes were alone, I would go and live with him", she answered, ""But with Goya, that owl with tits...! I couldn't handle it!"

"Grandmother", I offered, "If you want, I can try and see if I can rent a room for you where I'm living. At least, you would be with me there!"

She smiled. "What would you do with an old woman on your back, Miguel?", she replied, "Don't worry, son, you've got enough with your studies! Lidia and Chuchú want me to come and live with them in Los Remates, and that's what I'm going to do".

And seeing that I was a little taken aback, she added: "But that doesn't get you out of your promise. We are going to expect you to come and spend Christmas in Los Remates with us, with your family, as it should be".

A short time later aunt Lidia arrived, and was very happy to see me. After the customary hugs and kisses, I gave her the wedding present that I had bought for her in Sabana, for which I had to dip into my savings. There were tears in her eyes when she made me promise that I would come and spend Christmas with them.

As for me, when I realized that I wouldn't have to be looking at Sóstenes or his old snub nose of a wife, the house looked a little less somber. Besides, for lunch, grandmother had made Spanish rice, which I liked very much. When we sat down at the table, my mental state was quite different from that which had overcome me that morning, when I returned to the old house.

While we were having lunch, I asked my grandmother what was to become of the house.

"We are going to sell it to `Yambembe', the loan shark", she answered, "He offered me eight thousand pesos fcr it. From that I have to give Sóstenes three thousand for what he has contributed, and some repairs he had done to the kitchen and the bathroom".

"What a miracle that he's not charging her for the rice and beans", I thought.

Late in the afternoon I showered, had a cup of coffee and went out to take a walk around Helena. Strolling along without any particular objective, I arrived at the city park. I had just crossed it, and was walking along the city hall colonnade, when I heard someone calling me. It was Ramón García, one of my former high school classmates, whom we used to call "the Spaniard". Ramón and I had been good friends.

"Hey, Miguel, what are you doing here!? I didn't think you would ever again come to this frigging town!"

I explained the reason for my visit to Helena. "And what have you been up to, Spaniard?", I asked, "I haven't seen you around the University".

"I stayed in Helena", he replied, "I had to help my parents! I got a job as a clerk in the 'English Bazaar', and I'm still there".

"Last year I enrolled in the CPA program at the University", he went on, "They let me go to Sabana for the examinations. But let's talk a little, buddy! You've got the time, right?"

We went to the park, sat on one of the benches and reminisced about our high school days and the friends we hadn't seen for along time. I learned from him that three of them had died. One, just recently, under tragic circumstances.

Ramón told me some of the later gossiping circulating around Helena, among which was the scandal that the Pontevedras' cook had caused.

The Pontevedras were a middle class family that lived on San Jacinto Street, close to the high school. Their daughters had been girlfriends of God knows how many generations of students.

This family had, without a doubt, delusions of grandeur. They put on aristocratic airs, and their names appeared frequently in the "Waves of Helena", the society column of "The Marine Herald", because they cultivated the friendship of Pocholo del Jardín, stretching their purse strings every year to keep the "croniqueur" happy.

The Pontevedras had a cook, Nina, a woman who had worked for them for more than twenty years, and with whom they had unlimited confidence.

But, as they say in the United States, "familiarity breeds contempt". And that confidence, generated through the years, little by little got out of hand. Finally a lack of respect developed, and according to what one witness said, when Nina gave a sharp answer to Don León Pontevedra, the latter cried:

"Suck my royal cock, Nina!"

And Nina answered: "Fuck you, sir!"

As things went, something serious had to occur one day, and finally the inevitable happened. Doña Aleida Urrizarte de Pontevedra, and Nina, began to argue over some change that Doña Aleida said the cook hadn't given back to her, while Nina claimed that she had left the money for her mistress on a table in the entranceway.

In the heat of the discussion, the matron of the house, infuriated, called her servant woman "a thief", and Nina answered calling Doña Aleida "an old whore".

The accusations and the insults were getting worse by the minute and finally Doña Aleida, beside herself, fired Nina and kicked her out of the house.

"But things like that happen everyday in Helena", I observed when Ramón finished, "It's nothing out of the ordinary, nothing special".

"It's because I haven't told you what happened next! You know that the Pontevedras live on a very busy street! Well, Nina stood in front of the house and screamed that Doña Aleida was cheating on her husband, because Don León only had a scrawny little thing that was completely useless. And that she knew, because the old man had tried to screw her in the kitchen and he couldn't do anything, because he couldn't get it up! Oh, and also that Angelica and Matildita had been to Sabana several times, to have abortions!"

"I can imagine how that must have raised the roof!", I said.

"Man! They say it looked like a political rally! But what bothered Doña Aleida the most was what Nina said about the feathers!"

"What do you mean, 'the feathers'?"

"Listen to this! The Pontevedras always went around with their nose in the air. As you well know, chickens are very expensive here! Well, Nina screamed out to the world that, when the Pontevedras eat chicken, they save all the feathers and put a few of them in the garbage can each day so that the passers-by, seeing the feathers, would think that in this house they ate chicken every day!"

We kept chatting for a while. When the clock on city hall struck six o'clock, I said good-bye to Ramón, with the excuse that I still had to go and see Jorge.

I was planning to pay a visit to Higinio that night, not that I really wanted to, but because I knew that someone would get to him with the gossip that I had been seen in Helena. I didn't want Arturo's father to think that I was snubbing him.

I had been very careful to keep in contact with Arturo, calling him regularly at Leticia's house, going to see him at the medical school and getting together with him at the student's canteen.

Sometimes we took a couple of girls to Masanabo Beach; this, of course, behind Leticia's back, as she seemed to be more possessive and jealous of him every day.

I did all that to have something to tell Higinio, who, in spite of the fact that I wrote to him every month telling him how well things were going for his son, still called me sometimes on the phone. And I didn't want him to find fault with me in any way, for I depended on him for the money to keep coming every month.

That night, I left immediately after dinner, and headed for the Menéndez's house.

Arturo's mother was skinnier than she was the last time I saw her, and had also lost much of the thinning hair that she had then, so it wasn't possible for her to cover up her cyst. Mrs. Menéndez met me with the same affection as always.

"Come in, Miguel, and sit down", she said, after giving me a wet kiss on each cheek, "I'll tell Higinio that you are here".

I felt a shiver go up my back bone when I saw Arturo's father enter the living room at a slow pace.

Higinio had become a walking skeleton. I figured that since the last time I had seen him he had lost at least forty pounds.

His enormous, purplish red nose, projected between the two deep creases in the wrinkled, ashy face. While we were talking, Higinio, every once in a while, had to catch his breath, and there was, at times, the sound of a foul and terrible cough.

Arturo's mother brought us some coffee, and Higinio asked me a few questions about their son, but this time I noticed they were rather mechanical, as though from habit, not from real interest.

All of a sudden he had an attack of coughing, so severe, that it left him doubled over in his chair, panting, with bloodshot eyes and a face full of fear. After the attack subsided, he got up, still bent over from the effects, and went into the bathroom, from which we could hear him hawking and spitting.

Back in the living room, he sat down again on his rocking chair and lit one of those "supersticks" that he used to smoke. I couldn't contain myself, although I tried to be as diplomatic as possible.

"Why don't you try to cut down a little on your smoking?", I told him.

"The doctor has told him that one thousand times!", shrieked his wife, "But it goes in one ear and out of the other!"

"I'll cut down, I'll cut down!", promised Higinio, "But I have to do it little by little. I have been smoking for forty five years. I can't quit in one day!!"

"It's killing him", said his wife, turning to me.

"What do you mean, killing me!!?, cried Higinio, getting all upset, "All I've got is a little bronchitis, that's all!!

The woman shrugged her shoulders and said nothing. I changed the subject, talking about Arturo, and answered their questions.

Mrs. Menéndez was the one who asked the most questions.

Higinio seemed to be losing interest in the matter, and only listened, as if absorbed in thought. And even though he had a couple more of his coughing fits, he kept on smoking up a storm.

When the clock at city hall struck ten o'clock, I got up to leave.

"Excuse me if I have been boring you", I said, "But I really wanted to see you again".

"Don't worry about that", replied Higinio, "We are grateful for the peace that you have given us, taking the trouble to keep up with our son and keeping us informed".

"My God, Higinio", I responded, "Arturo is like a brother to me!"

I didn't tell him, of course, that, were it not for the money that he sent me every month, I couldn't care less if I learned that Arturo had been run over by a Sherman tank.

I left the Menéndez's house with a heavy heart, because Higinio's cough and his cadaverous aspect didn't augur well for my fragile finances.

A few days later, aunt Lidia and Chuchú got married.

After the ceremony, the newlyweds and a small group of well-wishers went over to the house where a cake and the usual goodies were waiting for them. A rental car arrived after the last guest had departed. Chuchú and Lidia left for Sabana, where they were to spend their honeymoon in a second class hotel near Central Park.

I had decided to stay in Helena for a few more days, helping grandmother to get things together. But we received a telegram from Sóstenes, telling us that they would be arriving the next day, and I changed my mind immediately.

I told my grandmother that I had a job interview in Sabana, got my bag ready, and that same evening I was riding a bus back to the capital.

CHAPTER XII

A POT OF BLACK BEANS FOR THE GOOD OLD BOYS OF HOME

The beginning of the new year at the University was a little sad for Goyito and myself, because we hadn't gotten used to the idea that our friend Ruperto would no longer be with us. Ruperto, who had graduated, went back to his home town. There, thanks to his uncle Eliseo, who lent him the money, he would buy old Campos' law practice.

One day when I had gone to the University in the hopes of seeing Perlita, a student that I had never met before sat down on the seat next to me. He was a man in his late forties, elegantly dressed, with his hair and mustache dyed a jet black. He had an expensive wrist watch, and on one of fingers sparkled a diamond of respectable size. About halfway through the class, the man leaned over to me and whispered:

"This is a load of horse shit"

"We agree on that", I replied.

Now that the ice was broken, we kept shooting the bull, while the professor, a skinny, leathery old man, kept lecturing. He seemed lost in an interminable and monotonous dissertation about the juridical nature of the fixed and cumulative dividend of preferred stock shares.

A couple of hours later I was sitting in the law school canteen when I saw the man with the dyed hair come in. He greeted me, and came over to where I was sitting.

"Let's have some coffee", he invited me.

I accepted. We spent quite a while there, drinking café con leche, talking, and exchanging comments about the charms of the girls that came in and out the place. If only half of what he told me was true, that guy had had in his life more sexual experiences than a rabbit. But, I got the impression that he was really a braggart.

"Well", I said finally, getting up, "I have to go. If I don't get to Cachita's in time, I don't get any lunch".

He told me they were expecting him at his office, in Sabana's old colonial section. We shook hands.

"It has been a pleasure to make your acquaintance", he said, "I am Alejandro Ayer. And you?" I told him my name.

In the plaza, in front of the law school, Ayer walked toward a beautiful Cadillac, of the latest model. He offered to take me to the boarding house, an offer that I declined, because Cachita's house was right next to the University.

Ayer left in his Cadillac, and I headed for the boarding house, looking forward to the usual beans.

When I got to the dining room, there was Cachita, exchanging screams and insults with some of her guests, who were protesting against something their mistress had done.

Cachita used to warm Cucuíto's bottle by putting it in the caldron of beans, but that day the bottle had broken into pieces inside the caldron.

Cachita wasn't perturbed in the least; she ordered Etelvino, the cook, to remove the pieces of glass from the pot and serve the beans. That the beans were mixed with the spilt milk, or that there might be fragments of glass left in the caldron didn't seem to worry her at all.

The problem aroused when Bebo, who wasn't getting along well with Etelvino, went with the story to Teodulfo. He told him that it had been the cook who had the idea to serve the beans mixed with Cucuíto's milk and glass chips.

Teodulfo wasted no time in telling the story to Goyito, and so before lunch everyone knew what had happened. But, instead of confronting Etelvino, a big black man who would easily have slapped us around, they went to Cachita with the problem.

"You don't have any conscience!!", cried Julieta, a pharmacy student.

Cachita, it seemed, tried to come up with an adequate response, and not finding one, shouted:

"And you are nohing but a whore!!"

"Fellow students!", hollered Lenín Sánchez, a communist that was studying law, "We have been at the point of being sacrificed by this dragon lady, and all for the sake of saving a few miserable pennies!!"

"She wanted to puncture our tripes!!", yelled some other guest from around the corner.

"We are eating glass and beans while you are playing a joke on us, you bitch!", seconded another one.

The students were shouting their heads off roaring, screaming, yelling. Lenín Sánchez got up on a chair and, getting everyone's attention, addressed the small crowd.

"Are we animals?", he asked.

"NOOOO!!!", they all screamed in chorus.

"Are we human beings?"

"YEEEEESSSS!!!

"Well, then", Lenín went on, very formal and serious, "Then we should demand to be treated that way. We'll form a student committee right now, over which I offer to preside, and let's go right now to formulate a complaint of these deeds before thc competent judge!!"

Lenín stopped for a few seconds, inhaled deeply and then continued his harangue.

"If we don't do that, fellow students", he screamed, "Then, this entrepeneur must offer us, first, an explanation, and then a monetary compensation for the risk we have been subjected to. And also for the emotional upheaval we have been through, for all of which she is resposible!! What do you say, Madame?", he concluded, turning to Cachita.

She had been listening, biting her fists in rage, to the stupidities uttered by the student "leader".

"I'm not afraid of judges, not the police, not even the president of the republic!!!", she thundered, facing up to the rebels, with hands on hips. "There is nothing wrong with the beans!! They're the same as you eat every day without complaining!!"

"All right, then!", she continued, "I am too old to be blackmailed and taken advantage of!! Those of you who don't like this house, go and look for another one!! Even if you all leave, it doesn't make any difference to me, not at all!! The next day I'll have the house full again!! So there you have it! If you want to eat what there is, fine; if not, that's OK, too!!"

"And as for you", she cried, turning to Lenín Sánchez, "Your month expires tomorrow. So get your things together and get the hell out of here!! I don't want to see you around here after noon tomorrow!!!"

"Madame", replied Lenín, in a choked voice, "You have misunderstood me! There was never any intention of carrying this to a personal level. I have only tried to defend the rights of my fellow boarders, motivated only by my principles!"

Cachita stared at him for a few seconds, disdainfully, with utter contempt.

"I don't want to see you here after noon tomorrow!", she repeated.

"All right then, but at least give me a little time to look for a place to live!", begged Lenín, "Where am I going to go?"

"You can go and get stuffed!!", roared Cachita, turning her back on him and leaving, "You little shit!!".

The silence that followed was broken by Goyito.

"People", he said, "Let's not behave like a bunch of assholes!"

And he went over to where the caldrons of food were located. Everybody followed him, and Bebo began serving lunch without uttering a word. Even today, on occasion, I look for pieces of glass in my black beans and rice.

During the weeks and months that followed, whenever we met in the classroom, Alejandro Ayer and I sat together. We soon became friends.

Ayer was a short guy, slightly bow-legged and pot-bellied, with a thin mustache. He had a square, fleshy face.

We never knew exactly how old he was, because his age was a secret that he carefully guarded. We figured, nevertheless, from the stories that he told, that Ayer was about forty five years old.

Ayer considered himself a tropical Don Juan. He made passes at the girls, invited them for refreshments and used to drive around in his Cadillac, "cruising for babes", as he used to say.

We often studied together. He lived on the first floor of a big house on Estoque street. The Ayers had no children. Elida, his wife, was a tall, bony woman with a sour face, who had a habit of constantly biting her upper lip.

Her sister who lived with them, was a little, dark-skinned woman with stringy hair and a vacant expression, that slipped around the house like a shadow, without talking or making any sound.

Ayer and his wife hardly spoke to each other. Their conversation was reduced to the strictly indispensable words needed to communicate for the few domestic affairs in which Ayer's opinion or consent was required.

Once I had courage to ask him what was the reason for such behavior. He told me that his wife had a very conflictive personality.

"She's got a hell of a bad temper!", he added.

Later, as our friendship grew, I came to realize that the marriage was held together only for appearances. They had not divorced, and continued living under the same roof, but that was all.

Mrs. Ayer and her sister had good government jobs. Besides, their father had left them plenty of money and several properties in Sabana. Ayer didn't have to give his wife anything, and the household expenses were evenly divided between his wife, his sister-in-law and himself.

My friend, who also owned real estate in the capital, spent money left and right. Like we say in the United States, "he'd got it made". Many times I asked myself how he made his dough.

His parents, as far as I knew, weren't rich, and though he claimed to be in the import-export business, he didn't seem to work at it very much. The office he kept in Old Sabana was almost always closed.

The answer to my question came to me one night while we were studying in the dining room of his house.

Taking a break, we put the textbooks to one side and began talking about politics. The conversation centered on the period that followed on the fall of president Mechado's government.

Letting himself get carried away by the flood of memories that came to his mind, he revealed to me that he was a corporal in the army when Mechado fled the island.

According to Ayer, he had taken part in the siege of Hotel Capital, in which many army officers were massacred by their own troops. Ayer assured me that he knew and had worked with general Majencio Bautista, who later became dictator of Yagruma, when the general was nothing more than a simple sergeant.

Ayer had been one of the many military men who, following the overthrow of the Mechado regime, had the chance to get connected to "the pipeline".

When the time came to divide the spoils, he was promoted from corporal to lieutenant colonel and, shortly thereafter, appointed managing director of the National Mental Hospital at Zamorra.

He went to his bedroom and came back with an old photograph taken at Zamorra fifteen years before. They showed a younger Ayer, dressed in uniform, with officer boots, campaign hat and a Colt forty five on his belt.

He spoke to me frankly. His job at the National Mental Hospital lasted a little over three years. One fine day, a transfer order arrived, sending him to a provincial garrison.

Since he wouldn't even think of living outside Sabana, Ayer asked for, and was granted, his release from the army. Then he bought the house where he now lives, and invested wisely the "little money" that he had "scraped together" during his years at Zamorra.

For Ayer, the Yagruman dream had become reality. That is getting a lot of money, no matter how, and then living the good life.

Probably from force of habit, although he didn't need it, Ayer kept riding the gravy train. He held, at that time, a highly paid job at the National Development Board, an institution unknown to most Yagrumans.

This Board was one of many offices created by the government to justify the juicy salaries paid to certain political protégés, much higher than those earned by the regular bureaucracy.

Alejandro Ayer was a good friend to me. Had it not been for him, only God knows what direction my life might have taken.

Next door to Cachita lived a mulatto whom everybody called "Chaveo", but whose real name was Rubén Iznaga.

Chaveo was the political delegate from La Colina district to the Liberal Party's Municipal Assembly. He was an important figure in local politics, especially at that time, when only a few weeks remained before the crucial elections in which the people of Sabana would choose their next mayor.

One Saturday afternoon, when we were having our siesta, Teodulfo woke us by shaking and poking us.

"Wake up, you guys!!", he yelled, "Come on, Antonio Elío is here!!"

"What's `Supercousin' doing here?", asked Goyito, getting into his pants in a hurry.

"He's probably come to buy Chaveo", I ventured.

"Birds of a feather flock together", said Teodulfo.

Antonio Elío was a first cousin of Carlos Elío, Yagruma's last constitutional president. It was said that they were like brothers, which was probably true, because the first thing that president Elío did after coming to power was to appoint Antonio Minister of the Treasury.

The president assured the people of Yagruma that he had given Antonio that post in his Cabinet, not because he was his cousin, but because of Antonio's impressive background and experience as a financier and an economist. But the truth was that the new Minister's only experience in those fields was the twenty years that he had worked as a bank clerk.

Minister Antonio, in accordance with the traditional and time-honored practices of Yagruman politics, made himself a multimillionaire in less than two years. Now, with his cousin's backing, he was running for mayor of Sabana.

We rushed to the balcony, where other students were also waiting for Antonio to come out of Chaveo's house, in front of which were parked the usual Cadillac limousines. Antonio's bodyguards were standing on the sidewalk.

We didn't have to wait long, because in about ten minutes the front door opened and we saw the mayoral candidate come out, respectfully preceded by Chaveo. Antonio, whom we knew only by his photographs in the newspapers, was an insignificant looking guy, with button eyes, a big nose and the indispensable black mustache. He really did look like a bank clerk.

"Down with Antonio!! Down with the Elíos!!!" cried several of the students.

Antonio walked toward his limousine, without looking at us.

"Thief!! Louse!!, cried others.

Antonio, who fancied himself a popular guy, stopped, turned around, and waved his hand at us.

"Scoundrel!! You stole the people's money!!", roared Teodulfo.

Antonio stared at him , smiling.

"So would you, if you could!! You are just envious!!!", he hollered.

Back in the room, I lay down on my cot, with my eyes closed. But I couldn't get back to sleep.

A little voice was telling me that something terrible would have to happen some day to a country that had, in charge of its destinies, men like the Minister of Commerce, the Black Market Czar; the Minister of Education who carried off, in suitcases, the public funds, and the Minister of the Treasury, Antonio Elío, whose pockets were overflowing with the people's money.

How long would the Yagruman people accept this status quo of graft and corruption?

Outside, a tin can clanked ahead of a drunk as he staggered down the road.

CHAPTER XIII
GODPARENTS FROM HELL

A few days after the big scene at Cachita's house, I ran across Arturo, who told me that Higinio had been taken to the hospital. I about shit in my pants when I heard that.

If the man kicked the bucket, my monthly money order would evaporate!! That was my only means of support. What was going to happen to me? I would have to leave Sabana, because in our seductive capital, so kind and friendly to those that had it made, there was no room for the have-nots and the ill-fated.

"I can't let myself face up to that", I thought, "I have to put a patch on it before it gets out of hand! I've got to get moving now...!

"What's the matter with your father?", I asked Arturo.

"The old man does not take care of himself", he answered, "He has chronic bronchitis. Besides, the way he smokes, he's also got emphysema. That's what I think!"

"What do the doctors say?", I insisted, "He's in the hospital, so it must be serious!"

"They are running tests on him and taking a lot of X-rays", replied Arturo, "I'm leaving for Helena, tonight, to talk to the doctors. But I hope it isn't anything serious. I'll bet you the old man will be back on his feet in a few days".

"How is your mother taking this?"

"That's a different matter", said Arturo, "She's convinced that father has cancer. I talked to her last night, and she was all broken up. I am going to stay with her until papa gets out of the hospital".

"Let me know, as soon as you come back", I said, "And, if there is anything that I can do, call me, and I'll come right away".

"Thanks!", he answered, "But you'll see that it isn't anything serious".

We parted company. When I was going up the University stairway, I saw Perlita Shell coming down in the opposite direction. She was wearing a clingy goldenrod dress which accentuated her coppery complexion. I had to catch my breath.

I stopped, leaning against the stone wall, to watch her pass by. I would have given twenty years of my life for a glance from those big, amber eyes, but she didn't even notice my presence.

She passed by on one side, indifferent and cool, as if she hadn't seen me. Or, at least, that's what I thought.

Time was passing, and I had no news about Higinio, nor had I heard anything from Arturo. I wrote and phoned to them several times, but my letters and calls went unanswered. And although the money orders continued to arrive punctually, I was worried. I still lacked two more years to graduate. If Higinio kicked off before then, how was I going to solve the problem of surviving in Sabana?

Thinking about this, and realizing that in my twenty-one years of life I had not acquired any marketable skills, I decided to learn shorthand and typing in a commercial school. And since I had the need to learn, I applied myself to it and became a stenographer-typist in a very short time. I thought that this could be of great help to me if I had to work in an office, and soon enough time showed, that I wasn't wrong.

The blow finally fell, as I have been expecting. One afternoon, when I came back from the University, there was a letter, postmarked at Helena, waiting for me at Cachita's house. I opened it right away, and after reading it I felt weak in the knees.

The letter, signed by Arturo's mother, was to inform me of Higinio's death as a result of lung cancer. She also served me notice that I would no longer be receiving the money that Higinio had been sending me for almost three years.

Mrs. Menéndez also informed me that Leticia and Arturo were spending a few months in the United States. Leticia, the old witch wrote, wanted him to get his mind off things for a while, since the poor boy had suffered so from the death of his father.

According to the widow Menéndez, Leticia and Arturo were planning to be married. He was discouraged with his studies at the medical school, so Leticia convinced him to drop out and dedicate himself to the management of her assets after they tied the knot.

The letter ended, "I am going to be away from Helena for quite a while. I am not sure when I will be back".

My situation was serious. Higinio had gone to another life and his widow had shut off the remittance that kept me in Sabana. The unwritten message that she had sent me was clear and unequivocal, "From now on, take care of yourself as best as you can, and don't bother me!"

Since my arrival to Sabana I had opened a savings account, where I deposited as much as I could save from the sixty pesos that were left after paying Cachita.

I now had two hundred and forty pesos in the account. That would take care of four months of room and board, and I would still have forty dollars left to use in looking for a job, something very difficult for someone who, like me, didn't have any influential relatives, nor contacts, nor pull with anyone.

Suddenly, I smacked myself on the forehead. My godparents, whom I had forgotten, lived in Sabana, and were well "connected"!!

According to what my grandmother had told me, they became my godparents by pure accident.

They had happened to stop by the house, on their way back from San Miguel del Sulfuro, a couple of days before my father took me to Sabana, where I was going to undergo skull surgery.

Everybody was sure that I was going to die. Paula, who was to become my godmother, was a member of the executive committee of the Ladies of the Sacred Heart. She said that it was a crime and a heresy that I hadn't been baptized, and she and her husband offered to be my godparents so I wouldn't die a heathen. That was how I became the godson of Paula and her husband, the major.

Their Christian obligations complied with, my godparents forgot all about me. I had seen them only once in my life, when I was eight years old, one day when they were on their way to San Miguel. They stopped for half an hour at my grandmother's house to take a pee and have a cup of coffee. On that occasion my godmother gave me a quarter.

I have never seen my godparents again, nor have I known anything about them, although, at my grandmother's insistence, I wrote to them several letters that were never answered.

Nevertheless, I decided to call them. What could I lose? All I was going to ask was that they use their connections to help me find a job, so that I could finish my studies. That would cost them no money!

So I looked in the telephone directory for the name of my godfather and made the call. A servant answered the phone and told me that her lady had gone shopping and the colonel was at the club.

"What would be a good time to call them?", I asked.

"They'll be having dinner at home tonight", she responded, "Call them about six o' clock".

My godmother's name was Paula Bretón. Her husband, my godfather, a retired army colonel, responded to the sonorous name of Ramón Cordobán. All I knew about them was what my grandmother, who was a distant relative of Paula's, had told me.

Paula was the only daughter of Don Pío Bretón, a wealthy merchant who, in life, had been engaged in the textiles trade in Sabana.

During the last years of the nineteenth century, the Bretóns were living in Helena. One day, Paula's mother scandalized the good people of my town, leaving her husband and daughter for a mulatto who was the drum-major in the regimental band.

Don Pío, who never got married again, moved to Sabana with Paula, then a five year old child. There he bought a small store and dedicated himself to making money and taking care of his daughter.

Paula Bretón developed into an unattractive young woman. She was undersized, not at all pretty, with thin legs and abnormally voluminous buttocks. She never wanted to study, refused to take piano lessons, hated embroidering and didn't even know how to fry an egg.

Her forte was to gossip with her friends and read novelettes. She spent hours lying on a sofa, with a box of chocolates beside her, devouring romances by M. Dely and Florence Barclay.

But, in spite of her shortcomings, Paula counted her suitors by the dozen. As she used to say, putting her fingers together, "I've got them like this". It never seemed to occur to her that what really attracted all those men were not her physical or intellectual endowments, but rather the respectable fortune that her father had amassed.

Among the bunch of hopefuls at hand for the rich heiress were Yagrumans of all classes: doctors, lawyers, merchants, architects...But Paula's heart received Cupid's arrow one summer night, in the Sabana Yacht and Country Club, when the handsome major Cordobán, irresistible in his dress uniform, took her in his arms near a large potted hibiscus, and seeing that she returned his kisses, he put his hand inside her décolletage and fondled her breasts.

A year later, Paula and the major were married in the cathedral of Sabana, by the Archbishop himself.

It was a wedding "with all the trimmings", as they say. Paula even insisted that they had the canopy of swords, because she wanted to show her friends the picture of her and her husband leaving the cathedral arm in arm, under the arch of the gleaming blades.

The wedding was remembered for its luxury and for the splendor of the reception and the superb quality of the food served to the guests. Don Pío spared no expense.

Although I had seen him only once in my life, thirteen years ago, I remembered Colonel Ramón Cordobán quite well. I was impressed by his military presence and the severe expression on his face, framed by a thick, black beard. His stiff posture caused him to walk unnaturally straight.

Later, grandmother told me that the major was an old whoremonger who, in order to camouflage the ravages of time, used a girdle and dyed his hair.

In politics, major Cordobán had always shown unbreakable loyalty to every president of the republic. If the government party wanted to win the elections in some particular city or town where the possibility of losing existed, they sent the major to that place.

The day before the election, my godfather had the opposition leaders, the political delegates, and the most active antigovernment elements, arrested and taken to the army barracks, where they were stripped naked and held until the election was over.

Then, they were given back their clothes and turned loose.

Whenever anyone complained, my godfather, dressed in his full uniform, put the fear of God into them.

When Paula and the major were installed in the Bretón's chalet, on Fifth Avenue, in the exclusive section of Vista Mar, the major took the place of his father-in-law, who had always viewed him with a mixture of fear and abject admiration. From then on, Major Cordobán was the real master of the mansion.

As far as Paula was concerned, she would have thrown herself on the floor to be stepped on by her husband, if he had ordered her to.

Don Pío died the evening before the first anniversary of his daughter's marriage. Shortly thereafter, my godmother granted the major a power of attorney, so that he could manage the fortune that the old merchant had left.

Major Cordobán, who was growing tired of military life, put in for retirement, which was granted to him, but not as a major. In reward for his services to the country, he was promoted to colonel, and with this rank and pay he was retired.

My godparents lived well, as all rich people do. Their time was divided between their social activities and their trips to San Miguel del Sulfuro, where they went several times every year to treat their arthritis and other health problems.

The couple had two "children", Leopoldina and Tután, who lived with their parents. Leopoldina, from the beginning, had shown clearly that she liked girls more than she liked boys.

My godparents couldn't do anything about their daughter's strange friendships, nor could they keep her from receiving some "intimate" friends in her bedroom, where they spent hours on end.

Tután, the older of the two, was a lazy leech. He had been studying engineering at the University for the last twenty years without completing a third of the courses necessary to graduate. Tután lived happily. His parents gave him a home and food, dressed him, and provided him with pocket money.

The more I went back into my memory, the more apparent it became to me that my godparents weren't going to help me. "But", I thought again, "I've nothing to lose by trying".

At six o'clock, as I had been advised, I phoned again. This time a different servant answered the phone, who wanted to know who I was and what I wanted.

"Would you tell Mrs. Cordobán", I asked, "That Miguel Baró, her godson, needs to talk to her?".

I waited, with my heart pounding. After a short while, a raspy, slightly tremulous woman's voice came to me through the phone.

"This is Paula Bretón de Cordobán. How can I help you?"

"Godmother", I said, "This is your godson, Miguel. Do you remember me?"

The coldness of her answer couldn't have been less encouraging.

"Oh, yes, Miguel! Long time no see, eh? How is your grandmother?"

"She's well, thank you", I lied, "When I told her that I was going to call you, she told me to be sure and give you her best regards".

"Poor Cándida!", commented my godmother, "It's been a long time since I have seen her! But, imagine, with the life that one leads! And besides, we are getting old...it's getting difficult even to move! But, tell me, to what do I owe the miracle of this call?"

My mouth and throat had turned dry.

"Godmother", I said, "I need to talk to you and my godfather. When could I come to see you?"

Her reply was cautious.

"Well, son", she replied, "We would be delighted to see you. But, why make the trip all the way from Helena? Couldn't you tell us by phone what it is that you want?"

"I'm not calling from Helena", I answered, "I've been living in Sabana for some time".

"Oh, yes?", meowed the old woman, without denoting any surprise, "How nice! Well then, you'll have to come and see us one of these days! What are you doing? Are you working?"

"No", I answered, "I'm studying law".

"Oh, how nice!", she said again, "Cándida's grandson, a lawyer! Who would have thought that!" But I noticed that there wasn't much enthusiasm in her voice.

"Godmother", I asked, once more, "When can I come and see you?"

"Son", she answered, smoothly, "That's going to be a little difficult right now, because your godfather and I are leaving for San Miguel tomorrow. We'll be spending a couple of weeks there".

It was clear that she was putting me off. But I wasn't going to give up, and I insisted.

"Son of a gun, that's too bad!", I replied, "But, then, that's OK, I'll see you when you get back. Of course, I'll call you before I come over".

"Look", she retorted, "We are not really home very much. You understand, one has a social life...it is not because we like it, but at home one gets bored... We are almost always at the club, or on a trip. I'll tell you what, give me your telephone number and when we get back, I'll call you. Don't try to call us".

You didn't have to be very smart to see that the blasted woman was trying to get rid of me. But as it was, I decided to force the situation.

"I've got an idea", I said, "I know where you live. I can be over there in less than an hour. Right now it's only a quarter after six. I realize that we hardly know each other, but, after all, you are my godparents! And, look, I'm going to be frank with you. I need your help!"

"Oh, son, how sorry I feel for you!", was her answer, "But, we won't be home tonight! The Navy's Chief of Operations, who is a good friend of your godfather's has invited us to dinner. Imagine! We couldn't refuse him!"

"I understand," I replied, "I'm sorry to have bothered you".

Something in my voice must have moved her.

"No, son, it's not a bother!", she assured me, "But, listen, can't you tell me what your problem is? How can we help you? We are not rich, although people say otherwise, but if it is a matter of a few pesos, count on us. I'll leave it with one of the servants".

That was the way it was! With thirty or forty pesos she would wipe her hands clean of me!

"I haven't called you to ask for money", I replied, "I need a job, so I can finish my studies. I thought that your husband, who knows so many influential people, would be able to do something for me!"

And during the next few minutes I explained the situation in which I found myself, and the need I had for a fixed income to survive during the next two years. She listened to me patiently, interrupting me only to express her sorrow about the problems that I was facing.

"Oh, you don't know how much it pains me to have to tell you this", she said when I had finished, "But, let me tell you, Ramón is very shy! He doesn't like to inconvenience his friends, asking them favors...I hate to let you down, but don't count on him for anything".

"He might want to help me if you talked to him", I suggested.

"Well, I can try", she replied, grudgingly, "But don't get your hopes up. I know my husband very well!"

"I wasn't wrong about what I had suspected,", I thought, "They won't do anything for me, I can see that. Let's cut it off! To hell with it!"

"Very well", I said, "I appreciate your being frank with me. Well then, good afternoon. I won't be bothering you anymore!"

"Good night", she answered, "It's been nice to hear from you. And, listen, if you think of coming to visit us some day, call us first, OK?"

"Sure", I replied, hanging up.

Disillusioned and saddened, I returned to the solitary melancholy of my room. My first effort had yielded no results, and I didn't see any chance that something else would manifest to solve the tremendous problem that was now coming toward me.

Next morning I went out and bought a newspaper. Back at Cachita's, I went to the living room, sat down, and opened the Help Wanted Section.

As I read it, I felt even more pessimistic about my chances of finding some kind of work, because the job ads were mainly for domestic help and skilled laborers, such as carpenters, plumbers, bricklayers and truck drivers.

A couple of ads "guaranteed" excellent earnings to active and diligent young men willing to "sweat the shirt". That same morning I went to the first of the two locations, which was not too far from where I lived.

The address belonged to a two-story building. There were two apartments on each floor, with balconies that looked over the street. I went up to the second floor and knocked on the door of number four.

"It's open, come in!", answered a sour and screeching voice from within.

In the apartment's small living room, I saw two men sitting in folding chairs. One of them was fleshy and chubby-cheeked, with black hair, in ringlets, and a narrow, depressed forehead. He had on a pair of wrinkled pants and a cheap guayabera, so tight, that his fat belly was showing.

The second individual, a dark-skinned country man, was tall and thin, with the evasive and suspicious look so common among our peasants. He was wearing a long sleeved shirt of an intense blue color with enormous yellow cuff links. A pair of pre-Columbian style pants completed his attire.

Standing in front of them was a third man, the guy with the screeching voice. This one had a mustache and a violet colored nose; he reminded me of Higinio Menéndez. Half of his face was covered up by a pair of immense sun glasses and, when talking, he showed a gold tooth and a gap between his front teeth.

The man's expensive linen guayabera, open at the neck, displayed a thick gold chain from which hung an oversized medal with the image of St. Lazarus. As was to be expected, on the fourth finger of his right hand sparkled a chunky gold ring with an enormous stone.

"Sit down, my friend, sit down", he said to me, indicating a chair, "I'll be with you in a minute. Let me finish with these gentlemen".

I sat down, and looked around The furniture consisted of ten or twelve folding chairs, a filing cabinet and a desk. Leaning against the wall and piled on the floor were picture frames of all sizes and styles and, in the corners, stacks of boxes, probably containing frames, too.

The one with the screeching voice directed himself to the two other individuals.

"So, what are you complaining about?" he asked, "These frames sell like hot cakes! The problem is, if you want to sell, you have to apply the methods that I taught you!!"

"No offense intended, Cheíto", replied the country guy, "But it seems to me that this merchandise doesn't have as much outlet as you assured me. One can't even earn enough to eat in this business!"

Cheíto gave him a sympathetic look.

"How many times do I have to tell you that, in order to sell, you have to use psychology?", he replied, "You have to apply selling techniques, that's what you have to do!"

"Women don't like to be bothered at home", retorted the country man, "They raise a big fuss about door to door salesmen. Many of them have told me to just go fuck myself! And there I am, taking all that crap, loaded down with the goddamned frames, hot and sweating, and playing the fool! What the hell! I don't see the point in all this!!"

"The problem is that you haven't used the sales psychology that I have taught you", protested Cheíto, again.

"Look, Victoriano", he went on, "When the woman opens the door, you have your samples in your hand, you give her a big smile, and you say, `Madame, this is something that everybody needs, and I'm selling it for about a third of what they would charge you in the store. You save money, you save the trouble, and you save the expense of the trip to the store'!"

"Out of ten women, scarcely one falls for that story", replied Victoriano.

The fat one, who until now had not opened his mouth, put his two cents in.

"You know, Cheíto, a lot of housewives tell you to go to hell just because you are a door- to- door salesman".

"Well, then", squealed Cheíto, trying to appear proud and arrogant, "That's when you throw the check book on the table and you say: `A salesman, and an honorable one! Call this bank and ask them who Toribio Malpica is'! You'll see, that way, that they don't tell you to go to hell!!"

But Malpica didn't agree with Cheíto's ideas on salesmanship.

"I don't have no bank account!", he cried, "Years of hunger, that's what I have!! What fucking check book am I going to throw at anybody, pal!!??"

"You could throw it out there if you had listened to me!", Cheíto yelled, "I have tried to pound that into your head. there's no sales without psychology! But as for you, it goes in one ear and out the other!!"

"Excuse me if I correct you", meddled Victoriano, turning to Cheíto, "But, what do you do when you knock at a door and someone comes out and says they don't need any picture frames?"

"Well, it's very simple", he replied, "You say, 'I can't believe that you don't want to have a picture of your mother on that table in your living room! Look, I have beautiful things here! If you will just permit me a moment, I'll show you how you can transform your living room with the picture of your dear mother in this classic Italian frame...'"

From what I had seen and heard, I decided that I didn't want to walk the streets of Sabana, selling Cheíto's picture frames door to door. I got up and left the apartment, without saying good-bye, while the promoter and his two salesmen continued their discussion, getting more worked up by the moment.

The other address turned out to be a life insurance company. They were looking for salesmen. The candidates took a one-week training course, and afterwards the company spread them around the area to sell insurance, door to door. Not too different from Cheíto and his picture frames.

I left the company's office without even filling out an employment application, because the jobs were on a commission basis only, a commission so low that I figured that I would have to sell no less than two hundred policies per month to just make ends meet.

Back in my room at Cachita's, I saw that Goyito had left me a note on the night table. Alejandro Ayer wanted me to call him. Since Ayer never got home before seven, I called him after dinner. He came to the phone right away.

"Listen, Miguel", he said, "How are you with contractual law?"

"Great!", I answered, "I know the stuff by heart. I got a hundred on the last exam!"

"I'm all screwed up", he replied, "My head isn't working like it used to. Do you think you could come over tomorrow night and help with this garbage?"

Of course, I told him yes, because Ayer had always been up front with me, and I owed him favors.

That night, on my back, in bed, I reviewed my situation again, trying to see if there was any possibility that I hadn't explored. It seemed that I didn't have any other choice but to go to Los Remates and beg Lidia and Chuchú for their help. At least, with them I would find secure shelter.

I might even get into the army, as a soldier, if Chuchú wanted to help me. If so, I could finish my last two years of law school and then, at least, be promoted to second lieutenant. Nevertheless, this plan, born out of desperation, didn't really appeal to me. I have always hated uniforms.

But if I made that decision, I would have to leave Sabana right away, so as not to waste the little money that I had left, and arrive at my uncle's house with a few pesos in my pocket.

Then, and I don't know how it didn't occur to me before, the idea popped up in my mind.

Alejandro Ayer could be the solution to my problems! Ayer had been very well "connected" in past years, during a hot period of my country's history, and so would still have the friendship of some fat cat, some old buddy of his. For some reason he had that good position in a government office!

"Tomorrow I'll hit him with the problem", I said to myself, "What can I lose?"

The following night, after I had reviewed contractual law with Ayer, I spoke to him about the tight fix I was in, of the anguish of my financial situation and of the avenues that I had explored trying to resolve the problem. He listened to me with his full attention.

"I'm discouraged, Alejandro", I said at the end, "I can't think of anything else to do. But the idea of ending up down there, in Los Remates, is driving me crazy!"

Ayer didn't answer me right away. He sat there for a few minutes with his eyes on the floor, his right arm resting on the table, and his forehead furrowed, as he meditated.

"I'm ashamed to have come to you with my problems", I exclaimed, "But I didn't know what else to do. I've come to you as a last resort!"

"The hell with being ashamed!", answered my friend, "It makes me feel bad to hear about your situation! I really wish I could help you!"

That answer sank me deeper in despair. It looked like my friend Alejandro was also going to fail me.

"Don't give up hope yet", he added, seeing the discouragement written on my face, "There may be still a chance for you".

I looked at him like a shipwrecked man would look at a floating plank.

"I am with the Office of National Development", he told me, "The Office is something like a fifth wheel on the wagon. They just changed the name. Now it's called the National Council for Economic Promotion".

"Up until now", continued Ayer, "It served no other purpose than to justify the paychecks of a group of bench warmers. There are no more than fifteen or twenty employees in the office. I am the managing director".

That didn't sound too encouraging.

"But things are going to change real soon", he went on, "In a couple of years there will be presidential elections in this country, and Los Puros are putting forward Carlos Selvia as their candidate".

The Yagruman Revolutionary Party was the party of the government, and its members were known as "Los Puros". But I couldn't see what that had to do with my problem, and I said so to Ayer.

"Very simple", he replied, "The banking industry wants Selvia for president of Yagruma. He's going to be appointed president of the National Council for Economic Promotion, and then the banks will lend one hundred million pesos to the Republic of Yagruma, for public works that will foster the economic growth of the country".

"I can guess the rest", I said, "The millions are going to be administered by the Council"

"You got that right", replied Ayer, "We will be the ones to decide which works are going to be done, and also the ones to grant the contracts. Thousands of jobs will be created. You can imagine what all this means to Selvia's candidacy!"

"Of course!, I answered, "That'll make Selvia unbeatable! And you think maybe you'll be able to get something for me out of that?"

"I think so", he told me, "But it's going to take a little while. First of all, they will have to restructure the Council. There will be a lot of jobs to fill in the central office, and that's where I would like to see you get in. Can you type?"

"You bet!", I answered, "And I can take shorthand, too!"

"I have been told that a couple of my friends will be appointed to high positions in the Council", Ayer said, "If it turns out that way, your problems will be over. I'll find something for you".

I began thanking him, but he didn't let me finish.

"I haven't done anything yet", he warned me, "But don't despair. Things in government move slowly!"

Time continued passing by with nothing happening of what Ayer had told me about. Whenever I saw him I asked him, and his answer was always the same, "Be patient. Things in government go slowly". Uncertainty and the lack of faith began to grow in me.

One morning when I sat down to read the paper, I saw, on the front page, the announcement that Carlos Selvia had been designated president of the National

Council for Economic Promotion. All that was lacking now was for the banks to come up with the money.

And the money wasn't long in showing up. A few days afterward, in the presidential palace, the papers for the loan of one hundred million pesos were signed by president Elío, by Carlos Selvia, and by the representatives of the banking industry. The money, that of course, was to be administered by the Council for Economic Promotion.

For me, that was the light at the end of the tunnel. In my savings account, after paying Cachita, there was scarcely enough left for one more month in Sabana and still get to Los Remates not flat broke.

I went to the University, looking for Ayer, but I couldn't find him anywhere. I called him to his office that afternoon, but nobody answered the phone. Finally, I located him at his home, that night, and I asked him about my chances of working for the Council.

"Look!", he told me, "You have to learn to have patience. I told you that! The reorganization is already under way. I've been appointed office manager in one of the new departments that have been created".

"The director", he went on, "is Delmiro Esquerra, an old friend of mine. We'll see what can be done! Don't worry, I'll keep you informed".

What Ayer told me was reasonable and sensible, but my anxiety and worry were so great, that it all appeared insincere and fabricated, and for a moment I thought that my friend was giving me the run- around.

I hung up the phone and sat down to think about what I should do. Should I take my few pesos out of the bank and head for Los Remates, or follow Ayer's advice and stretch out my stay in Sabana for as long as I could, in hope of some results from his plan?

Finally, after kicking the problem around in my head for a while, I decided that the best thing for me to do was to wait.

I remember that I slept little and poorly that night. After breakfast I went back to my room and tried, unsuccessfully, to study. Finally, at mid-morning, trying to combat the depression I was feeling, I was off to law school.

Upon entering the classroom, I chose a seat in a corner of the last row. From there I could hear the monotonous and sing-song voice of the professor, like an annoying buzzing that reached me from far away.

I couldn't focus on anything that was going on around me, nor think about anything else except the uncertainty of my future.

It made me sick to think of having to settle into a life at Los Remates, a dirty and hateful village, as hostile as the swamp near where it was located. That would mean that I would have to forget all the plans that I have made for my life, and bury myself in the gray and miserable routine of that God-forsaken place.

There was still the possibility of getting into the army, as an ordinary soldier, if Chuchú could help me. But that possibility was somewhat remote.

All of a sudden the professor's voice stopped. I heard the sound of the chairs being pushed back, and the steps and murmur of voices of the students leaving the classroom. But I didn't get up from my seat. Unaware of my surroundings, I kept brooding, lost in my sad contemplation.

Suddenly I sensed the presence of someone. A soft voice with a slightly nasal accent pronounced my name.

"Excuse the intrusion", said that voice, "But you have a terrible look in your face today. Can I help you with something?"

I looked up, there was Perlita Shell.

CHAPTER XIV
BUT TO SEE HER WAS TO LOVE HER

Standing next to my seat, Perlita looked at me with a mixture of curiosity and interest. I can't express what I felt when I realized that she was talking to me. All I remember about that moment is my heart pounding crazily inside my chest.

She sat down beside me, and for the first time in my life I was close to her; so close, that the edge of her skirt brushed against my pants.

"Don't you feel like talking?", she said, seeing that I sat there, silent, "If you want, I'll go and leave you alone".

I would have liked to tell her that what I wanted was for time to stand still right then, so I could stay there, close to her for an eternity, or until the universe came apart. But I bit my tongue to restrain myself, and tried to find some adequate words.

"No, of course not! How could I want such a thing!?", I uttered, finally, "On the contrary, I appreciate your interest. Please, don't go!"

"You always sit here, alone, lost in God knows what thoughts", replied Perlita, "Today, I am worried about you, with such a tragic face!"

"Only two persons had ever worried about me", I responded, "You are number three".

"Who are the others?", she asked. It seemed as though there was a little tension in her voice.

"My grandmother and my aunt Lidia. They live in the country".

"Oh, I thought you were talking about girl friends", she said.

"Girl friends are a luxury that I could never afford", I replied.

She stared at me, smiling, but didn't say a word.

The classroom, meanwhile, had been filling up with students arriving for the next class. We couldn't stay there.

"Do you have anything to do right now?", I asked.

"No", she answered, "I took the day off today".

"Well, would you like to go into the canteen?", I suggested, "We'll have a cup of coffee and talk for a while. How about it?"

"Good idea!", she answered, "Let's go! You see?", she added, "You are already looking more relaxed".

The law school canteen was almost deserted at that hour. We sat at a table and ordered coffee.

"You are a strange guy, Miguel", Perlita said, all of a sudden, "You don't mix with anybody in the class, nothing makes you laugh, you are always so serious! Let's see, why do you have that funereal face today?"

I was on the point of asking why someone like her would be interested in what could be happening to a guy like me. But I changed my mind. It would be better to enjoy the pleasure of that encounter, perhaps our first and last.

I told her then about the loss of my only source of income, my fruitless efforts to find a job and my now dead hopes of finding work at the Council. There seemed to be no other way for me than bury myself at Los Remates!

"If something doesn't come up real soon", I concluded, "In two or three weeks I'll have to leave Sabana for the countryside".

Perlita assured me that every problem had a solution, something which I didn't believe, although I didn't say so.

"Don't give up!", was her advise, "Look, a lot of things can happen in two weeks. Ayer is right, you know. Have a little patience, don't do anything rash! Besides, I can talk to my boss. He might find something for you".

"OK", I interrupted, "Up until now we haven't talked about anything except me. How about you? All I know is your name, nothing about your life".

"My life has been really boring", she said, "I was born here in Sabana. As a girl I went to Medina High School, and now here I am, studying law. That's about it".

"But you have a job", I observed, "Where?"

"In the Caribbean Petroleum Corporation", she responded.

"That's an American company, right?"

"Actually, it is multi-national concern", she explained, "It has interests in the United States, England, Holland, Venezuela...a big mixture!"

"Well, you have been lucky", I observed, "Those companies pay very well. And think of all the business connections you can make there! You won't have any problems when you graduate".

"I hope you are right", Perlita said. She glanced at her wrist watch. "It's twelve o'clock already!", she exclaimed, "I have to go, Miguel!"

"Why? I thought you didn't have to work today!", I protested.

"No, no!", she replied, "I'm off for the day! But I have a date for lunch". Was it just my imagination or did I detect a slight disturbance in her voice?

I tried to hide my feelings. "Thanks for your interest", I said, "And good luck!"

"I'll see you soon", she told me, getting up. The few men sitting at other tables followed her with their eyes while she walked across the room, with the carriage of a queen.

Without the spell of her presence, the magic of that interlude was broken. Now alone, I forced myself to overcome the agitation that was invading me.

I tried to analyze what I thought was nothing more than a fleeting relationship. But my practical approach to things didn't help to find answers to the questions I asked myself. Reason and common sense seemed to have left my mind, defeated by the eyes and lips of Perlita Shell.

The next day was Friday, and I left early for the University with the hope of seeing Perlita and trying to narrow the bonds of our emerging relationship. But she didn't come to class that day, nor did she appear at the University during the following two weeks, and I wondered what might have happened to her.

I would have sold my soul to Satan in exchange for being with her, for having her close to me again!

Perlita's number didn't appear in the Sabana telephone book, so, after thinking about it for a while I decided to phone the company where she worked. I had very little success, because the secretary who took my call only told me, in a dry and professional voice, that Miss Shell was on vacation, that they didn't know when she would be back, and that they had explicit instructions not to give her unlisted phone number to anybody.

"Could I leave a message for her?", I asked. My voice must have revealed my anxiety, because the woman said now, in an almost friendly voice, that, yes, I could leave a message.

I gave her my name and phone number, and begged her to give it to Miss Shell as soon as she returned.

Perlita didn't seem very friendly with the "aristocrats" of our class, although she sat amongst them. The one closest to her was a pretty brunette called Josefina, and I asked her if she had heard from our friend.

"No", she answered, "The last time I saw her, she told me she was going to Mexico, on company business, but I haven't heard anything more from her".

"When I called the company, they told me she was on vacation", I replied, "And now you are telling me that she went to Mexico. With whom did she go? She and who else!?"

"Baró, what makes you think that I would know?", she replied. Her eyes swept over mine. "Maybe she's changed her plans. You find out!"

I was sure that Josefina was hiding something from me, but I didn't want to insist. After all, what right did I have to look into what Perlita had or hadn't done, nor with whom?

Seeing that time passed without hearing anything from Ayer, I had written a long letter to Aunt Lidia, telling her, in detail, what had happened to me, and asking her if there was a place for me in her house, where I could ride out the storm and try to find out some new directions for myself. When I returned to Cachita's, I found my aunt's answer. It went, more or less, like this:

"My dear nephew: I received your letter on the tenth of this month, which made a deep impression on me, as well as on your uncle Chuchú. It is really a shame that you have to leave your studies, after burning the midnight oil for so long. But, actually, who knows what can happen tomorrow? I don't have to tell you that you will always be welcome in our house; I have a room, although small, all fixed up and ready for you, and you'll be as comfortable as one can be in Los Remates. By chance, Dr. Primitivo López, who is the only lawyer in this village, is looking for a clerk, and Chuchú is going to talk to him about you. You might even be picking the credits you need. Don't worry, and remember that God squeezes, but He does not choke. Love from your aunt, Lidia".

My fate seemed to have been decided. All that remained was for me to notify Cachita of my impending departure, take what little money I still had in my savings account, and pack my bags. It was the twenty fifth, so I still had six days in Sabana, because I always paid Cachita at the end of the month.

I had some textbooks and lecture papers from class that I wouldn't be needing now. The following morning I went to the University to see if could sell them to some student. I had to let them go for five pesos.

Then, when I was leaving Law school I saw a green Mercedes-Benz parked on the other side of the plaza. There were a man and a woman inside the car. From that distance I couldn't tell who they were, but when she got out of the Mercedes and started walking across the plaza, heading toward the school building, from the rhythmic cadence of her walk I recognized Perlita, immediately.

To see her getting out of that car was, for me, as though I had been hit on the head with a paving stone. Who was that man? Was he a friend, a fellow worker, perhaps a boy friend?"

I tried to calm myself down and consider my situation realistically. To face up to the uncertain future that was waiting for me at Los Remates, I had to keep a clear head.

After all, as much as the fire burned in my heart at the memories of Perlita, what justification did I have to think that she could feel anything similar for me? The short time we spent together in the law school canteen? Please, don't make me laugh, I've got a cracked lip!!

"I'm stupid", I said to myself, "I'm a poor bastard that has to walk to save a six-cent bus fare. I can't even dream of falling in love with a woman who is so high up the ladder!"

I was really playing the fool. I had to forget that craziness before it became an obsession.

The body of happiness is skinny, as the saying goes.

I would leave for Los Remates on the thirty-first of the month. I had notified Cachita, closed out my savings account, and packed my bags. That night, as a going away celebration, Goyito and Teodulfo invited me to dinner at a nearby cafe.

The dinner was sort of sad, because, as Goyito said, with my departure the group would disintegrate.

"Ruperto and Abilio are gone, already", he complained, "Now we are going to lose you. It isn't going to be the same without the group".

Teodulfo, somberly, agreed.

"That's for sure", I said, "By the way, what have we heard about Abilio? I haven't seen him since he graduated".

"I ran across him in the cafeteria of Radio Mundo, a couple of weeks ago", said Teodulfo, "Since he's a lawyer now, he's been promoted to second lieutenant".

"Each one goes his own way", I thought, "Life is parting us".

During the dinner we talked little and drank a lot, with the eternal excuse of drowning our sorrows. When we finished, Teodulfo invited us to go to the Hong Kong, but Goyito and I, saddened and depressed by the alcohol, declined the invitation. It was close to nine o'clock when we went up the stairs of the boarding house. I had just put a foot into the living room when I heard Cachita's voice from the balcony.

"Miguel!", she cried, "You've got a message! Call Alejandro Ayer right away!"

I rushed to make the call. Ayer answered the phone.

"It's me, Miguel", I said anxiously, "What's going on, Alejandro?"

"Do you know where the offices of the Council are?", he asked.

"Yes", I replied, "On the corner of Alameda and Fourth Street".

"That's right. Look, on the opposite corner, across Fourth Street, there is a cafe that has a green marquee over the main entrance. It's called "La Rosa de Medina". Be there tomorrow morning at nine o'clock!"

"He's got me a job!", I thought, crazy with happiness, "Now I won't have to leave Sabana!"

"Alejandro", I begged, "Tell me if you found something for me!"

"No, nothing on the phone", he replied, "I'll tell you about it tomorrow, at nine o'clock". And he hung up.

I lay awake almost all that night, turning and tossing in bed. Although I hadn't yet spoken to Ayer, I was sure that there was a spot waiting for me at the National Council of Economic Promotion. Lying back on my bed, looking at the ceiling, I began to build castles in the air.

I would attach myself to the fat cats of the Council, those who floated around Selvia and were called to be, without doubt, ministers and important people in the new administration. With Selvia as Yagruma's president, I was going to be in clover!

Besides, I still planned to take the entrance examinations to the judiciary. And with my connections, coming up with one of the highest grades would be a piece of cake.

At six o'clock in the morning it was impossible for me to stay in bed any longer. I showered, shaved and got dressed. It was seven o'clock now. I was so excited and impatient that I didn't want to wait for them to begin serving breakfast. I had a cup of coffee at a small place near the University and then walked a couple of blocks to the next bus stop. A half hour later I arrived to the corner of Alameda and Fourth Street.

I found the "Rosa de Medina" right away. It was full of people. Standing outside, on the corner, I waited for a while, which seemed like a year, until finally, in the distance, I saw Ayer coming out of the Council building.

"Let's go inside", he said as he came up to me. We went in, looked for a convenient place, and after ordering coffee for the both of us, Ayer made the announcement.

"Here it is!", he announced, "Tomorrow you start working at the Council!"

"Alejandro", was all that I could say, "I don't know how to thank you for what you have done for me. You have saved my life, brother!"

"Forget that!", he answered, "You don't have to thank me for anything! All I did was talk to Delmiro Esquerra, the engineer, who was the one who got you the job".

"Esquerra and I are old friends", continued Ayer, "We worked together at the Census Office, years ago. He has just been named Director of the Diverse Projects Bureau, and he wants me to be his office manager. I told him that I needed one more clerk, and recommended you. That's how you got in".

We finished our coffee and Ayer rose from his chair.

"Esquerra put you in as a staff employee", he said, "Your name is already on the payroll. Well, then, let's go over to the office so you can meet him, and get acquainted".

When we got to the Diverse Projects Office, we were told that Engr. Esquerra had called to inform that he wasn't coming in to the office that day. Ayer then introduced me to the other members of the staff. They were a typist and three draftsmen. Also assigned to the Office were an architect and a civil engineer.

That same day, after briefing me about my clerical duties, Ayer put me in front of a pile of specifications that had to be typed. I spent the rest of the day on that monotonous occupation. At six o'clock the office closed, and everybody rushed to Personnel, to punch the clock and get the hell out of the building.

If I were lucky, and they didn't fire me to give my job to some fat cat's protege, my room and board were assured for the scarcely eighteen months that remained for me to graduate. Then, I would see what I could do.

Once more, I thought of Perlita Shell. Our paths surely would separate forever after we graduated. And now, working at the Council, I wouldn't even have the opportunity to see her every once in a while.

"Why did she come to me that morning?", I asked myself again, "What could she want?"

That night I let Cachita know that I wasn't leaving after all. Then, to erase Perlita from my thoughts, I sat down at the table and wrote a long letter to Aunt Lidia, telling her how my situation had changed and I had decided to stay in Sabana and finish my studies. I thanked her and Chuchú, once again, for their generous offer. But, as I finished the letter, Perlita's eyes were still burning in my mind.

The following morning I met my boss, Engr. Esquerra, who showed up at the office about eleven o'clock. He acknowledged my greeting with a nod, and I had begun to tell him how grateful I was for his help when he, without saying a word, turned his back to me and left.

Esquerra was an apathetic and slovenly man, who really liked his brandy. He was always complaining about being a bureaucrat, a wage earner, as he said. He used to swear that he was going to quit his job, where he earned more than a thousand pesos per month, something fabulous in Yagruma, at that time.

"Is that a fact?", Ayer asked him, sarcastically, "Are you going to quit, Delmirito? And, prey tell, where will you go?"

"Out there, to make big bucks!", shouted Esquerra.

But he never quitted his job.

The engineer belonged to a highly renowned and influential family, whose members, it appeared, had a permanent and preferential lock on the juiciest positions in Yagruma's bureaucracy. The Esquerras, who ever since the Spanish domination had been feeding off the nation's budget, continued to be in clover after the republic was proclaimed.

Working for the National Council for Economic Promotion acquainted me with the sacred practices, uses and customs of Yagruma's bureaucracy; practices, uses and customs that endless generations of bureaucrats had created, observed and kept unchanged since time immemorial.

The Council's employees, according to this tradition, could be classified into two groups: Those who worked, which were the minority, and those who loafed around. The first group was comprised of employees who had no solid political recommendation or backing from sponsors with "pull".

Those poor souls always went around in fear of losing their jobs. They tried to make themselves indispensable, working restlessly from eight o'clock in the morning through six o'clock in the evening. Sometimes they had to stay in the office, working late, doing the other people's jobs.

The loafers who comprised the majority had been hired because of the recommendations of politicians, army officers and influential friends and relatives. These people, thanks to the fear that their sponsors commanded, had carte blanche. They did whatever they wanted to, without anybody daring to raise their voice to them.

Since there was always someone who would punch their time cards, they usually got to work late, and they left whenever they wanted to. At the office, they told stories, read pornographic magazines or talked on the phone with their friends.

They also spent lots of time at "La Rosa de Medina", eating breakfast, lunch, drinking coffee, snacking and talking politics.

It isn't that I criticize them, much to the contrary. What wouldn't I have given to be allowed to do the same!

But my only sponsor was Ayer, who, aside from his friendship with Esquerra, had no other connections. And Esquerra himself, as I soon found out, really wasn't one of the most influential ones in the Council.

It is not strange, then, that like most of my memories, those of my days at the Council were not exactly happy ones. While Ayer arrived at ten in the morning and left at about two in the afternoon, the draftsmen lounged in the cafe, and the engineer and the architect were in some unknown place, the typist and I spent the day glued to the typewriters.

All the castles in the air that I had built when I dreamed of working at the Council had collapsed. None of the low-ranking employees had any access to Engr. Selvia or any of his cohorts.

As Goyito would say, "Monkeys can't dance in the tiger's den".

CHAPTER XV
THE QUESTION BEING, UNREQUITED LOVE?

One evening when I returned to the boarding house from work, Cachita told me that a Perlita had called and left her phone number, and I was to call her.

I immediately forgot my determination not to have any more impossible dreams and not permit passion to blind me to reality. I flew to the telephone and dialed her number. Her voice came to me through the wire.

"It is I, Miguel Baró", I said, "Remember me?"

"Of course I do! Don't be silly!", she responded, "Say, where have you been? I don't see you at the University anymore! What's happened?"

"Several days ago I called you at your office", I replied, "I left you a message".

"Yes, I know", she said, "I'm sorry, but the switchboard operator forgot to give it to me. I found out today, and I called you as soon as I could".

"I'm surprised that you didn't tell me you were going on vacation, when we were at the Law school canteen".

A few seconds passed by before Perlita replied. When she did, she went around my question.

"I spent a few days in Mexico", she said, briefly. "Tell me", she went on, still avoiding the matter, "I haven't seen you at school! Where have you been? Did you go to see your aunt?"

"No", I replied, "I finally got a job. So I'm staying in Sabana".

"Oh, that's good news!?", she exclaimed, "Don't you remember that I told you that a lot of things could happen in two weeks? You see, Lady Luck is on your side now!"

When I told her that I was working at the National Council for Economic Promotion, Perlita was all excited.

"That's wonderful!", she exclaimed, "If you can get connected with those in the inner circle there, when Selvia becomes president, all your problems will be solved".

"All those fat cats are surrounded by a wall of flunkies and body guards", I observed, "They let no one get through. And ass-kissing is not my specialty!"

"You see?", said Perlita, "You are beginning all wrong! Miguel, in this life one has to have ambition. If not, you are left behind! But, listen, you haven't told me why you called me at the office".

"You would laugh at me if I told you", I replied.

"No, why should I!?", she said, "On the contrary, I think you are being more serious about this than I thought. So, tell me!"

Those words finally brought down the wall that my common sense had been trying to keep between my reason and my dreams.

"The other night", I said, "I was in my room, lying on my bed, when all of a sudden I realized that the only thing I could think about was you. I could see you, hear your voice, breath your perfume. And I wanted to tell you, I wanted you to know that!"

Perlita pretended to take it lightly. "You are a romantic", she replied, "You don't belong in this century. I'm not going to answer you, because I know that your fever is going to pass in just a few days. By the way, how are you going to go to the University, if you are working?"

I couldn't get over the fact that I had had the courage to tell Perlita how I felt about her. I was floating on air, my heart was beating wildly. Nevertheless, I didn't persist.

"They'll give me permission to go for the exams", I said.

"Look, I'm still at the office", said Perlita, "Take down my home number: 2-17-44. OK? All right then. Call me tonight. Not after eight o'clock, because I am going out. OK?"

"I'll call you about seven thirty", I said before hanging up.

That evening I waited, in suspense, for seven thirty to arrive. When the time came, I rushed to the phone. Perlita answered.

"I'm sorry, but I can't talk very long", she whispered, "I have to leave. I want to ask you, what would you think about us studying together? I know that you are a good student. I heard you once in class when you were talking about the failure of our penal system, and you did it very well. You know, studying by myself, it takes me longer, and I waste a lot of time. Well, what do you say?"

I struggled so my voice didn't reveal my excitement. "I would be delighted", I responded, "When do you want to start?"

"How about tomorrow?", she asked, "From eight to ten fifteen or ten thirty. Is that OK?"

"Fine!", I said, still struggling to keep down the agitation that possessed me, "But I don't know where you live".

"That's right, you don't", she replied, "Do you have a pencil and paper? OK, write down, 413 Avenue of the Patriots. That's between twenty one and nineteen streets. Have you got that? Yes? OK, I have to leave, they are waiting for me. See you tomorrow!"

I couldn't believe what was happening. A great exhilaration overcame me, but the shadow of a memory entered to disturb my happiness.

"With whom is she going out tonight?", I wondered. While I sat, lonely and frustrated in my dirty room at Cachita's, was she going around Sabana's pleasure spots, in the company of that man with the Mercedes?

My jealous mind worked overtime with my imagination before it finally allowed me to drift away into an erratic sleep.

The following morning, when I woke up, the first thing that came to my mind was that I would be with Perlita that evening.

When I put on my shoes I couldn't help but notice that, besides being old, the points were twisted and the soles had holes.

I would rather be dead than show up in her house with those disgraceful things on, so I bought a new pair at a nearby shoe store.

I had imagined that Perlita would be living in one of the many modern residences that were built on both sides of the Avenue of the Patriots, but I was mistaken. Turning east on Nineteenth Street, heading towards the Avenue, her house was the second in a row of two-story dwellings that were probably more than thirty years old.

Perlita pushed the button from up above to open the street door for me. Leaning on the railing, smiling, she watched me come up upstairs.

"How punctual you are!", she exclaimed, "I like that! What shall we study today?"

"Let's begin with intestate succession", I decided, "Actually, it's the only tough one that we have. The rest of it is easy".

"I wish I could have the same confidence!", she replied, "But, come in, come in!"

We went over to a corner of the living room where I saw two big chairs and an old mahogany table on which piled several books, an antique lamp with a silk shade, and a statuette of Mephistopheles, with his lips fixed in a strange smile. Perlita had never looked so beautiful to me, in her sleeveless blouse that revealed the smooth, golden skin of her arms.

A hoarse voice called from the adjoining living room.

"Perlita! What are you doing? Who is there?"

"I'll be right there, grandmother", she answered in a loud voice, "Just a minute!"

"I want you to meet her", she said, "Come with me".

The living room was plainly furnished. In one corner there was a television set, something which, in those times, most average Yagrumans could not afford.

Perlita introduced me to her grandmother, a lady close to eighty years old, whose hair was white like cotton. She was sitting on a big rocking chair, in front of the television set , which was turned off. The old lady cast a suspicious glance at me and then turned to her granddaughter.

"Who is this young man?", she asked.

"He is a classmate of mine at the University, grandma", she explained, "We are going to study together".

"Why don't you come and study in here?", inquired her grandmother, "You can bring the lamp in from the other room, and put it over there", she added, pointing with her finger at one of the corners of the room.

"No, grandma", explained Perlita, patiently, "We can't do that, because when you turn on the television the sound will interfere with our studying".

The old lady couldn't but agree with her, although grudgingly, judging by the face she put on.

"Well, all right", she said, talking to Perlita, but looking at me, "I can't miss watching my programs. You can go, but I'm going to tell Sofía to go by and look in every once in a while".

"Of course, grandma, of course", Perlita replied. "Wait a minute", she added, seeing that her grandmother wanted to get up, "I'll turn it on for you".

We went to the big chairs in the other room, sitting next to the table. The light from the old lamp bathed Perlita's body, embracing her as though trying to protect her from the surrounding darkness.

That night she had on a short skirt that came about to her knees and revealed her splendid legs. I looked at her, as though bewitched, until her voice brought me back to reality.

"OK, let's go to work!", she said, "Intestate succession, right?"

I told her yes, but actually it didn't make any difference. For me, the only thing of importance was that we were both there together, very close to each other, in the little oasis that the cone of light from the antique lamp opened in the darkness of the room.

We studied for a little more than two hours. About ten thirty, we ended our session.

"Would you like something to drink?", she asked, "Café con leche, a soft drink, something?

I thanked her, but I did not accept anything. I didn't want her grandmother, nor her aunt, who had looked in on us that night, to think that I was trying to be too familiar.

For the next few minutes we talked about trivial things, and finally separated. "We have to get up early", she said, "The poor have to work. I'll see you tomorrow at the same time".

Walking back to Cachita's house that night, I kept looking up at the sky. It seemed to me that sky was deeper and the stars shone more brightly.

The next day was Friday. That evening, before beginning to study, we started talking about other things, and I took the opportunity to ask her about something that had been weighing heavily on my heart.

"You haven't told me about your vacation", I said, "How was the trip to Mexico?" From the change I could notice in her eyes, and a certain tightening at the corner of her lips, it seemed to me that the question had disturbed her.

"Well, it was not exactly a vacation", she said after a few seconds, "Caribbean Petroleum has entered into an agreement with Mexico. There was a meeting in Mazatlán which Mr. Eniesta, our executive vice-president, had to attend".

I didn't say a word. Just kept staring at her.

"Marketing techniques were to be discussed" she went on, "And that is my department. Mr. Eniesta asked me to go with him, because he could use my help. Really, I couldn't say no to him. He is my boss! But, man, what's the matter? Miguel, don't look at me like that!"

"Your boss, the vice-president, does he drive a green Mercedes?", I asked her.

Perlita bit her lips.

"Well, yes, but, what does that have to do with it?" Her voice sounded uncertain.

"I saw you get out of that car a few days ago", I said, getting angry, but trying not to raise my voice, "At the University, in front of the plaza".

"Sure, that's true!", she protested, "He gave me a ride to the University! So what!?"

"So you are his assistant, huh? You go on trips with him, go around with him, in his car...What else do you assist him with?", I sputtered, furiously, "Do you sleep with him too?"

It seemed like my head had become empty. I felt as though something had come over me that I could only describe as a black velvet darkness in which millions of scarlet flies were buzzing. It wasn't the first time that that had happened to me. I sat motionless on the big chair, with my eyes closed, waiting for it to pass. I was soon feeling OK. When I opened my eyes, Perlita spoke to me.

"Are you all right?", she asked.

"I'm fine", I answered, "It was nothing".

"Has that happened to you before?"

"Yes. A couple of times".

"Have you seen a doctor about it?"

"Yes", I lied, "He told me it's all emotional".

"Oh, sure! You found out that I went to Mexico with the same man you saw me with later. And you blew your top! But, Miguel, you don't have any right to criticize me! I go where I want to, and with whomever I feel like! Who are you, to demand that I explain myself?"

She was raising her voice to me, something which I wouldn't permit anyone to do. I grabbed my books and stood up.

"You don't have to yell", I said, "If I have behaved like a fool, it's because I'm in love with you, something which I'm sure you have known for some time! Well, this is the end of the studying. Good-bye!"

I turned my back and started toward the stairway. Without saying a word, she let me go.

I spent the following days trying to overcome my feelings and gain control over myself. I had to forget Perlita Shell, for my own good. I buried myself in my work, whose load increased by the day, and in my studies.

The dredging of the port of Violeta, and other works of great importance were assigned to my department. From the time I got to the office, until the time I left, I spent my time taking, in shorthand, the specifications that Esquerra and other engineers dictated to me, and later typing them out. Then I put together sets of mimeograph copies.

When I got back to Cachita's house, I showered, ate dinner and studied until one or two o'clock in the morning, when I flopped down on my cot hoping that sleep would come in a matter of seconds.

But Perlita was hard to forget, and sometimes I tossed and turned on my cot until three or four o' clock, unable to erase her image from my memory.

Several days went by without knowing anything about her. One afternoon I was in the office, typing like crazy to finish a mountain of specifications that were urgently needed, when the telephone extension on my desk rang. When I answered the call my heart turned over. It was her.

"Miguel", she said, "It's been several days since we hurt each other, for no reason. That was really stupid! We are not a couple of teenagers! Will you please forgive me?"

"Only if you will forgive me", I replied, "You don't have any idea how I have felt these past few days, every time I thought of what I said to you".

"We have to talk", she said, "Can you come over to my house tonight?"

"Perlita", I replied, wishing with all my heart that reason would prevail over my feelings, "What are we going to accomplish by seeing each other? It would be better if we just left things the way they are. You know how I feel about you, but you and I are never going to have anything together. We live in different worlds".

"The only thing that I can say to you", Perlita responded, "Is that you have to change that attitude that you have towards life. That's one of the things that I want to discuss with you. As far as the rest of it is concerned, we'll talk about it".

I was silent.

"I'll be waiting for you tonight, then", she said, "You're going to come, right? Or don't you want to be with me now?"

I couldn't contain myself any longer.

"Are you going to ask the dead man if he would like a mass?", I retorted.

She laughed. "OK, then. I'll be expecting you. Come early!"

Sofia, Perlita's aunt, met me when I arrived at the house that evening. She was about fifty years old, a well formed woman, with graying hair that she arranged in a fresh and attractive manner.

She took me to that corner in the room where Perlita and I had been studying a few nights before, and after assuring me that her niece wouldn't be long, she left me alone. On the desk, in the milky light of the old lamp, Mephistopheles kept displaying his equivocal smile.

I had worked very hard that day at the office, and was tired. I lay back on the big chair, closed my eyes, and tried not to think. My head was nodding from exhaustion, when fragrance from a perfume that I knew very well brought me back to reality. I opened my eyes and saw Perlita at my side.

"I'm sorry to wake you up", she said, "But we have to talk".

She sat down, facing me, and for a few seconds we were both silent. She was the one that broke that silence.

"You make me feel bad with your pessimism, with that negative attitude that you have about things", she said to me, "Besides, I don't see that there is so much difference between what you call "our worlds", and I can't understand why you say that they are incompatible. You are young, you are intelligent, you'll soon be a lawyer! If you have any ambition, you can get what you want!"

"You may know a lot about petroleum and marketing", I replied, "But you don't really know what life in this rotten island is about. Here, if you are born a nobody, you'll never get far, unless you get into politics, marry money or become a rip-off artist. And I don't have what it takes to do any of those things".

"I wasn't born into a golden crib!", she protested.

"You have been lucky enough to get into a big international corporation", I told her, "You have done very well there! You make good money, travel, have made good connections! And the law degree will help you to climb higher and higher in this world that's opening up for you".

"Well, then", asked Perlita, "What are your plans for the future? Because with that negative attitude of yours, so defeatist, it seems to me that you aren't expecting your life to change very much when you get your degree".

"It will change", I replied, "But not a lot, maybe, at least I'll be a little better off. My boss is very happy with my work. He promised me that as soon as I graduated he would help me to get a civil service job"

"If so", I added, "I could get along until they hold entrance examinations for the judiciary. Then, I'll be a judge and go wherever they send me".

"And you'll be happy with that? I can't believe it!", she exclaimed, "Make your life in the country! What a thing! Nobody wants that!"

"I wouldn't be unhappy with it", I replied, "I've always wanted to write. Being a country judge, I'll have plenty of time for that".

"Well, nobody can accuse you of being ambitious", murmured Perlita.

"Miguel", she went on, "If you should find somebody here in Sabana that would help you to succeed in your profession, to finally become somebody, wouldn't you accept that help?"

Our eyes met, and in hers I saw a beseeching smile. Perlita didn't want me to vanish from her life!

"Is it so bad to have ambitions?", she asked, "Is it bad to want to prosper in this life?" Her voice seemed to come from far away.

I suddenly remembered the nights in Helena where, walking on the deserted beach, I imagined that I heard a voice coming on the wings of the wind, from the other side of the bay.

Without answering I went to her, took her in my arms, and searched for her mouth with mine. But, it seemed, during her years in the business world Perlita had learned a lot, because she reacted instantly, forming with her arms a barrier between our bodies, pushing me away preventing me from kissing her.

I opened my arms and let her go, choking with frustration and anger. Perlita understood what was happening to me.

She came up to me and took me by the hand.

"We can't even think of that", she said, "That's the wrong thing to do. The only thing we should think about now is graduating".

"This is what I want to propose to you", she went on, "We get along well studying together, so let's continue as we are, like two good friends. We'll study together, and we graduate in June! We'll see what happens afterwards. What do you say?"

"In other words", I replied, "I have to behave myself, isn't that right?"

"That's right, at least for the time being", she answered.

"I don't think I can do it", I said, "I don't think I'm capable of spending the nights beside you with my nose stuck in a book!"

"I have been dreaming about you since I saw you for the first time, at Law school. How can I be just a good friend to you!? Love excludes friendship!"

"And why do you think that you are here, now, at this moment, in my house, talking to me?", she exclaimed, "Why do you think I called you and asked you to come back? It's because I care deeply about you, because you have made an impression on me that even I can't explain!"

Perlita had admitted that she wasn't indifferent to me! Spurred by passion I went to her, but she kept me away with her arm extended.

"If you don't want to lose me", she said, coldly, "You have to prove that you can control yourself. Let's concentrate on one single thing: to graduate in June! Then you and I are going to sit down and talk about the future, and whether you and I are going to face it together. But don't push me, man. Give me time! All right? Are we in agreement?"

"I'll be here tomorrow evening", I answered, "We'll review the penal code".

"It's a deal! Now", Perlita added, "There is something that I want to clarify. Something that even now is bothering you, although you wouldn't admit it".

I guessed what she was talking about. "You don't have to explain anything to me", I replied, "Can't we forget that?"

"No!", was her answer, "You have this idea stuck in your head, and that's something that will poison our relationship. I want things to be perfectly clear between us".

She took out a pack of American cigarettes from one of the table drawers and offered me one. I refused, thanking her, and took one of my own Yagruman lung busters.

"How horrible!", she exclaimed when she saw them, "How can you smoke those things? They'll kill you!"

"It's a poor man's cigarette", I responded, "One gets used to anything".

We smoked in silence for a few seconds until she, comfortable in the big chair, began to talk.

"I want you to understand this clearly", she said to me, "I owe my job to that man of whom you are so jealous. His name is Felino Eniesta. He has done nothing but help me, worry about my future, and protect me. If I went to Mexico with him, it's because he thought that the experience would be useful in my career, with the corporation. Besides, Miguel, how can you be jealous of a man that is almost fifty years old, married, and lives with his family?"

"My love", I said, without her objecting that I called her that, "I believe you. I believe everything you say".

"But", I went on, "Not age, nor a wife, nor children, are barriers to keep a man from getting involved with another woman. Look, in Helena, I knew Don Rufino Márquez, an old guy, seventy one years old. He owned a noodle factory. Everybody respected him; he was a very honest and serious man, married, with children and grandchildren. Well, one day Don Rufino left his wife for a seamstress from Barrio Nuevo, with whom he lived for the rest of his life".

And since I thought I could see the beginning of a protest on Perlita's lips, I hurried to add:

"Of course, I'm speaking in generalities! I'm not thinking of your boss! You said you owe him your job. How's that?"

"There you go again! Miguel, how malicious you are!", she exclaimed, "I'll have to apply myself to pulling out those weeds that are growing in your mind!"

"I'm not thinking anything bad", I protested, "I'm just curious!"

"Don't tell me that!, retorted Perlita, "My father worked for Caribbean Petroleum. He and Mr. Eniesta were good friends. I was ten years old when my father died. A short time later my mother married again, to a guy that I never liked and who never inspired any confidence in me. My life in the home of that man was a living hell; after a few months, with my mother's blessing, I came to live here with my grandmother".

I asked myself where this story was going to end.

"When I graduated from high school", continued Perlita, "I entered law school. I liked the good things of life. Nice clothes, club life, playing `canasta'...you know! And, with what my mother and grandma gave me, I didn't have enough to even begin".

"And then", I interrupted, "You decided that you had to find a job. You went to "Caribbean Petroleum", talked to Felino Eniesta, and you were hired on the spot."

"Something like that", she replied, "I have been working for him since then. He's taught me everything I know, has sheltered me from the envy of those who didn't like to see me promoted, and made the arrangements so that I could go to the University whenever it was necessary. Miguel, that man has been like a father to me!!"

I didn't say anything. I had just remembered a story that Ruperto once told me. It was the story about a peasant from his area. They called him "Cabecita". The man, who was a widower, had eleven children, six boys and five girls.

The boys worked on the cane fields from dawn to dusk. "Cabecita" stayed at home, in bed with his daughters.

As much as I desired, there was no way I could tell Perlita this story. It seemed that the burning query in my mind would remain unquenched and silent.

CHAPTER XVI
BUT, FOOL AS I THEN WAS...

During the following months I continued living according to a established routine. Weekdays I spent working at the Council; in the evening, after dinner, I went to study with Perlita. During all this time, she refused my efforts to convert our relationship into a love affair.

"We have to finish our studies and graduate", she would say, "After that, we'll see".

My love for her, with the passing of time, grew more and more intense. Jealousy and self doubt made living hell out of the weekends that I couldn't see her and my heart told me that she was with someone else. Could it be that she was with that rich bastard she worked for?

I had written a letter to Aunt Lidia some time ago and I was wondering why she had not answered it. At last, one evening, back at Cachita's, I found a letter from Los Remates. It was Lidia's answer, and read:

"My dear nephew, it has made us very happy to hear that now you don't have to leave Sabana nor abandon your studies. Everyone has been praying to God to help you, and perhaps our prayers have been heard. We were very excited thinking that you would be coming to live with us, because as you know, we love you very much. But if that is not to be, and the change is for your own good, we are happy. We are always here to help you as much as we possibly can. Chuchú sends you a hug. Kisses from your Aunt Lidia. P.S. Your grandmother is coming to stay with us. She was living alone in a rented room, in Helena, and I didn't want her to continue like that, because she is not well. She also sends many kisses".

"I'm going to have to go there and see grandmother", I thought.

And, as it turned out, a few weeks later I went to Los Remates to see her. But she had died, a heart attack had taken her from this world.

Aunt Lidia called to give me the news and tell me that they would be expecting me to be there for the funeral. "Hurry up and get here!", she urged me, "We have to bury her as soon as possible". In Yagruma's heat, corpses begin to rot in less than forty eight hours.

As soon as Aunt Lidia hung up, I called Ayer and informed him of what had happened. After telling him that I wanted to leave that same night for Los Remates, I asked if he could talk Esquerra and get me a few days off.

As I had figured, Ayer didn't have any objection. "Take all the time you need", he said, "And don't worry about anything here! I'll explain everything to Delmirito".

"Listen, brother, don't forget to punch my time card", I reminded him.

"I told you to go!", he replied, "Go ahead, there will be no problems! OK, go, go, go!"

I had figured on spending four or five days in Los Remates. Almost a whole week without seeing Perlita! I had a crazy feeling that I needed to talk to her, and I called her office.

"Miss Shell can't come to the telephone right now", answered a secretary, "She is in conference with Mr. Eniesta, and I have instructions not to forward any calls".

A wave of bile rose in my mouth, but I constrained myself, and left a message for Perlita to call me as soon as she could.

Two hours later she called.

"I'm sorry about the delay", she said, "We had a terrible day at the office today. Problems and more problems!"

"Why do you have to shut yourself up in that guy's office and leave instructions not to be bothered?", I asked, furiously.

"Because he is my boss, and I work directly with him. We have important matters to take care of", she answered very calmly, "That's why we leave instructions not to be interrupted. Besides, as far as I know, you aren't my husband, to be asking me explanations! Miguel, you are acting like a child again! But, tell me, what happened? Why did you call me?"

"My grandmother died", I said, "I'm leaving tonight for Los Remates".

"Oh, Miguel! I know how much you loved her!", she exclaimed, "Oh, you don't know how sorry I am! Listen, don't leave without seeing me, OK?"

"You know very well I won't", I replied, "That's why I called you. I'll stop by your place about seven. Is that OK?"

"Of course!", was her response, "Don't be late!"

When she came to greet me that evening I saw, gleaming in her eyes, the green sparks that only appeared when Perlita was under some real emotional stress.

"I've never been very good with words", she said, "It is not easy for me to express my feelings. But you know I'm feeling your sorrow, don't you? Even if I don't know how to say it with beautiful words!" And I saw tears run down her cheeks.

Taking her hand, I led Perlita to her big chair. She sat down quietly, drying her tears. In her violet dress with the low neckline that revealed the cleaving of her firm, full breasts, Perlita, by the gentle light of the lamp, was a sensual reverie. I looked at her, fascinated.

"When do you leave for Los Remates?", she asked.

"The bus leaves at eight thirty", I told her, "I can't stay very long".

"I'll bet you haven't had anything to eat! If you like, in five minutes I can fix something for you. Do you want it?"

"No, thanks! I'm not hungry. I'll have a bite to eat when I get to Helena".

"How long is it going to be before I see you again?", she asked.

"I'll be back here about the end of the week", I told her, "I'll call you as soon as I get back".

"Why so long?", Perlita protested, "After the burial, what else do you have to do in that town? Fooling around with some country girl?"

"No,", I replied, "No country girls. For me, there is no other woman in the world but you".

"Now, perhaps", she retorted, "But, if I were weak enough to return your love, how long do you think that passion of yours would last? Sooner or later you would be running around after some other woman".

"To convince yourself that you are mistaken, all you have to do is love me in return", I said, "Do it, and you'll see how all your doubts disappear when you understand how I feel about you".

Perlita, eluding a reply, changed the subject.

"Well then", she murmured, "I'll put Successions to one side and stick to Criminal Procedure while you are gone. We'll go back to Successions when you return".

I nodded in agreement. What did I care about the studies at this moment? In my heart and mind there was room only for her.

I couldn't handle that situation any longer. Perlita's evasions were making me desperate, as were her abrupt changes of attitude towards me. To think of the world where she dwelt and functioned saddened and filled me with despair.

Yet, in spite of all, I felt that life without Perlita would mean nothing to me.

A few minutes went by. Perhaps she guessed what I was thinking, because she tried to distract my attention making small talk. But I looked at her without hearing what she said. My obsession was to have her in my arms, right there, in that room, smothering with kisses the empty chattering with which she was trying to appease me. I rose to my feet.

"I have to go", I said, "It's getting late".

"But, Miguel, it's only seven forty", she said, "You can stay a little longer!"

Without answering, I walked to the entrance of the stairway.

"But, honey, what's the matter?", she asked, alarmed, "Why are you leaving like this? Wait a minute!"

I waited, leaning against the iron gate. She stood in front of me, looking at me with a worried face.

"Let's see now, what have I done?", she said, "Why are you acting this way with me?"

"You know very well what you're doing", I answered, "What do you think I am? Your puppet?"

She locked her eyes with mine. "We can't go on this way", she replied after a few seconds, "We have to sit down and have a serious talk when you get back".

She had moved closer to me. So close that I could feel her breath on my face.

"If I leave here without kissing you", I told her, "I'll never come back. I can't keep on like this, loving you the way I do, if you're never going to be mine".

I put my hands on her shoulders. Perlita didn't try to pull away. She stared at me, silently.

"Perhaps it would be better if we didn't see each other again", I concluded, "After all, graduation is around the corner, and then we'll take different roads. The hard fact is that I could never forget you. You have found a place in my heart".

Saying that, I turned half around preparing to leave. But she stopped me, grabbing me by a sleeve.

"Tell me that you'll be back", she murmured, "Promise me!"

I could see that she was trembling. Then, without saying a word, I put my arm around her waist and pulled her to me, and we were lost in an ardent embrace. We kissed anxiously, restlessly, and while holding her in my arms I could feel her breasts, hard against my chest as though they were a promise.

"Don't ever leave me", I whispered in her ear, "I couldn't live without you!"

"Never, my love, never...!", she murmured. And she kissed me again, leaving on my face a trail of her tears.

CHAPTER XVII
ON THE LONESOME ROAD

It was ten o'clock at night by the courthouse clock in Helena when the bus stopped in front of the ancient cathedral. I got off, suitcase in hand, and hurried to the nearby park, which was a gathering place for the drivers of the jitneys that went from Helena to Los Remates.

That night there were only three drivers at the park, waiting to see if some late travelers came along.

At that time of night, "El Teniente Morocó" was the only driver going as far as Los Remates, where he lived.

"How many passengers do you need before you'll go?, I asked him.

"At least three", he answered, "And that will only pay the expenses".

The jitney fare from Helena to Los Remates was one peso. "OK, I'll give you the three pesos,", I said, "But if you pick someone along the way, I get a discount!"

He said that was OK, but kept sitting there, without moving. I was impatient to get going.

"Well, what are we waiting for?", I asked, hurrying him, "Let's go, let's go! Those tires are made for rolling!"

"El Teniente Morocó" got up, without much enthusiasm, from the bench where he was sitting, picked up my bag, put it in the trunk and, motioning for me to get in, sat behind the wheel.

It must have been a long time since that guy had seen soap and water, judging by the stench that he gave off. To be farther away, I got into the back seat, pretending that I was tired and wanted to try to get a little sleep along the way.

The car was an old clapped-out Chevrolet. The interior stank of tobacco and sour sweat. Some passenger, a tobacco chewer, had spit on the floor some black and stinking gobs. The windows wouldn't close.

I sat on the right side, resigned to the inevitable, and the car finally started. "El Teniente" drove slowly, with the hope of getting some additional passengers, while the hiccups and protestations of the old motor broke the silence that reigned in the poorly lighted and empty streets.

We stopped for a moment at the market plaza to pick up a passenger. He was a peasant man, short and leathery, dressed in a guayabera and gaiters, with spurs and a black mustache that looked as though it had been dyed with shoe polish.

The driver introduced me to the new passenger, who happened to be from Los Remates, and the man spent the next fifteen minutes telling me the story of his life. His name was Bartolo Hernández, although in those parts everybody knew him by the nickname of "Salsita".

Bartolo Hernández was a small land owner. He had only a couple of acres of sugar cane, so, to make some extra money, he grew vegetables and raised a few pigs. "Salsita" finished his monologue when he realized, by my attitude, that his conversation didn't interest me.

Shortly thereafter, upon arriving at an intersection, the driver turned to the left, and minutes later we were riding in the countryside.

In the moonlight, the highway to Los Remates shone like a silver ribbon. The royal palms, along the lonely road, silhouetted against the crystal sky; the frogs broke with their croaking the silence of the night, and the call of the nocturnal birds came to us, every so often, across the deserted fields.

Finally, the emotions of the day and the fatigue of the trip began to make themselves felt, and I sank into a deep sleep.

The voice of our driver brought me back to reality.

"Chief! Hey, chief!", he said, "Let's go, get up, we've arrived!"

I got out of the car and looked around. We were stopped in front of a dilapidated small cafe, on a narrow street, dirty and badly paved, lined by a double row of small wooden houses, all wretched looking.

"Poor Lidia!", I thought, "Stuck in the planet's ass-hole!"

"Chief", the driver said to me, "I don't want to bother you, but I've been busting my butt since six o'clock this morning, I want to go home and to bed. If you'll do me the favor and give me my money..."

I realized then that I hadn't seen Bartolo again. "Where is Hernández?", I asked, "Did he pay you already?"

"Bartolo's stop is farther along, near the Quevedo switch", he explained, "When he goes to Helena, he leaves his horse with a friend who lives nearby. That's where he got off".

"OK, then, it is two pesos", I said, giving him the money.

He walked over to his jitney, to go, when I called him.

"Wait a minute! How do I get here?" And I gave him the paper with Aunt Lidia's address. He took a look at it.

"Uuuhhh! That's a long way off, chief!", he protested, "You are going to have a long walk! Look, this house isn't in the town. It's the sergeant's house, right?"

And it was already past eleven o'clock at night! That's all I needed..!

"What do you mean by `a long way off'?" I asked.

"Well, you have to go along this street to the end", he replied, "That's where the town ends. You'll see a mill, go along there until you get to a railroad crossing, turn to the right, and keep on until you get to a guardhouse. The sergeant's house is about two miles up, on the same road".

"Son of a bitch!", I thought, "I'm not about to start on that trip".

"How much would you charge to take me out there?", I asked.

I'm sure he had anticipated my question. "Half a peso", he answered.

Lidia and Chuchú received me with affection. Lidia took me to the last room in the house, and there, surrounded by four candles, was the coffin. She left me alone there.

Somebody had wrapped a rosary around the cadaver's bony hands, which were deformed by arthritis. My grandmother's face, pale and lined by death, did not have its usual fatigued expression. Standing by the coffin, looking at her for the last time, I remembered my childhood years, when I helped her fight against the rats, and she, from Sóstenes' old clothes, made me shirts and pants so I could go to school.

When I was leaving the room, they called me from the kitchen. Lidia had prepared café con leche and sandwiches, and while we ate I asked her about Sóstenes.

"He sent word that he couldn't come to the funeral", Lidia informed me, "He says he is sick. Something about his prostate, or his bladder... I don't know!"

"What about Goya?"

"Goya has the perfect excuse for not coming", Chuchú said, "She says she has to stay to take care of the old guy!"

Aunt Lidia could see that I was falling asleep and she suggested that I go to bed. So I did. Ten minutes later I was sound asleep.

I woke up early the following day. Approaching one of the room's windows, I saw that it was a clear and beautiful day, and, after washing and getting dressed, I went out to the patio to take a look around. Aunt Lidia's house, though modest in appearance, was larger than most of the neighboring ones.

Jasmines, bougainvillea, and hibiscus grew along the low fence surrounding the house.

They had only been waiting for my arrival to bury grandmother, so my aunt had sent notice to Jose, the owner of the hardware store. Jose was also the only funeral director in the area, and his pickup, which usually carried rolls of fence wire, pipe and other hardware items, also served as a hearse.

My grandmother's funeral didn't take much time. Short and sweet, like Jose said. He arrived in his pickup at ten in the morning. Gathered in front of the house, besides my aunt and uncle and myself, were several rural guards, a storekeeper and a few peasants, friends of Chuchú. There were also three or four women who stayed in the house to keep Lidia company.

We put the casket in the pickup and Jose drove slowly through a few alleyways until he finally came out at the road that led to the cemetery. We all followed on foot.

The cemetery of Los Remates, small and poor, showed signs of neglect. Most of the headstones were covered with weeds, and quite a few were broken. The priest had arrived, and was waiting, sitting in the shade of an enormous mahogany..

When we got close to the grave, I was surprised to see that the hole they had made was more than eight feet in depth.

"Why so deep?", I asked Chuchú.

"We have to make the graves real deep here", he explained, "If we don't, the wild pigs will come at night to dig up the bodies and eat them".

Everything went fast, because the sun was cooking our brains. The funeral was over before twelve o'clock. As soon as father Emilio had said the benediction, the coffin was lowered into the grave, and when the first shovelful of dirt hit it, we all began to leave. After seventy five years, that's all there was.

I had planned to spend three or four days in Los Remates with Lidia and Chuchú, but the memories of Perlita and the kisses that we had exchanged the previous night, made me change my mind. Having her in my arms again was all I could think of.

That night, when we sat down to eat, I told them that I had to return to Sabana the following morning, because I had been given only three days off from work to go to the funeral.

"You understand, Aunt Lidia", I concluded, "What it would mean to me to lose my job, now that I only have a few more months to go until graduation". She agreed, and made me promise that after I graduated I would come and spend a few days with them.

The following day, at noon, I was back in Helena, and was lucky enough to catch a bus about to leave for Sabana. The first thing I did when I got back to the capital was to phone "Caribbean Petroleum", to talk to Perlita.

"Miss Shell went out with Mr. Eniesta", a woman's voice said, "She won't be back in the office today".

That was like getting a bucket of cold water poured over me.

I spent hours pacing in my room, like a caged animal. At six o'clock I called her at home.

"Perlita hasn't arrived yet", said her grandmother, "Call her around eight, maybe she'll be back by then".

When I phoned at eight I still had no luck. I waited, anxious and angry, until ten thirty, and called again. This time it was Sofía who answered the phone.

"Perlita just got back ten minutes ago", she told me, "But she went into her bedroom. She said she is tired, and doesn't want to talk to anybody".

"Sofía", I asked, "Tell her that it's Miguel". She didn't know that I was going to be back so soon!"

"Wait a moment!", she responded, "Don't hang up!"

She returned in a few minutes.

"Perlita asks that you will please excuse her, but she has a severe headache. She says for you to come and study tomorrow at the same time".

For a moment I thought I was going to explode with rage. But I restrained myself, and with my last bit of remaining reason I thanked the woman and hung up the phone.

The following morning, when I got to the office, I found a mountain of papers and estimates. I went to work in silence, mechanically, answering in monosyllables when someone asked me a question or told me to do something. All my thoughts were on Perlita. Had she taken advantage of the fact that I was away to go out with Eniesta? Christ, why was she home so late last night!!?

In the evening that followed, exasperated and angry, I headed toward her house. Jealousy was devouring me. It was as though Perlita hadn't realized that her world had changed when I entered it.

I had to make her see very clearly that I was ready to do whatever necessary if someone or something tried to separate us!

But when she was in front of me, and I had her in my arms again, the uncertainty and worry that had been torturing me disappeared, like those storms clouds that the wind sweeps away. I kissed her anxiously. She returned my kisses, caressing me, giving me little bites, and searched for my tongue with hers.

"We can't go on like this, my love!", she said, breathlessly, when our lips separated for a moment, "We have to study! We are going to fail".

She released herself from me, softly pushing me away. I followed her to our usual place, near the mahogany table. She looked at me, smiling.

"We are insatiable!", she exclaimed.

Her smile and those words brought once again to my mind the insecurity and suspicions that had been tormenting me.

"Yesterday, I spent hours trying to get in touch with you", I said, "What happened? Why did you get home so late?"

The question, contrary to what I had expected, didn't seem to bother her.

"I had to go the American Bank", she explained, "One of their marketing experts came from New York to conduct a seminar for executives of American corporations in Yagruma".

"And why did you have to go?", I asked, "You are not a senior executive. Not yet, at least".

"You'll understand very shortly", she replied, very seriously.

"You went with Eniesta, right? Naturally, he needed your help!", I said, with sarcasm.

"With him and other people from the Company", she responded, unruffled.

"Are you going to tell me that the seminar lasted until nine or nine thirty in the evening?", I protested, "Where did you go afterwards? Whom were you with?"

Perlita rose from her chair and, without answering my questions, walked to the living room and sat on the sofa.

"Come here, and sit down with me!", she asked, "Here, at my side!"

"So you will calm down", she went on, "I'm going to tell you where I was last night. I was at the Casino Español, with some friends . I got to the Casino about seven. We were playing canasta for a couple of hours, I ate dinner at the cafeteria and then I got the bus and came home. Do you need witnesses? I can get them for you!"

Love had made a complete fool of me! I wanted to believe her story, I swallowed everything she told me!!

"If she had known that I was going to get back sooner than I had planned", I rationalized, "She surely would have been waiting for me".

Perlita was staring at me.

"We can't go on this way!", she exclaimed, "I'm going to talk to you very seriously, .up front with the truth, since we haven't gotten too far in our relationship. I'm going to ask you something without which I don't see any chance for us in the future. Listen to me, and tell me what you honestly decide!"

"I love you very much, my dear", she continued, calmly, measuring her words, "I'm yours since that night, when you left for Los Remates. I want you to understand that I've been interested in you since the first time I saw you in class. You had such sad eyes! I asked myself: Who can that be? Where does he come from? Tell me, didn't you ever notice?"

"I would have never dared to even dream of it", I replied.

"You have to get out of your head those suspicions and all that jealousy of yours", she added, after a pause, "First of all, because you don't have any reason to feel that way, and also, because you are insulting me by having those thoughts. I have come along with you this far because I love you. You are the man I want! But you have to have faith in me, you have to believe me... don't offend me with your jealousy and your suspicions!!"

I moved even closer to Perlita and started to put my arms around her, but she pulled away from me and kept her distance with an extended arm.

"No!", she said, in a decisive tone of voice, "No more of that until you promise me that you'll never doubt me again, that you'll never make me unhappy again with your absurd suspicions!"

I would have cut off my tongue with my teeth at that moment, had she asked me to.

"I promise you", I murmured.

"Are you sure?", insisted Perlita, coming closer to me, "Look, if you don't keep that promise, what we have will never last!"

I saw the look in her eyes. And so close, the scarlet flesh of her lips. If I had had to sell my soul to the devil to have Perlita, the agreement between Satan and I would have been signed, sealed and delivered in a matter of seconds.

I took her by the shoulders.

"I swear to you", I whispered in her ear.

Transported to another world, we kissed and caressed each other. I felt her heaving breasts in my hands, and she pressed herself against me.

"They are yours, my love!", she sighed, "Yours! Nobody else's".

CHAPTER XVIII

CLOUDS THAT GATHER ROUND THE SUN

Perlita wanted me to talk to her grandmother to formalize our situation, to which I agreed without objection. Her request seemed to remove any doubts that I might still have in regard to her sincerity.

So, upon asking the old lady for her granddaughter's hand, I was admitted to the house as Perlita's fiancé.

Perlita got busy calling all her friends and associates to tell them about our engagement, and announcing that we were planning to get married as soon as we graduated.

Shortly before Christmas, one night when we were together, she mentioned the dinner party that "Caribbean Petroleum" gave for its employees every Christmas Eve, adding that she would like me to go with her on this occasion, to meet some of her associates. I told her yes, although I wasn't overjoyed at the idea.

The party was held in the blue room of Sabana's International Hotel. There, Perlita introduced me to her boss, Felino Eniesta, the man who had helped her so much to move up in the company and who, according to what she assured me, had been like a father to her.

Eniesta was a corpulent, gray-haired man in his late forties. His features were regular, except for the lower lip, thick and protruding like a horse's.

He extended his hand and told me that he was delighted that Perlita's choice had fallen on someone like me and wished us all kinds of happiness, but I got the impression that his words were not sincere.

I looked sideways at Perlita and it seemed to me that she had blushed lightly, avoiding Eniesta's glance. But I finally decided that it was all an excess of my imagination.

After a few minutes Eniesta excused himself, saying that he had to talk to a well-known banker who had just entered the room. Perlita followed him with her eyes, until she realized that I was watching her.

"He's fantastic, that fat guy..!", she said, sighing.

Of all of my fiancee's associates that I met that night, very few impressed me favorably. I noticed that some of them looked at me askance, with a deriding half-smile.

Among those that I met at that party, one of the very few that I liked was Pino Osorio, a veteran executive who worked with Perlita in the marketing department, also reporting directly to Eniesta. Osorio was a likable man, tall and thin, bald as a billiard ball. He had been with the corporation for more than twenty five years, and had known Perlita's father.

I had the impression that, instead of the foolishness and the trivialities that were talked about in that group, he would have preferred to sit down with me and talk about other things.

Although everyone that attended the affair had brought their spouses or friends, nobody accompanied Eniesta. That hit me as rather suspicious.

"How strange that Eniesta didn't bring his wife!", I commented. Perlita's answer was brief.

"They are separated", she told me.

"I am sorry", I replied, for lack of anything else to say, "Is there any chance they'll get together again?"

"I don't think so", she replied, dryly, "He's talking about getting a divorce. But Mr. Eniesta's private life is none of my business".

"Nor mine, either", I concurred, "Let's forget it".

"That would be best"", replied Perlita. And wrapping an arm around mine, she offered me her lips.

Some weeks went by, with nothing disturbing my happiness. We got together in the evenings to do our studying, combined with breathtaking passion. On Saturdays we used to go the movies, since I couldn't afford more. Sofia was our chaperone. Life, for the first time, appeared friendly to me.

But cloudless skies don't last very long. It happened one Saturday night, coming back from the theater, saying good-bye to her with a last kiss.

"I'll see you tomorrow, my love", I said.

She had her reply ready.

"No, dear heart", she answered, "Not tomorrow. I promised to go to the Casino on Sundays, to play canasta".

That hit me like a kick in the stomach. I felt my temples throbbing.

"Promised!?", I exclaimed, "You don't have obligations to anyone but me!"

"No, Miguel, don't be like that", was her response, "I have lots of friends in the Casino Español, you know that! And sometimes I can't say no!" "Well, you have to learn how to say it!", I protested, "It can't be that you prefer to get together with those parasites instead of being with me!"

"Love, I don't have any choice!", she exclaimed, "Imagine, Conchita Pérez wants to play with me as her partner!"

That made me furious. "And who the hell is Conchita Pérez?", I yelled, "It must be something real important if you prefer to be with her!"

"Well, she's Polito Souza's wife", she cried, "He's the vice-president of the Casino. A very rich man! Very influential!"

Conchita Pérez! Now I remembered the story that Teodulfo Montes had told to Goyito, Ruperto, Abilio Castro and me one night, at Cachita's house.

"This guy, Polito, does he own a store on Arcángel Street?", I asked.

"That's the one!", she responded, surprised, "Don Polito Souza, the owner of `La Preferida'. Do you know him?"

"No, and I don't want to", I said, "But someone who knows them very well has told me the story of this couple. Polito Souza got rich by sucking the blood from the people that fell into his pawn shop business!"

"That's what you say, but he got rich!", cried Perlita, defending the Souzas with an energy that surprised me, "Now, with his money, Polito Souza is a personage! Money washes everything!"

This attitude of hers should have made me reflect on that side of her nature that I was now discovering. But I wouldn't face the truth, for love had blinded me.

Seeing that I was silent, she returned to the matter.

"Let's suppose that Don Polito has been unscrupulous and a blood sucker, as you say", she argued, "What does Conchita have to do with that? Does that make her a blood sucker too, just because she's married to him?"

"No, she is a blood sucker in her own right", I responded, "That woman has the moral fiber of a whorehouse madam!"

And without omitting any details, I told her the whole story of the love affair between Conchita and Souza.

"That's your friend Conchita!", I concluded, "So, now what? Do you still want to go to the Casino and play canasta with her?"

Far from being shocked, as I had expected, Perlita gave me a compassionate look.

"What kind of a world do you live in?", she asked, "Chico, wake up and smell the coffee! Miguel, I don't know what these people have done to get where they are, and I couldn't care less!"

"The important thing", she went on, "Is that they have climbed the ladder, and way up there, too! I wish you could see the diamonds that Conchita wears to the Casino! They are big as chick peas!"

Listening to her, I felt a certain uneasiness. That enthusiasm she had for money and ostentation was bringing to the surface the doubts and suspicions that still remained in the depths of my soul, like a slime that had settled there.

"Be tough with her", Ayer had advised me once, "If you let her get the upper hand, you're lost. Show her that you're the man here, or she's going to make a rag out of you!"

I appreciated his advice, which I never had the courage to follow. The idea of losing her devastated me. I thought that I would never be able to fill the vacuum that my life would become if she left me.

So, Perlita went out with her friends, every Sunday, to the Casino Español, to play cards with Conchita Pérez de Souza, "the one with the diamonds like chick peas", and alternating with other distinguished figures of Sabana's high society. I, meanwhile, at Cachita's house, eaten by suspicion and jealousy, sat alone in my room, trying unsuccessfully to concentrate on the textbooks.

I was sleeping peacefully one morning, in May, when Goyito woke me up, shaking me by the shoulders, with the news that Generalissimo Majencio Bautista, Yagruma's former dictator, had successfully staged a coup d'etat, deposing the constitutional president, Carlos Elío, and taking the reins of power.

Generalissimo Bautista, according to radio and television broadcasts, had the full backing of the Yagruman armed forces.

The transition from a democracy to a military dictatorship took place in a peaceful way. The few that had hoped for a citizens' rebellion in defense of democracy and the constitution were sadly wrong. All over the island, people stayed at home.

Typical Yagrumans are born political turncoats, so the general concern now was how to "get connected" with the new mandarins.

There were exceptions, of course. Colonel Quintín Arenas, commander of the military garrison in my province, refused to accept the new regime and called on president Elío to join him and his troops in the defense of freedom.

He almost succeeded, because, according to rumors, for a few minutes president Elío considered the possibility of joining the colonel and fight the usurper. But they say that his cousin Antonio, who was a typical Yagruman, was able to make him change his mind.

"Fight!? Don't be stupid!", they say he told the president, "We've got it made, man! Let's get the hell out of here! We might get killed, you know!"

Such practical advice didn't fall on deaf ears. His cousin's words cooled President Elío's patriotic ardor.

Hours later, the two Elíos, and their families, were to be found installed in a luxury hotel in Miami, probably doing their arithmetic to see if they could live comfortably in the United States with the few hundreds of millions of dollars that they had been able to put away during their years of public life.

A few days after his ascension to power, the Generalissimo convoked the Yagruman people to a mass congregation in front of the presidential palace, to let them know, as he said, what the real causes of the coup d'etat had been. Yagruman television would carry the great event, live.

Naturally, it would have been a discredit to the new government if only three or four poor cats showed up for the meeting. So, in order to awaken the people's civic interest, and see to it that they came to the gathering arranged by their leader, it was announced that, following the meeting, roast pork sandwiches would be distributed, free, to all those who attended.

The day of the assemblage, at the appointed time, the dictator, flanked by generals "Pancho" Bodeguilla and Basílides Sota de Mesada, appeared on the balcony of the presidential palace, with the purpose of explaining to the public the reasons they had for subverting the constitutional order.

General Bodeguilla spoke first, in incendiary patriotic tones, finishing his speech with this encouraging message to the Yagrumans:

"From today on, nothing will be done in Yagruma without the previous approval of our three parties: the one in yellow, the one in blue, and the one in white!!"

Upon hearing this, a claque of soldiers, policemen and sailors who had collected in front of the crowd, began, with loud cries, to shout "Viva el Presidente Bautista!!", applauding roaringly.

Following that, General Sota de Mesada, who was, not only a brilliant military man, but also an inspired poet, at least according to his immediate subordinates, recited one of his poems, titled "Let's Love and Praise Our Flag".

But the poem, to tell the truth, was not received with much enthusiasm by the crowd.

Generalissimo Bautista delivered the closing speech. According to him, the military had taken over the government of the island because they were convinced that it was their civic duty to protect the people, and especially the youth of the country, from the bad examples set by the Elíos and their gang.

"The conduct of these people", he assured his audience, "was a denial of the firm and severe moral principles on which the social organization and the family structure of the Yagruman nation rests".

Upon finishing his discourse, the Generalissimo saluted militarily and disappeared from the balcony, followed by his two cohorts.

Of course, everybody in Yagruma knew very well the real reasons that the Generalissimo had for breaking the democratic and constitutional rhythm of the country.

Years before, Bautista had been Yagruma's dictator for a long time; he and his closest associates had hundreds of millions of dollars in American and Swiss banks when they left the island, specially the Generalissimo, who, for quite a few years, lived better than the Maharajah of Kapurthala.

But, as the proverb goes, what comes easy, goes easy. And one fine day, Generalissimo Bautista and his friends found out that they only had a few miserable millions left.

"If, in order to fill up the sack again, one has to sacrifice himself for the country", the Generalissimo must have thought, "Well...that's the way it goes!"

And, no sooner said than done, he and his buddies orchestrated the takeover, and a short time afterwards he was again the head honcho in the happy island.

From the very first moment he could count on the support of the armed forces. Among his principal collaborators were brilliant military strategists such as generals "Pancho" Bodeguilla, Basílides Sota de Mesada and Mamerto Hernández Piranda, and also bright, totally scruple-free lawyers like "Papucho" Pérez and Neptúneo López Albo.

As always happened in Yagruma when there was a change in government, the Generalissimo's cabinet didn't waste any time in beginning massive lay-offs of public employees, filling the vacant jobs with cronies and protégés of the new military elite and of Bautista's "collaborators".

I couldn't sleep, for worrying about it. What was going to happen to me if I got fired? And of the plans that Perlita and I had made?

My anguish, however, didn't last very long. Probably, God felt sorry for me; I can't explain it otherwise. It so happened that Engr. Mardoqueo López Rastro, the new president of the National Council for Economic Promotion and my boss, Eng. Esquerra, were old friends and former classmates at Sabana University.

Esquerra went to see López Rastro and spoke to him about Ayer, Mrs. Llanes and me.

According to López Rastro's secretary, who witnessed the interview, Esquerra asked the new boss to overlook us in the firing.

"I need those three with me", said Esquerra, referring to us, "They are the ones that keep the department going. I don't care what you do with the others!"

"Tomorrow, when you see them", answered López Rastro, "Tell them not to worry. And, tell them also that they are lucky to be working for you".

CHAPTER XIX
LOVE LOST, BETTER THAN NONE AT ALL

At the beginning of May, classes were resumed at the University, which had been closed for about three weeks because of the military coup.

By the end of June, Perlita and I had passed all the remaining examinations, and a couple of months later, after complying with the requirements of the thesis, we graduated as lawyers.

Aunt Lidia, during that time, had called me to announce that Captain Cotrina, who before the coup was chief of the rural guard squadron at Los Remates, had been promoted to general and was now assigned to the army's general headquarters in Sabana.

Since Chuchú and Cotrina were good friends, the general had arranged for my uncle-in-law to be promoted to the rank of captain. Chuchú was given the command of the squadron at Chirimoyas, a town in the neighboring province of Las Gavillas, and Lidia and he were getting ready to move to their new destination.

The day that we went to the Law School to receive our diplomas, Perlita observed that it didn't look correct that I should continue working as a clerk at the National Council, now that I was an attorney

"It just so happens", I replied, "That this job is all I have to live on. If I don't pay Cachita, she'll kick me out on the street, lawyer or no lawyer!"

"Who said anything about quitting?", she said, "What you have to do is to begin to move up, to look for something that is consistent with your level and, above all, that will give you more money!".

"Three or four years from now I'll take the entrance examinations for the judiciary", I reminded her, "Time flies! By then, you'll be my wife, and you won't have to work anymore. Except in bed, of course!"

"Is that your only ambition, Miguel?", protested Perlita, impatiently, "To spend your life as a judge in some country town?"

"No", I responded, "If I become a municipal judge at age twenty-six, rest assured that before I'm forty I'll be in the appellate court. Do you know something? I'd like to be a justice at Helena's court of appeals. We'd live in one of those beautiful old houses by the sea!".

"That's all you want to be?", she said, contemptuously, "How do you know if I'll be willing to follow you, to share such a mediocre existence?"

"You will", I said, "If you really love me".

She looked away. "Three or four years is a long time", she observed, "Who knows what the future will bring us?"

Perlita, because of her work, had to deal with some of the most important law offices in Sabana. One night she told me that Azagaya, Mosteiro, Basolo and Nabochea, the attorneys for "Caribbean Petroleum", were looking for a recent graduate to join their firm.

"I think you may have a chance", suggested Perlita, "Look, I know Dr. Basolo, and I'm going to talk to him about you".

"Those big firms wouldn't care for an `out at the elbows' like me", I told her, "They want people from the upper classes, with good social connections. I appreciate what you are trying to do for me, but you are wasting your time".

"You are always so pessimistic!", she exclaimed, "You were a good student, you always got good grades! Besides, you also were a student of Dr. Azagaya's! Surely he remembers you!"

"Yes", I replied, "I got a hundred per cent on his final exam. But for guys like him, people like me don't count".

"I am going to talk to Basolo", she insisted, "And ask him to put in a good word for you with Dr. Azagaya. We'll see what happens".

I shrugged my shoulders. "If you want to", I said, "But don't get your hopes up".

A few days later, a sad and sorrowful Perlita informed me about the results of Basolo's efforts.

"I'm really sorry to have to tell you this", she began, "But I've got bad news for you!"

I stared at her.

"Dr. Basolo came to see me today at the office", she continued, "He told me that Dr. Azagaya remembers you as a very intelligent and correct student. He said that it would give him great pleasure to consider you for the position, provided you are a practicing Catholic and a member of at least three of the clubs of the Big Seven".

The Big Seven was the name given to the seven most exclusive private clubs in Sabana.

"Well, was I right or not?", I asked Perlita.

"Yes, you were", she replied, "But, remember, when one door closes, another may open".

"I'm not discouraged", I said, "I've had my plans made for a long time. You know what they are".

In the look that she gave me I thought I had read a hint of disdain.

One thing was for sure: my law degree entitled me, at least, to earn more than I was earning at the Council. I thought then of talking with Chuchú to see if it could be possible for his friend, the general, to recommend me.

I had always been able to count on my in-law, and without giving it any more thought, the following day I phoned Los Remates. When I told Chuchú of my problem, he said that he would talk to general Cotrina to see if it would be possible to get me into the Army's legal service as a second lieutenant.

"Cotrina and I are good friends", Chuchú told me, "And he owes me a few favors. I'll get in touch with him. I'll call you back as soon as I have news for you".

I thanked him and hung up. But for a few moments it had occurred to me that perhaps Chuchú was giving me the run around. People change when they get promoted.

Next Saturday, when I went for her to go to the movies, Perlita was bubbling over with happiness. She ran to me and gave me a big kiss.

"I've got something to tell you!", she announced, "See if you can guess what it is!"

"I give up", I replied.

"I got a promotion at work!", she cried, "And I got a raise, too!"

"And more and more her work and ambitions will be getting between us", I thought.

"Just imagine!", she exclaimed, jubilantly, "Now, I'll be in charge of all of our contracts with national retailers. When I graduated, Mr. Eniesta recommended me for it".

This last part I had already imagined. The kindhearted Felino, who took care of her like a father!

Perlita was very agitated. She seemed to be prey to unusual excitement.

"OK, then", she went on, "Tonight we are going to celebrate! Mr. Eniesta, Pino and Aurelita have asked us to have dinner at ‘La Valenciana’, and afterwards we'll go to 'Tropicalia' to see the new show, 'Abasí Abacuá'. They say it's a wild show, really exciting!"

"I'm not going to get mixed up in all that", I replied, "Don't count on me!"

She faced me, seething with fury.

"What!? What are you saying!?", she cried, "You can't do that to me, Miguel!! What are those people going to think!!?? We can't be rude to them!!"

"As far as I am concerned, they can think whatever they want to", I replied, trying not to lose control of myself.

"You can't talk to me that way!!", she spluttered, indignantly, "Not with that sluggish manner! And, if it isn't too much to ask, will you please explain to me the reason why you can't go?"

"Sure!", I replied, "I don't want to be your pals' laughing stock, that's all!! I am not going to those places, the most expensive in Sabana, with a few miserable pesos in my pocket!"

"If that's what's bothering you", she answered sarcastically, "You should know that we all are Mr. Eniesta's invited guests!"

That put the frosting on the cake.

"I don't need anybody to invite me!!", I roared, "That mother-fucking Eniesta can go to hell!! And listen well to what I'm telling you: I'm fed up with that bastard!! From now on, you'll limit your contacts with him to the office. Do you understand me!!??"

Instead of being intimidated, Perlita stood up to me with a fury the likes of which I would never have thought her capable.

"When you speak of that man that way you'd better wash out your mouth!!", she screeched, "Everything I am today I owe to Felino Eniesta, do you hear!!?? I owe him a debt of gratitude! And don't you ever use those words in this house again!! What do you think I am, anyway?"

"I'll tell you what you are, in case you have forgotten!!", I shouted, "You are my fiancee!! You are the woman that I am going to marry!! Your relationship with Eniesta may be as innocent as you claim it is, but I won't permit it!! You can have only one man in your life, and that's me!!"

Suddenly, Perlita's attitude changed. Fury had disappeared from her voice. She answered me with incredible calm and coolness.

"I beg you to lower your voice", she said, "You are frightening my grandmother".

In my blowup, I had forgotten the poor old lady. "I'm sorry", I apologized.

"You are kicking a dead horse, Miguel", she continued, "You have promised me, several times, that you would control your stupid jealousy. But you haven't done it! Besides, I don't owe any obedience to you. I am your fiancee, not your property! You are begining to think that I belong to you, and that you can manipulate me any way you want to!!

"Of course I'm jealous!", I interrupted, "How can I accept having to share your attention with someone else who influences your life as much, or more, than I do?"

"Well, we are right back in the same place", she replied without changing her frigid tone of voice, "Chico, I think it would be better for both of us if we don't see each other for a few days, to seriously think over what we have between us".

"Then", she went on, "We'll decide what we should do: if we can reach some kind of understanding to save our relationship, or to separate and each of us look for happiness in his own way".

I felt as though a bolt of lightning had struck in front of me! Perlita was talking about us separating, of not seeing each other! She was telling me that I might no longer have her kisses, nor the spasms of passion that I was accustomed to!

"My love", I exclaimed, "That won't be necessary ! Come here and sit by me! There's nothing that you and I can't work together!

"It isn't your love that is in doubt", she replied, "Rather if you're capable of making me happy. It's better if we take a few days to think over what we are going to do".

She glanced at her watch.

"It's almost eight o'clock!", she cried out, "Those people will be here any minute! You better leave, Miguel!"

I couldn't believe it. She was kicking me out of her house to welcome Eniesta and his gang! But I was such a slave to my passion that, shamelessly, forgetting my dignity, instead of telling Perlita to go to hell and leaving that place forever, I asked, abjectly:

"When will I hear from you?"

"We'll see", she responded, "These things usually take care of themselves".

Prolonging my stay there was humiliating. But I lowered myself even more. I grabbed her by the arm and tried to kiss her, but she rejected me with a shove.

"There's no time for that now!", she protested, "Get going, get going! I don't want those people to see you here!"

That night I didn't go directly back to Cachita's house. I entered the first bar that I found open, and did what countless men have done in moments like those. I got drunk.

I didn't hear from Perlita during the next several days.

Whenever I called her at the office, all I got was some secretary telling me that doctor Shell was at a meeting and had left instructions not to be disturbed. If I called her house, they would tell me that Perlita had gone out without saying where.

Since she usually went to the Casino Español on weekends, I called there several times, but wasn't able to contact her.

It finally got to the point where Perlita was all I could think about. All my desires, all my yearnings were concentrated on one single thought: to have her in my arms again.

One night, unable to remain closed up in the boarding house, I went out into the street and began walking aimlessly along Las Tunas Avenue. At some corner, a cafe attracted me with its lights and music from a jukebox. I walked in and went straight to the bar.

An hour later, half stewed, I left the cafe. Pushed by an unhealthy feeling, I headed toward Avenue of the Patriots, without really knowing why, nor what I was going to do once I got there.

In spite of the "load" I was carrying, I remember that it was a hot, humid night. When I got to the corner of Nineteenth Street and Avenue of the Patriots, I could see that although Perlita's house was dark, the stairway light was still on, proof that she hadn't returned yet.

"I have to see her!", I said to myself, "I'm not leaving here until I talk to her!" I decided then to go and sit on one of the benches on the Avenue, across from her house, to wait for her to arrive. But, as I got closer, I noticed a car parked along the sidewalk, in front of the house. It was Eniesta's automobile.

The thought of what I might find left me paralyzed for a moment. Then, driven by a morbid impulse, I walked back to the corner, and under the cover of night, without being seen, I crossed the avenue, stood next to Eniesta's car and looked inside.

A man and a woman were on the front seat, their bodies entwined in a close embrace. And, in spite of the darkness, I recognized them as clearly as though the sun had suddenly come out, lighting up the interior of the Mercedes.

They were Perlita and Eniesta.

I was instantly cold sober. Upon noticing my presence, the two separated swiftly and looked at me as if they had seen a ghost. Eniesta, motionless, seemed petrified with surprise. And, strangely, in that moment, instead of exploding in a rage, all I felt was an irrepressible urge to get away from there, from the wretchedness hidden in that car. I felt a desperate need not to see them, to be by myself.

Dumbfounded, devastated by the betrayal that had sent tumbling down the house of cards of my illusions, I walked away from the place. I could hear the voice of Perlita, calling me. But that voice resounded in my ears like the toll of a death-knell.

Back at the boarding house, I went straight to my room, took off my shoes and lay down on bed, still dressed. Exhausted, I fell asleep instantly.

It was after nine when I woke up. I went to the telephone, called the Council and told Ayer that I wouldn't be in to work, because I had a bad cold. Then I went back to my room and, sitting on the edge of the cot, I faced reality.

My life had changed. Now I could see that, from the very first moment, Perlita had been playing me for a sucker. While exchanging kisses and passionate caresses with me, her thoughts and desires were flying somewhere else, to the other guy, the one upon whom she could count for the protection, the security and the prestige that I was in no condition to offer to her.

Things that I had only confusedly perceived before appeared now to me very clearly.

Perlita and Eniesta had, surely, been involved with each other since God knows when. Pretending to go along with my love, becoming my fiancee and announcing that we were planning to get married after graduation, Perlita was only trying to inflame and heighten the passion of her aging lover, pressuring him to hurry up with his divorce in fear that she, tired of promises and waiting, would decide to stay with me.

Yet, I couldn't cry for the death of that love that I had feared so much to lose.

Perlita's treason was the kind that excites hatred rather than tears, that is never forgotten nor forgiven. On my night table I had a picture of her that she had given me when we were lovers. I grabbed it, tore it into a thousand pieces and threw it into the waste basket.

A couple of days went by before I returned to work. Perlita had been calling me at Cachita's house, but I didn't want to talk to her.

When I went back to work, the switchboard operator gave me several messages that Perlita had left, asking me to call her. I put them in a big ash tray that I had on my desk, touched a match to them, and watched as the pieces of paper burned, twisted and turned to ash.

Life had taught me to be patient. Someday I would laugh about the whole affair. I had always believed in the truth of the old Arab proverb: "Sit patiently at your tent's door, and you'll see your enemy's dead body borne before your eyes".

Cachita was waiting for me that evening, when I came back to the house. She called me out to her balcony, with a mysterious air, to tell me, in a low voice, that she had taken a telephone call from the Army General Headquarters.

"Lieutenant Julio Núñez called you", she whispered, "He wants you to call him tomorrow. Is he a friend of yours?"

"Never screwed him", I answered, rather amused to see how scared she was.

"Drop the bullshit, Miguel!", exclaimed Cachita, "Listen, are you in some kind of trouble?"

"No, of course not! Nothing like that!", I assured her. "It has something to do with some inquiries that my uncle, Captain Reyes, is making".

Cachita, calm now, gave me the piece or paper where she had written Lieutenant Núñez's phone number, and went off to supervise the preparation of dinner.

"Well", I thought, "It seems that Chuchú hasn't failed me. Let's see what comes out of this!"

The following morning I called the lieutenant, who turned out to be one of general Cotrina's assistants. He told me that the general wanted to see me in his office at the Army General Headquarters, and asked if I could be there at three in the afternoon. When I told him that I could, the lieutenant told me to report to sentry-box number eight. The sentries would be notified of my appointment with the general.

Esquerra gave me permission to leave work at one o'clock. After eating lunch at "La Rosa de Medina", I caught a bus that let me off a couple of blocks from the Army General Headquarters. There was a jeep driven by a sergeant waiting for me at sentry-box number eight.

He took me to one of several enormous buildings guarded by soldiers armed with Garands and machine guns. The sergeant and I went in, and he led me to a large room where a lot of people were waiting, sitting on chairs lined up against the wall. My guide told me to take a seat and wait.

About a half hour later, a tall, skinny officer with a thin mustache appeared at one of the doors and called my name. I answered his call. He was lieutenant Núñez, and told me that the general would see me as soon as he finished a meeting that he had to attend.

I had been now waiting for more than two hours, and was beginning to think that they had forgotten about me, when the lieutenant came out again and announced that the general awaited me in his office.

Cotrina, unlike what I had expected, was a polite man of calm and composed manners.

"Glad to meet you, Dr. Baró", he said to me, "Your uncle, Captain Reyes, is a good friend of mine, and I want to do whatever I can for him".

The general sat down, inviting me to do the same.

"Chuchú", he went on, "Asked me if I could get you a place in the army's legal service. Unfortunately, I can't help you in this.. In the first place, there aren't any vacancies at the present time. Besides, many soldiers and non-coms have earned law degrees, and we have to give preference to our own".

I listened to this with indifference. I had never been very optimistic about Chuchú's help and, besides, the idea of the military never appealed to me.

Thanking the general for having received me, I began to get up to leave, when he stopped me with a gesture.

"Not all of the news that I have is bad", he announced with a smile, "You see, a couple of days ago, talking with the Minister of Commerce, I mentioned to him that I wanted to do something for your uncle. By coincidence there is an opening in the legal department, and the minister, who owes me, offered it to me. Are you interested?"

Was I! It meant more money and less work. In Yagruma, public offices opened at eight in the morning and closed at one o'clock in the afternoon.

"Of course I am!", I told him, "General, I don't know how to thank you for your help. You can be sure I'll never forget it!"

"Don't be thanking me", he replied, "Thank your uncle, who has shown a great interest in your case". He scribbled a few lines on a piece of official paper, folded it, put it in an envelope and gave it to me.

"Be at the Ministry tomorrow morning", he told me, "Go to the personnel department and ask for Pedro Billot. Give him this note. He'll take care of everything".

Minutes later I got out at sentry-box number eight and left the Army Headquarters, heading to the bus stop.

CHAPTER XX
MERCEDES' WHOREHOUSE

Pedro Billotte, chief of personnel of the Ministry of Commerce, was a freckle-faced, red-haired short man. His face had that peculiar expression, mixture of anxiety and despair, that one can see on the faces of those suffering from constipation.

Like most bureaucrats, Billotte thought he was the center of Creation. To the employees under him, and to the ordinary citizens who came to his office, he was rough and despotic; not so with his superiors or with the rich and powerful, whose asses he kissed.

When I showed him the letter from general Cotrina, Billotte immediately dropped his arrogant manners and asked me into his private office. He even treated me to café con leche and sweet cakes.

"Your papers are ready, Dr. Baró", he announced, "Tell the general that I, personally, took care of it".

And he gave me a copy of the decree by which I was appointed assistant attorney in the legal department of the Ministry of Commerce, assigned to the Office of Trademarks and Patents, with a salary of one hundred and seventy five pesos per month, which at that time was considered a decent salary. Not only that, but I was protected in my position by the Yagruma Bar Association, which meant that I now enjoyed the blessings of job security.

"I might as well go on up to my office today and take charge", I told Billotte, "Whom should I see?"

"Doctor Alonso Aura", answered Billotte, "He is the Director".

As I was leaving, the chief of personnel offered to assist me in a any way that he could be useful, wished me good luck, and reminded me not to forget to tell general Cotrina how well he, Billotte, had treated me.

The Office of Trademarks and Patents was on the third floor of the ancient building occupied by the Ministry of Commerce. The elevator was so old, and in such bad condition, that I decided to used the stairs.

The office occupied the whole dilapidated floor. There were decrepit desks, grimy tables and rusty filing cabinets everywhere, and swarms of bureaucrats loafing around the place.

Some of them walked leisurely around the office, stopping every once in a while to chat with their pals. There were also small groups gathered around some of the desks, telling jokes, probably, because of the way they laughed; still others were sitting idly, drinking coffee or talking on the phone about matters that, apparently, were not official business.

Only a few employees were working, glued to their typewriters.

I asked a janitor where I could find Dr. Alonso Aura.

"That's his office over there", answered the man, pointing towards a sort of raised enclosure in one corner of the room. "But", he added, "If you want to see Aura, you'll have to talk to Faldas, first".

"With whom?", I asked.

"With Dr. Evelio Faldas", replied the janitor, "As a matter of fact, look, here he comes right now! Hey, Bello, this guy wants to talk to Aura!"

From the center of the office came a guy of medium height, about forty years of age, clothed in an expensive, well cut linen suit. A long, chrome cigarette holder was sticking out of one of the corners of his mouth.

Faldas, who had metal taps on his heels and on the points of his shoes, strode heavily, to make an impression. He walked with his head held back, but upon getting close to me he lowered it and looked me up and down.

"The director is very busy right now", he told me, with a voice that reminded me of the cawing of a crow, "What can I do for you?"

"I'm Dr. Miguel Baró", I answered, "I have been assigned to this office, and I am reporting for work".

"Oh, yes!", he replied, making an effort to seem friendly, "You are the one recommended by general Cotrina".

I took out my letter of appointment, which he took and read carefully.

"Welcome aboard!", he said, finally, extending his hand, "I'm Dr. Evelio Faldas. But come on, come on so you can meet Dr. Aura!"

I followed him into the director's office, at the other end of the room. Faldas knocked on the door and, without waiting for an answer, opened it and went in, making motions for me to follow.

The space had, for all its furniture, a rather beat up desk, two chairs and several metal cabinets, rusty and full of dents. Behind the desk, sitting on a wooden swivel chair, I saw a small man with an expressionless face. He had shifty, small black eyes under his bushy eyebrows, and two or three strands of hair carefully distributed over a shiny bald head. Dr. Aura was about sixty years old.

"Director!", greeted Faldas, "I would like to introduce Dr. Miguel Baró, who has been assigned to this office!"

Aura stared at me for a few seconds.

"Oh, yes!", he finally uttered, "Pedro Billotte called yesterday to tell us about you".

"You'll be in charge of him, right?", he said, turning to Faldas, "Bring him up to date, and explain to him how we do things here, and give him something to do". He turned back to me. "A great pleasure to meet you, Dr. Baró. You are in good hands here", he added.

And with nothing more, he turned back to the papers on his desk.

After leaving Aura's hideaway, Faldas took me to a corner of the office, where there sat a prehistoric desk, covered with dust and litter, half hidden behind rows of old metal cabinets, arranged in line to form a partition.

"This is your cubicle", he said, "There are enough pending cases in these cabinets to keep you busy for the next twenty years. But don't overdo it, OK? Take it real easy!"

"What are the work hours here?", I wanted to know.

"Whatever is most convenient for you!", responded Faldas. With a gesture of his hand he indicated the employees coming and going through the place.

"The clock and the time stamp are for the slaves out there!", he said, "We, the lawyers, come in at any time that pleases us, and we leave when we feel like it. How does it grab you?"

"Great!", I told him, "By the way, I have a few errands to run today, so if it's all the same to you, I'll be leaving now".

"No problem!", said Faldas, "Get going, get going! We'll see you tomorrow!"

That afternoon, at the Council, I quit the job that had made it possible for me to finish my studies. Afterwards I went and talked to Esquerra and Ayer, to fill them in on my new position and thank them for the help they had given me.

Now that I had a secure job and a little more money each month, the idea of moving to a boarding house of better quality, or possibly renting a room in a small hotel occurred to me. But so many memories tied me to Cachita's house, that I decided to stay there, provided that the owner would agree to rent me a room by myself.

Cachita not only put up no resistance, but gave me a big room with a large and comfortable bed and lots of furniture in pretty good condition, for just a few more pesos than I had been paying her. Breakfast, lunch and dinner were still included in the deal.

Besides Faldas and myself, there were three other lawyers in the office. Two of them were never around; the third one was an obese man, very talkative, who passed along his work to me so I could correct his numerous spelling mistakes. The fat lawyer's name was Silvino de Córdoba.

During the first two or three months I showed up early at the office, sat down at my desk and went to work. Faldas had given me a mountain of cases to be studied and brought up to date. So, with my excellent memory, in just a few weeks I learned the P's and Q's of trademark and patent legislation.

Like those three wise monkeys, I didn't see anything that I didn't want to, didn't hear anything that wasn't my business, and didn't talk about what I shouldn't.

The bus that I took every morning to go to work left me off at the corner of Traficantes and Congoja streets, right in front of a clothing store named "Gentle Sabana". From there, I walked along Traficantes Street to the ministry, that was three blocks away.

One morning, after I got off the bus, a man rushed out of the store and came up to me.

"Counselor", he asked, with a heavy Galician accent, "If you would be so good as to give me a few minutes".

I was immediately on guard. "What does this guy want?", I asked myself.

"I am Manuel Nogueira, the owner of "Gentle Sabana", said the man, "I need a lawyer, and I have thought of you. Could we go in the store and talk?"

I agreed, and followed Manuel Nogueira into the store. Still surprised at the way in which the merchant had approached me, I stopped to take a better look at him. Nogueira was between fifty five and sixty years old, short and pot-bellied, with a reddish face and gray hair, cut short. He was wearing a silk shirt and linen pants and vest. A heavy gold watch chain glittered over his abdomen.

I couldn't believe it. This Galician, who smelled of money, wanted to be my client!

I went with him to the enormous storage room in the rear part of the building, where he led me into a small office, improvised with wall-board partitions in one of the corners. In this office, besides a modern steel desk, there were a couple of filing cabinets and several chairs.

Nogueira sat down, inviting me to do the same. He was the first to talk.

"Well, counselor", he said, "I have a serious problem that I want to talk to you about, to see if you would like to handle it".

"Excuse me, señor Nogueira", I interrupted, "But, how is it that you want to use my services, without even knowing me?"

"I knew you were a lawyer by the badge you have in your button-hole", he said, "And from my friends at the Ministry I found out that your name is Miguel Baró, and that you are in the Trademarks and Patents Office. Isn't that so?"

"That's correct", I replied, "But, to be honest with you, before I make any commitments I want you to understand that it's been only a few months since I graduated, and my experience as a lawyer is very limited".

"Your honesty", declared Nogueira, solemnly, "Convinces me more and more that I haven't made a mistake in choosing you for this matter. Let me explain the situation!"

"I own", he began, "An apartment building on Naves Street, between Hospicio and Jovellanos, that gives me a pretty good income. Good tenants that pay punctually, never any problems...until one day! I'm sure you remember that musical group, `Los Chicos de Iberia', that became very popular in Yagruma".

"I sure do", I replied.

"Do you also remember when one of the group's musicians ran over with his car the madam of a high-class bordello?"

"Yes, of course! It was in all the newspapers, and on television; they had to give her a ton of money to put the matter to rest!"

"Exactly", agreed Nogueira, "As you know, it's been two years since the government declared war on prostitution".

"You are right. The police have closed down every brothel in the red light zones".

"Well", said Nogueira, "A few months ago, a well-mannered, respectable-looking lady came to see me. There was a vacant apartment in my building, and she wanted to rent it".

"The woman", he went on, "Had excellent references, didn't quibble over the rental price and gave me a month's rent deposit and two months' rent in advance. Man, with that, who's going to object?"

"And so what happened?", I asked, although I had a good idea of what he was going to say.

"Well, the woman moved in", the storekeeper answered, "But she has brought several young women into the apartment, and that wasn't in the agreement that she signed with me".

"Now, men are going in and out of the apartment at all hours", he continued, "The record player doesn't stop, and there is a traffic of all sorts of strange people! To make a long story short, a whorehouse is now operating in the apartment!"

"And, of course, you investigated and found out that the nice-looking lady was none other than Mercedes, the madam!"

"You are right", said Nogueira, "And now I have all the other tenants, and the neighbors, complaining about this situation! My tenants are threatening to move out if I don't get rid of Mercedes and her whores. They call the police, they call at home, at the store, constantly...my life has turned into an inferno!"

"But, well", I said, "You are a business man, a man of affairs, of wealth! You must have a law firm that takes care of your legal problems. Why don't you take this one to them?

Nogueira scratched his head.

"The truth is I'm ashamed to", he confessed, "Dr. Acosta, my lawyer, advised me to verify the credentials and the background of this woman, before agreeing to rent the apartment to her. But, well...you know, it was such a tempting offer that I didn't follow his advice. And now you see what I've gotten myself into!"

"You sure have a problem", I concurred, "The woman is now protected by the rental law. It's going to be difficult to get her out of there. And now you don't feel comfortable in going to see Acosta, after failing to follow his advice, right?"

"Yes, that's right", admitted Nogueira, "Now you know why I want you to take care of the matter".

"Very well", I said, "As I told you, it's going to be difficult to get Mercedes and her stable out of that apartment. Difficult, but not impossible. Now, there are hundreds of experienced lawyers in Sabana. Are you sure you want me to handle the case?"

"Maybe you don't have a lot of experience", answered the Galician, "But you have all the requirements for this job. You are young, you have energy, and you need to make some money".

"OK, we'll see what can be done", I replied.

"What do you have in mind?", he wanted to know.

"First, I'm going to talk to Mercedes", I explained, "Perhaps it'll scare her if I threaten her with a criminal proceeding if she doesn't agree to vacate the premises. If this doesn't work, we'll have to take her to court".

"Whatever you say, counselor", replied the storekeeper, “You are the lawyer!"

"My fee will be one thousand pesos, plus expenses", I made clear to him, "Agreed?"

"Absolutely!", declared Nogueira, adopting the most solemn air that he could, "You've got my word of honor!"

"It's been agreed, then", I said, "I'll start working on your case today".

Prostitutes, since they usually work nights, spend the mornings sleeping, so I decided that it would be better if I arrived at Mercedes' in the afternoon.

I stayed in the office until one o'clock, working on some old papers, to kill time. Then, after having lunch at a nearby restaurant, I caught a bus that left me off a short distance from Naves street.

Nogueira's building was a marble, concrete and glass dinosaur. It was three stories in height, with two large apartments on each floor. I went to the second floor and knocked on the door of the apartment, where, according to my client, Mercedes conducted her business.

From the other side of the door, through the peep hole which someone had just opened, came a young woman's voice, asking what I wanted.

"If you'll do me the favor", I replied, very seriously, "I have to see Señora Mercedes".

"Can I tell her what your business is?", asked the voice.

"It's a private matter", I replied, "I am Mr. Nogueira's attorney. Do me the favor of telling Mercedes that I have to talk to her".

"Wait a moment", she replied.

A few minutes later the door opened, a girl appeared at the threshold. She was about fifteen years old, dressed only in a thin, see-through blouse. Despite her youth, her pretty face, and the innocent smile of her fleshy lips, she already had the air of a veteran prostitute.

"Come in and have a seat", she said, "Mercedes will see you soon". I entered and sat in a very comfortable recliner.

The apartment was larger than it looked from the outside, and was furnished tastefully. From the far end came women's voices and laughter, and the noise of china and silverware clanging. Mercedes' girls were probably gathering strength for the evening's work.

A woman in her late fifties, dressed in a flimsy robe and slippers, walked into the living room and stood in front of me.

"You wanted to see me, son?", she asked, "What can I do for you?"

Neither her figure nor her appearance indicated the kind of business she was in. Mercedes was a woman of medium height, a little heavy, with her gray hair pulled back in a bun. She had very expressive black eyes and a friendly, almost motherly, attitude.

"Señora", I stated gravely, "I am Dr. Miguel Baró, Mr. Nogueira's attorney".

My doctorate didn't seem to impress her very much. "Yes, my boy?", she replied, "And, what is it that you want?"

"You are operating a house of prostitution in this apartment", I said, "And that's a serious crime. If Mr. Nogueira had known what you were planning, he would have never rented the apartment to you. Your falsehood has rendered that contract null and void!"

Mercedes was looking at me with a compassionate and mocking smile.

"This activity of yours is damaging to my client", I went on, with all the pompousness and the pedantry that only a rookie lawyer is capable of, "Not only are the other tenants threatening to move out if you don't put an end to this situation, but the value of the property is depreciating because of your activities!"

Mercedes, patiently, had let me get it all out.

"Well, my lad, I'll ask you again", she said, "What is it that you want?"

"I have come here to advise you that you have ten days to move out of this apartment and turn over the key to my client", I declared, putting on a tough face, "If not, I'll be forced to take you to court and, in that case, let me advise you that we could be talking about a possible criminal case!"

I had hoped to scare Mercedes with this last bit, but, to my surprise, she began to laugh out loud.

"Oh, my dear", she finally exclaimed, "That old queer has no shame to have hired such a decent and sweet boy! Look, my lad, do you know why he has gotten you involved in this? Because he could not find any other lawyer who was willing to face up to Mercedes!"

"Look", she went on, "Very important and influential people visit this house of prostitution, as you call it. Dr. Torres Borrás, for instance".

Torres Borrás was one of the justices of Yagruma's Supreme Court. He had a reputation of being an incorruptible judge, and also a man of high moral principles.

"Well", continued Mercedes, "He is one of my customers. Torres Borrás has a taste for the unusual, and here, in my house, he finds what he likes. I'm going to give you some advice, because I don't want to see you wasting your time. If you know someone in the police force, verify first who my customers are. When you find out, it is going to make you week in the knees".

Now I was getting worried, thinking that there might be some truth in what Mercedes was telling me. But I managed not to loose my cool. I rose and faced Mercedes.

"Señora", I said, trying to look and sound stern, "If within ten days you haven't vacated the premises, we are going to bring charges against you. Good afternoon!"

"Whatever you like, my boy", she responded, in a friendly manner, "Remember: you are always welcome here!"

Back at Cachita's, I called my old friend Abilio Pardo, who was now a lieutenant with the police department.

By good luck, Abilio was home. I explained the case I was involved in, and asked him if he could verify, by means of his contacts in the police department, whether or not Mercedes was, as she said, above the law.

"I hate pestering you", I told him, "But this is the first client that has come my way, brother, and I don't want to come out looking like a fool".

"Always glad to help my friends", answered Abilio, "Let's see what I can do. I'll get back to you, OK?"

I was on my way to the shower when I had a telephone call. It was Sofia, Perlita's aunt.

"I have something here for you", she said, "When can you come by for it?"

My heart was pounding. "Tonight, if that's convenient", I answered.

"That's fine, come by about eight", she told me.

"I'll be there", I said and hung up the phone.

When I got to Perlita's house, Sofia was waiting for me at the door. She had an envelope in her hand.

"Excuse me if I don't ask you in", she said, "But mama isn't well, and she'll get all nervous if she hears you".

"That's all right, that's fine", I replied, "Sofia, could you please ask Perlita to come down for a moment?"

"Son", she replied, sweetly, "Follow my advice and forget Perlita. She doesn't live here anymore. Before she left, she gave me this letter to deliver to you. Well, excuse me, but I have to go. I don't want to leave mamá alone".

I took the envelope that she handed to me. "Sofía", I asked, "Where is Perlita?"

"I don't want to talk about that", she responded, "After all, Perlita is my niece".

And with that, Sofía went back into the house, closing the door behind her.

I returned to the boarding house and, back in my room, I opened the envelope and took out the letter, which was dated two days before. It was only one page, neatly typed, without errors or corrections. Every one of its words are forever engraved in my memory.

"Dear Miguel", it said, "When this letter reaches your hands, I will have arrived in Macuto Beach, Venezuela, where Felino is waiting for me.-- He is attending a series of meetings that top executives of the petroleum industry are holding in Caracas.-- Felino is taking me with him, because we are going to get married as soon as his divorce decree is final.-- Marco Antonio Ermitas, the president of Caribbean Petroleum in Yagruma, will be retiring in a few months, and it's a sure thing that Felino will be his replacement.-- I don't doubt it, because he is a very influential man, with fantastic connections. I don't have to say any more than he is a personal friend of generals Bodeguilla and Sota de Mesada!--"

"Felino Eniesta has been my protector, my advisor, my support.-- He made me a woman, I gave him my virginity long ago.-- Nevertheless, I deeply cared about you. When you and I became engaged, Felino, who didn't want to lose me, started the divorce proceedings, and things changed.-- He talked to me, and convinced me, and finally I decided to take the steps that I have mentioned above.--"

"You and I, perhaps, might have been happy together, if you had been a strong and ambitious man.-- But your idea of happiness was to become a country judge, living on a salary, and I want much more than that in my life. I wish you a lot of luck in whatever road you take, and I'll say good-bye to you from one who hopes to continue to be your friend, Perlita".

Incredibly, that letter didn't unleash a tempest of fury in me. I only felt myself belittled, for the sad part I had played.

Abilio Pardo called me the next day, at the office.

"Listen!", he said, "Mercedes was telling you the truth. Don't try to fight her, because you'll be wasting your time! Not only Torres Borrás, but other Supreme Court justices and several Circuit Court judges are customers of hers. Besides, all kinds of important people go there: the inspector general of the army, big-time lawyers, senators... a lot of fat cats!"

"What I'm going to tell you is absolutely confidential", he added, "The police have orders not to bother Mercedes and to ignore all complaints made against her. Another thing that I found out: your client, Nogueira, had contacted all kinds of lawyers before you, and none of them could do anything. Well, listen, I have to go. The major is calling for me!"

I said good-bye to Abilio, left the ministry and walked the three blocks to "Gentle Sabana". There I faced Nogueira and told him about my experience with Mercedes, and what Abilio had revealed to me.

"For the time that I have wasted in this matter", I said, "My fee is five hundred pesos".

"Not five hundred, not even five pesos!", he screamed, "You haven't done a damn thing!"

But when I grabbed the old bastard by his tie and dragged him over to a corner of the store telling him that I was going to show him a thing or two, he agreed to give me three hundred pesos.

I put the money in my pocket and went to my favorite bar.

When I got back to Cachita's house, I was drunk. Once in my room I took off my clothes, lay down and fell right to sleep.

That night I dreamt that I was again in Mercedes' bordello. The door to one of the bedrooms opened, and out came Perlita, dressed in a white gown that gave her an almost virginal air. I wanted to take her in my arms, and kiss her, and take her away from that place. But she pushed me to one side and went over to sit on the lap of a scrofulous old man who was waving around a big stack of bills while crying out to her from his chair.

CHAPTER XXI
THINGS YOU LEARN ALONG THE WAY

The cost of living had been rising steadily in Sabana, and the salary that I earned at my government job barely stretched out to cover the month.

It would be at least three years before the entrance examinations for the judiciary were held, and even supposing that it came out well for me, I would have to wait some time before my appointment as a judge in any of the provinces.

I was thinking about how I could find the means to make some extra money when, one day, I stumbled upon Dr. Humberto Gastaigorri, whom I had known since I was a child. Gastaigorri was then a law student. He used to come to Helena every weekend to visit his fiancee Yadira, the daughter of our neighbor, Selfas, the Moor.

Once in a while, grandmother or Aunt Lidia made tamales or pumpkin fritters. On these occasions they invited Yadira and her fiancee to come and try them, and that's how I came to know the future attorney.

Two years after Gastaigorri graduated from law school, he and Yadira were married. The newlyweds went to live in Sabana, "subsidized" by old man Selfas, who had made a lot of money with a silk and small goods shop he had in Helena.

It was said that Gastaigorri had acquired the habit of disappearing from public view three or four times a year and going, God knows where, to plunge himself in drunken binges, only to reappear after a few days, fresh as a daisy, to resume his professional duties.

That was the only reason why the old Moor was never happy with his daughter's marriage. If he reluctantly gave his consent, it was due to the pressures from his wife and his sister-in-law, a pair of shrews who were the ones that wore the pants in that family.

Selfas was an important stock holder of the "Alliance of Merchants, Inc.", a major insurance company headquartered in Sabana, and he used this leverage to put his son-in-law in touch with Cándido Alvires, the chairman of the board.

In order to please Selfas, Alvires, who was a nationally known figure in Yagruma's political world, found some legal work for Gastaigorri to do. The young lawyer accomplished his task so quickly and efficiently that Alvires, impressed by his talent, finally ended up appointing him legal counsel for the insurance company.

When Dr. Ramón Arau Santín, Yagruma's president at that time, made Alvires his Minister of Public Works, the latter took Gastaigorri to the Ministry with him.

Minister Alvires, during his tenure, increased by several millions his already respectable fortune, with the help of Gastaigorri. A new and important department, the Office of Technical Assessors, was created in the Ministry, with Gastaigorri as its director. The man was in clover, permanently.

Frankly, the idea of going to see Gastaigorri in his office had never crossed my mind. Not expecting anything from anybody had already become part of my nature.

One afternoon, before returning to the boarding house, I walked into a cafe, to have a beer. I was standing up at the bar when someone put a hand on my shoulder.

"Miguelito Baró", said a voice, "Long time no see, huh?"

I turned around. Humberto Gastaigorri was standing beside me. He hadn't changed much since I had last seen him, in my grandmother's house, ten years before.

"Tell me", he went on, "How's life treating you? What are you doing? OK, let's have a beer. On me!"

We sat at one of the tables and had a beer together. In a few minutes, in generalities, I told him what my life had been in Sabana, leaving out, among other things, my sad affair with Perlita.

Gastaigorri listened to me, frowning.

"Miguel", he said, when I had finished my story, "How would you like to come and work with me, at the law office?"

His offer, naturally, caught me by surprise. But it didn't keep me from considering it, and I told him that I would be delighted.

"Let me explain", Gastaigorri went on, "I don't have the time to personally take care of much of the business that they bring me. That's money lost! You would be in charge of those cases".

"How come you don't have any associates working with you?", I asked.

"I had in the office a young lawyer that handled those matters", he answered, "But the son-of-a-bitch married a rich farmer's daughter. His father-in-law bought him a law practice in San Gumersindo, where they are from, and the fellow is there now, living like a king".

"Well, thanks for the opportunity you are affording me!", I replied.

"I want to be sure that you understand", he said, "I can't offer you a salary, not any guarantee of a monthly income. But, for each case that you handle, or in which you intervene, you will get something. Besides, with me, you will be gaining experience, and that's worth money".

"No problem!", I answered, "When do I start?"

"Tomorrow", he said, "Be there before ten o'clock!"

He gave me his card, with his office address and telephone number.

"I'll be there!", I promised as I left.

The following morning I spoke with Faldas and, after telling him of my agreement with Gastaigorri, I informed him that, beginning that same day, I would be devoting a good chunk of my time to private practice.

"Don't worry, brother!", he assured me, "Come by here every once in a while and, of course, don't forget to come on paydays to pick up your check. You know how it works! Today for me, tomorrow for you! One hand washes the other, and they both wash your face!"

My work as Gastaigorri's associate opened my eyes to the realities of the practice of law in Yagruma. One day, shortly after I began working for him, Gastaigorri called me to his private office.

"Miguel", he said, "Go to the Sabana North district court and see Blasco, the chief clerk. Tell him that I need him to hasten the sentence in the Fundora-Villapol divorce. We won't get paid until we have a sentence! Tell him that if he speeds it up, I'll owe him a consideration".

That kind of errand worried me, still a greenhorn in the field. I was sure that the chief clerk would take offense at that proposal, because Gastaigorri's offer smelled of bribery.

When I arrived at the court the following morning, I was nervous, scared. I didn't know how to deliver the message.

Finally, it was my turn to speak with the chief clerk. José Hernández de Blasco was a short man, fat and flabby, with a cautious manner. He dressed smartly, and was saturated with cologne.

"What can I do for you, counselor?", he asked.

I didn't know how to begin.

"Mr. Blasco", I finally said, almost stammering, "I am an associate of Dr. Gastaigorri's. I bring you a message from him".

"Yes?", replied Blasco, "What's the matter with Gastaigorri?"

"It has to do with the Fundora-Villapol divorce, that has been heard by this court", I began, as cautiously as I could, "Dr. Gastaigorri needs the final settlement in the proceedings, so that he can collect his fees".

I stopped here, thinking of how I could arrange it so as not to appear too abrupt. But I couldn't think of anything.

A few seconds went by, and realizing that the chief clerk seemed to be growing impatient, I swallowed dry and got right down to it.

"Gastaigorri asked me to tell you", I told him, "That if you would hasten the sentence, he would owe you a consideration".

I was in a cold sweat.

"They are going to kick me out of here on my ass", I thought. I looked at Blasco, waiting for an explosion, but the guy didn't appear to be offended. Much to the contrary!

"A consideration?", he asked, "How much, counselor?"

I gave a sigh of relief. "That, he didn't tell me", I replied, "But, remember, Mr. Blasco. Gastaigorri never eats alone".

Blasco smiled. "Tell him not to worry", he said, "I'll have the sentence ready in a couple of days".

I learned a lot from Gastaigorri during the years that I worked for him.

Gastaigorri, intelligent and astute, knew how to get around the "incorruptible" chief clerks, how to "earn" the good will of the judges, and how to "convince" experts and witnesses to inform and testify according to best interests of his clients.

He never practiced criminal law, and had nothing but contempt for criminal lawyers, who, according to him, were a bunch of ignoramuses, good only for bribing policemen and buying up judges and justices.

After having worked for some time in his law office, I had learned by memory all the trickery, the chicanery and the crooked ways, the mastery of which was indispensable to any attorney who wanted to build a successful practice in Yagruma.

When the time came to pay for my services, Gastaigorri showed his true colors, because when it came to money, he was a miserable and niggardly bastard. I have seen few people that suffered so much over coughing up a few pesos.

Nevertheless, Gastaigorri would forget his sordidness once in a while, and became munificent, even splendid to the people that worked for him.

On one occasion, representing one of the workers of a pasta manufacturer, we filed suit against the employer's insurer, alleging that the flours used in the industrial process, acting as allergenic agents, had caused our client a dermatitis of the most severe kind.

Well then, the day that there were three Supreme Court rulings declaring that allergy was a professional illness, and therefore to be indemnified, insurance companies were due to suffer considerable losses.

It hardly needs to be said that it was enough to know that the word "allergy" was written in the claim, for lawyers for the National Association of Manufacturers to come running to Gastaigorri. It wasn't long before they reached an out-of-court settlement.

I never knew how much money he got from that arrangement, nor how much he gave to our client. All I know is that I got a check for five hundred pesos, so he must have pocketed at least ten thousand. And in those days ten thousand pesos was a ton of money!

He had to have noticed the face I made when I took a look at the amount written on the check he gave me, but said nothing. That evening, when I was getting ready to leave, he called me from his private office.

"Hey, come here!", he said, "Do you have any plans for the evening?"

"Nothing", I replied, "The same as always! Eat, read a little and...to bed!"

"Then, you are not in any hurry!", exclaimed Gastaigorri, "Wait a minute, buddy! We're going on down and have us a drink!"

I didn't feel much like drinking, but I couldn't tell him no. After all, in that place, he was my boss, and the extra money that I earned working for him was really welcome.

When we came out of the building, Gastaigorri's car, with the chauffeur at the wheel, was already waiting for us. We went a few blocks from the office, to the Club Lafayette, one of Gastaigorri's favorite watering holes.

The bartenders, who knew what he liked, put a bottle of Chivas Regal in front of him. I ordered Barbancourt with tonic water, and there, in the quiet atmosphere of the bar, almost deserted at that hour, we talked of whatever came to mind: politics, literature, philosophy, women.

Gastaigorri was a cultured man. I listened to him with pleasure, but when the bottle was showing its bottom, he was slurring his words, and upon getting up to go to the men's room, I noticed he was walking unsteadily.

He came back to the table, stood next to me and put his hand on my shoulder.

"Miguel", he asked, "How long has it been since you `polished your saber'?"

"I'm way overdue", I replied.

"Well, listen", he said, "Finish your drink, and we're going to a place that I know, so we can have a `tune up'. OK?"

"I hope it won't be too expensive", I said.

I had to save my money; when I began to study to prepare for the examinations I wouldn't be able to take any cases, and this would make quite a hole in my finances.

"You're not going to spend anything, buddy!", cried Gastaigorri, putting his arm around my shoulders, "All this is on me! We are celebrating today's victory!"

"It's nine o'clock", I advised him, "What time do you have to be home? Yadira is going to have a fit!", I exclaimed.

"Don't worry about Yadira, or her fit!", he replied, "She left yesterday for Helena and will spend several days with her folks!"

"OK, then, let's go!", I agreed.

Gastaigorri paid for the drinks, and we left the Lafayette. The chauffeur was waiting for us, leaning against the car.

"Listen, Godín", said Gastaigorri, giving him a ten peso bill, "Go, eat, and then catch the bus home. I'm going to drive now".

Godín, evidently, was accustomed to these escapades of his boss, because he showed no surprise. He put the money in his pocket, thanked Gastaigorri, and asked him what time he should report for work the following morning.

"Be in the office at eight o'clock!", he was told.

Godín said good night to us, and off he went.

"The owner of the place where we are going", Gastaigorri informed me, "Has been a client of mine for many years. There is no luxury there, but it is comfortable, and he has a doctor that examines the women regularly. Ah, and the ‘cattle’ are first class!"

The car was weaving its way through the horrendous Sabana traffic. My friend drove safely, in spite of all the alcohol he had consumed. Twenty minutes later we stopped in front of a two-story house of ordinary aspect, on San Francisco street.

The front door was ajar. Gastaigorri pushed it open and we went up the dark and steep stairway until we came to an iron gate that kept us from entering.

The place reminded me of the nights, now long past, when I went to study with Perlita and she ran to open the grating of the stairway, also steep and shadowy, at the house on the Avenue of the Patriots.

Gastaigorri pressed the bell button, that was recessed on the wall. Seconds later, a man's high pitched voice came down from above.

"What do you want?"

"Manolo, it's I", cried Gastaigorri, "I've brought a friend! Please open the door!

"Oh, yes, doctor, yes, indeed!", replied Manolo, "Do me the favor of closing the grating behind you!"

We heard the sound of an electric buzzer, and the gate opened. Closing it behind us, we continued our ascent until we reached the second floor level, where a tall man awaited us. He had long, unruly blond hair, rouged cheeks and lips painted a coral red. Manolo's shirt was pink, with pleated cuffs. The women's black panties he had on were showing through the thin fabric of the white trousers that he was wearing.

Manolo greeted Gastaigorri, shook my hand, and we proceeded into the living room.

"Make yourself right at home", he told me, "I hope you spend a few pleasant moments here with us. The doctor knows this place well, so you see, you could hardly have a better recommendation! And now you will have to excuse me. You know how it is, you have to circulate. Love makes the world go round!"

And he left us, his massive buttocks shaking rhythmically as he walked.

One didn't have to be a Frank Lloyd Wright to see that the house had been remodeled in order to adapt to the needs of the business. Three additional rooms had been built inside of its area, leaving the living room half its former size. What used to be the family room, "la saleta", was now a well supplied bar, juke box and all.

"Well, let's have another drink!", said Gastaigorri. I declined the invitation.

"No, thanks", I responded, "I'm going to sit in the living room for a while. I want to see what kind of goods your friend has here".

"I'm going into the bar", he replied, "If you need me, you know where to find me".

I saw no prostitutes chatting with the clients, and the doors of all the bedrooms were closed. Manolo's girls were busy taking care of other customers. There were six men in the living room, sunk into their rocking chairs, waiting for the women to be available.

I picked a chair that looked comfortable, lighted a cigarette, and began to observe them, reservedly. Three of the men looked like bureaucrats or store clerks; the fourth, a red-faced, pudgy fellow sitting in front of me, had the appearance of a shopkeeper. The fifth was a smartly dressed Chinese, with lots of rings on his fingers. I don't know why I figured he was a loan shark.

Finally, sitting by my side was a bald man of about fifty years old. With his well ironed white "guayabera" and his black-framed eyeglasses, he cut a serious and respectable figure. He might have made a favorable impression on me, had we not met in a whorehouse.

After a few minutes, two of the doors on the hall opened, and from each room a woman and her john came out. The men, still adjusting their pants, headed for the stairway; the two prostitutes came into the living room. One of them, a young girl, still an adolescent, walked right up to my neighbor, the bald man of honorable aspect.

With a note of absurd deference in her voice, she asked him:

"Sir, are you going to screw?"

"Not now", answered the `caballero', gravely, "I'd rather wait until Estela is available".

The refusal didn't seem to bother her, because she turned around without insisting and went towards the fat man with the brick-red face, who was whistling, calling her over. Fatso sat the girl on his lap, and whispered something in her ear. She gave a forced laugh, nodding in assent to whatever the man had proposed.

They both got up. He put his arm around the girl's waist and off they went, to the room that she had left just a few minutes before.

The other woman was sitting in one corner of the living room, not too far from me. I watched her closely. She was a slim mulatta, with fine features and short, well arranged hair. I was attracted to that woman. She noticed this and, returning my look, slightly winked an eye.

"Let's get it over with!", I said to my self. A brothel's atmosphere was far from being my favorite milieu. Besides, it was late now, and the following day I had to go to work. Fifteen minutes with her would be more than enough!

Afterwards I would get dressed, and go home to get some sleep. If Gastaigorri, who was still stuck in the bar, completely smashed, wanted to stay there, let him!

But when I came nearer, and saw her close up, my heart began to pound. The woman's eyes had a yellow glow, like those of Perlita. Waves of memories flooded my mind, nights in the past, with her, our first kiss, the night I caught her in the arms of her boss.

The voice of the prostitute brought me back to reality.

"What's the matter, my friend?, she asked, "Am I so ugly that you wouldn't even talk to me?"

"No, of course not!", I answered, feeling somewhat ashamed, "You are a very beautiful woman. Please excuse me! Sometimes, things come to my mind that I shouldn't be thinking about".

She looked at me with those beautiful eyes, but she wasn't smiling now.

"I know", she said, "I have the same problem. Listen, won't you buy me a drink?"

Naturally, I said yes, and we went to the bar. She ordered a "depth charge", and I had more Barbancourt.

"I remind you of someone, right?", she asked me after the first two swallows.

"Yes, it's true", I admitted, "How did you know?"

"In this job, you learn to know people", she said, "A woman dumped you, right?"

"Something like that", I replied, "Let's talk about something else".

"You know", she confessed, "The guy who broke my heart was white like you. We were together for three years".

"And what happened?", I asked, "He left you high and dry?"

"No", she responded, "He died". She put the empty glass upside down on the table. "Well", she said, "Shall we go?"

"May I know your name?", I asked.

"Rosario", she answered. And seeing that I couldn't keep from smiling, she added, very seriously, "Really, that's my name. Why would I tell you a lie?"

When we left the bar, she took my arm and we proceeded that way towards the room.

A night-light tinged the room with a soft pink dimness that kept the shadows away from the bed.

Rosario held me close, and I put my arms around her waist.

"Kiss me", she whispered, "Don't be afraid, I'm healthy".

We kissed, with long and moist kisses. Our tongues caressed each other's and entwined, but my mind was far away. She noted this, and pushed away from me.

"Tonight you are going to forget everything", she told me, "I'll guarantee you that! Come on, come with me!"

Softly, Rosario pushed me towards the bed, and amid caresses and kisses she helped me undress. When she saw me naked, lying on my back, she got up.

"Look!", she said, letting her dress fall to the floor.

She stood there, motionless, for a few seconds, bathed in the lamp's rosy glow. Rosario made a perfect nude. She was slim, but had a marvelously formed body, with small firm breasts and fantastic buttocks, high and solid. The light reflected the points of her breasts and the black, curly triangle of her sex.

She came towards the bed, leaned over me and searched for my tongue with hers.

"Lover", she said, "I'm going to take you out of this world!"

And that's exactly how it was.

CHAPTER XXII
THE MONKEY DANCES FOR MONEY

My life revolved around the Ministry of Commerce and Gastaigorri's law office. Sometimes, on Friday nights, I used to take Rosario to a little hotel on the beach, where we would spend the weekend playing the newlyweds. So that's how my days went by, only disturbed, once in a blue moon, by memories of Perlita.

About three years after I had begun working for the government, the public competitive examinations for entrance to the judiciary were finally announced. I had to go around, getting together the certificates, affidavits, credentials and other documents that were required for admission to the exams.

The material that I had to study consisted of several thick volumes that covered all the civil, criminal, business, labor, constitutional and administrative legislation that was currently in force in the Republic of Yagruma.

I realized that I was going to have to tie my pants and knuckle down with the books. True, I had been devoting some time studying at night, but upon seeing the program I realized that there was no other way but for me to get at it if I wanted to pass the exam.

The following day, at the Ministry, I explained my situation to Faldas. I told him that in three months I was going to sit for the exams, and that I needed all my time to prepare myself.

Faldas, as usual, smoothed the way for me.

"Go home right now and tie yourself to your books", he told me, "Don't come here anymore except to sign the payroll and pick up your paycheck! And good luck, brother! Listen, Baró, remember me when you get to the Supreme Court!"

Gastaigorri also made things easy for me.

"Take the three months off!", he agreed, "I'll get by here as best as I can".

I left the law office heading towards a nearby pharmacy, where I bought a good supply of Benzedrine sulfate to keep me awake and alert during the long sleepless days that awaited me. Back at the boarding house, I showered, had dinner and closed myself up in my room.

Cachita had given me a great big old desk. I arranged on it the piles of books and other printed material that I had to study for the exam, and I sat down to work.

For more than three months I was tied to that desk and those books, without getting up for anything, except to go to the dining room at meal time, and to the bathroom.

Some time after the exams were held, the scores with the names and grades of the passing candidates would be published. The judgeships, then, were awarded as the openings occurred, with those highest on the score being the first to be appointed to the available positions.

The ones on the middle and lower ends of the scale might have to wait two, three or even four years until their turn came. I didn't shelter any illusions, because it was an open secret that, in order to be high on the score, you had to be recommended by a Supreme Court Justice or by one of the really fat cats.

My hope was to pass the exam with a decent grade. That would place me in the score high enough not to have to wait more than a couple of years to be appointed to a judgeship. And in order to make this possible, I studied furiously, day and night, sleeping three or four hours a night, sustaining myself on coffee and Benzedrine pills. I had heard it said that some of the examiners were merciless.

That year, the examination tribunal was composed of three justices, doctors Marco de la Cerna, Ramiro Jar, and Roderico Fernández Orejón. The first two were, reputedly, fair and honest men. Not so Fernández Orejón, who, according to what I had heard, was a crotchety old despot. Rumor had it that he was a tubercular, and, to tell the truth, he looked like a walking mummy.

The examinations were oral.

Fernández Orejón presided the tribunal. He used to throw the most difficult and complicated questions at the candidates, and seemed to enjoy immensely the anguish and bewilderment of his victims.

A couple of weeks after the process had begun, it was finally my turn to take the exam. Jar and de la Cerna asked me several questions on topics that I had no difficulty answering. Afterwards, Fernández Orejón took over and began his query.

He covered every subject. But I had studied and memorized those damn books so thoroughly and exhaustively, that I knew them from left to right, from right to left and from top to bottom. He had hardly finished asking me a question, when I would spout out all the correct answers, without hesitating or faltering.

Finally, apparently convinced that he couldn't fail me, the old bastard called it off, and I was dismissed.

Two months later, the scores were published. Of the more than five hundred candidates taking the exam, only a hundred and seventy six passed. I was number ninety nine, which meant that I would have to wait about three years before being appointed to a judgeship.

Nevertheless, I didn't feel discouraged, because I was twenty six then, and becoming a judge at age twenty nine went according to the plans that I had forged for the future, when I was still a high school student in Helena.

With my salary from the Ministry of Commerce, and the extra money that I made working for Gastaigorri, I had more than I needed to live on. It didn't bother me that I would have to wait; life had taught me to be patient.

Meanwhile, under the Yagruman sky, things were happening that would have worried the citizens of any country where civic conscience and political maturity were not, as in my native country, outlandish ideas.

Generalissimo Bautista and his clique already had spent too much time feeding at the through. Now it was time for them to let go and make room for others that had been denied this luxury for some time, and were anxiously waiting for a chance to "get theirs". As one of the opposition leaders used to say, "We are also God's children, damn it!"

The anti-Bautista groups were becoming more daring every day, more audacious. Now, they not only planted bombs in public buildings in Sabana, but also began to attack the police and throw Molotov cocktails at patrol cars.

The anti-terrorist bureau and other police units tried to contain the wave of terrorism, torturing and killing suspects right and left, with little success. The Generalissimo had the scare of his life when the caravan that was taking him to a political gathering in a nearby town was attacked by an action group with grenades and machine guns.

Bautista escaped uninjured, but some of the soldiers in his escort were killed, and others wounded. The reprisals were bloody; the following day, the bodies of twenty suspected terrorists, riddled with bullets, were found on the streets.

The people, though, didn't seem to care about the tragedy in their country. They kept on going to the ball games, festivals and cabarets as though nothing was happening. Restaurants, theaters and bordellos were always full, and money was pouring in as never before in taverns and motels.

Something happened, then, that captured the attention of the news media for several days, and even awakened some interest in the exceedingly small number of citizens that worried about the country's future. A group of anti-Bautista exiles, led by Casto Cruz, a former Sabana University alumnus, had landed on Red Beach, in the easternmost province of Levante, determined to bring down by force of arms what they called "Bautista's bloody tyranny".

Upon launching their boat toward Yagruma, the expeditionary invaders left behind a number of their compatriots who, like them, wanted to go to the island to get in on the shootings, so that they, too, would be entitled to their share of the spoils when the regime fell.

But, as it could be expected from my fellow citizens, those that were left behind, anxious to get their vengeance and screw up the invaders, had called the Yagruman military and denounced their comrades' plan. And so, when the expedition landed on the beach, there were special units of the Yagruman army waiting for them.

A few minutes later, the Republic of Yagruma had eighty one more names to add to its list of "martyrs". But Casto Cruz who, as usual, was in the rear guard, could escape, along with nineteen invaders who survived the army's deadly barrage.

In Yagruma, the Red Beach event didn't appear to make a big impression on the people.

"They are just a bunch of lunatics!", some said.

"They'll wipe 'em up in a couple of days!", others offered, talking about those that had escaped.

"Is he some dumb SOB, this man?", Gastaigorri asked me, talking about the rebel leader, "When they catch him, they'll make mince-meat out of him!"

With the passing of time, the landing on Red Beach was no longer front page news. And in Sabana, as in the rest of the island, it was business as usual, again.

Casto Cruz either had one of the most powerful amulets that santería priests could make, or he made a pact with Satan, because, under circumstances in which others would not have survived, he and the remaining invaders managed to evade the net extended by the army. Finally they took refuge in Sierra Dómine, the great massive mountain range in the south of Levante province.

In the Sierra, they ran upon a band of convicts and cattle rustlers led by Florencio Pérez, an old criminal that had become a legendary figure in the area. Florencio used to say that, in Sierra Dómine, he was the bull that bellowed the loudest.

Florencio and his boys lived by robbing, cheating and extorting money from the area farmers, merchants and industrialists. The military couldn't catch them, because Florencio's gang knew more secret paths, footways and hideouts in the Sierra than any veteran army trackers.

The bandits took the invaders to an almost inaccessible place in the heart of the Sierra, out of the reach of Bautista's soldiers. There, during the first few days, Casto Cruz, who had remarkable persuasive powers, was able to convince Florencio, an illiterate, that his revolution was going to succeed.

In a ceremony held on a barren ground in the midst of the tropical jungle, Casto Cruz accepted the rank of Generalissimo that the revolution conferred on him, and named old Florencio a colonel in the insurgent army.

Afterwards, the men enjoyed a hearty meal with plenty of rum and beer, and the company of a pack of country girls from the area, brought there for the enjoyment and relief of the insurgents.

The small army of convicted felons, now converted into idealistic guerrilla fighters, built Casto Cruz's headquarters in a recondite spot, high in the Sierra. Now installed there, without having to worry about possible attacks from the army, Generalissimo Casto Cruz turned his attention to the procurement of the funds that he needed to get his revolution going.

He began levying "war contributions" on farmers, cattlemen and industrialists. His men also extorted money, under threat of death, from the area's bourgeoisie.

By use of radio equipment that sympathizers in the United States had sent, Generalissimo Casto Cruz exhorted the citizens of Yagruma to unite with him in the fight against the "tyrant" Bautista.

A few hundred Yagrumans responded to this call. Among them were unemployed people who had lost any hope of finding work, ex-convicts, adventurers and opportunists who were beginning to see a possibility for the revolution to succeed.

There were, of course, some doctors without patients and quite a few starving lawyers.

Those who wanted to be admitted as guerrilla fighters in the Sierra had to have credentials issued by Casto Cruz's agents operating in the cities. Once the permission was granted, they had to travel to San Jaime, capital of the province of Levante, and wait, in hiding, until an emissary came to take them to the foothills of the Sierra. There, a group of hillbillies were waiting to take them to the august presence of the Great Leader.

The country folk, with its proverbial hatred of the cities and the government, cooperated with the rebel forces, selling them provisions, acting as spies, and giving misleading information to Bautista's army, that lost a few men in ambushes prepared by the guerrillas.

A year after his arrival in the Sierra, Generalissimo Casto was at the head of a force that was calculated at about four hundred men, equipped with modern weapons. Casto had been extending his operations, and now controlled a large portion of Sierra Dómine.

Money overflowed the revolution's coffers. Close to the insurgent's head-quarters, an airport had been built where planes landed every day, loaded with bags full of money sent from the United States by Pro-Casto Clubs and other leftist groups. Besides, the income from "war taxes" had swollen as the size of the rebel-controlled areas steadily increased.

Also, all over the island, merchants, planters, cattlemen and industrialists were beginning to consider the possibility that "that Casto shithead" would actually accomplish the overthrow of Generalissimo Bautista. So, they began sending tons of money to the man in the Sierra, to earn the good will of the possible future "macho".

Meanwhile, from Sabana, Bautista and his cohorts tried to create the impression that they were putting up a real effort to finish off Casto Cruz and his bunch.

More than thirty thousand soldiers were sent to Levante and other places around the island where other groups, upon seeing that those in the Sierra were getting ahead of them, felt that they needed to rise up in arms so as not to lose out in the final sharing.

Bautista's military leaders "were under strict orders to destroy the few remaining insurgents still roaming Yagruma's countryside", General Sota de Mesada announced, in a televised press interview.

Still, at this time there were those who wondered how was it possible that a handful of terrorists could keep at bay and defeat thousands of well trained and superbly armed soldiers.

Quevedo's proverb answers this question: "Mr. Money is a powerful gentleman".

The officers commanding the troops, after arriving at their positions, received orders to "limit as much as possible the encounters with the enemy", and "proceed with extreme caution".

Those children of Mars, who were nobody's fools, began to smell what was cooking in far away Sabana. Since they knew their leaders well, they realized that Bautista and his clique would be skipping the country any day, leaving them high and dry.

From that moment on, the motto of the military commanders in charge of the campaigns in the Levante and Las Millas provinces was "FILL YOUR POCKETS!" And it was all so easy! It was done by manipulating, in collusion with army suppliers, the requests for ammunition, materials, food, equipment, tools and medical supplies; by not reporting the names of the soldiers who got killed, whose paychecks they cashed, pocketing the money, and by exacting "protection" money from business, farms, sugar mills and cattlemen, following the example of their enemy, Generalissimo Casto Cruz.

Another important source of income for Bautista's officers was what they called "transit permits", a name coined by General Cheo de Varas, a veterinarian turned guerrilla fighter who had landed with Casto Cruz in Playa Roja.

Cheo de Varas remembered having read that, according to Napoleon, the only three things needed to win a war were money, money and money.

That stuck in General Cheo's head, so he decided to find out if the Great Corsican was right.

The case of army colonel Obdulio Goñi, executed by firing squad in La Barraca fortress shortly after the overthrow of the Bautista regime, is proof that money was the determining factor in the triumph of Casto Cruz's revolution.

Dr. Gastaigorri was the lawyer who defended colonel Goñi before the revolutionary court that sentenced him to death.

Gastaigorri told me that Goñi had confided to him that, one night, lieutenant Recaredo Pijuán came in, very excited, to his office. At that time, Colonel Goñi was in command of the forces stationed at Camarones, a town in western Levante.

"Colonel!", cried the lieutenant, "There's an insurgent in the guard house that wants to talk to you! He says he has a message for you from general Cheo de Varas!"

Colonel Goñi was a sluggish and apathetic man.

"Well, bring him in, then!", he ordered, "Let's see what he wants".

The lieutenant went out and returned a few minutes later with a pair of soldiers escorting a tall, skinny and long-haired man, with a long tangled beard that reached down to his chest.

The man with the beard gave a military salute, which the colonel did not return.

"If you have something to tell me", said the colonel, looking at his watch, "Spit it out now, because in five minutes we are going to shoot you".

"Colonel", responded the man, unruffled, "I bring you a message from my chief, general Cheo de Varas. But I have orders from my general to deal with you in private. I mean, no witnesses! I assure you, colonel, that you will not be sorry to hear what I have to tell you!"

"Well, I hope that's true, for your own good", replied Goñi, "Wait outside!", he ordered the lieutenant, who left immediately with the two soldiers, leaving the rebel alone with the colonel.

"C'mon, I don't have time to waste!", said the latter, "What's the message?"

"As you surely know", replied the insurgent, "Generalissimo Casto has started the invasion of Yagruma, from Levante to the West. The final objective is the taking of Sabana, which will precipitate Bautista's fall".

"Everybody knows that!", interrupted the colonel, "Is that what you have to tell me?"

"No, it's not only that", replied the other, "You know, this morning general De Varas and his column will be marching toward El Guareao, to link with the forces of General Canuto. Tomorrow night we'll be crossing by less than two kilometers to the north of Camarones".

Colonel Goñi didn't seem to be impressed by the news.

"Column, my ass!", he responded with his usual calm, "For your information, we know that your chief has no more than fifty men with him. If they try to pass by here, there won't be one left alive. We'll wipe them all out!!"

"That's exactly why general Cheo has sent me to talk to you, colonel", explained the courier, "If you try to stop the column, they'll return fire. And then, you know, there's going to be dead and wounded. Who needs that? We'll all lose!!"

The messenger fell silent for a few seconds.

"Suppose there is a confrontation and you force us to retreat", he went on, talking to colonel Goñi, "We'll just have to change our route. And, do you think Bautista is going to thank you for it, or reward you with a promotion? Don't make me laugh! The man has very little power left, because no one can stop the revolution. You can bet anything that right at this moment he is making plans to flee the country!!"

"The bastard is telling nothing but the truth", thought Goñi, "What could he want?"

"My colonel", continued the emissary, who seemed to be reading Goñi's thoughts, "We can come out of this in good shape, without anybody being the loser. Not very far from here, one of my comrades is waiting, with ten thousand American dollars in a packet. If you change the sentinels and the patrols so that the column can pass tomorrow night without being bothered, this money is yours".

Colonel Goñi figured that after the triumph of the revolution, he would be kicked out of the army. And the ten thousand dollars would be a Godsend in Miami!

"When do I get the money?", he asked. Emotion and greed made his hands shake perceptibly.

"Come with me to where my comrade is", said the man. "And the packet will be yours. Of course, you'll have to sign a receipt for us as a proof that you received the money in payment of your services".

The colonel opened the door of his office.

"Lieutenant Pijuán, bring the jeep right away!", he ordered.

When the lieutenant arrived with the jeep , the colonel and the rebel were waiting for him in front of the building.

Colonel Goñi called the lieutenant to his side. "This man has promised to provide us a very valuable service", he said, "But one has to be on guard all the time with these mother-fuckers. Grab your machine gun and get in the back. If they try to pull anything funny with us, blow their heads off!"

Lieutenant Pijuán was habituated to obeying orders without asking questions. The colonel got behind the wheel, with the courier at his side; the lieutenant installed himself on the back seat with the machine gun on his lap, and the jeep disappeared in the darkness.

Sócrates Govín, my former classmate at Helena High School, had joined Casto Cruz forces since the beginning, and made lieutenant colonel. But months after Casto' s triumph, Sócrates, who was not a communist, took refuge in the Embassy of Costa Rica where he spent two months until, finally, Generalissimo Cruz agreed to provide him with safe conduct to leave the island.

I met Sócrates once, in Miami. We had lunch together, and there he laughingly admitted to me that the money from the United States, and the "transit permits", opened the road for Casto Cruz and his boys during the "invasion".

I asked him if he ever had to go into a real battle.

"Well, yes...once!", replied my friend, "It was in central Las Millas, close to Santa Clotilde. Incredible, but the officer in charge of that detachment was a commander that wasn't for sale!"

"And how did that end up?", I asked.

"We won", said Govín, "Because the town's people, seeing that we had arrived there, realized that Bautista was on his way out.

"They not only threw people on the streets to help us, but the mayor and his councilmen asked the commander to cease fire and surrender, because Casto Cruz was the hope of the country!

"Great patriots, these Yagrumans!", he added, laughing.

CHAPTER XXIII
SHADOWS OVER PLEASURE LAND

Casto Cruz forces, divided into three columns, had entered the province of Sabana and were getting closer to the capital. Bautista's army, totally demoralized, didn't even try to stop the insurgents.

Generals Cheo de Varas, Cirilo Seisdedos and Juan Negrón, respectively, were each in command of a column. Generalissimo Cruz, worried about the possibility that someone might take a pot shot at him, stayed at his headquarters in Sierra Dómine.

Though the rebels were equipped with the best in modern armaments, the three generals' best and most effective weapons were the bundles of dollars that Casto Cruz had given them to "convince" Bautista's army officers to let the three columns pass by without a fuss.

Boy, and were those dollars effective! When an insurgent column passed by to the north, the army was looking for them in the South; if the column was to pass near a town, most of the garrison would be previously routed to some distant area, with orders to "search and destroy the enemy".

The few remaining soldiers in town wouldn't dare to venture beyond its limits. And that was the way it was!

The "castos", as the people already called them, entered into the province of Las Millas and linked with other insurgent groups from the neighboring Sierra Guirigay. In a matter of hours, Santa Blanca, the provincial capital, surrendered to the "castos". When this happened, there wasn't a single Yagruman left who didn't agree that the days of generalissimo Bautista were numbered.

In the cities and towns that fell into the hands of the rebels, a "revolutionary" militia was immediately organized. The militia, a paramilitary corps created by generalissimo Casto Cruz, had the mission of preserving order in the "liberated areas", replacing Bautista's army and police, that were disbanded at once.

As could be expected, thousands of Yagruman carpetbaggers were joining the militia, with the laudable intention of having revolutionary credentials to show when the hour arrived for the struggle over the spoils.

According to reliable sources, the taking of Santa Blanca finally convinced generalissimo Bautista that his head smelled of gunpowder. Witnesses have confirmed that Bautista, alarmed at the way things were turning, called an urgent meeting of the most important figures of his regime.

All of them agreed with "el Presidente": the future couldn't look more sinister. Casto Cruz had sworn that when he captured Bautista and his gang he would put them at the disposal of the revolutionary tribunals created by a new constitution dictated by him.

And generalissimo Casto had already made known that the only sentence that he would permit the tribunals to pronounce would be "guilty", and the only possible penalty would be death by firing squad.

"It seems to me", said general `Pancho' Bodeguilla, who was one of the first to arrive, "That there is only one solution. If you, my general", he said, looking at Bautista, "Insist on continuing the fight against that rabble, blood is going to run down the gutters in Yagruma. And you know how it is: fathers without sons, sons without fathers, wives without husbands, husbands without wives, hate between brothers! Goddammit! We can't let that happen in our beloved country!"

Bodeguilla's words were enthusiastically applauded by Major General Oberto Hernández Piranda, Bautista's adopted son.

"Jesus Christ, Pancho, that's what I call a hell of a speech!", he cried, "Listen, you guys, we better get the hell out of this fucking island! If those bastards grab us, they'll make flour from our bones!"

"What Oberto is saying is exactly what I was going to propose!, exclaimed general Bodeguilla. He addressed generalissimo Bautista.

"You, señor Presidente", he said, "Have half a billion dollars in Swiss and American banks. That's not counting your real estate holdings in New York, Florida and Spain. We..."

Days later, on a TV program, an eyewitness to the meeting stated that Bautista, evidently, was bothered by this reference to the awesome amount of wealth accumulated by him during his second dictatorship. He interrupted general Bodeguilla.

"OK, let's get to the point, let's get to the point!", he cried, "Pancho, what should we do!?"

"Gentlemen, we are comfortable", replied Bodeguilla, now addressing the group, "I've got my little nest egg, in the United States and in Switzerland, the same as all of you. What the hell, the worst of us has thirty or forty million bucks on the other side of the pond! OK, I can have a couple of planes ready tonight at the military airport. I say we'll get in them and leave for Miami. All the good things of life will be waiting for us!"

"But as for me, I feel sorry for the friends that are going to be left behind, those that have been at my side!", protested generalissimo Bautista, "What's going to happen to them when they fall into the hands of those sons-of-bitches?"

Major General Hernández Piranda was so nervous that he dared to raise his voice at his adoptive father.

"Papá", he shrieked, "This is every man for himself! You have to think of yourself! Fuck the others! They'd do the same to you, if they could!"

Dr. Neptúneo López Albo, Bautista's Secretary of the Treasure, interrupted.

"I admire your noble feelings, señor Presidente", he said with his usual sugary intonation, "But I dare beg you to seriously consider the gravity of the situation: if we evaluate the data..."

"Cut it out, will you!?", yelled Bodeguilla, giving López Albo a shove, so hard, that the latter stumbled into a corner.

"Señor Presidente", he urged Bautista, "I'm going to say it as clearly as I can. We either leave tonight, or in a week those mother-fuckers will be pissing on our dead bodies!!"

Generalissimo Bautista did not waste any more time. "Get things ready!", he told Bodeguilla. He then turned to his wife, who had kept silent during the whole discussion.

"My dear", he said, "We'll only need a couple of bags! Put in some winter clothes, because it's blowing like hell up North!"

That night, shrouded in utmost secrecy, generalissimo Bautista, his wife and children, left Sabana on board a military plane, heading for the United States. Leaving in the same aircraft were generals Hernández Piranda, Bodeguilla, and Sota de Mesada, with their families.

A second plane, also loaded with members of Bautista's innermost circle, took off minutes later.

Very early next morning, Yagruma radio transmitted a message that generalissimo Bautista had recorded before his departure. In it, the former dictator told the Yagruman people that he had taken the painful decision to abandon the fatherland.

"I have chosen the rocky and bitter path into exile", he stated, "To put an end to the flow of Yagruman blood".

After Bautista's getaway, a provisional government was formed, with general Eudosio Cantrillo as its leader. Cantrillo, in a matter of hours, surrendered unconditionally to the rebel chiefs advancing toward Sabana, and placed himself at their disposal.

Uniformed militia began to appear immediately all over Sabana, commanded by so-called leaders from the underground, and in a couple of days what was left of the Yagruman armed forces had been disarmed and garrisoned.

The week after, generalissimo Casto Cruz, the new dictator of Yagruma, made his triumphal entrance into the capital, followed by his army and also by thousands of militiamen from the "liberated" provinces. When the newspapers published the names of the general staff of the revolutionary army, to my surprise, I saw among them, with the rank of colonel, that of my old friend Abilio Pardo.

Casto Cruz didn't delay in showing his intentions. By his orders, revolutionary tribunals began functioning in Yagruma, constitutional guarantees were suspended, and the writ of habeas corpus was abolished.

They began to execute people left and right all the length and the width of the island. Those who were accused of conspiring against the regime, those suspected of being anti-Communists, and those who openly expressed their opposition to the new order, went to stand, helpless, against the firing squad wall.

The Casto Cruz regime began the confiscation of the assets of everybody and everything that was considered counter-revolutionary. Shortly afterwards, all banks, foreign as well as domestic, were nationalized.

Private property was abolished, and all business and industries of the country were also nationalized or confiscated.

As a result of these policies, food soon became scarce in Yagruma. It could be obtained in limited quantities, and only by those who had the ration book issued by the government.

Opposition to the new regime had been organized clandestinely, and to combat this new threat to his rule, Casto Cruz created, in cities and villages, what were called "vigilant committees". There was one on every block.

Their mission was to watch carefully the activities of their neighbors and whatever was going on the block, and to report to the authorities anything they deemed suspicious. These committees functioned twenty four hours a day, seven days a week.

A year later, generalissimo Casto's government and the Soviet Union signed their first economic treaty. Casto Cruz had shown his true colors, turning Yagruma into a tropical satellite of the U.S.R.R.

Meanwhile, dozens of Yagrumans were executed every day. The names of the "enemies of the people" that had been put to death by order of the "revolutionary" tribunals appeared daily on the official newspapers, and in one of those lists I saw the name of general Cotrina.

The following week, Radio Free Yagruma announced that the Republic of Argentina had granted political asylum to a group of former Bautista associates who sought refuge at the Argentinean embassy in Sabana to escape imprisonment or death at the hands of the new rulers.

The names of Felino Eniesta and his wife, Perlita Shell, were on this list of political refugees.

Hardly a year had passed since the communists had come into power when the Yagrumans, frightened by what was happening on the island and by what they could see coming, began to leave the country.

The rich were the first to leave, after them went the middle class, and lastly, citizens of humble origin also began leaving Yagruma by the thousands.

One morning, upon arriving at the law office, I found Gastaigorri taking down his diplomas from the wall and putting them into a cardboard box.

"What are you doing?", I asked, as a matter of course. I imagined what his answer was going to be.

He kept on putting into the box a variety of objects that were on his desk: a pair of onyx book-ends, a pen and pencil set and a table lighter.

"We are finished, Miguel", he said, "There's nothing more for us to do here. We don't have any clients left! Some of them have been executed, others have been put in prison, and of those who haven't been killed or imprisoned, the communists have confiscated everything they have or nationalized their business".

I tried to cheer him up a little.

"Well, don't be discouraged!", I ventured, "This thing can't last. Things have to change!"

But Gastaigorri shook his head in disagreement. "Apparently, you haven't realized what's happening", he replied, "We are under the Russian boot already! And, what the hell can lawyers do in a communist regime?"

"Well, then what can anybody do?", I replied, "The regime's repression gets worse every day, the watchdog committees don't spare anybody, the people are terrorized!"

"We have to get the hell out of here!", exclaimed Gastaigorri, "That's what I'm going to do!"

He stared at me for a few seconds.

"I was going to tell you, anyway", he went on, "Yadira and I are leaving for the United States this weekend. We got our exit permits yesterday".

"Son-of-a-bitch!", I thought, "He's been real quiet about it".

"Let me give you some advice", continued Gastaigorri, "Apply for your passport right away, and as soon as you get it, go to the American consulate and get a visa. I know someone that can help you with that. But you must hurry, because I have a feeling that the United States is going to sever diplomatic ties with Yagruma very soon".

"I'll do that", I assured him, "Thanks for the advice. But, listen, what the hell are you going to do in the United States? What are you going to live on? You folks don't even speak English!"

"Don't worry", he replied, "We'll sweep floors, clean toilets...whatever! We won't starve!"

Gastaigorri scribbled a few lines on a piece of paper which he gave me.

"Apply for the American visas as soon as possible. Then go to this address and ask for Anita. She will know who you are, because I'm going to see her tonight and I'll tell her about you. Anita can speed up the visa for you. She's got the connections that you need for that".

He finished putting his things in the box, and carefully closed it.

"I'm going to leave it with my parents', he explained, "I might use the stuff again, if I ever come back to this shitty island".

He looked at me. "Well, until we meet again!", he exclaimed. "May God protect you!", was all I could say. We shook hands. Gastaigorri left the office with the box under his arm.

Although the idea of leaving Yagruma had never crossed my mind, I decided to follow Gastaigorri's advice. A paralegal that I knew handled all the paperwork at the Ministry of Foreign Relations, and as soon as I had my passport, I went to the United States Consulate and filed an application for a tourist visa.

That evening I got in touch with Anita, who turned out to be a woman in her early sixties, very cultured and friendly. She told me that my visa would be ready in no time, and that she would call me as soon as she got my passport.

After the closing of the law office, the only income that I had left was my salary from the Ministry of Commerce. Faldas and I had been transferred to the legal department, due to an administrative reorganization.

Since Casto Cruz and his communist lackeys became the absolute masters of the island, more than a million Yagrumans had joined the militia to keep their jobs, now that the state was the sole employer in the country.

In my place of work, many employees showed up dressed in their militia uniforms and proclaiming their adhesion to communism. They sometimes went to really blatant extremes in their praise of the regime.

I remember one day when Guillermo López, a functionary turned militiaman, called out to one of the clerks, who was a skinny, bow-legged girl in a militia uniform that had been chatting with some other employees beside the water cooler.

"Comrade Dania!"

"Yes, comrade!"

"A ship from the mother country, loaded with canned meat, has just arrived! Let's see if we can get it unloaded today! Get busy with the paper work! Right now!"

Many militiamen, in referring to the Soviet Union, called it the "Mother Country".

"Russian!?", shrieked the girl, rolling her eyes, "If that meat is Russian, I'd eat it raw if I had to!"

"I'll see you eating shit, you cocksucking bitch!", I said to myself.

Faldas was among the first ones to become "integrated" and join the militia. He was rewarded with a private office and a shapely blonde secretary. The first thing that one saw upon entering his office were the portraits of Karl Marx and Lenin hanging on the wall. Over them was a placard with the inscription "IF CASTO IS A COMMUNIST, PLEASE ADD MY NAME TO THE LIST".

There was also a poster representing a street scene in a Czechoslovakian town, with Czech folks smiling agreeably at the camera. A sign at the bottom read: "CZECHOSLOVAKIA, THE FRIENDLY COUNTRY".

Stapled to another of the walls was a past issue of "Rebellion", the official paper of the Casto Cruz regime. On the front page, in large letters, the Yagruman people were informed that in the past century, during the war of independence from Spain, two Russians had figured in the rank and file of the liberators.

One morning, when I got to the office, I found on my desk a memorandum from Faldas, notifying me that he wanted to see me "at my earliest convenience". When I entered his office, my friend pulled over a chair and signaled for me to sit down.

The blonde offered me a cup of coffee, which I accepted, because I had already used up the monthly quota allowed by my ration book. Faldas appeared confused, upset. He kept playing with his fountain pen, without saying a word. Finally, I decided to break the ice.

I took out the memorandum and showed it to him.

"So, what's up?", I asked, "What do you want to see me about?"

Faldas didn't answer immediately. He seemed to be trying to find the right words.

"Chico, Yagruma is running out of soap!", he exclaimed at last, "And it's all the fault of those gringos! They won't sell us any tallow!"

"Of course they won't!", I replied, "This regime has nationalized the soap industry and we haven't indemnified the Americans for the loss of their factories! What makes you think that they would send tallow for us to operate the factories that we stole from them?"

"Look", said Faldas, "We are under orders from our great leader to find a solution to this problem. I want you to explore the possibilities of importing tallow from Argentina, and have a report ready for me by Friday".

"Our comrade minister", he went on, "Will meet with generalissimo Casto, and this is one of the matters they are going to discuss".

"Very well", I answered, "The report will be on your desk on Friday. But if they think they are going to solve the problem by bringing tallow from Argentina, they are full of shit"

"Oh, really!", retorted Faldas, "I didn't know you were an economist".

"No, I'm not, but when Perón nationalized the railroads in that country, England took Argentinean beef as payment. The cattle industry in Argentina was ruined! Even today, Argentina wouldn't be able to supply the tallow we need".

"Even if they could", I concluded, "Just imagine the shipping costs! A little bar of soap would cost three or four pesos!"

"OK, OK, we'll see!", replied Faldas, somewhat upset, "The problem will be solved, one way or another! We can always count on the help of the socialist block!"

I was about to tell him what I thought about the help that we could expect from the Commies, but I held back. In those days, one had to be very careful with what one said.

Assuring Faldas that I would have the report for him on Friday, I was about to get up to leave his office. But he stopped me with a gesture.

"Wait a moment!", he said, "I've got something to tell you!

"Yes? What is it?"

Faldas looked really disturbed. "Chico", he said, "A couple of days ago, the political under-secretary called me to his office to talk to me about you. There are several lawyers in this ministry that haven't joined the militia".

"Yes", I answered, "And since I'm one of them, he's ordered you to pressure me into joining that shit!".

"Miguel, what's so terrible about putting on the uniform and going to the practices twice a week?, protested Faldas, "I'm telling you this for your own good, my friend! They've got their eyes on you".

I did not say a word.

"For these bastards", he kept on, "Refusing to be a militiaman is the same as being an enemy of the revolution. Don't provoke them, brother, make it easy on yourself!

"Tell them that I'm not joining anything, nor am I anybody's enemy", I replied. "All I want is for them to leave me alone".

"No, I wouldn't tell the under-secretary that", protested Faldas.

"Well then, tell him that I didn't spend years of my life studying just to carry a rifle marching in ranks with a bunch of imbeciles! Besides, as far as uniforms go, I don't even like the bus driver's"

Faldas' face darkened. "You can take a horse to the water, but you can't make him drink", he sighed, "Well, at least, I did all I could to keep you out of trouble!"

That night, I got a phone call from Anita. "I've got the complete works of Ernest Hemingway", she told me, "Let me know when you can come by and pick them up".

With that she was telling me that I had the US visa in my passport.

It must have been my guardian angel that put the words in my mouth. "I won't be able to come by there during the next few days", I answered, "Please hold on to them until I can come by and get them".

"Of course!", replied Anita, "And how is it going? Everything OK?"

"Lovely!", I said, "Everything is lovely! OK, I'll see you!"

"Good night then", she responded, hanging up.

But, very soon, things would cease to be OK, because life was going to put me through a terrible test.

CHAPTER XXIV
A MASSACRE

For several days, Yagruma's television had been announcing that the great leader of our glorious revolution and president for life of the Yagruman nation, generalissimo Casto Cruz, would be appearing before the cameras. He would reveal to the nation the satanic plan that the revengeful capitalist refugees living in exile in Miami were plotting and scheming against the Yagruman people.

In his television speech, Casto Cruz did nothing but to confirm what everybody in the island already knew. According to him, the enemies of the country, with the assistance of the American imperialists, were preparing to start a civil war in Yagruma.

The conflict, the red leader announced, would begin with the arrival of an invasion force supported by American planes and ships. Casto Cruz told the nation that the attack was imminent, and that there were traitors hiding in the shadows, ready to join the invaders.

"But our great revolution will have no mercy on them!", generalissimo Casto roared, "We shall overcome! The patriotic and revolutionary spirit of the Yagruman people will prevail over the treachery and wickedness of the imperialist monster!"

"The rebel army and our courageous militia have received their orders and are anxiously awaiting the moment when they can smash those bastards".

"Yagruma sí, Yankees no!", he bellowed, concluding his message, "Long live the glorious Soviet Union!"

Evidently, discretion is not one of the virtues of my countrymen. No matter how solemnly a Yagruman swears to faithfully guard a secret that has been confided to him, in less than an hour that secret will have been made public.

All over the island, militiamen, members of the spy committees and the "revolutionary" courts, and informers of all sorts were shitting in their pants with fear.

They had been getting phone calls from some of their former victims, now living in the United States and Central America.

"We are coming down with the invasion!", was the average message, "We are going to hunt you down, you motherfuckers! We'll tear off your heads!"

It was also a common matter that someone would approach someone else and say to him in a low, mysterious voice:

"Listen, brother, I'm involved in this "thing" up to here!", and he would raise his hand to his neck, "If you notice that I disappear, you'll know what happened! Now, brother, that's just between you and me, do you hear? Not a word of this to anyone!"

"What's the matter with you, brother?", the other one would respond, "Am I a man or what!? Your secret is safe with me! What you have told me, I'll take to the grave!"

And as soon as the "conspirator" left, the recipient of the confidence would head straight for the cafe or the store, itching to reveal the "secret" to everybody.

Also, with the story that the "fiesta" was going to be in full swing at any moment and they would be risking their lives fighting the enemy, quite a few militiamen were able to convince their fiancees to lose their virginity to them.

"I'm committed, my little one, I have to go! And what if they get me? Be good to me, my love! Don't let me go off like this! Look at the state I'm in!"

There wasn't a single Yagruman that didn't want everybody to believe that he was involved in "the thing". Every day, more and more rumors circulated, which raised the level of "secret" information divulged by the supposed conspirators, and kept Casto Cruz's spies busy twenty four hours a day, seven days a week.

In public and in private, the people openly talked about the hundreds of thousands of citizens that were ready to rise in support of the invaders, as soon as the landing took place.

Things like the following were heard all over, at street corners and coffee joints, in offices and shops, in cafes...everywhere! The invasion was now an open secret.

"My cousin Pepe called me last night from Miami. He told me "the thing" will be here sometime next week".

"Heliodoro and Chiquitico are already in Guatemala. Their old man says that "the thing" will `explode' soon!"

"Juan the militiaman better get lost. My son says that as soon as "the thing" gets here they are going to hunt him down and cut out his liver!"

"I've got targeted that old bitch in my block's spy committee. As soon as the `mambo' gets going, I'm going to cut her throat!"

And so on and so forth. All over the island the people were guessing, conjecturing and hoping.

It was about the middle of April, and while working at the office, I fell ill with the flu. I was granted permission to take a few days off until I could go back to work.

When I got home I went right to bed, where I stayed for four days without getting up. Luckily for me, a cargo of little, skinny Bulgarian hens, of the kind the Yagrumans called "Alicia Alonso" because of their long skinny legs, had been distributed in those days by the government. Cachita had managed to get two of the hens, and made chicken soup for me.

By then, all the pharmacies in Yagruma had run out of aspirin. But the resting, and Cachita's soup, worked miracles, and soon I was feeling much better.

The fifth day I knew that I had licked the flu, but I decided to take the rest of the week off. That morning, in robe and slippers, I was shaving in front of the bathroom mirror when I heard the noise of what I thought were claps of thunder. Cachita's outcries, coming from the living room, made me realize my mistake.

"This is it!", she screamed, "The invaders hit the beaches!

"They have landed! Miguel, Rosalina, the `mambo' is on!"

I ran to the living room. Now Cachita's cries were muffled by the sound of the engines of rapidly approaching airplanes. She was in the balcony and had raised the awning in order to see better. I got there at the moment when two World War II relics, two B-26 bombers passed overhead, flying so low over the roofs of Sabana with a deafening roar.

Seconds later Rosalina, uglier than ever in her yellow negligee spotted with coffee stains, joined us, bawling, in a hysterical fit. Cucuíto followed her, picking his nose.

"Oh, Holy Virgin of Lourdes!", squealed Rosalina, "Oh, Sacred Sacrament, protect us! Protect us, Lord!"

Her mother turned toward her, furious, giving her a scorching look.

"Shut up! What you should be doing is pleading to God for the invasion to be a success, and that they tear the head off all those sons-of-bitches!"

"Look! Look over there!", cried Cucuíto, pointing with his finger.

Far away, to the North of the city, thick columns of black smoke could be seen, slowly rising against the pale blue sky. Sabana had just been bombed.

"Fiesta" time had finally arrived!

"Radio Yagruma" and "Rebel Television of Yagruma" began immediately to tell the public their versions of the events.

The long-awaited invasion force had finally arrived, landing at Cenagales Beach, in the south of El Guije Province. American military airplanes had been reported flying over the area, but so far they were not taking part in the action.

It was also announced that several divisions of the glorious rebel army, supported by select contingents of the national militia, were now on the way to Cenagales, ready to crush the mercenaries "paid by the Yankee gold".

The Great Leader of the People, Generalissimo Casto Cruz, had assured the people that the tanks, armored carriers and artillery sold to the Yagruman people by their generous friend, the Soviet Union, were now at the inlet, ready to be used against the enemies of our heroic revolution.

We were sitting in the living room, listening to the news, when the telephone rang. Cucuíto answered it.

"Miguel, it's for you".

That gave me a bad feeling. I went to the phone.

"Yes?"

"Is this comrade Baró?"

"Dr. Baró speaking", I answered.

"Comrade, this is Benito Becadas".

"What can I do for you, señor Becadas?"

Becadas was our new chief of personnel. He had replaced Billotte, who had been accused of "crimes against the state" and sentenced to death by a "revolutionary" court.

"Our country and freedom are in danger, comrade! You must report at once to your labor center!"

"But, señor Becadas", I responded, "I'm on sick leave! I'm really not well enough to go out!"

"Comrade!", roared Becadas, "Come down here immediately! You have a duty to defend the revolution! If you don't report to me without delay, you will suffer the consequences!"

"Son-of a-bitch!", I thought, hanging up the phone.

I explained to Cachita what had happened.

"Are you going?", she asked.

"And put my life on the line for these bastards? Not me!", I said, "I'm not a Commie, and I'll never be! I hope the Americans come and shoot all those assholes!"

"What are you going to do?"

"I'll stay right here, watching television, until they announce that the invasion has succeeded, that the Great Leader has had his head torn off, and that a provisional, anti-Communist government has taken over".

"May God hear you!", sighed Cachita, "OK then, let's go to the kitchen. I'm going to make some coffee with what I have left. We have to celebrate!"

During the rest of the day, the radio, television and newspapers did nothing else but to repeat that the army and the militia were fighting heroically against the forces of imperialism.

Finally, before midnight, tired of listening to the same thing, we went to bed. "Tomorrow will be another day", said Cachita, "Good night!"

About two o'clock in the morning I was awakened by a terrible clamoring from the street. There were people screaming and dealing tremendous blows to the street door.

My mind was still foggy from sleep. For a minute I thought that it was a nightmare, but my head cleared when I heard them calling my name.

"Baró!!", they cried, "Miguel Baró!! Open the door immediately!!!"

How many things came to my mind as I leaped out of bed and put on my robe and slippers! I hurried through the hall. Cachita was already out of her room and came running towards me. She threw her arms around me, crying.

"Don't let them get you, Miguel! Run and hide in that room on the roof!"

"You think these people are stupid?", I said, "They will search the house until they find me, and then you'll get involved in the mess, too".

The blows kept on raining on the street door.

"Oh, my God! Miguel, why do they want you? What are they going to do with you?"

"Calm down, calm down", I told her, "Nothing is going to happen to me! I'm not involved in anything, they have nothing to use against me!"

Down below, in the street, the cries and blows on the door intensified.

"Baró", cried a voice that I thought I recognized, "If you don't open the door at once, we'll break it down!!"

"I'm coming!, I cried, "Wait a moment! Wait 'til I put something on!"

Cachita, terrified, pressed against me. I softly pushed her to one side and went down the stairs.

When I opened the door, a group of soldiers and militiamen armed with pistols and Soviet submachine guns pushed me aside and ran upstairs, calling my name.

Among the militiamen, I recognized two of my fellow employees at the Ministry of Commerce. One of them was a young, pimply-faced man that worked in Personnel. The other was Dr. Silvino de Córdoba, the fat lawyer who used to work with me in the Trademarks and Patents office.

They were so anxious to put their hands on me, that they didn't realize that the person who had opened the door for them was the very one they were looking for. Only when they had gone halfway up the stairs did de Córdoba realized that he had passed me by. He stopped abruptly, and pointing at me cried:

"There he is! Look over there! That's him!"

"Surrender, and don't move!", cried the leader of the group, a young mulatto in an army uniform. He motioned to one of the men, who came to me and searched me thoroughly, making sure that I was not armed.

"Who else lives here?", asked the mulatto, who had corporal's chevrons on the sleeves of his uniform.

"The owner of the house, with her daughter and her grandson".

"Are you the boyfriend of any of those women?"

"No, I am only a guest in this house".

"OK, go on up!", he ordered, "We are going upstairs!". Cachita, trembling like a leaf, was waiting for us at the top of the stairs. She faced the mulatto.

"Oh, corporal, you have been misinformed! This is a serious, law-abiding young man! I'm telling you, I know him well! He's been my guest for almost fourteen years!"

"Madam", replied the corporal, "I have orders to arrest Miguel Baró, and I have to follow these orders. I give you my word that, as long as he in my custody, nothing will happen to him".

"Hey, Fernández, let's not waste any more time", interrupted de Córdoba, "We still have to catch those two guys at the Calzada, and that other one in Santa María!"

"That's right", said Fernández. "Angelito!", he called out. One of the soldiers, a young, lanky peasant, came over to us.

"You and comrade Silvino! Go to Baró's room and search it thoroughly. Take anything that looks suspicious. This woman will take you to the room".

"I swear to God...", Cachita began to say. But Fernández didn't let her finish.

"Shut up and do as I tell you", he exclaimed, "Or I'm taking you along with us, too!"

"Do as he says, Cachita! Make it easy on yourself!", I begged her. Sobbing, she went on down the corridor, followed by Fatso and Angelito.

Fernández turned to face the rest of the men.

"Search the rest of the house!" he ordered. The men started moving.

Angelito and de Córdoba returned a few minutes later. The latter was carrying my television set, an almost brand new Phillips, something that could no longer be found in any store in Sabana. Angelito was wearing my Omega chronometer on his left wrist.

"Did you find anything?", asked the mulatto.

"This television set might have been smuggled in", said de Córdoba. "Have you got the sales ticket?", he asked, turning to me.

"I had it in my desk, at the law office", I responded, "I don't know where it can be now. The government confiscated the building and converted it into a house for the homeless."

"Where did you buy this set?"

"I bought it at `Casa Gerona', but the government nationalized the business some months ago. I tried to get a copy of the sales ticket, but they had thrown away all the records".

"Well", said de Córdoba, "I'll see what can be done, if anything. If everything is cleared up, we'll give you back the set. But, to tell you the truth, don't bet on it".

Angelito didn't bother to explain why he was wearing my wrist watch.

Protesting and demanding that they give me back the TV set and the watch they had just stolen would only make things worse. I shouldn't antagonize these people; I was at their mercy. They could do with me whatever they wanted to.

"OK, let's go down", ordered Fernández.

"Where are you taking me?", I wanted to know.

"You'll soon find out!"

"I'm in my night clothes", I exclaimed, "At least, let me change!"

The mulatto wavered for a few seconds.

"You've got two minutes", he said, finally. "Go with him!", he ordered Angelito.

I got dressed in less than two minutes and, with the pretext of getting a handkerchief, opened the drawer of my dresser. My wallet, with fifty pesos inside, was missing. Probably, Fernández, Angelito and Fatso would be dividing it up later, along with the rest of the booty.

"OK, OK, you are dressed now", said Angelito, "Let's get the hell out of here!"

He took me back to the living room. The other bastards were returning from their search. One of the militiamen carried a brown bag.

"What did you find?", corporal Fernández asked them.

"They had twelve bars of soap in there", replied the one with the pimply face, pointing at Rosalina's room, "We seized them because now that's a crime, right?"

"Sure!', answered de Córdoba, "That's hoarding of an essential commodity!"

"If they clear up this matter about the soap", Fernández told Cachita, "They'll return it to you!"

The soap would surely become part of the booty. Cachita, of course, knew this, but she didn't say anything, so as not to provoke my captors.

"OK, let's go! We have already wasted a lot of time!", ordered Fernández.

Cachita couldn't stop crying. I hugged her and then went down the stairs with my captors. The mulatto went in front, followed by three of his men. I walked behind them, followed by the rest of the party.

Parked in front of the house were two Cadillac limousines from the Ministry of Commerce. Fernández took me by the arm towards one of them and made me sit in the back, between him and a militiaman. Angelito got behind the wheel, with de Córdoba next to him holding on to my television set.

"Let's go, step on it!", ordered Fernández.

The limousine sped through the streets of Sabana, which were deserted except for other government vehicles that we encountered. They were certainly on similar missions to ours.

Again I asked corporal Fernández where they were taking me.

"To the Sports and Conventions Arena", he answered. We didn't speak any more for the rest of the trip.

I really didn't think that my life was in danger, because if they had wanted to kill me, they could have just stopped at any isolated spot and filled me full of lead. No questions asked.

The front of the Sports and Conventions Arena was blocked by a multitude of cars and military vehicles. Angelito had to park at some distance from the entrance.

"Here we are!", said Fernández, "Let's get out!"

I stepped out of the car and followed him, flanked by Angelito and Fatso.

Around the building, groups of prisoners, surrounded by soldiers and militiamen with fixed bayonets, waited to be taken inside. The mulatto and his men worked their way through the crowd until we arrived at one of the gates that gave access to the basket ball court. It was guarded by several soldiers under the command of a lieutenant.

Fernández called the officer to one side and spoke with him, pointing his finger at me several times while the officer nodded in agreement. Minutes later, two of the soldiers came and took me into the basket ball court.

The floor was crammed with prisoners, some standing, others sitting or lying down. Some spoke and gesticulated, others were quiet, with somber and worried faces, still others cried silently. I looked over towards the bleachers. They were full of militiamen armed to the teeth.

"Go out onto the floor!", ordered one of my escorts, pushing me with the butt of his rifle.

I obeyed and walked in among the people collected there, taking care not to step on those lying or spread out on the floor, until I got to a space slightly less congested, where I stayed.

"Hey, how is it going out there?", a tall, mustached man at my side asked me, "What can you tell me about the invasion? They grabbed me around seven. I'd just got home!"

That guy could very well be one of the informers that Casto Cruz had probably infiltrated among us. One had to be careful.

"According to the last news that I heard at eleven o'clock last night", I said, "It seems that they were still fighting around Cenagales".

"My only hope is that the Americans will come in", he commented.

I said nothing. That guy had an honest face, but that didn't guarantee that he was not a scoundrel.

"What are they going to do with us?", it occurred to me to ask.

"That's the sixty four thousand dollar question", he responded.

"They'll skin us alive if they see that the invasion is going to be a success", said a black man that was close to us and had heard us talking.

"Kill us in cold blood? Without a reason?"

"Sure! The Great Leader knows that we are against him! And he certainly isn't going to let us get out of here alive to help the ones that came to oust him!"

"As much an assassin as Casto Cruz is, I don't think he would be capable of a crime like that!", I said

"They are a bunch of motherfuckers, all of them!", replied the black. "Look", he exclaimed, pointing at a lunch box on the floor, beside him, "I was coming home from work when they grabbed me. I wanted to leave the lunch box at my home, two doors away. But they laughed at me, and kicked me in the ass!"

"The only thing we can do", said the man with the mustache, "Is ask God to..."

He was interrupted by the desperate screams of a woman that was coming down from the bleachers towards the floor of the court, yelling like one possessed, struggling with the militiamen that were trying to stop her.

"My daughter!", she shouted, "My daughter! "What have you done with my daughter, you murdering bastards!?"

"Let her go!", the prisoners cried out from the floor, "Let her go, you sons-of-bitches! You cocksucking Commies!!"

As they dragged the poor woman out of there, I happened to glance up toward the top of the bleachers, just to see two militiamen stand up and aim their weapons at the crowd.

"Get down on the floor!", I cried to those around me, setting the example, "They are going to machine gun us!"

Then all hell broke loose.

From the bleachers, the militia opened fire against the defenseless prisoners. They were shooting at us with everything they had: machine guns, rifles, carbines, semi-automatic pistols and revolvers.

The shots rang through the court, with deafening noise. Face down on the floor, I could hardly believe that what I was living in those moments was not a nightmare. But it was terrifying reality. I could hear the impact of the bullets hitting the wooden floor.

"As long as I can hear it, I guess there is no problem", I thought, "What I don't hear is what's going to get me!"

Suddenly, not far from where I was lying, I heard a loud groan. Out of the corner of my eye I noticed the black man twist for a few seconds and then lie still. Blood poured out of his chest, soaking his shirt, and formed a rapidly growing puddle at his side.

Then something happened that showed me that there were still men with balls in Yagruma. Near us a young man, almost an adolescent, got up, and running over to the wounded man, picked him up, threw him on his shoulders and walked with his burden over towards the seats, under a hail of bullets.

"Sons-of-bitches!!", he roared at the militia, "You are killing our own people, you bastards!!"

I closed my eyes. I was sure that that young man would be killed, and I didn't want to watch it. But seconds later the firing stopped, and when I turned to look, I saw that the militia had begun to leave the bleachers. A contingent of soldiers had entered and were taking positions around the court.

A group of militiamen had come out and was carrying off the bodies of several men that lay dead on the floor, the black among them.

Shortly afterwards, the soldiers took us up to the front of the building, where a caravan of buses of the urban transit lines was waiting for us.

"This smells bad to me", murmured the mustached man at my side.

I hadn't cried since I was a child, but as I was leaving that place of death, my eyes filled with tears when I saw, lying in a puddle of blood, the lunch box in which that poor black man had carried his last meal.

La "fiesta" had swooped down upon us with apocalyptic swiftness.

CHAPTER XXV
A CASTLE IN THE SKY, HORRORS BY AND BY...

The buses were waiting with their motors running. The soldiers, after separating the men from the women, packed the prisoners inside the vehicles. Besides the driver, several soldiers, heavily armed, were riding each bus.

There were no empty seats when I got in, so I had to ride standing up, hanging on to the straps on the ceiling. Next to me was my new acquaintance, sucking on his mustache.

It seemed that the busloads of prisoners were to be taken to various detention centers, because the buses were separating along the way and taking different directions, until finally there were only three vehicles left from the original caravan. They were escorted by two armored personnel carriers, loaded with soldiers.

A sepulchral silence reigned inside our bus. It felt as if the prisoners knew that some terrible fate was awaiting them.

About twenty minutes later, that nightmare of a trip ended. The three buses came to a halt, and the soldiers stepped down, with their weapons readied. They were joined by the troops from the armored carriers.

"Don't anybody move!!", they hollered, "Wait for your orders!!"

A lieutenant, pistol in hand, came up to our bus, making a signal with a motion of his hand to the driver, who opened the front door. The officer, standing up on the first step, addressed the prisoners.

"When I give the order, all of you get out", he shouted. "Come out one by one, and don't run!" He got out to join the other soldiers standing by the bus.

"OK, let's go!!", he yelled, "Now!!"

We obeyed. A few yards away from the parked buses, a bunch of shabbily dressed people began hurling threats and insults at the prisoners.

"Cockroaches!", they hollered, "Fatherland or death!"

"The firing squad for the bourgeoisie!"

"Now you are going to get it in the ass, you bastards!!"

We were in front of Arosategui Hill, on top of which, bathed in the pallid light of an ashy dawn, rose the massive structure of El Infante castle, built centuries before by the Spaniards and made into a prison by the republic.

Access to the castle was possible by means of a wide and steep stairway that went up the side of the hill. After being warned that there were orders to shoot anyone who tried to escape, we slowly climbed the old worn cement steps, flanked by the soldiers, who had fixed their bayonets on us.

There were heavy machine gun emplacements protected by sand-bags around El Infante's main entrance, and we could also see anti-aircraft batteries set up in ramparts and parapets. In addition to machine guns, the soldiers were armed with hand grenades.

The lieutenant moved on ahead and talked briefly with a sergeant who appeared to be in command. Minutes later, still flanked by the soldiers, we entered the fortress, and crossing a large open area, we came to one of the castle's defense towers, beside which the lieutenant ordered us to wait.

One opening in that tower gave access to an outside stairway that ran down the side of the wall. The lieutenant ordered us to form a single line.

"We're going down here!", he said, "No talking!"

The stairway was so narrow that we could descend it only single file. The lieutenant lead, followed by some of his men; behind them went the prisoners and, lastly, the rest of the soldiers.

The steps were worn; a lot of them were broken. We wended down little by little, carefully, trying not to stumble and fall. Fear and despair was reflected in many faces. Others, though, showed no emotion at all. They walked like zombies, totally removed from what was happening to them.

The stairway went down to the castle's basement. The soldiers led us directly to a an iron-reinforced door at the end of one of the walls and called out, hitting the iron bars with the butt of their rifles.

Several militiamen opened the door.

"OK, everybody inside!", yelled the lieutenant.

My new friend, the mustached guy, extended his hand.

"We won't get out of here alive!", he told me, "My name is Manuel Gutiérrez, so you know with whom you are going to the other side".

"My name is Miguel Baró". I replied. I tried to find some words of encouragement, but I couldn't. I was convinced that our appointment with the grim reaper was, at best, a matter of hours.

"Let's go, let's go! Don't fall back! Inside, inside!", bellowed the lieutenant.

We crossed the grate and found ourselves in an enormous hall, dusky and damp, scarcely illuminated by a few electric lamps hanging from the ceiling. A throng of prisoners that had been brought in there before we came were sitting or lying down on the floor. Some were sleeping with their backs leaning against the walls.

In a distant corner of the gloomy hall I saw what appeared to be the mouth of a narrow tunnel, closed off by an iron door.

The soldiers had stayed outside. We were now in the hands of the militia. Their leader was a man of about fifty years of age, who didn't seem to be very happy with his job of jail keeper.

I approached him.

"May I ask you a question?"

"You may", he answered, "But I don't know if you'll get an answer".

"How long are they going to keep us here?"

"I don't know", he answered, "I haven't the slightest idea. The orders come down from above, all we do is obey them".

"There's another thing", I said, "And I'm asking you to tell me the truth, man to man!"

"We'll see"

"The rumor is going around that Casto Cruz has given orders that all of us are to be killed if the invasion is a success". The man looked me in the eye for a few seconds.

"Do you believe in anything?", he asked.

"Yes!", I answered, "I worship Saint Barbara".

"Well then, you better pray to Her that the invasion is a failure", replied the man.

The place was so full of people, that you had to walk with extreme care not to step on the bodies of the prisoners sitting or spread out on the floor. Near the corner, where that tunnel's mouth was, I saw Manuel Gutiérrez and two other men, sitting with their legs spread out, and their shoulders against the wall.

Gutiérrez introduced me to his companions. One of them, fat and bald, with pale blue eyes, was Dr. Mora, a renowned Sabana ophthalmologist; the other was a young man of about twenty some years of age, named Jesús Acebal. He wore a pair of steel-rimmed glasses that slipped constantly down his nose.

"We saw you talking to that bastard. What did he tell you?", asked Jesús.

I didn't have the nerve to tell them what I had heard from the lips of the militiaman.

"Miguel", said Gutiérrez, "You don't have to hide the truth from us. Elías, that guy that's standing in front of the group over by the grating, talked with another of the militia, and he told us what's going on".

"Don't listen to rumors", I replied, "And don't be influenced by all the stories that are going around. Nobody here knows anything!"

There was a Canadian priest among the prisoners, a tall, thin man in a white cassock. He stood in one of the corners, hearing confession and giving absolution to a group of prisoners that, "just in case", were preparing to die.

I looked around me, at the men lying or sitting close to us. Some cried in silence, others were sobbing noisily, and every once in a while I could hear groans and shrieks of desperation coming from those bodies packed in there. The militiamen, taking pleasure in the anguish of the prisoners, had spread the news that our lives depended on the outcome of the invasion.

What could possibly happen in that large and gloomy place didn't scare me, because I had always thought of death as the solution to all my problems. I lay down on the floor, beside Manuel, and closed my eyes.

"Hey, what are you doing?", he asked.

"I'm going to sleep. I'm so tired I can't stand it!"

"But, you are crazy, brother! Haven't you heard that we probably won't get out of here alive!?"

"Well, maybe so", I replied, "But maybe not! Wake me up if something happens!"

I turned over on my side and with an arm beneath my head, like a pillow, in less than a minute I fell asleep.

Voices screaming and shouting, and the shoves that Manuel and Jesús were giving me, woke me up. I looked around and saw the militiamen coming and going, waking the sleeping prisoners and pricking the lazy ones with the bayonets. The victims cried out as though they had been run through.

"Everybody on their feet!", yelled our jailers.

I noticed that the iron door that guarded the entrance of that mysterious tunnel had been opened. The militiamen didn't let anybody get near there.

"The invasion has failed!", Manuel told me, "They say we're going to live, but I'm not too sure about it, I don't know why!"

"Who gave you the news?"

"A soldier came to the grate a few minutes ago and made the announcement".

"Well, if that's true", said Dr. Mora, "I imagine that they'll let us go free soon".

"Of course!", exclaimed Jesús, "After all, why are we locked up here? I haven't committed any crime! The only thing I've done..."

I didn't let him finish.

"Shut up! God knows how many informers there are among us!"

"Hey", interjected Manuel, "I don't know about you, guys, but I'm famished! I'm playing the unfinished symphony with my guts!"

"I'm feeling really weak!, said Dr. Mora.

"So am I", complained Jesús, "I'm craving food! How about you, Miguel?"

"Same here!", I replied.

"Perhaps these sons-of-bitches want to starve us to death" exclaimed Jesús.

At that precise moment we heard the sound of the entrance door being opened, and the lieutenant, followed by a half dozen soldiers, entered the hall and walked to the mouth of the tunnel, stopping beside it.

"All right! Form a single line and start going in!!"

Upon hearing this, an infernal pandemonium erupted inside the detention hall. All hell broke loose, with the prisoners yelling, screaming and shouting like wild beasts. They, who had been hoping to soon be released, were once again seized with terror.

"They want us in the tunnel to put us to death!!", some of them were crying.

"They don't have the balls to shoot us, so they'll starve us to death inside the tunnel!! screamed others.

"Yagruma sí, Russia no!!", roared the prisoners, "Long live the United States! Long live Christ the King!!"

"They'll machine-gun us again!", I said to Manuel.

"I told you we would never get out of here alive!", he replied.

The soldiers grouped around the lieutenant, aiming their rifles and sub-machine guns at us. A couple of militiamen ran towards the grate, probably to look for reinforcements.

One of the prisoners, standing on an empty wooden crate, managed to get the attention of the crowd.

"This tunnel is full of dynamite!!", he shouted, "Don't go in there, people!! They'll blow us to pieces and put the blame on the Americans. Men, if we're going to die, let's die like men!! Let's..."

Two shots rang out and the man fell dead, with two bullets in his chest. The lieutenant, smoking pistol in hand, turned to the horrified prisoners.

"All right!! Anyone else wants to protest?", he shouted.

Once again the door opened. Two squads of soldiers entered the cave, but by now the reinforcements were not necessary. The lieutenant, single-handedly, had put an end to the rebellion.

Two militiamen grabbed the prisoner's corpse by the ankles and dragged it outside.

"Go on in!", roared the lieutenant, "Keep your mouths shut and stay in order! Don't do anything to make me mad!!"

The soldiers, with the butts of their rifles, were pushing the slow ones and the stragglers. Little by little, we went inside the tunnel, like a herd of sheep driven by the shepherd's dogs.

Manuel, Jesús, Dr. Mora and I were among the first to enter the dreary gallery.

We found ourselves in a vaulted passage, about eight feet wide and, at the most, seven feet high, built in the castle's basement probably to help in the defense against the attacks of pirates and buccaneers.

The only ventilation came from some loopholes opened in the thick stone walls. Through these slits one could see part of a vast inner yard limited by a huge rampart.

Semi-darkness reigned in that place. The shafts of light that filtered through the loopholes, together with the weak glow of the few light bulbs hanging from the roof, could not completely disperse the shadows that filled the gloomy corridor.

We had walked eighty or ninety feet when we came up to an iron gate that prevented us going any farther. Some of our fellow inmates piled up behind us.

A murmur of voices could be heard coming from the other side of the grate.

"Hey!", yelled Jesús, "Who goes there?"

A group of men of various ages, races and appearance, materialized on the other side of the bars.

"Gentlemen, where are we?", asked Dr. Mora.

"In a corridor that goes all around the basement of the castle", responded one of them, a bald man with a hook nose, "It's divided into sections by grates like this one".

"They fucked Satan here, and he didn't even cry for help! He knew that nobody would hear him!", added a mulatto dressed in white from head to toe. He had several strings of beads around his neck.

"How many people are there in your section?"

"There's space here for about three hundred men", said the bald guy, "But they have jammed in close to five hundred!"

"That's bad", commented Dr. Mora, "If they don't take us out of here, soon we'll be dropping off like flies!"

"When did you get here?", one of our group asked, an old man with a white mustache, dressed in a business suit.

"About a couple hours ago", they answered.

"Have they given you anything to eat?", Jesús asked, "We are starving!"

"A militiaman told me that the food was coming pretty soon!", said a dwarf whom the bald guy had helped up on the grate.

All of a sudden an authoritative voice, coming through a loudspeaker, resounded through the gallery.

"Food call! Form a single line up to the entrance of your section!"

"Let's go! The grub is here!", said the bald one to his group. The men left the grate and went to line up to get the food.

"I hope I'll see you again!", said our new friend.

"I hope so, brother!", responded Manolo.

We started to line up along the length of the passageway. Nobody talked. Terror and hunger had most of the prisoners in a stupor. Slowly, the line of men made their way toward the slop.

CHAPTER XXVI
A DREAM ITSELF IS BUT A SHADOW

Several convicts, armed with big ladles, were serving the food from metal drums placed at the mouth of the gallery. Each of us were given a tin plate with the warning not to lose it, because there weren't any more.

The food was scarce and slimy. Each prisoner was served a ladleful of cold, sticky rice and another of some kind of muddy looking soup in which a few black beans floated. A small sweet potato completed the meal.

Some poor bastards, spurred by hunger, wanted to go for seconds; others protested, complaining about the trashy grub. They were clobbered and kicked out of the food line by the militiamen.

We had been given neither forks nor spoons, so we used our fingers to eat the rice and the sweet potato. Then we took the plates up to the mouth and sipped the foul soup. After gulping down that slop, we started talking, to kill time.

"Well, what do you think is going to happen?", asked Jesús, "What are they going to do with us?"

"That's anybody's guess", answered Dr. Mora.

"But, this can't be!", exclaimed Jesús, "The government can't do this to us! I'm a citizen, brother! One has rights!"

He turned to me.

"You are a lawyer", he said, "Tell me, am I right or not?"

"Forget about your rights", I replied, "Now, in Yagruma, the only ones that have rights are the Commies. You say they can't do this to us? Well, as you can see, here we are, locked up!"

"But I'm not a criminal and I don't get mixed up in politics, for God's sake!", cried Jesús, "Yes, I had a few drinks and I talked a lot of horseshit, but that's all!"

"Then they got you for being a loud mouth", said a Spaniard who had been crawling over to get near the group.

"We don't know why they have brought us here!", replied Dr. Mora, making signs to Jesús to shut up.

He understood the signs. "I'm not a politician!", he exclaimed, "I'm a family man! My wife, my kids and my job, that's all I care about! As far as politics go, don't even mention it! It doesn't interest me!"

"Why don't we try to sleep a little?", suggested the doctor, "Who knows what will be waiting for us tomorrow!"

"That's a good idea", agreed Manuel, standing up, "But, first, I have to take a leak".

"Me too!", I added, getting up with difficulty. My tailbone was hurting after sitting for so long on that hard surface.

Needless to say, there were no toilets in the dungeons of El Infante. After first arriving there, we prisoners, as if per some tacit agreement, relieved ourselves in a far corner of the corridor, close to the grating that separated us from the other section.

But with so many people doing their job in the same place, at the end of the first day that corner was an enormous swamp of rotting urine with masses of excrement rising from its bottom, like brown hills emerging from the strata of a greenish-yellow lake.

And so as not to get our feet in this nauseous mixture, when we had to relieve ourselves we looked along the wall for clean spaces, as far as possible from the other prisoners.

When we came back and rejoined our friends, Jesús and Dr. Mora were still awake, talking. The Spaniard had disappeared.

"Where is the `gallego'?" I asked, "What happened, didn't he like your company?"

"We gave the bastard the cold shoulder!", replied Jesús, "The doctor was right, you have to be really careful with the stool pigeons around here".

"Look over there", said Manuel, laughing.

Gradually and to nobody's surprise, many of the prisoners, according to their origins, occupations and associations, had formed cliques in different parts of the tunnel. With pieces of charcoal that were found scattered around, each group marked on the floor the boundaries of their territory. Written on the walls, in large letters, were the names of the cliques: "Pacheco's Platoon", "The Cocks from Lunayó", "The Bachicha Tigers" and others of that sort.

"The Cocks from Lunayó" had installed themselves along the opposite side of the wall, a few yards away from us. And sure enough, there was the Spaniard, sprawled out on the floor, laughing at the jokes that Elías Ledón, the leader of the "Cocks", was telling.

"Perhaps the man is not a stool pigeon, not even a bastard!", said Manuel.

"Just in case", I replied, "The best thing is to keep your mouth shut. You can't tell who's who in this place".

"I agree with that", said Jesús.

"We don't get any sunshine here", exclaimed Dr. Mora, "And there isn't any ventilation. Some of us will not leave this dungeon alive".

"I heard that there are quite a few people with the flu in the other section of the tunnel", commented Jesús.

"If we get sick, I bet these sons-of-bitches won't take us to the infirmary!", said Manuel.

"Judging from what I have seen, they surely won't", replied Dr. Mora, "Another thing", he added, "Those hoses are two real sources of infection".

Through the loopholes, from the outside, they had passed two garden hoses to provide water for more than three hundred prisoners caged in our section.

The men, at first, cleaned the nozzles before drinking, but soon stopped doing that, as if the possibility of catching a contagious disease had stopped being a matter of concern to them.

"I'm going to ask you guys a favor", said Manuel.

"Well, it depends", responded Jesús, "What is it?"

"No one knows what it is that they want to do with us. I think that we are going to be facing some terrible days in this cave, and I want to ask you, before I go to sleep, to say a prayer with me".

"And what good is a prayer going to do?", I asked, "Is that going to get us out of here?"

"Maybe not", replied Manuel, "But at least it will prepare us for the worst".

Now I was ashamed of my stupid sarcasm.

"You are probably right", I said, "But I don't know how to pray".

"That doesn't make any difference. You just repeat after me. Are you guys ready?"

"Yes!"

We sat down close to each other, forming a tight circle.

Manuel began, “The Lord is my shepherd; I shall not want" "He taketh me to lie down in green pastures" "And leadeth me beside still waters..."

When our friend had finished, all of us were moved. Jesús had his eyes full of tears. Perhaps he was thinking of his wife and children.

"Well then, let's get to sleep", said Manuel, "We'll see what tomorrow brings".

I lay down with my head toward the wall and fell asleep right away, because I was physically and emotionally exhausted.

Now I was in an opulent neighborhood in Caracas, standing in front of a beautiful, colonial style mansion.

I walked to the front door and noticed that it was not closed. Giving in to an uncontrollable impulse, I pushed the door and walked in.

I found myself in a large, red-tiled entranceway leading to a tastefully decorated family room, with a door and windows that opened to a flowering garden. To my right, on the wall of the entranceway, there was an oaken door with an antique bronze lock that had a big keyhole.

I was trying to decide what would be the best thing to do.

Should I explore the place, that seemed to be deserted, or get out of there before someone appeared and took me for a thief? Then, all of a sudden, I heard voices behind the oaken door, and prodded by curiosity put my ear to the keyhole.

Weak "ohs", deep sighs and cries of pleasure came from the lips of a woman. From someone else were coming smacks and grunts similar to those made by pigs when fed a good portion of milk and grain.

Then I knew who they were, and why I was there! Some obscure and mysterious force had sent me to that place!

Using extreme care not to make any noise, I pushed the door slightly open, to look through the interstice.

But all I could see through the narrow gap was one of the corners of an elegant living room and some expensive pieces of furniture, and on the wall, an array of arms displaying a battle ax and two daggers.

The woman's sighs and moans were getting louder, more yearning, more anxious, coming from some other corner of the room.

"Don't let go! Keep going, keep going! Don't stop!", she pleaded.

I entered the room silently and locked the door from inside with a key that was hanging on the door frame. I put the key in my pocket. They were not aware that a visitor had arrived, such was the fever of their passion!

I stopped for a moment, watching them. Perlita, her eyes closed and her legs spread, lay naked on a red damask sofa, amid convulsions of pleasure that made vibrate her full, firm breasts. Eniesta, also nude and on all fours, was also on the sofa, with his face buried in Perlita's pubis, his pendulous belly swinging with each motion that he made.

Very carefully, not to make any noise, I went to the display of arms and took down one of the daggers. But I had the bad luck to stumble over a table, throwing to the floor a crystal vase that broke into pieces.

Perlita was the first to realize what was happening, and jumping up from the sofa, ran to the door. But when she found out that she couldn't get it open, knowing that there was no way out, she began to cry in desperation.

I lunged toward her with the dagger raised, but Eniesta, in spite of his corpulence, moved fast. Placing himself in front of Perlita, he shielded her with his body and tried, by kicking, to keep me at bay.

I was a thousand times more agile than he was, and easily eluded him. With the thrusts and slashes of my dagger, I was slowly forcing the pair into the corner where I wanted to kill them.

Fat old Eniesta had put too much food down his throat. He soon stopped kicking, and leaned against the wall, gasping for air and pressing his chest with his hands. Perlita kept crying like the damned, hiding behind the big, sweaty body of her lover, and begging me to spare them, in the name of the Blessed Virgin and the Holy Sacraments.

I hadn't uttered a word, because talking would have been a waste of time, on my part. Besides, there was nothing to talk about. I was going to disembowel them, and that was that!

She had read my mind, and her terror knew no bounds. "Have mercy!", she was shrieking now, "Miguel, I did love you, remember!? I'll do whatever you want me to! I'll be yours again, yours for....!"

I thrust the dagger, up to the hilt, inside Eniesta's stomach, and without taking the blade out of him, with a firm and steady hand, drew it down the length of his abdomen, severing the intestines. But something incredible, unimaginable, happened.

Not one drop of blood came out of the wound!

The man leaned against the table, staring with glassy eyes at his belly, opened by the slash of the dagger. Suddenly, with a savage scream, he grabbed both sides of the wound and began tugging and tearing until the guts began to pour out of the opening.

Perlita's shrieking ceased. She was wailing, howling and screaming like the damned probably do when facing, for the first time, the fires of hell.

Seeing that Eniesta was not falling, I let him have it again, this time in the heart. But when I pulled the dagger from his chest to stab him for the third time, a fast thickening cloud of black smoke began to flow down the ceiling, filling up the room.

I could hear Perlita's screams and Eniesta's moans, and clutching the dagger in my hand, looked for them in the darkness. But it was useless. The black cloud thickened even more; millions of dazzling scarlet flies scintillated in that dense fog.

I had the impression that the floor gave way beneath my feet and that my body fell into the vacuum and began to descend, slowly, floating in the shadows that surrounded me. The screams from Perlita were getting weaker, until they finally ceased altogether.

Then, suddenly, I felt the sensation of a hard, irregular surface under me. The fog had dissipated, and looking around I recognized the walls of the tunnel and my companions around me, sleeping. I had had a nightmare, that was all! With my handkerchief, I blotted up the sweat that covered my neck and forehead.

I was terribly thirsty. I got up and went to the hoses, for a drink.

By the hazy glow of the light bulbs I could see the rows of bodies spread out on the floor of the gallery, bringing to my mind the descriptions of the funeral houses of Ancient Egypt, where the embalmers prepared the corpses for their journey to the underworld.

CHAPTER XXVII
A FLEECING FROM A FRIEND

In the morning, the militia came in to pass inspection. We were told that, beginning that same day, the food would be provided in the afternoon, about two o'clock. When we wanted to know if they were going to give us some breakfast, all we got for an answer was laughter.

It had now been four or five days since we had lost contact with the outside world. Neither friends nor families knew where we were. Manuel and Jesús were being eaten up by the fear that something bad might happen to their wives and children.

Manuel's wife was furiously counterrevolutionary.

"I've told her so many times to keep her mouth shut!", he complained, "Well, there's no way to keep her quiet. She even got in trouble with the president of the spy committee in our block. They'll probably take her too!"

Jesús was more depressed each day. He was often found crying.

"If at least they knew that I am still alive!", he said.

The only one in this world that might be losing sleep over me was Cachita, who had told me that, after all these years, she had come to love me like a son.

Strangely, Dr. Mora didn't seem to worry much about the impossibility of communicating with his family. As far as that goes, we didn't even know if he had a family. The quiet man with inexpressive blue eyes never talked about his private life.

Besides our isolation from the outside world, we were facing other serious problems.

We were locked in that narrow and stuffy gallery, breathing its vitiated atmosphere. Neither sunshine nor air entered the gloomy corridor.

Besides, we were always hungry.

Some of the militiamen, if they were paid for their services, would go to a nearby store and buy guava paste, crackers and condensed milk for the prisoners.

But not everybody could afford these services, since most of us had been robbed by the arresting soldiers and militiamen. Others had no money on them at the time of their arrest.

To make it even worse, Manuel, Jesús and I were smokers, and of the cigarettes that we had with us when we were arrested, only four were left.

Long before the invasion, I knew in my heart that things would be going from bad to worse in Yagruma. This premonition made me withdraw, little by little, three thousand and some pesos that I had in a savings account.

I gave this money to Cachita, for safekeeping. The only cash that my captors could make off with were the fifty pesos that Angelito stole out of the drawer of my cabinet.

Meanwhile, in the gallery, the cases of influenza were on the increase. To complete the picture, quite a few among us suffered from asthma and heart ailments; others had cancer, tuberculosis and venereal diseases.

The food that they gave us that afternoon was as skimpy and as bad as what they had been feeding us during the previous days. The only difference was that now we found some chick peas swimming in the soup, instead of beans, and it was yucca instead of sweet potatoes.

We wolfed it down in no time, because we were starving.

Just after we had lit our last cigarettes, I saw a police sergeant enter the tunnel, bayonet in hand. He was a short, black man, about fifty years of age, with a big belly and a scar on one cheek, under his right eye.

I recognized him. His name was Roque Almanza, and he was, like me, from Helena. In our hometown, this man earned his living selling lottery tickets and collecting bets for the numbers game. He was a frequent visitor at our house, because my grandmother used to gamble a few nickels every week.

I ran over to him, calling him by his name. Almanza, surprised and scared, turned around, with the bayonet thrust out. "Hey, hey! Stop right there!", he cried.

I stopped at once. Almanza came up to me, suspiciously.

"What's the matter?", he asked, "What's the problem?"

"Almanza, don't you remember me?"

"Nooo! And, how do you know my name?"

"I'm the grandson of Cándida Oropesa".

Almanza's face changed. Now he smiled, friendly. He came up to me as though to hug me, but when he realized that several pairs of eyes were fixed on him, he restrained himself to give me a pat on the back.

"Of course!", he exclaimed, "Miguelito, Doña Cándida's grandson! It's been a lot of years! Tell me, how is your grandmother?"

"She died a few years ago".

"Oh, the poor thing! She was a good person, Doña Cándida! She always invited me for a cup a coffee when I went to her house to collect for the numbers game! But, brother Miguelito, how have you ended up here?"

"Chico, I don't know! I'm not involved in anything, that's the truth, and I've never been shooting off my mouth! It has to be a mistake!"

"If that's true", replied Almanza, "Don't worry! You won't have any problem!"

"What about this uniform?", I asked, "How long have you been in the police?"

"Since the triumph of the revolution", he answered, "I had tried to get in before, but I couldn't. I had a criminal record, you know!"

"Then, how did you manage to get in now?"

"My brother Ortelio was in the hills with generalissimo Casto Cruz and...well, you know how it is!"

"I sure do!"

Almanza looked at his watch. "I better get going", he said, "The lieutenant will give me hell if he catches me screwing off".

He extended his hand.

"Listen, Miguelito, if there is anything I can do for you... No problem! Eh? We Helenos have to stick together!"

I saw the skies opening up.

"Well", I told him, "Now that you have offered..."

"What is it?"

"I live in a boarding house close to the university. The owner, of course, doesn't know where I am, nor if I am still alive. She is very close to me. Can you take a message to her?"

Almanza's face contracted. His nose and forehead were furrowed, and his eyes became two slits.

"Listen, brother, that's going to be difficult!", he replied, "The prisoners can't send messages to anyone outside. That order comes from up above!"

"And who's going to know?", I said, "That woman is a serious, responsible person! And you know that I'm not going to say anything to anybody!"

Almanza scratched his head, his eyes fixed on the floor.

"It's really dangerous!", he repeated, "If they catch me in this, they'll cut my balls off!"

I could see that the man, like a good Yagruman, wanted to be greased.

"Listen, Almanza", I said, "I know this is risky for you, but I'll know how to thank you for your help. How does that grab you?"

Almanza's expression changed. He was smiling again.

"Mr. Money is a powerful gentleman", he said.

"That's how it is!", I exclaimed, "Write down the woman's address!"

He took out a pencil stub and a package of cigarettes, on top of which he scribbled Cachita's name and telephone number.

"I'll call her this afternoon and make an appointment with her", he said, "What is it that you want?"

"First tell her where I am, and that I'm OK. Explain the situation to her. And tell her to send me a carton of cigarettes and one hundred pesos".

"And how much for me?"

"How about twenty bucks?"

"Brother, make it at least twenty five!

"OK, twenty five bucks! But, call her today!"

He took out the pack of cigarettes and the pencil stub again.

"Look, write something on here. I don't want the lady to think that I'm making this all up!"

I wrote on the package: "The bearer is a friend.-Trust him.-Miguel.-

"Can you leave me a few cigarettes?", I asked as I gave him back the package.

He took out five and gave them to me, and also a few matches.

"I'll see you tonight", he said as he left.

My friends got all excited when I told them about my meeting with Almanza.

"Do you think the man would like to do business with us?", they kept asking me.

"Let's wait until tonight", I told them, "If he comes through, I'll tell him about you".

Almanza came to our corner that night and gave me a letter from Cachita, the cigarettes, and seventy five pesos.

"Everything went OK", he said, "I called her and we arranged to meet at Central Park. She gave me my twenty five pesos, and from the hundred that she sent you, I took another twenty five. Is that OK?"

I felt like telling him to go piss on his mother's skull, but I smothered the impulse to say it. We needed this son of a bitch!

"That's OK, brother!", I told him, "You can take her another message in a few days, right?"

He nodded his assent.

"Another thing, I have three friends here, regular guys, very serious. They want to get in touch with their wives. What do you say?"

He scratched his beard. "I don't know, Miguelito. I'm worried. That's too many people, too much risk".

"No, listen!", I assured him, "I know these guys well. They are no loose tongues, I guarantee it! Besides, there's more money for you!"

This last seemed to be the most convincing.

"OK", he said, "But it's going to cost them!" "The grease is not a problem", I told him.

"OK, I'll come by here in a few minutes. Have you got some paper?"

"No".

Almanza took out a folded sheet of lined paper from his shirt pocket and gave it to me.

"Tell them to write down their names, their wives' and their telephone numbers. I'll talk to them about the rest when I come back. See you later, then!"

"Much obliged", I said.

CHAPTER XXVIII
INTO THE NIGHT FROM DANTE'S INFERNO

Almanza was not the only one to make a tidy profit from his "personal services". Other policemen, soldiers and militiamen were also engaged in the same business, filling their pockets with the money that they got for delivering cash and letters to the prisoners, or for makings trips to the store to get them crackers, guava paste or cigarettes.

We could even drink coffee, that some of the common prisoners sold us under the control of the militia. Those sons-of-bitches charged us two pesos for half a small can of watery coffee.

We were also informed by Almanza about the failure of the invasion. The American planes, supposed to provide air cover, never materialized, and Casto Cruz's air force took its pleasure in sinking the supply ships. The invaders had to surrender when they ran out of ammunition.

Many were massacred, on Generalissimo Casto's orders. The survivors were packed into sealed trucks and hauled off to Sabana. Those who didn't die of asphyxiation during the trip were locked up in a military fortress. The communists organized demonstrations that filled the streets of Sabana, demanding that the "worms" be given the firing squad.

Meanwhile, influenza was sweeping through our tunnel like fire through the brush, infecting a great number of prisoners. Three men died during our first day in the dungeons. Two of them, apparently, suffered heart attacks; nobody could imagine what happened to the third one, a man of seventy some years. Dr. Mora told us that the old man might have had a massive stroke.

By strict orders of the fortress' commanding officer, political prisoners were not to receive medical attention, and it was also expressly prohibited to bring them medicines of any kind.

We begged, implored and supplicated that some medical assistance be provided to us, but our entreaties were ignored. All we could do for the sick ones was to give them herbal tea, which the militiamen sold to us at stratospheric prices..

The Canadian priest helped the dying in their last moments. When somebody died, four of his fellow prisoners grabbed the body by the feet and the arms and, screaming that passage be opened throughout, dragged it to the mouth of the gallery and left it there, leaning against the iron door. Later on, the militiamen came and took away the corpse.

Ten years have gone by, and still, in my nightmares, I see those men, carrying their sinister loads through the gloomy corridor. These images will never be erased from my memory; they are alive, engraved forever in my mind.

Many of the captives could not cope with the situation. After the first week of imprisonment they were completely "burnt out". One of those was Dr. Heiser, that old man with white hair and mustache, dressed formally, who had been one the first, along with Manolo, Jesús, and I, to enter the sinister gallery.

Dr. Heiser had completely lost touch with reality. He spent hours sitting on the floor, with his legs crossed as if he were doing Yoga, mumbling incoherently meaningless things. We even had to help him urinate, opening his pants; if not, he would pee on himself. We also had to take away his dentures, to keep him from swallowing them.

I remember another case, that of a young man who spent his entire time sitting down, motionless and glassy-eyed, with his legs extended. He didn't speak nor grimace. Nothing seemed to make any impression on him. We had to fetch him food and make him swallow it, or he would have starved to death.

When we thought that this young man needed to relieve himself, we carried him away, took down his pants, and waited 'til he was done. Then we took him back to his place. Nevertheless, there were times when we miscalculated, and the poor man soiled himself.

During the first few days of our captivity, when we had to relieve ourselves we went to the farthest extreme of the place, where the iron grate separated us from the next section of the tunnel.

But, soon, that area was covered with feces and pools of urine, so that we had to look for another spot to take care of our bodily wastes, until the new site came to be in the same conditions as the first. The same occurred with the next place selected, and the next, and the next.

The juggernaut kept advancing, threatening the men with having to sleep on layers of excrement and pools of rotten urine. The prisoners, then, stopped those who were about to do their job near them, pushing and shoving the poor bastards, and often beating the daylights out of them.

Elías Ledón, the leader of "The Cocks from Lunayó", was the one who solved the problem. Elías was a man of medium height, but muscular, strong and fearless. According to his followers, he was a tough son of a bitch.

Escorted by some of the "Cocks", Elías walked over to where the excrement had finally reached, and with a piece of charcoal drew a line on the floor, from wall to wall, separating the dry part of the gallery from that part which we had been using as a latrine.

"From now on, everybody is going to crap and piss on the other side of that line, where it's already fouled up!", he bellowed, "Do you hear me!? If we catch anybody shitting or pissing on this side of the line, we'll cut him in half!! And we've got the balls to back it up!!"

Most of us were in agreement with Elías. We had a problem that had to be solved, no matter how!

Because of the lack of ventilation, the cigarette smoke hung in the air, floating like a mist that put a veil over the weak lights in the tunnel.

Since there was no way we could bathe, or even wash ourselves, the hundreds of bodies stored there were soon giving off sickening odors. This stench was combined with the fetid and foul odors from the excrement and the stagnant urine that covered the area designated by Elías Ledón as our latrine, which we used to call "Xochimilco".

There was an endless traffic of prisoners going into and out of that area. Once inside, the men went around looking for a slightly less filthy spot to take care of their needs. But they couldn't avoid treading through the feces already accumulated on the floor, mixed with vomit, urine and other matter.

Soon, in "Xochimilco", the floor disappeared beneath mounds and layers of shit and other human excretions. It was a dreadful stew of filth and loathsomeness, whose level and thickness kept growing by the hour.

I had never felt more humiliated, more insulted, more outraged, than when I first entered "Xochimilco" to do my job. But, under certain circumstances, human beings can easily be made to lose their self esteem. A few days later, we calmly dropped our pants and shorts, sank down above our knees into the sinister and fetid mass and relieved ourselves, in a state of total indifference.

On one of the walls of the tunnel, somebody had written with charcoal, in large letters, two lines that accurately reflected our feelings:

"The blood in my veins seems to be lying dormant; inside my breast the heart seems no longer to beat".

We were getting weaker by the day in the sickly environment of our foul smelling enclosure, deprived of sunshine and fresh air, eating the scarce and vile food that our captors fed us. Gaunt and wasted as we were, we could have been likened to a legion of lost souls wandering in the caverns of hell.

Death had become a daily occurrence in the tunnel. But it was no longer a matter of four or five deaths in a week; now, every day, we had two or three bodies carried to the iron gate. One of the last to die was a young man, freckled and red-haired, whom we knew by his nickname of "Titico".

According to some other prisoners who at that moment were in "Xochimilco" moving their bowels, Titico had entered the area in a big hurry and was taking down his pants when, all of a sudden, he began to scream, clutching his abdomen with both hands.

Several of us, at hearing him, ran over to see what was happening. When we got to "Xochimilco", Titico was writhing on the layer of feces and foul matter that covered the floor. Blood poured from his mouth, mixed with what I thought were particles of his insides.

The cries had stopped. Now, only a muted, persistent complaint issued from his lips.

"Oh, my God! Oh, my God! Oh, my God!"

"We better take him over to the grate", said Elías, "At least, so he won't die here, covered in shit!'

Elías and I, together with two other prisoners that were friends of the sick man, lifted up the convulsing body and carried him up to the front, next to the iron bars.

"Militia!", roared Elías, "Militia, here, at the entrance!

"We've got a sick man here! Hurry!"

To our surprise, our calls were answered, not by militiamen, but by a police captain followed by several cops.

"Let's see, what kind of emergency is this?", he asked "Who do you think you are? What's going on?"

"Captain", answered Elías, pointing at Titico, "This boy is very sick! He needs a doctor right away!"

"Chico, were it up to me, we'd take him to hospital right now", replied the captain, "But you know the orders we have. Besides, the commandant is away, and he won't get back until next week!"

"Who is in charge, then?"

"I am, until the commandant returns".

"You seem to be a man with feelings, captain", I begged, "Have a heart! Please, see that this man is taken to a hospital!"

"If you could just talk to one of the doctors and get him to come here to see our friend", urged Elías, "You'll be doing a good deed, and good deeds are always rewarded".

The captain seemed to think it over for a few seconds. "Very well", he said finally, "Let's see what I can do. I'm not promising anything, but I'll try my best".

And he left, followed by the others. Elías squatted down beside Titico, who had stopped complaining. He took his pulse and passed his hand over his forehead. All of a sudden, he stood up and looked at us, moving his head.

"He's gone", he said.

One didn't have to be a doctor to see that the man was dead. He was lying on his back, with his eyes wide open and a pleading expression on his face. His convulsions had stopped, and blood no longer flowed from his mouth.

Almost an hour later the captain returned with his men and an army lieutenant who had the insignia of the medical corps on his uniform.

"The doctor has come to see your friend", said the captain.

"You got here a little late", replied Elías, "The man is now chatting with Saint Peter".

The captain said nothing, but it seemed to me that he had been somewhat shaken by the news.

"Let me see him", said the doctor, "Guard, open up!"

He entered and kneeled down beside the motionless body, examining it for a few moments.

"You are right", he told Elías, "He is dead".

"What do you think happened to him, doctor?"

The doctor became evasive. "Frankly, I don't have an idea", he replied, "An autopsy will have to be done. What's his name?"

"Ramón Aldazábal", answered one of the deceased's friends. "Captain", he added, "I'd like to clean his face before they take him away. May I go to the hose to wet my handkerchief?"

"OK, but hurry!", said the captain.

The handkerchief that the man took out of his pocket had been white, but now it was the color of chocolate. He was back in a couple of minutes and, with the wet handkerchief, wiped off the crusts of excrement stuck to the face and hands of the cadaver.

At a sign from the doctor, four militiamen lifted up the body and carried it out of the tunnel.

"I'm really sorry about this", said the captain, "Believe me, I did all I could!"

"We appreciate that, captain", I assured him, "This is the first time that a doctor has come to see one of us".

"Very well", he replied, "We have to go. I hope that you won't have to be in here very much longer. I've heard it said that in a few days they are going to set you all free".

He was getting ready to leave, followed by the doctor, when Elías stood in front of him.

"Captain" he said, "You have shown yourself to be a man of conscience. And the same goes for you, doctor. That's why I want you to know that if they won't let us go out into the courtyard, for some fresh air and sunshine and get a little exercise, the dead ones in here are going to be in bunches".

"What we are asking", he went on, "Is that you talk to whoever you have to, to obtain permission for us to be allowed to get out, at least in the daytime. We are not going to make trouble, captain! We're not criminals! I don't know why they have us locked up here! We are all working men here, honorable men, men with dignity!"

"I don't know", answered the captain, "I'll do whatever I can. But we have to be very careful. You may not believe it, but everyone is being watched here, including us".

The doctor was silent, constantly looking around to be sure that nobody was getting close to us.

"Dr. Quevedo and I will talk to our superiors about the conditions down here", the captain finally said, “Of course, I can't promise you anything".

And without waiting to hear another word, the two officers left the tunnel.

I don't know if it was the result of what the captain had promised us that he would do, but a few days later we were informed by a voice on the loudspeaker that, beginning the following morning, we would be allowed to go out in the yard, from eight o'clock in the morning until eight o'clock at night. We were delirious with happiness.

"Maybe what the captain heard was true", commented Manuel, "It is very likely they will release us soon".

From the next day on, as soon as we got up, we went out to the yard. The filth, the sour sweat, the shit and the urine from "Xochimilco" that we had encrusted on our clothes and shoes, gave off a repugnant odor.

Early in the evening, it began to get cooler in the yard. The militia sold us, at an outrageously elevated price, burlap sacks which we used to cover ourselves and also on which we slept.

We looked like an army of beggars: emaciated, bearded, stinking and in tatters, with the tin plates at our belts and the burlap sacks over our shoulders.

Some guy from one of the groups at the end of the tunnel came to see Elías to tell him that he and some of his friends were planning to revolt when they got outside in the yard.

Their plan was to subdue the guards and take their arms. Then they would shoot their way out of the fortress and go into hiding in Sabana.

The man wanted Elías and his followers to take part in the mutiny.

"You guys do whatever you want to", replied Elías, "But neither myself nor my friends are going to get mixed up in that".

"Come on, Elías! What's the matter? No guts?"

"Look up there!", said Elías, indicating the machine gun emplacements on top of the stone walls that circled the patio, "Or haven't you seen them?"

"Well, so what!? That's what we have balls for!"

"As big as they are, what good are they going to do you against the machine guns?"

"God damn it! Look at the condition I'm in, Elías! Look!! I'm starving, showing my ass through my ripped pants, having to get into that shit up to my ears when I have to take a crap! Who wants to keep on living like that!!"

"Well, I do! Who's going to put food on the table for my wife and children if they wipe me out, eh? Tell me!!"

"Then we can't count on you?"

"No!", answered Elías, "There's no point in discussing it. Look, wait it out, brother. We'll be out of here soon!"

The other turned his back and left, grumbling and cursing.

Elías told us about it later. "I don't like that bastard", he said, "I'd be surprised if he wasn't a Casto Cruz agent!"

In the afternoon of the twenty fifth day of our stay in the dungeons of El Infante, orders came through the loudspeaker for all of the prisoners to go out into the yard immediately. Upon leaving the tunnel we saw several tables arranged at the side of the main hall's entranceway. There were stacks of cardboard boxes on the tables.

Following orders given to us on the loudspeaker, we lined up and kept silent. An officer that we hadn't seen before, probably the fortress' commandant, spoke to us through a bullhorn.

"The militia comrades have a list with the names of the persons detained in this place", he announced, "In a few minutes, the comrades are going to begin calling names, in alphabetical order!"

"When you hear your name, come at once to have your record checked, be fingerprinted and, then, released. You have..."

The commandant couldn't keep on talking. The clamor of hundreds of voices with which the announcement was received drowned out his words. The prisoners screamed, yelled and whistled, jumping up and down.

Finally the commandant was able to continue.

"We aren't going to begin until there is order and silence", he cried, "If you don't shut up and calm down, nobody will go anywhere!"

His words pacified the crowd, and a few minutes later, the first name on the list was called.

Although the militiamen worked non-stop, it was nighttime before they called my name. When I arrived at the tables, one of them took my fingerprints, checked my name and address and, after asking me several questions and jotting my answers in the file, he ordered me to join a group that was waiting beside the stone steps, guarded by several soldiers.

Fifteen minutes later, I had left behind me the towering mass of the fortress and descended the stairway downhill. We were free again, but, for how long? When would it please Casto Cruz to have us live another nightmare like the one we had just suffered? Would he, this time, put us against the wall, to face the firing squad?

Chapter XXIX
THERE'LL BE NO RETURN

Night had already fallen over Sabana when I arrived at Carlos IV Avenue. No cars were passing by. There was not a soul to be seen anywhere.

I was worried. I looked like a tramp, and my body and clothes gave off a nauseating odor. Some busybody might take me for a prowler and throw the cops on me.

At the end of the block I could see the lights shining from a bar, "Las Palmas Nuevas", and that's where I went. The place was empty, except for the bartender, who was leaning against the counter smoking a cigarette, with a cup of coffee in front of him.

I went over to the guy.

"Where's the telephone?", I asked.

"Did you come from the hill?"

"Yes".

"The phone is beside the men's room, over to your right", he replied, motioning with his hand.

I still had money from Cachita's last remittance.

"Listen, brother", I said, laying a five-peso bill on the counter, "I'm so hungry, it's killing me. While I'm phoning, fix me a ham and cheese sandwich, with Dutch cheese, and give me a real cold beer".

"Ham, there isn't any", he told me, "The little bit there is goes to the top Commies. If you want, I have a few small pieces of pork roast left".

"OK, that'll be all right, make it with the pork and the Dutch cheese".

"There isn't any Dutch cheese, either. You won't find any Dutch cheese in Yagruma even if you offered to pay a thousand pesos a pound for it. The only ones that can get any Dutch cheese in Yagruma are the top Commies".

"Well then, what do you have?"

"I've got some domestic white cheese. It's a little sour, but, like the man said, 'our cheese is sour, but it's our cheese'."

"All right then, the pork and the white cheese. It will taste like pheasant from India, compared to the shit they fed us at the castle! "

I went over to the phone and called Cachita. She answered the phone herself.

"It's Ruperto", I said, "Do you have visitors?"

That was a code that we had agreed on in he past.

It was a warning to be careful of what we said.

"No, we are watching television", she answered, "How's it going with you?"

"OK. Listen, I'm here at the corner of Carlos IV and Soberana, in a bar called "Las Palmas Nuevas". Get Pérez right away and come and get me. I don't want to walk, my arthritis is acting up".

"All right, don't move from there!", she said, and hung up.

The bartender had served the sandwich and beer at a table in a dark corner, behind large curtains.

"Nobody passing by on the street can see you here", he said, "It's safer that way".

I put away the sandwich and the beer in no time, and stayed quiet in that corner, separating the curtains from time to time to peer out to the street. Finally, I saw old Pérez's taxi, a '55 Dodge, come around the corner and slowly approach "Las Palmas Nuevas".

I left the bar and walked toward the taxi. But, even though I was sure that Cachita and Pérez had seen me, the car passed by without stopping.

"Pérez!", I hollered, "Cachita! It's me, Miguel! Open the door!!"

Fortunately, Cachita had lowered a rear window and could hear me. Pérez stopped the car, without shutting off the motor, but didn't open the car door. I ran over to them and stuck my head in the window.

"What's the matter? Don't you know me!?"

"Miguel!! Is that you!!? I'm sorry, son, we didn't recognize you! You look like a beggar! Christ!! You smell like something rotten!!

"My God!", complained Pérez, "You are going to stink up the whole car!"

When I got in the taxi, Cachita and Pérez rolled down the windows. Cachita held a handkerchief over her nose because, like she said, I was a walking sewer.

"OK, tell me everything!", she asked, "The stories going around here make one's hair stand on end. Oh, by the way, you have a letter from the Ministry and a manila envelope that a lady left for you!"

"Did she say what her name was?"

"Anita. Is that a new conquest?"

"No, no! Anita is a friend of my aunt Lidia. She's keeping some papers for me. Nothing important!"

"We'll talk tomorrow", I promised her, "First, I'm going to disinfect myself and get rid of all this shit from up there. And after that, I'm going to bed, to sleep! I've been sleeping on the floor for nearly a month".

When we got to the house, I took off my clothes and my shoes, leaving on my shorts, only. I made a bundle of all of it.

"All this has to be thrown in the garbage", I said to Cachita, "When do they pick it up?"

"The day after tomorrow", she told me.

Cachita grabbed the bundle with one hand, and holding her nose with the other, rushed downstairs. She was back in couple of minutes.

"Is there any hot water?", I asked.

"Yes. I lit the water heater before we left to pick you up. I put a clean towel for you".

I went into the bathroom, filled the bathtub with warm water and sank myself into it, with ineffable pleasure. Leaning my head on the edge, with my eyes closed, I enjoyed the sensation of indescribable well-being.

I was awakened from that glory by someone pounding on the door, and then, Cachita's voice.

"Miguel! You've been in there for more than an hour! What's going on? Are you OK?"

"Everything's fine!", I answered, "It's just taking me a long time! I've got a thick layer of crud to wash off!"

It was true. The crust of filth that I removed from my body was making the bath water into a dark and foul smelling soup.

I drained out the dirty water, rinsed out the bathtub with a sponge and filled it up again. Then, with a piece of kitchen soap and a bristle brush, I scrubbed my whole body again.

This time, the water didn't get so dirty nor so stinking.

But I still wasn't clean. I smelled less putrid, but I still smelled.

"Cachitaaa!", I called.

"What do you want?"

"Get me some laundry detergent, please! I can't get this stuff off with just soap!"

I opened the door a little and stuck out my arm. Seconds later she put the box of detergent in my hand.

"Don't waste it, son! That's all I could get with my ration book!", she warned me, "God only knows when there will be any more!"

Finally, after a good scrubbing with the detergent and brush, I was able to get myself reasonably clean. I put on my pajamas and went to the dining room, where Cachita was waiting for me.

"I couldn't fix you any café con leche", she said, "Now the government only gives milk to children under five years of age and old folks over seventy five".

Cachita had managed to get some eggs the day before, and she fried me a couple. That, plus some bread and a bowl of black bean soup, made my dinner that night.

"Come on, sit down and eat!", she urged me.

I tried to sit down at the table, but I couldn't do it.

"Cachita", I explained, "I've had to sit on the floor for so long, that I've lost the ability to use a chair. Let me sit on the floor now; tomorrow I'll try to get back to normal!

She looked at me with pity.

"Whatever you want, son", she said, "You are in your home".

Only then I realized that neither Rosalina nor Cucuíto were around, and I asked Cachita about them.

"They are in the countryside, in San Felipe", she answered, "My brother owns a little farm there. Nothing much, less than three acres. That's why the government hasn't taken it yet".

"And what gave them the idea of going there?"

"Well, for more than a month we have had nothing to eat but `Lumumba in his undies'. That's all there was!".

"Lumumba in his undies! What the hell is that!?"

"Black beans and rice! It finally got to the point where Cucuíto refused to eat. You know how he's been spoiled so by my daughter ".

"Will they eat better at San Felipe?"

"Yes, because my brother raises chickens and a few pigs. He also grows vegetables and plantains".

Cachita brought me up to date on things that had been happening during the time I was in prison. From her I learned that the United States had broken diplomatic relations with Yagruma.

She also told me about the invaders' fate, and the fact that more than three hundred thousand people had been arrested all over the island, on the day of the invasion.

While she was talking, I devoured the bread and eggs. I was falling asleep, so finally I got up to go to bed.

"Thanks, sweetheart", I told Cachita, "We'll talk tomorrow, when I come back from the Ministry. I have to find out what the hell they are planning to do with me".

"Oh, look!", she replied, "Let me get the letters that I have for you". She got up and left the room.

A couple of minutes later Cachita came back with two envelopes. One bore the seal of the Ministry of Commerce, while the other was a manila envelope. I put them in my robe pocket and went to my room, because I could hardly stay on my feet from fatigue.

I was so sleepy, and so tired, that when I got to my room I didn't want to bother opening the envelopes. I threw them on top of the chest of drawers, disrobed, and threw myself on the bed. I think I fell asleep as soon as my head hit the pillow.

When I woke up, my first reaction was one of surprise at not feeling beneath me the hardness of the floor, nor “Xochimilco's” fetid odor in my nose.

I had barely realized that I was back in Cachita's house when her voice resounded through the hallway.

"Miguel!", she cried, "It's ten o'clock in the morning! Aren't you going to the Ministry?"

Ten o'clock! I had slept twelve hours straight through!

Still in my pajamas, I stepped into the hallway.

"Did you make some coffee?", I asked.

"Yes. I saved some for you, son!"

Back in my room, I got the two envelopes, and opened them. As I had expected, in the manila envelope that Anita left for me was my passport, with a tourist visa issued by the United States Consulate.

The other envelope contained an official communication, through which I was informed that by decree of the Minister of Commerce, dated April 25, 1961, I had been dishonorably discharged from my position as an assistant attorney in the legal department of the Ministry.

According to the document, my counterrevolutionary attitude placed me among the enemies of the revolution and the people.

Now, that was serious! The damn paper, practically, sentenced me to ostracism. It made a pariah out of me; it changed me into an outcast.

Casto Cruz had abolished private property in Yagruma. The state had become the only employer, landlord and health care provider in the island. So, having been labeled as an enemy of the regime, the possibilities that I had of finding a job in my country were less than zero.

As far as working in my profession, I couldn't even dream of it! Of what use was a lawyer in Yagruma, where industry, commerce and agriculture were all nationalized, private property eliminated, and those accused of crimes tried by popular courts made up of illiterates?

Besides, taking into account the island's political climate, it was almost certain that sooner or later they would pick me up again, charging me with "crimes against the state".

The possibility existed that I would end up against the wall, facing one of the many firing squads that operated daily in Yagruma to remind the enemies of Casto Cruz that you didn't mess around with the Great Leader.

The future in my country, in addition to hunger, promised me more prison, and maybe death.

The United States was my only hope.

I went to look for Cachita, who was in the living room, mending a pair of pants for Cucuíto. She was surprised to see me.

"Oh, I thought that you had gone to see your bosses!", she said to me.

I took out of my pocket the letter from the ministry and showed it to her. Cachita read it and gave back to me. She was livid with fury.

"Those sons-of-bitches!", she exploded, "Just like that! Without giving you an opportunity to explain or defend yourself! Bastards! And, what are you going to do now?"

"I don't know. I'll think of something."

"Remember, son, this is your house! You can stay here for as long as you want to".

"Thanks, love! I know that! Listen, did Anita leave any kind of message for me?"

"Yes, now I remember! She said to tell you that she was leaving for New York the following day".

I left Cachita's house and began to walk aimlessly down the street. When I got to Grillo park, I looked for a bench in the shade and sat down to rest, trying to decide what to do.

Only two things were certain. First, I had to get out of Yagruma as soon as I could; second, the United States was, at that moment, the only country in the hemisphere that would take in and help whoever managed to escape Yagruma's communist regime.

The American visa that I had in my passport only took care of part of my problem. In order to leave the island, one had to have an exit permit issued by the police. This permit, invariably, was denied to anyone that was, like me, listed as an enemy of the regime.

Abilio Pardo had been in my thoughts since that morning. He had been in the mountains with Casto Cruz's. Now a colonel, Abilio was nothing less than deputy chief of police. He could help me to get out of Yagruma.

But now Abilio was a big shot and, as the saying goes, "with the glories, one forgets the memories".

Could he have forgotten our bohemian student times, the party nights in Sabana, our gatherings at Cachita's house? And, above all, would he be willing to risk his position, and even his life, by helping an enemy of the people?

But, pondering and brooding over fears and suspicions wasn't going to solve my problems. I realized that I had no other choice but to talk to Abilio, face to face.

I would explain the situation that I was in and ask him to help me, in the name of our old friendship.

"The iron has to be beaten when it's hot", I said to myself, getting up, "It's in the hands of God!"

I walked to a nearby stop and caught a bus that went close to the steel and concrete building that housed the headquarters of the national police force. When I got off the bus, I walked to the building's main entrance, which was guarded by several policemen and militiamen armed with rifles and submachine guns.

"I'm Dr. Baró", I said, showing them my ID from the Sabana Bar Association, "I have to see Colonel Pardo".

"Go to the end of the hallway", was the answer, "Talk to the lieutenant in charge".

When I told him what I wanted, the lieutenant motioned to a bench, and told me to sit down. From there I saw him talk on the phone for a couple of minutes, after which he asked me to follow him.

"Come with me, comrade. The colonel will see you now".

He took me to the elevator. "It's on the second floor, the third door on the right", he said.

Abilio, very elegant in his uniform with colonel insignia, was waiting for me, standing beside a mahogany desk. As soon as he saw me enter, he came towards me with his eyes wide open, and putting a finger over his lips, indicated with the other hand toward the ceiling, to let me know that the room was bugged.

"Miguel, for God's sake! Long time no see!"

"That's right", I replied, keeping up the acting, "Four years at least, my friend!"

Without saying a word, he took a small piece of paper from the top of his desk, folded it up, and put it in one of the pockets of my guayabera.

"Well, so how goes it?", he asked, winking an eye, "To what do I owe this surprise?"

"Chico, I'm trying to see if a few of those of us that were classmates at law school could get together and organize a reunion of the graduates from our class".

"And you", I went on, "With your revolutionary prestige and your official position, could help out a lot. Are you interested?"

"Listen, Miguel", he answered, "You can't imagine how much I would like to help you out in this project, and even be a part of the organizing committee".

"But I'm so busy now", he concluded, "My responsibilities are such, that I'm no going to lie to you. I can't tell you yes, you can count on me, and then, later, leave you dangling!"

"Man, if it's like that, don't say any more!", I replied, "I can imagine how busy you must be! But I said to myself, what the hell, nothing is lost by trying!"

"Listen, if there is anything I can help you with...", he said.

"Sure!", I responded, "You're not going to get rid of me that easy!"

"Someone told me you are still living at Cachita's house".

"Yes. I don't have any family, I never married...Where was I going to go?"

"What happened to Perlita?"

"Irreconcilable differences", I answered dryly.

"I wish I could give you more time", said Abilio, "But in a few moments I have a meeting with general Almejero".

"No problem", I replied, "I know you don't have a lot of time".

"Come by another day!", added Abilio, "We'll see if we can have lunch together!"

We said good-bye with a handshake.

I left the police headquarters and, after having walked several blocks, took out Abilio's note. He had printed an address and a short message: "**EIGHT O' CLOCK TONIGHT.-I'LL BE WAITING**".

The address that Abilio wrote in his note was F Street, number 1725, between 15 and 17.

It was located in El Venado, a section where, for many years, Sabana's tropical aristocrats and the wealthy bourgeoisie used to live.

During the last twenty years, El Venado had been decaying. The aristocracy, the well-to-do and the blood-sucking politicians now preferred to live in the new developments that had been built on the outskirts of Sabana.

The houses, in these new and exclusive neighborhoods, were more luxurious, more ostentatious, and infinitely more expensive than those in El Venado.

Nevertheless, the old quarter still had remains of its past splendor. Here and there could still be seen sumptuous old mansions, apartment buildings that were master works of Yagruman architecture, and romantic, stone-paved streets lined with poplars and royal palms.

I took a bus that let me off at the corner of 17th and F.

Turning down F street towards 15th, I walked the full length of the block, asking heaven not to awaken the suspicions of the busybodies in the block's spy committee.

At last, I found myself in front of number 1725. It was a pretty villa, painted white, with blue windows and surrounded by an artistic wrought iron fence. There were two automobiles and a jeep parked in front of the villa.

The gate of the fence was ajar. I opened it, and went down a paved pathway that led to a door. Suddenly, four men carrying Russian machine guns came out of the house. Two of them went behind me, preventing my retreat, while the other two stopped my advance.

"Are you Dr. Baró?", asked one of the men.

Nothing surprised me any more. "The same", I responded.

"You'll have to excuse us, doctor", said the man, "But we have to search you".

"Are you from the police?"

"Yes, from colonel Pardo's personal escort. I'm sergeant Sevilla. OK, Kin-Kan, search the doctor!"

Kin-Kan was a black man, about six and a half feet tall and weighing close to three hundred pounds. He searched me with the rapidity and skill of a real expert.

"He's clean", he said to the sergeant.

"You may go into the house, doctor", he told me, "The colonel is waiting for you".

When I called at the door, Abilio in person came out to greet me.

"Brother, at last we can talk!", he said, putting his arm around my shoulders, "It's been a long time since we have had a chance to talk. Well, let's go into the living room!"

Walking through the lobby, I mentioned my encounter with the four gorillas. Abilio laughed.

"Don't take it the wrong way! Sevilla searches everybody that comes to see me, even if it is my own father! Look, Miguel, these men of my escort are the only ones I can trust".

"Are you having problems, Abilio?"

"No! But the top Commies around the Great Leader suspect their own shadows. We in the military are under special surveillance".

"Are you kidding me?"

"I'm not, believe me! The party doesn't lose sight of a single footstep we take, even as loyal as we are to the revolutionary government. One has to be very careful with what one says".

"Now I understand why you went through all that farce in your office".

"Exactly! Everything that is said there, is recorded".

"Are you serious, chico? And what do they do with the recordings?"

"All the information is sent to military intelligence. They have Russians, Bulgarians and Romanians working there. Those are the ones in charge of counter-espionage in Yagruma. What do you think of that?"

I would have liked to tell him what I thought of Casto Cruz, his revolution and his Commies, but I kept my trap shut. After all, Abilio was a colonel and a friend of Casto Cruz.

The living room of the villa was spacious, and furnished with luxury and good taste. The two lighting fixtures that hung from the ceiling, and the fine, custom-made mahogany furniture with velvet-lined seats and backs must have cost a fortune.

We sat down on some enormous, varnished mahogany rocking chairs. On an ebony table, inlaid with ivory, was a box of Yagruman cigars. Abilio opened it, took our several cigars, put one in his mouth and slipped the others into the pockets of my guayabera.

"Light up, it won't be long until there's no more of these", he told me, "Yagruma needs foreign currency".

We lit up, and smoked in silence for a few minutes, enjoying the delicious aroma of the cigars.

"It's true that the revolution devours her own sons", Abilio said, "But, before swallowing us, she treats us nicely".

I didn't know how to begin explaining the problem that was facing me.

"I heard that you got married", I commented, for no other reason than to have something to say.

His brow furrowed, as though he hadn't appreciated my remark.

"Yes, three years ago", he responded.

"Well, I hope I'll meet your wife before I go", I ventured.

His brow furrowed even more.

"That won't be possible, my friend", he said, "My wife isn't here".

"How could that be? She is not home at night? Without her husband?"

Abilio took a deep breath and tightened his shoulders as though saying: "Son-of-a-bitch, here we go again!"

"Look, I'm not going to make up a story for you", he said, "This isn't my house! A good friend of mine, Lula Castillo, lives here. I knew her in the Sierra, and...you know how it is! I brought her back here to Sabana with me and...well...we are living together!"

"Where is she from?"

"She's from El Solibio, a village to the south of Levante".

"So, in other words, you brought her to the capital and set her up in this house...but that must have cost you tons of money!"

"Well, the truth is that it didn't", replied Abilio, "This is one of the mansions that the revolutionary government took away from the rich, to give the people".

"I see. Since your girl friend is part of the people and you are a colonel from the Sierra, you were able to arrange that the house be given to her".

"That's the way it was. Listen, Miguel, how much do you think she pays the state for the rent of this house?"

"I have no idea. How much?"

"Forty pesos! Forty lousy pesos!

"Don't tell me, chico! That's a gift! And you pay for that, right?"

"Hell, no! The revolution pays for it! I managed to put her on the payroll, in the Ministry of Public Works. Two hundred fifty pesos a month! All she has to do is show up at the end of the month and collect her paycheck".

"The revolution hasn't changed the Yagrumans", I thought.

"Of course", Abilio then said, getting serious, "Don't repeat any of this to anybody! If I'm telling it to you, it's because I can't be a hypocrite with you, nor with Ruperto, nor any of the old gang!"

The cigars had gone out in the ash trays. Abilio took his, lighted it again, and leaned back in his rocking chair. I did the same and we smoked in silence for a few minutes.

"Well, Miguel", Abilio finally said, "Now tell me why you wanted to see me. How can I help you?"

"The moment of truth has arrived", I thought, "From here, either I leave for the United States or this son-of-a-bitch will have me arrested".

"I've thought it over for a long time before deciding to talk to you", I began, "If I do it, it's because I think that you still are the same Abilio that was my friend years ago. I..."

Abilio interrupted me, impatiently.

"Stop beating around the bush, chico! Tell me what's wrong. What's your problem?"

"This is it!", I said to myself. And I told my old friend the story of my arrest, and the weeks that I had spent as a prisoner in the dungeons of El Infante.

I also explained to him, without concealing anything, the situation that I was facing, and the steps that I had been taking in my efforts to leave the island.

"You know very well that the visa isn't any good to me", I said, "If I don't have the exit permit from the police, and a seat on the plane to Miami".

Abilio was silent, thinking.

"I can see that you have a problem", he said, after I had finished my story, "They'll take you prisoner again any day. And then it will be much more than three or four weeks. Twenty years, maybe, or who knows!"

"With that decree from the Minister of Commerce", he went on, "They now have enough to grab you, and accuse you of some crime against the fatherland, or against the revolution, or some shit like that!"

"I saw many prisoners dying and losing their mind in that hell", I replied, "Thank God, I came out of it unharmed, this time. But another experience like that will probably do me in. I would rather die. That's why I have come to ask, in the name of our friendship, that you get me out of Yagruma. You can do it".

Abilio didn't answer me at once. With his eyes focused on a spot on the ceiling, he kept chewing his cigar, moving it from one side of the mouth to the other. Finally, he lowered his gaze and stared at me.

"When do you want to leave?", he asked.

The relief that these words brought to my soul was indescribable. Happiness left me mute; I didn't know what to say, I couldn't find the words to show my gratitude.

"As soon as possible", I managed to say at last.

"OK", replied Abilio, "Bring me your passport, tomorrow morning. Be here at seven o'clock. Then, go back to Cachita's and wait there for news from me. And get your things ready! I'm going to get you out the country as fast as I can".

"Brother", I said with feeling, "How can I ever repay you for what you're doing for me?"

"Don't be silly, Miguel", he exclaimed, "I'm one of those Yagrumans that believe in friendship! Did you think I had forgotten the good times we had at Cachita's, eh? All the hell raising we did together?"

"My heart told me no", I replied, "But you, better than anybody, know what is happening in Yagruma. Things have changed in this country, Abilio! The people aren't the same!"

I wasn't totally at ease. There was still something that made me nervous, something that I hadn't discussed with Abilio, and could--I thought--weaken his resolve to help me.

"There's something that we haven't talked about yet, Abilio", I said.

"Yes? What's that?"

"I've been told that, in cases such as mine, the police charge ten thousand pesos to get somebody out of the island".

"That could be true" he said.

"I don't have that kind of money, nor any place to get it. All I have is two thousand pesos, which I'll bring you tomorrow, with the passport. I'll send you the rest from the United States, as soon as I begin to work".

Abilio looked at me in the eye.

"I thought you knew me better that that", he said, "I don't sell favors to my friends! Keep your money!"

"I have put my foot in it!", I thought.

"Listen, man, I didn't mean to offend you", I replied, trying to repair the damage that my indiscretion might have caused, "It's that I feel bad that you are going to place yourself at risk for me!"

"Nobody is going to bother me for helping a friend", he answered, "Forget about the money!"

I was having a hard time believing that my problem was being solved that easily. So accustomed was I to finding nothing but obstacles and setbacks in my way!

"I'll never forget what you are doing for me!", I said.

"Not a word of this to anybody!", he warned me, "If a stool pigeon gets hold of this, you've screwed up your exit permit, and probably end in prison again!"

Abilio stood up.

"Well, I've got to leave you. Lula is in the other room, waiting for me. The poor thing just dies to be with me! Imagine, sometimes days pass by when I can't come to see her!"

I extended my hand. "Thanks for everything", I repeated.

"Enough of that!", he replied, "That's what friends are for! OK, be here tomorrow morning, at seven! If I'm not up yet, leave the passport with Sevilla!"

Under Casto Cruz's communist regime, the bus service had grown worse by the day. I waited almost two hours for a bus to pass.

It was after midnight when I got back to Cachita's. I was feeling happy: all indications were that Lady Luck was with me this time.

Still, one thing worried me: I couldn't find a scrap of paper that Elías Ledón had given to me, with the name, address and telephone number of his brother Eufemio, who lived in Elizabeth, New Jersey. According to Elías, his brother could help me to find work when I arrived to the United States.

CHAPTER XXX
FAREWELL WITHOUT REGRET

I was back at the villa the following morning at eight o'clock sharp. Abilio was getting ready to leave. I gave him my passport.

We stayed for a few minutes, talking. I was about to take leave when Abilio stopped me.

"I must warn you", he said, "That when you get to Miami, there is a chance that the Immigration people will send you to Opa-Locka".

"Opa-Locka!? What the hell is that?"

"It's a detention center, where they process the Yagrumans arriving to the United States. If you don't have communist connections, they'll let you go after they check your background".

"But", he went on, "If you were a member of the Communist Party, or if you are listed as a Commie by the United States government, then you are really screwed, brother!"

"I wasn't even in the militia".

"I know that, but you have worked for this government. Probably, they'll detain you to check you out".

"Well, if that's the way it is, I'll have to put up with it", I replied, "I can't stay here!"

"I don't think you're going to have any big problems", Abilio said, "After all, the American consulate gave you the visa!

"Oh, another thing", he added, "As soon as Immigration turns you loose, go to the Yagruman refugee center, in Miami. They'll tell you there what you have to do".

But, how was I going to get around without any money? I couldn't take even one dollar with me, because possession of American currency had been forbidden by generalissimo Casto Cruz. Whoever got caught with dollars faced twenty years of hard labor in the tyrant's Gulag.

"Take along rum and cigars", Abilio advised me, "And sell them in Miami".

In those days, the Casto Cruz regime permitted any citizen who was leaving the country to take with him a box of Yagruman cigars, famous the world over, and a bottle of "Totí", America's favorite rum.

According to Abilio, there were swarms of hawkers all over the airport and around the refugee center, buying the cigars and rum brought from the

Yagruman exiles. Later, the peddlers would resell the merchandise at several times the price they had paid to the new immigrants.

Sergeant Sevilla appeared, bringing a tray with two cups of black-coffee. Abilio sipped his and looked at his watch.

"You better go now, Miguel", he said, "I don't want anyone to see you here".

"When will I hear from you?", I asked.

"In a couple of days, maybe more. I've got your telephone number. Now go to Cachita's, and don't leave there. Remember: don't even talk to your shadow about this!"

Once again I thanked Abilio, and left the villa. When I got home, Cachita was on the balcony, waiting for me.

"What happened? Did you go to the ministry?", she asked when she saw me.

"Yes, that's where I was", I lied, "I was talking to Faldas".

"How did he receive you?"

"Fine! Friendly as ever".

"What did he say when you told him about your problem?"

"Well, it seems that the minister is pissed off at me. I have criticized the regime, I haven't joined the militia, and I didn't show up when they called me to stand against the invaders!"

"What about Faldas, then? Can he do something for you?"

"Well, he is going to talk to the minister, to try to convince him that my punishment has been too harsh, and that I'm now ready to embrace the cause of the revolution. Of course, he couldn't promise me anything, but there's always hope".

"Supposing they let you go back to work, will you have to join the militia?"

"I don't know. It's possible!"

"Miguel! You in the militia! I don't believe it!"

"Chica, one has to wake up to reality!, I said, "What else could I do? Tend bar in a whorehouse? I have no other choice!!"

"What the hell! You are right, after all!", exclaimed Cachita, sighing, "Those sons-of-bitches have got you by the balls!!"

"They said they would give me a call to let me know", I replied, "We'll see what happens!" I got up, and after kissing her on the cheek, went to my room.

Not that day, nor the next, did I have any news from Abilio. I didn't leave the house, smoking like a stove and bursting with impatience, waiting for his call. Finally, early Friday morning, while still in bed, I heard the telephone bell ring.

Moments later, Cachita was knocking at my door.

"Hurry up, Miguel, you've got a call!", she cried.

"Tell whoever it is that I'll be right there!", I hollered, "I'm putting on my robe!"

I ran down the hall and grabbed the phone.

"Hello!"

"Doctor Baró?"

I had heard that voice before, but I couldn't guess who it was.

"This is Miguel Baró", I answered, "Who's speaking?"

"It's a friend of your friend", was the answer, "We have to talk. Ten o'clock, at Grillo Park. Sit on one of the benches facing the statue of Crispín Canteras. Understand?"

"I'll be there", I replied. The caller hung up.

Cachita had followed me to the telephone.

"Who was it?", she wanted to know, "Someone from the Ministry?"

"Yes, it was Faldas. He wants to talk to me. I have to be in his office at nine o'clock".

"Well, look, you have to hurry then! It is half past seven!"

"I'm going to shave", I said, and I ran off to the bathroom.

The grotesque-looking statue of General Crispín Canteras, one of the heroes of our Wars of Independence, stood at the center of Grillo Park.

I chose a bench in front of the monument, lit a cigarette and waited. A few minutes later I saw, coming toward me, the massive figure of Sergeant Sevilla. He had a folded newspaper in his hand.

Sevilla sat on the bench next to me and talked without looking at me.

"What you need is inside the paper", he said, "Nobody has followed you. When I go, grab it and get lost".

And leaving the newspaper on the bench, he got up and left.

My heart was pounding in my chest. I looked all around: there was nobody close by. With the most casual and innocent appearance that I could muster, I picked up the newspaper, put it under my arm and walked toward the bus stop.

I got off the bus before my stop and went into a government store where I bought a box of the best Sabana cigars and a bottle of Rum "Tot¡".

Cachita wasn't home when I arrived. She had left a note on the dining room table, letting me know that she had gone to a government store where they were distributing rice, one pound per family.

I put the cigars and the bottle in my suitcase, and unfolded the newspaper. Inside, secured with scotch tape, was my passport with the exit permit from the police, and a plane ticket with a seat reserved on flight 835 leaving for Miami the following Monday, at ten o'clock in the morning. My friend Abilio hadn't failed me!!

I threw myself down on the bed, drunk with happiness, clutching the documents to my chest. In less that seventy two hours I would be saying good-bye to Yagruma, to the bloody and stupid tyranny, and to the herd of murderers and mental midgets that supported it!!

When Cachita returned, the first thing she did was to ask me how things had gone at the Ministry.

"There is no problem with Faldas", I explained to her, "But he can't take care of it all by himself. He had arranged a hearing for me today with the under-secretary, but at the last minute the son-of-a-bitch had to run off to an emergency meeting and screwed up my interview.

"So, what then? How did it end up?"

"I'll have to be at the Ministry Monday morning, to talk to the undersecretary".

"Well, son, then you'll have to have patience! Everything will work out, you'll see! Oh! I didn't tell you! Rosalina called!"

"Yes? What did she say?"

"They'll be at my brother's farm until the end of the month. He asked them to stay a few more days".

I didn't like the news. The idea of leaving Cachita alone in that big house worried me.

It made me sad to think of leaving the house where I had lived for so many years without telling Cachita.

I didn't like having to lie to her either; she had been very good to me, after all. My feelings of guilt grew with every lie that I told her. But, if Cachita had known my plans, how could I be sure that she wouldn't let something slip? One indiscretion from her could send me to prison for twenty years, and maybe Abilio, too.

Cachita, since that Friday, had been fighting against the first symptoms of the flu. On Sunday she couldn't get up; she had a high fever, a sore throat and every bone in her body ached.

In lieu of aspirin, I gave her hot herbal tea and broth from sage, which was a remedy that my grandmother used in those cases.

So that she wouldn't be suspicious, I had planned to bring down my suitcase the night before my departure, and hide it in a closet beneath the staircase, where they stored the trash can and the cleaning utensils.

The next morning I would say good-bye as usual to Cachita, telling her that I was going to the Ministry. Then, I would go down stairs, grab my suitcase, and "adiós, muchachos!"

Now, with Cachita in bed with the flu, I didn't have to bother with those precautions.

During the wee hours of that Monday morning, I tossed and turned in the bed, unable to sleep. I got up when the first lights of dawn began to illuminate the sky of Sabana.

I showered, shaved, and got dressed. Then I went into the kitchen, made some coffee and took a cup to Cachita's room.

I knocked at the door. "Cachita, wake up!", I called, "I'm bringing you a cup of coffee!"

"Come in, son!", her voice was so weak and hoarse that I could hardly understand what she said.

I went into the room. Cachita sat up in bed to take the cup. Her eyes, bloodshot and full of matter, were inflamed and running; a stream of mucus ran from her nostrils. She must have had her nose all stuffed up, because I could see that she was breathing through her mouth.

"Ay, Miguel, I feel terrible!"

"How is it going?"

"Oh, my God, I've got a terribly sore throat! I can't swallow! And there isn't a bone in my body that doesn't hurt!"

"Well, you have to be patient", I advised her, "All you have to do is rest in bed and drink plenty of liquid. Just take care of yourself. I left plenty of sage broth in the kitchen for you. In a couple of days, you'll be feeling better".

"And you, what are you going to do today?"

"They tell me that they have received some Romanian shoes at one of the government stores. Let's see if they'll sell me a pair, that's all they allow per person! Then, I'm going to the Ministry. I have an appointment with the undersecretary, remember?

"Don't come back too late, OK? I don't like to be here all alone!"

"No, no! I'll be back about five o'clock. By the way, all I have on me is five pesos. Where did you hide my money?"

"It's in the wardrobe. Top drawer, on he right, under the bloomers".

I counted what was there. Exactly eighteen hundred and thirteen pesos. This money wouldn't be any good to me in the United States, because the Yagruman peso wasn't even quoted in the international currency market. But I still had to get a taxi to go to the airport and buy lunch; that is, if I was lucky enough to find a restaurant with food.

I took one hundred pesos and put the rest of the money back in its place.

Cachita, sound asleep again, was snoring noisily, rolled up in the blanket.

Standing beside the bed, I stared at her for a few moments. I had a lump in my throat; I felt as that night at Aunt Lidia's house in Los Remates, when I was alone in the room where my grandmother lay in her casket.

I would have liked to kiss Cachita on the cheek, as a farewell, but I stopped myself. I couldn't afford to run the risk of waking her and arousing her suspicions.

It was eight o'clock in the morning when I descended the stairs of Cachita's house for the last time.

There wasn't a taxi driver in the neighborhood that didn't know me. So, to avoid the risk of running into a busybody, I decided to go downtown and catch the first taxi that happened to pass by.

I finally got on a bus that left me at the corner of San Fermín and Fábrica, where a taxi driver agreed to take me to the airport for sixty pesos.

I had only been to the Granja Vaqueros airport once before, several years ago, when I went to see off some friends. At that time, the air terminal was a clean and well maintained building, totally air-conditioned, with shining floors and spotless rest rooms.

Now, the air terminal was dirty, with the walls defaced with graffiti and communist slogans, and the floors covered with cigar and cigarette butts, spittle, and all kinds of garbage.

It was sweltering, oppressively hot inside the building.

"The air conditioning system broke down", said an old gentleman who was walking beside me, "And they can't get the parts they need to repair it".

Loud speakers installed throughout the terminal building spewed torrents of insults against the Yagrumans that were leaving the island, calling them cockroaches, traitors, worms, mercenaries and scorpions who had sold themselves to the Yankee gold.

"The communists", said the old gentleman, "Have the Midas touch, but in reverse"

"What do you mean by that?"

"King Midas transformed into gold everything he touched, right?"

"According to the legend, yes".

"Well, everything the communists touch turns to shit"

"Sir, you have really spoken the truth", I replied.

"My name is Félix Cano", said the gentleman.

"I'm Miguel Baró. Glad to know you, Don Félix". We shook hands.

In the airport, Yagrumans leaving for the United States had to report to a large room, divided by glass partitions into several offices. They called it "the fish tank".

Inside, members of the army and the militia checked the passports and exit permits of the travelers before they were allowed to board their planes.

Don Félix and I entered the "fish tank". A militiaman that was on guard told us to sit down and wait until they called us from the adjoining office. We were there for a short time.

The old man told me that he was going to join his daughter, who had left Yagruma ten years before.

"She lives in Miami", he informed me, "You'll meet her for sure, because she's going to meet me at the airport".

"I am going to live with her", the old man went on, "I hope that you and I will meet again".

Don Félix gave me his daughter's address, which I wrote down on my notebook.

The old man had been living on a rental income and his retirement pension, until the communist regime "nationalized" all of his properties. His daughter, now a US citizen, had claimed her father, and sent him the air fare to Miami.

After spending a good while talking about his daughter, he wanted to start telling me the story of his life. But, fortunately, at that precise moment they called him from the adjoining office, and he had to leave.

Don Félix was taken care of in five minutes, and the guard signaled to me that it was now my turn.

I walked into the office. There were two desks in it, and sitting behind one of them was a militia woman with a .45 Colt pistol on her belt. A dumpy soldier, armed as though he was going to fight in the battle of Stalingrad, was at the other desk.

"Your passport and exit permit!", growled the woman.

Without a word, I laid them on the desk. The woman checked and rechecked them thoroughly, and finally gave me back the passport.

"Go and join the other passengers at the boarding gate", she told me.

I was on my way out when she called my name.

"Baró! Come back here a moment!"

I went back. My heart was pounding crazily in my chest; my mouth was dry.

"Let me have your passport again!"

I gave it to her, trying to keep my face from showing the tempest that was boiling in my brain.

She swiveled her chair around to the desk where the fat soldier was, and gave him my passport. The man took a glance at it, nodded affirmatively and gave the passport back to her. I was rooted to the spot, incapable of thinking or acting.

The voice of the woman shook me out of it.

"Take your passport!", she was saying, "You may go!"

I grabbed it and left for the boarding gate. Moments later I had joined the other passengers, all Yagrumans, that were waiting for the last "formality", the luggage search.

The militia in charge of this operation arrived a few minutes later, opened our suitcases and checked them thoroughly, taking out anything that in their opinion exceeded the limits authorized by the regime.

The one who searched my luggage hardly looked at what was inside. He was a serious, middle aged man who seemed embarrassed by the duty to which he had been assigned. Some of my companions, though, weren't so lucky; another militia man confiscated a satin sheet that a woman close to me was carrying, and one young girl was embarrassed when they opened up a bag of sanitary napkins.

The bastard that was doing the searching scratched the napkins with his dirty fingers, laughing and showing them to the others, pretending that he was doing this to make sure that there was no money or jewelry hidden inside the cheap Kotex imitation.

The nightmare was finally over. The flight crew of our plane came out of the terminal and placed themselves at the head of our group. The captain, a tall, blond American, gave us the orders that we were to follow.

Before long, we had all taken our seats in the airplane, and soon after, the Lockheed began to move slowly along the runway and then stopped and remained stationary for a few minutes that seemed like an eternity to me.

Finally, the plane started down the runway, with a deafening roar of the engines, and suddenly, quicker than you could say "Jesus", we were in the air.

When they knew that the plane was airborne, the Yagrumans aboard reacted in different ways. Some of the women cried, covering their faces with their hands; other passengers remained silent and serious. There were, nevertheless, some that, believing themselves now out of the reach of the communists, began to cuss out loud Casto Cruz, Cheo de Varas and the Commies in general.

Suddenly, the captain's voice came over the loud speaker.

"Control yourselves", he ordered, "We are still in Yagruman air space, and if the control tower ordered us to return to the airport I would have no choice but to do it!"

As if by magic, silence fell over all in the airplane.

Shortly afterwards the voice of the captain was heard again, informing us that we had now left the Yagruman air space and that we could now, without fear, unleash all of our emotions.

But the silence remained unbroken, except for the sobs of a few women. Even the loquacious Don Félix, who was sitting beside me, remained silent, with a furrowed brow, as though lost in somber meditation.

I stared out of the window as the green island of Yagruma grew smaller and smaller. Finally, Yagruma was gone; I saw nothing but my reflection in the glass as I wondered if and when I would ever see my native land again.

CHAPTER XXXI
A TURNING POINT

The Lockheed touched ground in Miami fifty minutes later. It was an incandescent afternoon; dark clouds were slowly gathering in the blazing sky.

My purpose had been accomplished; I was in the United States. Nevertheless, a strange feeling of uneasiness, an anxiety that I couldn't explain came over me.

The more I repeated to myself that Yagruma had been left behind, and that a new life was opening up to me, the more twitchy and ill at ease I felt.

All of a sudden I remembered what Abilio had told me about the possibility of being sent to Opa-Locka.

"Don Félix", I said to my new friend, "I'll have to ask you a favor".

"Well, if I can...", he replied.

"There is a chance that Immigration might hold me for one or two days".

"What do you mean, hold you!? Are you in any kind of trouble?"

"No, no, nothing like that! But I worked for the Casto Cruz government, and the possibility always exists that the FBI, or Immigration, might have my name on some of their lists".

"You're not going to be on any list! You are a decent man!"

"Thank you very much, Don Félix, but I have the feeling that these people will want to check on me before letting me in the country. Of course, like I said, it's only a possibility".

"Well, how can I help you?"

"I don't have any money on me", I explain, "Assuming that they confine me for a few days, could you and your daughter pick me up when they release me?"

"Of course", he answered, "With pleasure! My daughter will be delighted, I'm sure!"

The plane stopped in front of its assigned gate, and the captain gave the order to the passengers to leave the aircraft. There were no US citizens in our group, so the Immigration personnel had to check our passports and entry visas.

The passengers that preceded me were taken care of with dispatch, but with my documents they took longer. Finally, from a nearby office, a man in a blue uniform came out to me.

"Señor Baró", he said, in perfect Spanish, "I'm inspector González, from the Immigration Department. Please come with me".

I felt my backbone freeze up.

"Go with you?", I asked, "Where? What's the problem?"

"No problem", he answered, in a friendly manner, "You and a few other passengers will be held at the Opa-Locka detention center until we receive the information we have requested from Washington about you".

The memory of the days that I had spent in the castle were still fresh in my mind.

"In other words, I'm under arrest, isn't that right?"

"No, señor Baró", he replied, still friendly, "This is a routine procedure. I'm sure you won't have any problems".

"And, for how long will I be confined?"

"That depends on how long it takes Washington to send us the information about you. Now, come with me, please".

"At least, let me go to pick up my suitcase!"

"That has been taken care of. Please, Mr. Baró; we have to get moving!"

Resisting the man's authority was something that didn't even enter my mind. I followed inspector González to a parking lot outside the terminal, where a station wagon from the Immigration and Naturalization Service was waiting for us.

There were three other men in the vehicle. They kept silent during the whole trip, probably for fear of committing some indiscretion that would make things worse for them.

My stay at Opa-Locka lasted less than twenty four hours. The morning following my arrival, about ten o'clock, inspector González called me to his office and told me that the information from Washington had arrived, and that it confirmed my lack of ties with the communists.

"You were a functionary with the Casto Cruz regime", he added, "That's why you have been held in this center. Also, you have been seeing visiting Colonel

Abilio Pardo, at Sabana's national police headquarters, and also at the home of the dear colonel".

I wanted to explain, but he wouldn't let me talk.

"Like I told you", he continued, "Your record is completely favorable. You have never had any ties with Casto Cruz, nor have you ever conducted yourself as an enemy of the United States".

"As for Colonel Pardo, who helped you to leave Yagruma, we know that you two have been friends since your University days. Your relationship with him has been only one of friendship".

I was amazed.

"How did you know all that?", I asked.

The inspector smiled. "We have our ways", he answered.

He then opened a file that was on his desk and took out some blank forms.

"With the persecution that you have suffered in your own country", he said, "And the probability of being thrown in a prison again, I don't imagine that you would think of returning to the island. Am I right?"

"Inspector", I responded, "It's my intention to apply for political asylum in the United States. If that's granted to me, I will rebuild my life in this country".

González, without a word, took one of the forms, scribbled something on it and handed the form to me.

"Sign on the dotted line", he said, offering me his pen. I obeyed without hesitation.

He put the form away in the file folder, looked again in the pile of papers and took out a smaller printed chart, about four by five inches.

He wrote something on it, signed it and gave it to me.

"Until you become a lawful resident of the United States", he said, "This document will be your only identification. It's your proof that the Immigration Service has authorized your stay in the country. It also permits you to work in the United States".

He put the rest of the papers back in the file folder.

"That closes your case", he told me, "You are free to go now. When you leave this office, turn to your left and go straight ahead until you come to a door. Outside you will find a jeep that'll take you to the exit. Your suitcase will be in it".

"May I use your telephone?", I asked.

"I'm sorry", he replied, "But these phones are for official use only".

"Look", I replied, "I don't have a penny, and I'm not going to walk to Miami. I have to call a friend to come and get me".

He thrust his hand in his pocket, took out a pile of change, put aside three dimes and offered them to me.

"There is a pay phone next to the main gate", he informed me, "Take this so you can call your friend".

I felt kind of embarrassed, but I took the dimes and thanked him. Inspector González stood up.

"Good luck", he said, extending his hand.

Luckily, I hadn't lost Don Félix's phone number.

When I got to the detention camp's entrance, I found the telephone booth, and from there I called the old man. He himself answered my call, and sounded sincere when he assured me that he and his daughter had been very worried about me.

"Don Félix", I said, "I'm still at Opa-Locka. They just released me. Could you come and get me? I'm sorry to cause you so much of a problem, but I am so broke that I can't even afford the bus fare!"

"I don't think that will be a problem", answered Don Félix, "But my daughter is the driver here. Look, she is listening in on the extension; arrange it with her!"

"Dr. Baró", said a woman's voice, "This is Rita Cano speaking. How are you?"

"Very well, señorita, thank you. You have heard what has happened to me. Please forgive me for being such a pest".

"Oh, don't say that! We Yagrumans are supposed to help each other, right?"

"Well, thanks again. Your help is really appreciated!"

"You are welcome! It's a good thing I've taken a three-day leave of absence from work. Since my father was arriving, you know...! Well, we'll leave for Opa-Locka right away. Wait for us at the main gate!"

I still had some cigarettes left from those that I had bought at Granja Vaqueros. I lit one and sat on a nearby bench to wait for Don Félix and his daughter.

An hour and three cigarettes later I saw a shiny, late model Chrysler slowly approaching the gate. It was driven by a young woman, at whose side sat Don Félix. The woman stopped the car; she and the old man got out and came to meet me.

Don Félix gave me a big hug, stating that not for a moment did he think that I had had anything to do with the communists. The young lady had stayed behind him. I noticed she looked attentively at me, as though inspecting me.

"Miguel, I want you to meet my daughter", said Don Félix, "Rita, this is Dr. Miguel Baró, my traveling companion and new friend".

Rita Cano was about thirty five years old. She was tall and slender, with big brown eyes, exquisitely shaped lips and long, black hair that fell over her shoulders. She greeted me with a handshake, so soft and warm it felt like a caress.

"What are your plans, Dr. Baró? Tell me where you would like us to take you".

"My name is Miguel", I answered, "I left my doctorate in Yagruma".

She smiled. "I'm Rita. Well, where do you want to go?"

"I think the best thing for me to do is to go to the Refugee Center, and sign up", I said.

"I think so, too. Insist that they give you your check right away. Refugees get a hundred dollars every month, as assistance".

"And food, also", added Don Félix.

"Are you going to stay in Miami?", Rita asked me.

"I don't think so. Elías Ledón, a friend of mine, gave me the phone number and the address of his brother Eufemio. I have lost them, but I'm sure that the telephone company can find it for me".

"Do you remember the name of the town where Eufemio lives?"

"Sure! He lives in Elizabeth, New Jersey. He can help me to get a job".

"Really? How can you be so sure?"

"Elías told me that Eufemio has a lot of pull within his union".

"I hope your friend is right", she said, "Well, look, the Refugee Center will pay for your plane fare. On top of that, they will give you ten dollars for travel expenses".

"You are doing the right thing, Miguel", said Don Félix, "Rita has told me that things have gotten really tough, here in Miami. Jobs are very hard to find".

"Well, let's go!", Rita urged, "If we don't get there too late, Miguel could probably get his check today".

She handed me a piece of paper.

"Here are the directions to our house", she said, "When you get done at the Center, come on over. "You will stay with us until you get things arranged. OK?"

I was really moved.

"But I can't accept that!", I exclaimed, "How am I going to intrude your house and mess up your quiet? Besides, your father just arrived to Miami; you two have a lot to talk about!"

"You don't have a job, and the hundred dollars from the Center will only last you a few days, if that", she replied, "Where are you going to live? In the street? In one of those flea-bags where the refugees are sent?"

"I have a spare room at my house", she insisted, "You are welcome as our guest!"

Her offer was so tempting, and her reasoning so sound, that I couldn't decline any longer.

"You've convinced me", I said, "I promise that I'm not going to be a problem for you. Rita, I don't know how to thank you!"

"You don't have to thank me", she replied, "We three are here for the same reason".

The Yagruman Refugee Center was housed in an old building in the North East section of the city.

When Rita and her father left me there, the old man, before I could stop him, put a ten-dollar bill in one of the pockets of my jacket.

"No, Don Félix, please don't!", I protested, "You heard Rita, I am going to leave the Center with a hundred bucks in my pocket!"

"Oh, yes? And where are you going to cash the check? Now, suppose you don't get it today, what are you going to do?"

"Don't pay attention to him, papá", Rita told him. She looked at me, smiling, "See you tonight", she said as they left.

The employees of the Refugee Center were, for the most part, Yagruman exiles who had arrived to the United States with the first waves of refugees, during 1959 and 1960. The arrogance and despotism with which these Yagrumans treated their less fortunate compatriots was unbelievable.

Nevertheless, my status as a lawyer served me so as not to be mistreated. The clerk assigned to my case gave me a written order to the medical department, for a checkup. There, a young physician examined me, looked in my ears and throat, and certified that I was in perfect health.

I went back to the office and gave the medical certificate to the bureaucrat who was processing my papers. He read it and nodded his approval.

"Perfect!", he exclaimed, "This is all I needed! Your papers will be ready in a couple of hours".

"I understand that the Refugee Center will be giving me a hundred dollars a month, as assistance".

"Yes, that's right".

"I don't have any money. Could I have the first check today?"

"I don't know. I'll talk to my boss to see what we can do, but I can't promise you anything".

"Then, I'll see you in a couple of hours", I told him.

"We'll see what news we have then", he replied.

When leaving the Refugee Center, my stomach rumblings reminded me that I hadn't had anything to eat since my meager breakfast at Opa-Locka.

In a Royal Castle that was nearby, I had a bowl of soup and a hamburger, breaking the ten-dollar bill that Don Félix had given me. Afterwards, to kill time while I was waiting, I walked around the neighborhood, being careful not to get too far away from the Center. When I came back, the guy behind the desk gave me a sad look.

"I have good news and bad news", he told me, "Which do you want to hear first?"

"Give me the good news", I replied with a blank face. "Your papers have been finished and approved".

"And the bad news?"

"I couldn't get a check for you today. But it will be ready tomorrow! I give you my word!"

"After all", I thought, "Today or tomorrow, what difference does it make? Thanks to the Canos, I'll have food and a bed. And I still have eight dollars in my pocket. Besides, tomorrow I'll bring the cigars and the rum and sell them. Hey, it could be much worse!"

The clerk thought he knew the cause of my silence.

"If you don't have a place to stay", he told me, "I can give you a voucher for a hotel close by. It won't be a Holiday Inn, but the important thing is to have shelter".

That hotel had to be one of the flea bags that Rita had mentioned.

"I'm staying at the home of some friends", I replied, "Thanks anyway! What time shall I come tomorrow?"

"Your check will be ready about ten o' clock".

"OK, I'll see you at ten. Thanks again!"

Rita and her father lived in the Northeast section of Miami, in a big house along whose sides bougainvillea shrubs and sea-grapes grew. It was past five o' clock in the evening when I went up the three steps to the door and rang the bell.

I heard the quick footsteps of a woman. The door opened and in the doorway appeared Rita, recently made up, hair combed, and smiling. She was wearing a short green dress, with a very low neckline that really looked good on her.

"Chico, you had me scared!", she exclaimed, "I thought you had gotten lost! But, what are we standing here for? There's no admission charge here!"

Saying this, she grabbed my arm and, close by my side, took me into the living room. The house was clear and spacious, furnished with sober elegance.

"Make yourself at home", said Rita, "Sit down, relax! I'll fix you a drink. What would you like?"

"Rum. With quinine tonic, if you have it, please".

"Of course I do! One rum with quinine water, coming right up!"

She came back in a few minutes with the drink and sat down on the sofa, at my side.

"Well, tell me. How did it go at the Center? Did you get everything taken care of?"

I told her of my experiences that afternoon.

"You will surely have your check tomorrow", Rita assured me, "Don't worry! Listen, if you need money, I can lend you some, OK? Don't be bashful!"

That excess of generosity had me confused and somewhat embarrassed. It had been less than eight hours since I first met that woman, and now here was she, giving me food and shelter and offering me money!

"Tell me about yourself", she went on, "About your life in Yagruma, about everything that has happened to you. Everything!"

I did, omitting, of course, many of the things that I wouldn't tell to strangers. Rita, on her part, told me about herself.

Rita was a pharmacist. Shortly after her arrival to Miami, she found a job with a pharmaceutical industry. Now, ten years later, she held an executive position in the company.

Discreetly, I tried to get her to talk about her love life, and I found out that it had not been very happy or exciting. Five years before, she had been dating a Yagruman writer whom she finally married.

The man, though, turned out to be a lazy bum, a leech who tried to live off her, something Rita wouldn't tolerate. The inevitable divorce came less than two years after the marriage. Since then, Rita had dedicated herself to her job and her books.

"I find it hard to believe", I said to her, "That a woman like you, so beautiful, so attractive, so well-educated, could settle for this kind of monastic life".

"I won't be living like that for ever", she answered, "At least, I hope I won't".

She stared at me.

"I may still find the man than really tickles me. And then, if it happened, he could do with me whatever he pleased to", she said.

"What is this woman trying to do?", I thought, "Having some fun at my expense? Could she possibly get her kicks from exchanges of this kind?"

I had to be cautious. Without any comment, I finished my drink and put the glass on a side table.

"How about a refill?", she asked me.

"No, thank you! What I really want is to shower and change".

"Well, don't wait, then. I took your suitcase to your room and put it on the bed".

We left the room together, crossing the pantry and entering a hallway where I saw the doors to two bedrooms, one at each end. In between them, in the middle of the hall, was the bathroom.

Rita stopped in front of one of the doors.

"This is your room", she said, and indicating the other end of the hallway, she added, "That's mine".

"Boy, do I crave a nice hot shower!", I exclaimed. I went into my room and had taken off my shirt when I heard a knock on the door and Rita's voice, calling me. I put the shirt back on, unbuttoned, and went out of the hallway.

"I forgot to tell you", said Rita, "You have time to lie down for a while, if you want, because we eat about eight".

"That's fine. By the way", I asked, "What happened to your father? I haven't seen him. Is he all right?"

"Better than ever! He's in his room now, watching television".

Rita stood there for a few seconds, looking at my bare chest.

"How hairy!", she said, "You are a bear!" and she left for the kitchen.

Rita was an excellent cook. That night she gave us tossed salad, rice and black beans, Caribbean roast, fried ripe plantains and, for dessert, home-made guava pastries.

After dinner, we had strong Latin coffee; then, Don Félix took out a couple of cigars and offered me one, which I lit with pleasure.

During our after-dinner conversation, which was long and pleasant, I noticed that Rita's eyes lingered on me, with languid tenderness.

The following morning, when I was finishing shaving, someone called at the bathroom door. It was Rita, again.

"Miguel, are you going to have breakfast now?", she asked.

"Yes, I'll be ready in five minutes", I answered.

"Great! Then, I'll drive you to the Center!"

"No, please, don't bother!", I replied, "I can take the bus!"

"At this time of the morning you'll be caught in the traffic jam", she said, "Besides, you don't know Miami. It would be better if I take you".

"You are going to be late for work, because of me!"

"That's not a problem, chico! I don't have to punch the time clock! Hurry up, and we'll go together!"

It was useless to argue. I finished shaving, got dressed, and took out of my suitcase the box of cigars and the bottle of "Totí" that I had brought from Yagruma. I tore off a page from my notebook and wrote on it:

"Don Félix: I beg of you to accept this small gift as an expression of my gratitude for all the help you have given me.-Your friend, Miguel.-"

When I got to the kitchen, Rita was setting up the breakfast table.

"I prefer the Yagruman breakfast", she said, "Orange juice, café con leche, bread and butter. Now, if you want, I can fix you some ham and eggs, or pancakes. Whatever you want!"

"I prefer whatever you prefer", I replied.

"You are talking about breakfast, right?"

"I'm talking about everything that has to do with you".

Rita didn't answer; she only smiled. But when she served me the café con leche, she rubbed her behind against my arm. The perfume she was using that morning had a sweet, enervating fragrance that went to my head.

"I'll have to control myself", I thought, "Otherwise I'm going to take her right here on the table. And that can't be! She and her father have opened the doors of their home to me! What would they think of me?!"

"Where is Don Félix?", I asked Rita, "I thought he was an early riser".

"Papá has always had a problem with insomnia", she said, "He solves it with sleeping pills. But sometimes they are too strong for him, and he is often still snoring at nine o'clock in the morning".

We finished breakfast. I picked up the plates and put them in the sink.

"Papá will wash them when he gets up", said Rita, "Don't worry about them". Then she noticed the box of cigars and the bottle that I had left on the sideboard. "And these?", she asked.

I explained where the cigars and rum had come from, and the reason why I had bought them.

"But now I want to leave them as a gift for Don Félix", I added, "Because he has been so good to me".

She looked at me sharply.

"And I? Haven't I been good to you?"

I came close to Rita and took her by the hand.

"More than good", I told her, "When in my fantasies I dream of an angel, that angel wouldn't be anyone but you".

Then, in a burst of passion that I would never have thought possible in her, she freed herself and, putting her arms around me, kissed me anxiously, with biting and voracious kisses that I returned in the same way.

The sound of a door closing was heard, and the cough of Don Félix. Rita and I separated a few seconds before the old man came into the kitchen.

"Good morning!", he greeted us, "What's up? I see that you already had your breakfast. Did you sleep well, Miguel?

"Very well, like a log, Don Félix".

"Pap ", said Rita, "We are going now. I'm going to take Miguel to the Center".

"Very well. Be very careful, dear. The people here drive like they are crazy!"

"Don't worry, pap . I'll give you a call later!"

She kissed her father. "Don't open the door for anybody!", she warned him before leaving.

I sat beside Rita on the front seat of the Chrysler. Disconcerted, and somewhat confused, I tried to talk about what had happened between us in the kitchen. But she wouldn't discuss the matter.

"We'll talk about that later", she told me.

The rest of the trip we made in silence. Every once in a while Rita extended her right arm and took my hand, squeezing it and digging in her nails.

When we got to the Refugee Center, I was so confused that I didn't even know how to say good-bye. I turned to her.

"Thanks for the ride", I said.

"What are you going to do today?", she replied.

"First, I'm going to get my check", I told her, "Then, I'll go to the telephone company to see if they can find Eufemio's phone and address for me. If I can locate him, what he has to tell me will determine what I'm going to do".

"Are you still thinking of leaving?"

"Yes, if I can't find some way to get along in Miami".

"Then, I am not important to you?"

"You are going to be late for work", I said. And turning on my heels, I went into the Center.

The guy behind the desk made me wait almost a half hour.

Finally he returned with the one hundred dollar check. He also gave me a card that made me eligible for a couple of bags of free food, once a month. I cashed the check at a bank not too far from the Center.

I had, in writing, the directions how to get to the telephone company. There, a Spanish-speaking operator did everything she could to locate Eufemio's number in Union City. But her efforts were useless.

Little by little, a presentiment had begun to creep through my mind; a foreboding that my luck was about to change, that a good star had guided me to that comfortable and beautiful house, to Rita's side. Maybe for that reason I wasn't too disappointed when they informed me that the name of Eufemio Ledón didn't appear in the Elizabeth, New Jersey, telephone directory, and that neither had he an unlisted number.

Leaving the telephone company, I stopped at a Royal Castle for a cup of coffee and, after getting the "Miami News" and the "Herald" at a news stand, I took the bus back to Rita's house.

"Miguel", said Don Félix, who came to open the door, "I really appreciate the kindness that you have shown me, but you shouldn't have done it".

"That's all right, old man", I replied, treating him familiarly for the first time, "Forget about that! It's a pleasure that you can't deny me. Besides, I intend to help you use up the rum and the cigars".

"Well, if it's like that...", murmured Rita's father.

Night was falling when I heard he noise of the garage door opening. Minutes later Rita came into the family room, where I was reading the classified ads in the "Herald". But this time she didn't come close to me, nor did she try to kiss me. She sat on a rattan chair, laying her purse on the floor, beside her.

"How did it go this morning?", she asked, "Did you get everything taken care of?"

"Well, I didn't have very much to do", I responded, "I got the check and cashed it".

"What about your friend? Did they give you his phone number?"

I told her about my inquiry at the telephone company. Was it only my imagination, or did I see for a few seconds an expression of indescribable relief in Rita's face?

"Well then, what do you plan to do?"

I waved the "Herald" in the air.

"Washing dishes or sweeping floors in some hotel is all that I can hope for! Do you know why? Because I don't speak the language!!"

"But you can learn it", she said, "Besides, you must remember something from your high school English!"

"Sure!, I replied, "Tom is a boy; Mary is a girl; Rover is a dog! That's the only damn thing I can remember!!"

We were silent for a moment. Rita, with a furrowed brow, focused her eyes on the floor, as though she were concentrating on something that would soon come to her mind.

I broke the silence. "Tomorrow I'm going to hit the hotels and see if I can find something", I said, "Washing dishes or cleaning toilets, it's all the same to me!"

She looked at me face to face with her beautiful, big brown eyes, as though looking through me.

Her attitude shocked me. "Maybe I was wrong about this woman", I thought, "Probably all she wanted to do was play around with me, or maybe she just changed her mind and decided that she didn't want to waste her time with a tramp".

But I changed my mind again when Rita, came and sat by me on the sofa.

"Don't worry", she said, running her fingers through my hair, "Everything will work out; I'll make sure of that! But don't give up; be patient".

And she leaned over and kissed me on the lips, but this time softly, with a bland and tender kiss. I took her by the shoulders to bring her closer to me, but she didn't let me.

"Wait a minute, wait a minute", she said, in a low voice, "Don't get all excited! I have to go and get dinner ready. Do you know what I'm going to serve you today? Spanish omelet and pickled red snapper! Yagruman flan, for dessert! How does it grab you?"

After dinner, Rita went to her room, to work on a report that she had to submit to her boss the following day. Don Félix and I stayed in the living room, watching television, and shortly before midnight we went to bed.

Sleep didn't come easily that night. I turned over and over in bed, I lay on my right side, then on my left side, I lay on my back, crossed my legs...nothing, I couldn't get to sleep!

I was worried at my peculiar situation as a guest of the Canos. Whatever Rita might be feeling for me, I couldn't stay indefinitely in her house, living like a parasite.

"I must get some sleep", I thought, "In the morning, I'm going to make the rounds of the hotels, looking for a job!"

I wrapped up in the sheet, closed my eyes, and tried to force myself to sleep.

I found my self, once more, in Helena's red-light district, calling at a brothel's door. An incredibly repulsive old witch came to the door and let me in.

"The girl's free now", she grumbled, pointing at the door to the pigsty's only bedroom.

I went in. It smelled of sick flesh, of menstrual rags, of sour sweat and dried urine. The light from the front room filtered through the partly open door, and by its dim light I could see, hanging on the wall, a calendar advertising "Vigoril, the potent sexual invigorator", and a lithograph of the Sacred Heart of Jesus.

There was an old iron bed and, next to it, an ancient night table, upon which a flask of alcohol and a roll of toilet tissue had been placed. A bucket on the floor by the bed, and a decrepit chair in one of the corners completed the furnishing of that temple of Venus. A torn underskirt and a bra hung from the back of the chair.

Someone was stretched out on the bed. A labored breathing was coming from under the sheet, and at hearing it, a fear overcame me that I could not explain; for a moment I thought that the best thing would be for me to leave that place. But then I changed my mind, partly out of pride and partly because of the call of my hormones.

I came closer to the bed. A mass of wavy brunette hair rested on the pillow; I had to see who its owner was! But when I leaned over the bed, the sheet thrust to one side and two iron hands grabbed me by the shoulders, pulling me down.

Somebody, probably the old hag, opened the door of the room, letting more light into that pigsty. Then I would clearly see the frightful, fiendish specter that was embracing me!

The splendid brunette hair fell over her face, hiding it, and descended like a cascade over two bony shoulders. Her skinny body was wrinkled and stooped, with a sunken chest from which the skin fell in strips down to the almost hairless pubis.

The breasts, flaccid and wrinkled, with twisted nipples, were those of an octogenarian.

Nevertheless, she had the strength and vitality of an amazon. Overcoming my resistance, she threw me onto my back on the bed and sat astride me. Then, while pressing one hand on my chest, with the other she pushed back the mass of hair that covered her face. It was then, that terror paralyzed me.

The hairy face, furrowed and lined, looked like an old leather mask. Under the nose, curved like a parrot's, the toothless mouth, partly open with the expectation of pleasure, drooled down to her chin. But in that horrible face glowed two eyes of youth, two light-amber eyes with green sparks!

I don't know what passed through my mind. I tried to break loose and flee from the apparition that had imprisoned me, but my limbs did not respond. I couldn't move! Then I closed my eyes, and I asked God to help me!

The cold, drooling lips, pressed on mine, leaving a moist, glacial kiss that filled me with terror. And I felt on my genitals the trembling brush of a skeletal hand!!

God had to have heard my pleas. Because with unexpected strength, with my arms suddenly hardened like poles, I could push myself loose from the specter. And jumping up from the bed, I ran to the door.

But the other old harpy had closed it, latching it from the other side! I stepped back to get the impulse to kick open the door, but in that moment two arms grabbed me convulsively. It was her, it was Perlita, again!

Slipping out of her embrace, I turned to confront her. Perlita jumped at me, screeching like a she-demon. I waited until she was close, and then, with all my strength, I kicked her in the belly.

My kick threw her back, stumbling, until she crashed into the bucket and fell to the floor, hitting her head against the edge of the night table's marble surface.

Grabbing the chair, I went up to her, ready to let her have it, but Perlita didn't move. I noticed that her neck was bent over in a grotesque manner, forming a strange angle with the rest of the body. A little blood trickled down from her right ear.

All of a sudden, a bright, orange light flooded the tiny room, erasing with its glow the horror that surrounded me.

A warm, soft hand, was caressing my forehead. Someone spoke to me.

"Miguel, wake up!", said a woman's voice, "It's all right, sweetheart, it's all right! It's all gone, it's all right!"

Finally, with an effort, I could open my eyes. I was in my room. The lamp on the night table was on, and by its light I saw Rita, sitting on the edge of the bed. All she had on was a short nightgown, thigh length.

"What happened?", I asked, "What are you doing here?"

"You had a nightmare, my love. You were screaming so terribly! It scared me!"

Rita was in my room, half-naked, sitting on my bed, calling me "sweetheart" and "love". And I found it so natural as though it had always been like this!

She leaned over me.

"Who is Perlita?", she murmured.

I put a hand under her nightgown and touched her breasts. "Some one that I knew", I replied, "She died a long time ago".

Rita, with a rapid movement, threw off the nightgown and climbed in bed with me.

"Lover", she said between kisses, "I think you are going to stay in Miami".

EPILOGUE

My destiny and Rita's became one that night. We knew we would be together "for the duration". Like the wedding vow, "'til death us do part".

Rita found a job for me in the personnel department of the pharmaceutical complex where she was an executive. Later on, I began attending Law school at night. My English was steadily improving.

Officially, I was staying with the Canos as a friend, though Don Félix, I am sure, was aware of what was going on between Rita and me. He never complained nor voiced any disapproval.

Don Félix had a stroke three years after his arrival to Miami, and was told by his doctor that, sooner or later, he was bound to have another, and it would be fatal.

Back from the hospital, the first thing he did was talk to Rita and me.

"The doctors", he told us, "Are sure that it'll happen. It could be tomorrow, it could be next year. Who knows?"

"I'm not afraid to die", he continued, "But I worry about my daughter. I want to ask that you two get married; please do it, even if only to let me die in peace".

Marriage was something that Rita and I never considered before, for we never believed it necessary. But we wanted Don Félix's last stretch to be a peaceful one, so we tied the knot.

A few months later, one Sunday morning, he had the second stroke while pruning the ixora shrubs in the backyard. We called the ambulance and I drove Rita to the hospital, but they could do nothing for Don Félix. He died shortly after being admitted.

Meanwhile, things kept looking up for me. I had been promoted twice in my job, and a couple of years later, when I graduated from Law school, they appointed me Industrial Relations Manager for Latin America, with a great salary, bonuses, stock options, and all the other "goodies" that our corporations give to those who serve them well.

Rita and I were happy. Always in the mood for love, in a nice house, with late model cars, fat bank accounts and select stock portfolios. Life, finally, was good to me!

Driving back home one night through a decayed Miami neighborhood, I had to stop at an intersection where a traffic accident has just happened. A woman had been the victim of a hit and run.

I was overcome by a strange feeling that compelled me to push my way through the small crowd gathered around the scene, and take a look at the corpse.

The woman, fat and flabby in her waitress' uniform, lay on her back, with eyes closed, her long graying hair spread over the pavement. Threads of blood ran out of her right ear.

For a few moments I stared at the corpse, and in spite of the flaccid, lined face and the gray hair, I recognized the victim.

That cadaver lying on the street was Perlita Shell.

An old woman standing next to me happened to be Perlita's next door neighbor. From her I learned that fate had turned against my old flame.

Caribbean Petroleum International had ignored Felino Eniesta's requests for employment. The former big-time executive, now a hopeless, broken old man, wouldn't even think of working as a janitor or a dishwasher. Eniesta hanged himself in the dilapidated apartment where Perlita and he were living.

Perlita who was working as a waitress in a Biscayne Boulevard coffee shop, had turned to the bottle. Also hooked on drugs, she was behind in her rent, and facing eviction from her dingy apartment.

"I think it was better for her, this way", the old woman concluded.

I slipped a ten-dollar bill in her hand. And after looking at Perlita's corpse for the last time, I walked back to my car.

On my way home, I kept thinking of the truth in the old Arab proverb: "Sit patiently at your tent's door, and you'll see your enemy's dead body borne before your eyes".

THE END.